BY GEORGIA CLARK

Play It Again
Most Wonderful
Island Time
It Had to Be You
The Bucket List
The Regulars
Parched
She's with the Band

PLAY IT AGAIN

Play It Again

A Novel

GEORGIA CLARK

The Dial Press
NEW YORK

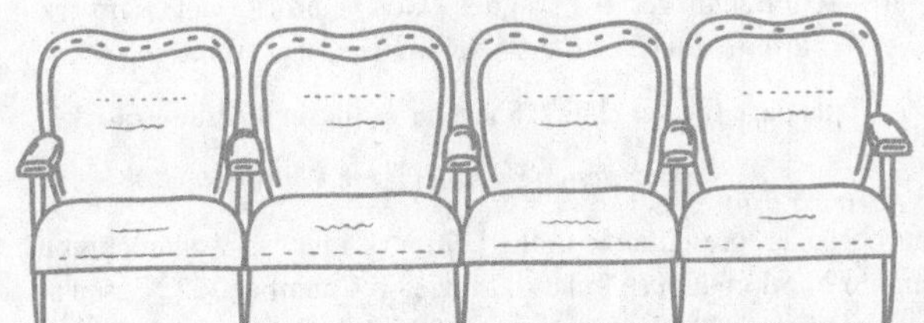

The Dial Press
An imprint of Random House
A division of Penguin Random House LLC
1745 Broadway, New York, NY 10019

randomhousebooks.com
penguinrandomhouse.com

A Dial Press Trade Paperback Original

ISBN 978-0-593-72910-6
Ebook ISBN 978-0-593-72911-3

Printed in the United States of America

1st Printing

BOOK TEAM: Managing editor: Rebecca Berlant • Production manager: Ali Wagner • Copy editor: Nicole Ramirez • Proofreaders: Cameron Schoettle, Caryl Weintraub

Title page theater chairs: Shorena Tedliashvili/Adobe Stock

Book design by Kim Henze Walker

The authorized representative in the EU for product safety and compliance is Penguin Random House Ireland, Morrison Chambers, 32 Nassau Street, Dublin D02 YH68, Ireland. https://eu-contact.penguin.ie

For queer dreamers, smitten kittens,
and forever theater kids

PLAY IT AGAIN

PART ONE

First Act, Second Thoughts

1.

ANNIE LIGHTFOOT COULD NEVER RESIST A STRAY. SHE EMPAthized with the sock that lost its other half at the laundromat, doomed for a life without its mate in a world that does not value single socks. Annie saved every orphaned sock to make mismatched pairs. She liked imagining them in an opposites-attract rom-com—no-nonsense navy meets bubbly pink. Initial clash, unexpected chemistry, then, despite their differences, a perfect match. Maybe even sole mates.

Anything lonely, lopsided, or unloved, Annie claimed as her own. That same soft spot for the underdog had pulled her back here to Rhodes, the small, overlooked Hudson Valley town where she grew up—short on cash, never on charm. The Groom Room, her dog-grooming salon, was the culmination of that instinct: a place that brought out the beauty in every pup while also making her hometown a little brighter.

The Groom Room wasn't large, but it had personality. White walls, hanging plants, and secondhand furniture made it feel bright, cozy, and cool. The services menu, designed in a groovy rainbow font, looked more like a handmade sign at a queer potluck than a glossy corporate Pride float.

Annie was folding a stack of tiny dog bandannas, wondering if glitter polka dots were too much or just enough (verdict: just enough), when the front door banged open. Deborah Buttrose burst in, a magazine raised like a trophy.

"This," Deborah declared, "might just *save our town*!"

Annie blinked at her neighbor—the owner of the nail salon up the street, a white zinfandel enthusiast who'd never met an oversize earring she didn't like. Deborah usually came in with her bichon frise, Spanky the Magnificent, but today she'd evidently left him behind for the breaking news.

"Let's dial the hyperbole back a bit, Deb," Annie said, even as her pulse quickened. "One write-up won't 'save the town.' Not that I'm saying we *need* saving . . ."

"We absolutely *do* need saving and it's not *just* a write-up," Deborah exclaimed, her flamingo earrings bobbing with every syllable. "It's the Best Small Town awards in the most widely read travel magazine in the country! And my neighbor's friend's cousin whose roommate works there swore that *Rhodes* gets a mention!"

"We know." Salvador Carson-Ruiz, aka Sal, Annie's best friend and part-time employee, poked his thick tortoiseshell frames up his nose with a sigh. He wore the same short-sleeved pink jumpsuit that Annie did. "You've only *mentioned* it every day for the past six weeks."

"And it's *finally* here!" Deborah thrust the glossy mag at Annie. "Ooh, I can't look!"

The Groom Room hadn't had a single booking all day, and they weren't the only struggling business in Rhodes. Annie's fingers turned slippery. "I can't, either."

"Give it here." Sal plucked the magazine with an eye roll and began flipping the pages.

Annie had poured her whole heart—and every last dollar—into the Groom Room. She woke each day with new ideas: themed promos, pun-filled posts, loyalty cards shaped like tiny bones. But business stayed slow, and Annie was out of solutions. She wasn't exactly a tourist draw—no one drove to Upstate to get their dog shampooed—but good press might mean the start of an upswing. Her future turning on a dime.

Because if something didn't change for the better soon, her story would end with failure. With letting Sal down. Letting herself down. Letting go of the one thing she'd built with her own two hands, from the rubble of everything else.

Finally, Sal stopped. His thick brows dipped down. "Oh."

"Oh?" Annie repeated. "Oh what? Oh yay?"

"Oh, we didn't win."

"Oh no." Annie deflated. "Who did?"

"Hudson."

"*Hudson?*" Annie and Deb spoke their rival town's name so loudly, Annie's rescue Yorkie, Socks, woke up in his dog bed with a surprised *woof.*

"As if they need more good press!" Deb exclaimed.

Only thirty minutes away, Hudson was Rhodes's buzzy, well-loved, effortlessly cooler older sibling. With its antique shops, art galleries, and excellent restaurants, Hudson was thriving. Meanwhile, Rhodes—walkable and charming but smaller and scrappier—was hanging on by a thread.

"Well, what about the write-up?" Annie angled over Sal's shoulder to scan the other categories. Best Small Food Town, Best Small Beer + Wine Town . . . "Maybe we got *something.*"

"We did." Sal tapped a breakout box. "We're on the Skip It list."

Annie exhaled in horror. "*No.*"

There, in black and white, the world's most devastating sentence. There's nothing really wrong with Rhodes (NY), but there's nothing especially right about it, either.

That was it.

That was it?!

The big, game-changing mention they'd spent the last six weeks getting their hopes up for? Annie's eyes filled. "Well, that's just *mean.*"

Deborah looked similarly shell-shocked, clutching her sequined tunic as she took in the snarky assessment. Like Annie's business, Deb's nail salon wasn't exactly turning away customers. "Oh, what do they know," she huffed. "No one even reads magazines anymore!"

Annie and Sal exchanged a glance. Not the time to remind Deb of her own words regarding the publication's reach and influence. "Exactly." Annie grabbed the offensive edition to dump it straight in the recycling. "They don't know us! And we *don't* need them!"

Deb was already halfway to the door, off to share the bad news with the next shop owner. The bell tinkled in her wake.

As soon as she was out of sight, Annie's smile dropped. The silence felt different now—less like peace, more like the start of an ending she did not want.

Was it time to admit the truth? That Rhodes might not be the town she'd hoped it could become? The idea felt like a betrayal. Someone had to believe in this place. She couldn't be the first to walk away.

Annie collapsed onto the sofa in the waiting area, scooping up Socks for a consoling hug. "At least I have a reason to skip speed dating tonight."

"Which is?"

"I'm depressed!" Annie exclaimed. "And it's always the same five lesbians, all of whom I've either slept with or have ghosted me. Plus, the whole town will know about the Skip It list in approximately twenty-eight minutes. People will need a shoulder to cry on."

Annie could feel Sal's disapproving look. He was twenty-nine, seven years younger than Annie, but he often felt older and wiser.

"Don't," she murmured. "I know what you're thinking."

"Do you?" Sal frowned, his slightly squashy face becoming even squashier. "What am I thinking right now?"

"That you want to do filthy things to a Hemsworth while inhaling a bag of Flamin' Hot Cheetos."

Sal narrowed his eyes. "That was actually spooky." He moved to one of the three silver wash basins, running a rag over its already pristine interior. "You need to put yourself first. You keep saying you want to meet someone."

"But do I?" Annie wondered aloud. "Do I really want to meet someone, fall for her, and have her move in with me only to have her dump me for some ceramicist from Brooklyn who makes vulva-shaped pottery? Or do I want to spend the night showing that pint of Chubby Hubby upstairs who's boss?"

Annie had moved into the apartment above the shop during the pandemic. The location of many a hot date with Ben and Jerry, especially recently.

Sal looked appalled. "Do I need to start a GoFundMe to save you from yourself? I will happily make the first donation."

Annie gave him a look. "Sal," she said. "Find something to do."

Sal sighed and turned back to the basin.

Plopping her rescue dog back in his bed, Annie wandered over to the record player in the corner, flipping through the stack of vinyl records—funk, jazz, funky jazz, jazzy funk—before landing on Amy Winehouse's *Back to Black*. A favorite. Annie picked the album up, feeling the same sweet sadness she always felt when holding Amy in her hands. Sometimes it felt like everyone Annie loved left her before she stopped loving them.

A needle dropped, and the opening of "Valerie" crooned into the salon. *Well, sometimes I go out by myself / And I look across the water . . .*

It was late afternoon. In the morning, sunlight poured in, but now Annie could see it only drenching the street out front, beyond the windows. Somehow, it was already July. The smell of last weekend's fireworks and vegetarian hot dogs were long gone. Summer was half over, and she hadn't even been to the McCormacks' water hole, let alone planned a vacation. Social media made it seem like every woman and her dog were drinking caipirinhas in Portugal or doing something adventurous like skydiving or performing at the Edinburgh Fringe. But this woman and her dogs were still here, in her skippable hometown. The most ambitious thing Annie had done all summer was dye her hair for Pride. Her choppy French bob and bangs were the same soft-shell pink as her jumpsuit. Hardly a big adventure.

Even though Annie loved Rhodes and her small business and Sal, some strange undefinable ache floated up from her belly, making her exhale into a sigh. It wasn't just that she was lonely—which she was. It was a feeling of being left behind. That a bigger, bolder life was happening somewhere else and she'd forgotten to show up. She'd always told herself she was happy here, and mostly she was. But sometimes Annie wondered if she'd let her simple existence shrink too much. Like she'd closed a door on a part of herself and left the key in a jacket she'd donated to Goodwill. Like she was playing a minor role in her own life.

As if sorting mail could sort her head, Annie began working through the pile on the front counter. The usual junk mail, catalogs for brands she'd bought one thing off of six years ago, some terrifying overdue bills . . . and then something that made her pause.

A bright red envelope, addressed to Annie Lightfoot in a looping cursive script. No stamp. No return address.

"Hey," Annie called to Sal. "Who dropped this off?"

Sal looked up from where he was topping off the shampoo bottles. "No idea."

Annie edged a finger under the envelope's lip. Inside was a note card illustrated with artsy line drawings of women's breasts. Across the top, embossed in bold gold letters, read FROM THE DESK OF JAZZ WHITAKER.

Annie sucked in a breath of surprise. Jasmine "Jazz" Whitaker. Annie hadn't seen or spoken to the artistic director of the Rhodes Playhouse since the early days of the pandemic. As soon as social distancing started, the theater closed. Jazz Whitaker had rented out her house and gone West to ride out lockdown with her ex-wife, Terry, with whom Jazz was still close. So it must've been six years, at least, since Annie and Jazz last spoke.

The handwritten note was brief.

Annie,

Please meet me at the Rhodes Playhouse this Sunday at four o'clock. I have something very important to discuss.

Fondly,
Jazz

That was it. No further clues.

Annie's pulse skittered like a startled rabbit. Her mind zoomed to the worst-case scenario.

Multilevel marketing.

Something messy with money.

Or worse—Jazz was . . . dying?

Just like Annie's beloved grandmother had, fourteen years ago, after a painfully long battle with heart failure. That had to be it. Jazz was dying and needed help or to say some sort of gut-wrenching goodbye.

Annie's throat tightened. A terrified "Oh no" fell out of her mouth.

"What's wrong?" Sal asked in alarm. "Who's it from?"

Or, Jazz was as healthy as ever and this "important" meeting was good news. Champagne to celebrate her return to Rhodes! She'd always had a flair for the dramatic, after all.

"Jazz Whitaker," Annie replied.

Sal frowned, trying to place the name. Unlike Annie, he hadn't grown up here. He'd moved to Rhodes after the playhouse closed.

"She ran the Rhodes Playhouse," Annie explained. "That old theater, over on Myrtle, at the other end of town? Jazz used to direct shows there—champion community theater. She lives—lived?—in this incredible Victorian ten minutes outside town." Annie hadn't pictured Jazz's rambling pink-and-purple dollhouse in years. "She's older, but we've been close since I was a teenager. Back when I was an . . ."

Annie pulled up short. She'd never told Sal about this chapter of her past. It wasn't a secret. It'd just never come up.

Sal, sensing a story, nudged. "Back when you were an . . ."

"An actor," Annie admitted. "A member of the Rhodes Players, the local acting troupe."

"*What?*" Sal stared at Annie with a look of disbelief and salacious excitement. "You? Were in shows? I knew you went to *see* plays but I didn't know you were *in* them!"

Annie blushed. "I wasn't very good. Honestly still don't know how I got cast. And all that was a million years ago."

"What were you in?"

"Just small parts—a fairy in *A Midsummer Night's Dream*. One of the shorter speeches in *The Vagina Monologues*." It was an effort to make all this sound somewhat trivial. Especially the next part. "And then, when I was sixteen—which I guess makes it twenty years ago—me and three other kids played the Tragedians in a gender-swapped version of *Rosencrantz and Guildenstern Are Dead*. By Tom Stoppard."

Sal gave an uncomprehending shrug: None of that scanned. "What's a Tra-gee-dee-uhn?" He spoke the unfamiliar word with vocal baby steps.

"Um, a troupe of traveling Elizabethan actors," Annie replied. "The story's sort of set inside the play *Hamlet* from the perspective of two of the minor characters." No easy feat to spontaneously sum up the absurdist, existential tragicomedy. "The four of us did mime and tumbling and physical comedy."

But of course, the teen quartet was so much more than just castmates.

"Look at you and your multitudes." Sal seemed impressed. He nodded at the note card in Annie's hand. "So, what'd Jazz say?"

Mysteriously little.

The Rhodes Playhouse had been little more than background scenery for years—until now. Memories surged, hot and fast, too big to shove back into the box she kept them in. She could almost hear the hushed murmurs of the audience. Feel the heat of the stage lights. See the secret spot in the green room backstage, where cast members scratched their names into the plywood. Was her name still there, next to the others'?

Queen bee Vicky, with her take-no-prisoners 'tude. Insecure Dylan, the baby of the group, who'd followed Vicky around like a lovesick puppy.

And, of course, Lola Wilson. The girl Annie had trained herself never to think about.

Warm hazel eyes the color of golden hour. The broad, stunning smile not many could summon. A brain even more exquisite than her face. Everyone knew she was going to be a star. And now, she was. Globetrotting on movie sets, leading a life that was light-years away from Annie's own.

The first girl Annie had ever loved.

The girl whose heart Annie had broken with a lie she'd never been brave enough to undo.

2.

"HERE SHE *ISSSS!*" LOLA'S PUBLICIST, KIMBERLY, SCREECHED the welcome, voice filled with delight. "Doll, you look *gorgeous.* Glam squad did *good.*"

Lola touched her blond, barrel-rolled curls that were so stiff with hairspray, they felt fake. Her stilettos were so high, she could practically sense the change in atmospheric pressure. "It's not too much?"

"It'll look great on camera," Kimberly assured her, examining Lola's face as shamelessly as an appraiser. "We might go heavier on the blush."

The press day for *Saturn Rising,* a multimillion-dollar sci-fi space battle, was underway at the Four Seasons in New York City. In the glitzy lobby, dozens of journalists from various media outlets were being told where to set up by busy production staff as hotel guests sipped morning coffee and lookie-loos openly stared. Oversize posters of the forthcoming blockbuster flanked the elevator banks. Under the sweeping title, six chiseled faces floated in order of importance. Lola's was the third. It was the biggest film she'd ever done: crew size, shoot length, paycheck. Her big break, even if right now she felt like a Barbie on stilts wearing too much blush.

"Brett's in sneakers?" Lola pointed to where her famous co-star was chatting up an enamored-looking receptionist. Brett Burns was in a T-shirt and jeans. *People* magazine's Sexiest Man Alive hadn't even shaved. Lola tugged down the hem of her short, tight dress, feeling the familiar sting of the industry's shameless double standards. "I didn't know we could wear jeans."

Kimberly waved this off. "But you look so hot! Like Charlize Theron's little sister. I would do murder for your jawline."

Lola didn't love that her colleagues openly commented on her appearance but that, apparently, was how things were done. "Could I at least wear my flats until I'm on camera?" Her feet were already pinched and throbbing.

"You're in *Louboutins,*" Kimberly enunciated. "Which means you've made it! C'mon, let's show the world how gorgeous you are."

"My face is probably the least interesting thing about me," Lola said, following the experienced publicist through the crowded foyer.

Kimberly laughed heartily. "And my connections are the least interesting thing about me," she joked back, stopping at an elevator bank and pushing the Up button. "Okay—I know this is more than you're used to, but you look great and you'll be fine. Just remember your media training. What's the most important thing?"

"Engage in meaningful dialogue that moves the cultural conversation forward and creates a more empathetic, deeply thinking society," Lola replied.

"*Smile.*" Kimberly gave the correct answer, demonstrating it in a way that made her look like a possessed clown.

Lola tried not to laugh. Her reflection in the silvered elevator doors was that of a stranger, her makeup as thick as a stage mask. "Of course," she said obediently, "that's what I meant."

They rode the elevator up ten floors, then navigated to a hotel suite. Even though it was balmy July in New York, the plush room was freezing, each window blacked out.

Lola arranged her body on a chair in front of blinding lights and a rolling camera, *smiling* at her first interviewer. Gemma Andrews was a peppy entertainment reporter in a candy-pink tube dress. "Lola, *hi.* So nice to meet you. Congrats on the film, I'm *obsessed* with it."

Even though this was Lola's first big press junket, she'd been in the industry long enough to know that *obsessed* could reasonably be interchanged with *aware of.* "Thank you, Gemma," she said. "And thank you for taking the time to talk with me today."

Gemma made an *aren't you sweet* face and glanced down at her clipboard. "So, this is, like, your big break, right?" she enthused. "How does it feel?"

Not how I thought it would was the unexpected answer that bubbled up in her head. Not the time to unpack it. "Wonderful," Lola dutifully replied. "I came up through the theater, starting in Rhodes, New York. I performed in plays for about a decade—lots of Chekhov and Ibsen—then made the switch to TV and film, as a way of opening up the sorts of stories I could tell."

"Also more money, amiright?" Gemma winked.

Inwardly, Lola cringed. Sure, but it'd sound too lofty to claim art was more important to her, even though it was.

"And you're *thirty-six,*" Gemma made it sound like Lola was one hundred and six. "You must have been wondering, 'Is this *ever* going to happen?'"

Lola's smile stayed frozen. Ageism wasn't absent in the theater, just less unapologetic. "I don't see life experience as an impediment."

"That is so brave," Gemma cooed. Her creaseless face suggested that, while likely born in the twenty-first century, she already got Botox, something Lola had so far managed to avoid. "You actually look way younger. Okay, so tell us about your character in the film—Zarina, right?"

"Yes, Zarina," Lola said. "She was quite a challenge to figure out."

"Why?"

Because Zarina was the most undeveloped character Lola had ever read. A blue-skinned alien whose plot function was two-fold: To seduce Captain Chris, played by Brett Burns, in a gratuitous hookup scene, prompting the male lead to realize who he *really* loved, his plucky second-in-command. And, second, to appear in a lot of skintight blue spandex.

"Zarina was a challenge to figure out because her backstory was so"—Lola avoided the phrase *nonexistent*—"mysterious. But that gave me room to build the character out myself. I had the freedom to make choices about her life and point of view."

"Amazing!" Gemma trilled. "Obsessed! Okay, now something a little more hard-hitting."

"Fantastic." Lola shifted forward as much as her dress would allow, eager to begin a meatier conversation.

"I have to know," Gemma said, "how did you fit into your costume?" She dropped her voice to a whisper. "Ozempic?"

What sort of questions was Brett being asked? Probably not how he fit into his space suit. "I worked out three times a week for six months," Lola replied. "But that brings up an interesting question. Zarina's look, her body—it's all very much defined by what we as a society find attractive. A product of the male gaze, no question. And yet, Zarina's from a different planet, a completely different culture. What does that say about the universality of these ideals? Is the male gaze something that exists beyond Earth, or is it just a projection of our own limited worldview? Even in a film that leans heavily on spectacle, I think it's important we engage with these larger, more philosophical questions."

Gemma blinked, glancing down at her clipboard with a puzzled frown.

Out of the corner of her eye, Lola saw Kimberly making a slashing movement over her throat while smiling demonically.

"Yeah, totally crucial . . ." Gemma tapped her pen against her lips. "So, Lola Wilson—who is your celebrity crush?"

Lola wilted like week-old craft services. One part of her knew to expect this. That this was the game and these were the rules, and she wasn't that naïve. But her most idealistic, committed, artistic part feared she'd made a much bigger misstep. "Celebrity crush?" she repeated in a monotone. "I don't have one."

"What about Brett Burns?" Gemma pushed. "I'm so jealous you got paid to make out with him—*goals.*"

Brett Burns kissed like a dead fish. Lola had been single for over a year. Trust issues, a therapist once diagnosed. *You leave them before they leave you even if they're not planning on it.* Brett was the last person Lola would have a crush on. But in the corner, Kimberly was giving two enthusiastic thumbs up.

Lola felt herself float up above the room, like a ghost with a SAG card. "Sure," Lola said, her mouth gamely twisted into a smile. "My celebrity crush is Brett Burns."

EIGHT HOURS AND twenty-five interviews later, Lola Wilson finally let herself back into her Tribeca loft. Sweet relief to get out of her nightmare heels and feel the solidity of wooden floorboards under her feet. She was exhausted. She was starving. And she was lost. Lola knew a day of TikTok and YouTube content creation was a far cry from her dream of being on *Fresh Air* with Terry Gross. But the lived experience of answering trivial questions designed for attention spans of three seconds or less left Lola feeling diminished and inconsequential.

After a long, hot shower, Lola dressed in jeans and an old T-shirt and wandered to the kitchen in search of a snack. Her fridge, like the rest of the apartment, was distressingly bare. She'd bought the loft last year, charmed by its high ceilings and exposed brick—everything she was supposed to want—but it never felt like hers. When she'd first moved in, she'd been filming on location, so she had an interior designer set it up with the basics, intending to finish it herself. Make it feel true to who she was: a lover of stories and big ideas. Lola envisioned a lush, creative oasis full of beautiful memories and lush plants and things that'd spark unforgettable conversations. A bookshelf filled with her favorite plays and memoirs, walls lined with framed playbills and art that moved her.

But Lola could never find the time or the inspiration. Her playbills were still in storage. The only plant she could keep alive was a cactus. And all her fridge was offering was a jar of dill pickles.

It was just after seven in the evening. Pickles would tide her over, and then, maybe she'd take herself out for dinner. Cheer herself up—and celebrate the movie—with a big bowl of pasta and a bigger glass of wine. In *sneakers.* When was the last time she'd allowed herself that? The thought almost made her giddy.

Lola's phone rang. It was Kevin, the hungry L.A. agent who'd wooed Lola off the stage and onto the screen, seven years ago. The next logical step, he'd said. And dream chasing implied ascension, didn't it? Forward momentum.

She tapped Accept. "Hey, Kev."

"Wilson. How'd it go today?"

Lola scooped up her phone and jar of pickles and padded over to her long white sectional, sinking gratefully into the soft cushions. "Think I really moved the needle on sci-fi space skirmishes as a metaphor for our divided world."

He chuckled warily. "Well, I'll look forward to a call from Kimberly about that. Anyway, I'm calling because I have news."

"About?"

"Hood."

A blockbuster reboot of the English folktale, but this time, Robin had superpowers and his merry men were ripped. Working tagline: *A legend reborn. A hood unmasked.* Lola was up for the role of Maid Marian, who did not have superpowers but did have the line, "I'd look under his hood." It was down to her and a total unknown, Sabina Waters. The role offered an embarrassing amount of money and was starring opposite Clay Russo, the good-guy A-list action hero who the internet drooled over.

"Oh?" Lola bolted upright, alert. "Yeah?"

Kevin let out a sigh of defeat. "I'm *so* sorry, dude, but they went with Sabina."

"What?" Lola felt a punch of shock. "But—all those auditions." Four rounds, all in L.A., each in front of more and more gatekeepers. "All that effort." For nothing.

"I know!" Kevin moaned. "Those fuckers. But we'll get the next one."

Lola waited for the crush of disappointment, the urge to burst into tears or demand that Kevin get her another shot. But all she felt was . . . relief.

Which was the wrong reaction. Completely wrong.

She'd been asked a dozen times today if she'd enjoyed making *Saturn Rising.* She'd answered in the affirmative, but each time, the words felt more hollow. Acting in front of a green screen while poured into blue spandex didn't feel like making art. It felt like making money, and everyone involved understood the assignment except her.

Sure, her theater years had been physically demanding and financially starved, but at least they meant something. Rehearsals were a time of passion and persistence, where every word was thoughtfully analyzed, every movement carefully considered. Feeding off a live audience during a performance used to make Lola feel profoundly alive.

But now her life was an endless treadmill of fighting for roles with no substance and no soul.

She hadn't enjoyed *Saturn Rising*'s preproduction. Hadn't enjoyed filming. Hadn't enjoyed the big, fancy press day. All that was left was the premiere, which from experience Lola suspected would be a too-long night of fake smiling in another uncomfortable dress.

Was this it? Was this . . . the dream?

An alarm sounded in her chest. One Lola hurriedly shut off.

Instead, she inhaled a defiant breath. It was far too late to turn back now. The sunk cost was titanic. Starting over? Impossible.

"You're right, Kev." Lola forced herself to sound optimistic. "Their loss."

"That's the spirit!" Kevin's tone became upbeat. "Let's talk about what's next." Shuffling papers sounded over the phone. "Oh, this is gonna be *huge*. Super edgy thriller that's like *Chucky* set in a Build-A-Bear Workshop. You're the unlucky hottie who picks the wrong bear."

"Pass," Lola said.

"All right, okay, what about . . . *Moon People*? *Massive* ensemble drama set in the first moon colony. Really gritty and grounded, maybe even Oscar-worthy!"

"And I'm one of the colonists?"

"No, you're the scientist who stays on Earth and just *watches* the colonists."

Lola rolled her eyes so hard she risked fracturing an eyeball. "Pass."

"Yeah, probably for the best, I think it's a lot of you looking into a telescope. Ooh, this is up your alley. A biopic of—wait for it—Marie Curie."

Lola perked up. "The scientist?"

"Exactly. The take is she's brainy *and* a babe. *Marie Curie: Radium Nights.* Tagline: *Science has never been hotter.*"

Lola cringed. "The woman won a Nobel Prize."

"Yeah, and imagine the poster. You in a lab coat, *glowing.* I have chills."

Lola had to laugh or she'd scream. It was bizarre that even though her career was peaking, she had so little control over it. "C'mon, Kev."

"Hey, these are all solid roles that pay well." Kevin sounded defensive. "*Marie Curie* will be massive! I busted my ass to get you in the mix!"

Lola rubbed her temples, feeling torn. "But like I keep saying, I want to be in things that are smart. Adventurous. Meaningful."

"I'm trying, dude! But you gotta play the game. One for you, one for them."

The idea that artists alternated one project for themselves, and one for "them": studios, mainstream taste, palms that needed greasing. "Feels like we're making every choice for 'them,'" Lola muttered.

"Because we're still breaking you out," Kevin said. "But *Saturn Rising*'s going to destroy opening weekend and then, we're gold, baby. In the meantime . . ."

The sound of more shuffling papers. A pause.

"You did actually get an *adventurous* invitation this week. Your old friend Chazz—or was it Jazz? No, I think it was Chazz—sent something. Here we go." Kevin began reciting. "*Lola, Please meet me at the Rhodes Playhouse this Sunday at four o'clock. I have something very important to discuss. Fondly, Jazz.* Oh," Kevin added. "Guess it was Jazz."

Lola had turned into Alice, tumbling headfirst down the rabbit hole, her world tilting into the surreal.

Jazz Whitaker. The first person to believe in her talent. Lola recalled, with absolute clarity, the way the colorful director had looked Lola in the eye after her very first audition and said, with rapt delight: *Oh, you're a* real *actor.* Jazz was enthusiastic and supportive; she was Lola's first mentor. When Jazz learned Lola was interested in directing as well, she'd taken Lola under her wing, let her shadow the production. And Jazz was the first person Lola knew who lived openly as a lesbian, proudly and without shame. Jazz changed everything.

"This Sunday?" Lola said. "She wants to meet in person?"

"At four," Kevin said. "My assistant tried to make it a Zoom, but he couldn't find a contact. Looks like the Rhodes Playhouse has been closed for years."

In her mind's eye, Lola saw the red velvet seats fanning out from the wooden boards of the raised stage. The silly but fun pre-show warm-ups. The adrenaline-fueled anticipation of walking onstage. *Five minutes to places!*

Lola hadn't been back to Rhodes in twenty years.

Was Annie Lightfoot still there?

Just thinking her name felt like conjuring a spell. Wishing for something impossible. Picturing Annie's sweet, open face evoked a muscle memory of longing and desire. Which hardened instantly into pain and sadness.

Annie had stolen her heart and had never given it back. Lola swore she'd never speak to her again. A promise, thus far, she'd kept.

"And it's just an invite for me," Lola clarified. "On my own?"

"Only addressed to you," Kevin said.

Lola felt a push-pull of relief and disappointment.

Annie Lightfoot. Vicky Fang. Dylan Rogers. They'd all been so close that summer. The closest, Lola realized, that she'd ever been to a group of friends. Before it all imploded. At the closing night after-party. When everything fell apart, for all of them. The drama scattered the tight quartet to the wind. To Lola's knowledge no one stayed in touch.

"Not to sound crude," Kevin said, "but odds are Jazz wants money, or some other favor, now that you're big-time."

"That's not Jazz's style." Lola spoke out of loyalty, but Kevin might be right.

"Well, if I had to guess," Kevin said, "a rinky-dink theater is trying to profit off your name, but of course, it's up to you."

Lola's heart thumped. She didn't just hear it—she *felt* it: every what-if, every if-only. She pictured Rhodes, with its charming cobbled main street and mom-and-pop shops. You always saw so much more sky, out of the city.

A siren outside wailed, making her jump. She was in Tribeca, in busy New York City, one hundred miles from her sweet and sleepy hometown. That was the past, one full of painful memories. And Lola had enough to deal with right here in the present.

"You don't have to worry," Lola said. "I'm not going back to Rhodes."

"Good. Now, do me a favor. Read *Marie Curie* tonight."

"Tonight?" Lola exhaled. "I was about to grab dinner." Pasta. Wine. *Sneakers.*

"Order in! This is your moment, Wilson. Things are gonna change. I can *feel* it!"

Who could argue with that? She was on a hard-won path, and everybody knew that meant sacrifices. "Fine." Lola relented. "Send *Marie* my way."

3.

"I'M GUESSING I'LL BE AN HOUR," ANNIE TOLD SAL, BOUNCING from foot to foot. "Maybe less. Maybe more?"

From the low stool by his station, Sal swiped the inside of a Rhodesian Ridgeback's ear with the focus one would give to cleaning the *Mona Lisa*. "Roger that."

Their slow Sunday afternoon was coming up alarmingly fast on four o'clock. Annie's excitement at her much-anticipated meeting with Jazz was undercut by sharp worry that her old friend would deliver bad news that'd break her heart.

"We don't have any more bookings," Sal added. "Take your time, boo."

Sal wasn't technically Annie's brother, but he might as well have been. They'd met over a decade ago, when Sal worked in palliative care, doing weekly home visits for Annie's grandmother Pearl in the final year of her life. Even back then, Sal struck a balance of care and snark, which made Pearl chuckle when little else could. They'd reconnected after Annie moved back to Rhodes. Sal was slinging beers at a gay bar in Hudson. Even staying six feet apart, in masks, they'd become fast friends. Sal was one of the first people to encourage Annie to start her own business, spending hours helping her sketch out blueprints and dreaming up the quirky, queer-coded menu. Their most affordable service? The Rose Apothecary Wash & Dry: *Treat your precious pooch to a luxurious shampoo, followed by a gentle blow-dry to leave their coat as soft as* David's *face!* Then there was the *Heated Rivalry* hairdo: *Get your fur baby's coat as springy as Ilya's curls!* Or the *Buffy* teeth brushing: *Love your pup as much as Willow loved Tara? Slay teeth decay with our gentle ultrasound cleaning!*

It was Sal's idea for employees to wear matching pink jumpsuits. When she'd presented him with a suit, hand-stitched with his name in curling lime-green font and asked if he'd be the Thelma to her Louise, Sal *almost* teared up as he agreed, stating that a lifetime of serving bitchy queens had prepared him for serving queeny bitches.

Annie trusted Sal, but now she was stalling, straightening a shampoo bottle by the front counter. "You sure there isn't anything that needs doing?"

Sal gave the Ridgeback a pat. "Well, you could help me express this good boy's anal glands."

Annie cringed. Not her favorite part of the job.

"Annie," Sal said, smile twitching. "Ever considered I might want to run the salon alone? More experience. More hours. More money."

"Oh. Right. Okay, I'm going."

Annie ducked out the back for one last fit check in her office, which was so small she had to shuffle sideways like a crab around her desk to get to the wall mirror.

At least she had a reason to wear her new outfit: a funky vintage sundress patterned with yellow flowers. Summer-groovy when paired with sky-blue sandals and a heart-shaped pair of sunglasses. She finger-combed her light pink bob, fiddling with the ends that skimmed the bottom of her jaw, and dabbed on some cherry lip balm. Meeting her own gaze in the mirror, Annie felt satisfied with what she saw—someone cute yet capable. She dropped into a curtsy, addressing her reflection. "M'lady." One must always have inside jokes with oneself.

Grabbing a straw bucket hat, Annie crab-walked her way around the desk and out the door.

IT WAS A beautiful Sunday afternoon. The July sun was bright, the humidity pleasant and not yet at the feeling-licked-by-a-Great-Dane stage. It was only a seven- or eight-minute drive to the theater, and Annie owned a yellow Volkswagen Beetle. But she needed the walk to calm her nerves.

Most of the town's shops and bars were clustered along this end of Henry Street, the Hudson River just beyond the train tracks. The Groom Room was close to the station—two and a half hours to New York City, but lately, Rhodes felt even farther. The theater was at the less busy, less populated end of town. The part that was encroaching on the "busy" end of town, little by little, year by year.

Not that Rhodes was written off just yet. The window boxes of the old general store, though neglected, still held tufts of stubborn marigolds, their bright orange petals catching the afternoon light.

Annie passed Clyde's Grocery, where she'd had her first job at age fifteen until Clyde fired her for letting too many senior citizens use expired coupons. (Annie believed women could do anything men could, except, in her circumstance, telling Betty Buford she could not have two dollars off her cat food.)

The store's long roller door was up. While most of the produce was inside, wooden bins of fresh fruit and vegetables lined the sidewalk. Zero customers, but that didn't stop Clyde saluting cheerfully from his position behind the counter. "Hello there, Annie!"

"Hello there, Clyde," Annie called back, pausing to sniff a peach.

"Where are you off to on this lovely afternoon?" Her neighborhood grocer still wore the red grocer's apron he'd had on since the store first opened, except his hair was now white and his belly was as large as his growing eccentricities.

"Just . . . getting some fresh air," she fibbed.

"Very nice." Clyde nodded. "Annie, have you ever heard of the Mothman?"

"Can't say I have, Clyde."

The grocer became animated as he explained that the Mothman was a half-man, half-moth who people claimed to see before a cataclysmic event. "But does the Mothman cause the disaster," Clyde posited, "or is he trying to warn us?"

"Bigger question, Clyde," Annie replied, "is the Mothman eating sweaters for breakfast? Scarves for lunch?" She waved. "Gotta run!"

Annie rarely came up to the far edge of town. Not only because she had no need to—the train station and exit to the city were closer to her salon—but also because this quieter end was close to Summerville Road. The street that Lola used to live on.

As teenagers, Lola and Annie had both lived in town: Annie, in the wisteria-covered cottage owned by her grandmother. It was snug, but they made it homey. Lola's single mother, Renée, rented an even smaller apartment that backed onto the train line. Annie remembered low ceilings and silverware rattling when the express train rocketed past. She and Lola, both sophomores, went to Hudson High, a public school.

Vicky and Dylan lived in much bigger houses outside of town and went to Riverstone Prep, a K–12 private school. Smart, fearless Vicky was a family law attorney now, working in Manhattan.

Annie couldn't find Dylan Rogers. There was another Dylan Rogers, an older British guy who was a bestselling author of an epic romantasy series. *Sorcery & Scales* centered on shape-shifting dragons and horny young magicians with names like Isolde Nightshade and Aric Flameheart. That Dylan Rogers made it finding someone with the same name, and as few details as Annie had, impossible to unearth.

Annie paused at the top of Summerville Road, gazing down on the unassuming red-brick apartment block. How many times had she taken this turn, her heart bouncing in happy anticipation? And how far it all seemed now from the Lola Wilson whom Annie would only ever see in an occasional Google search. Which, after a second glass of wine, she'd succumbed to last night.

On Annie's phone screen, a platinum Lola looked unrecognizably glamorous in a new interview, revealing her *celebrity crush*. Brett Burns—a paint-by-numbers leading man from a big sci-fi movie Annie would never watch.

A man. So, Lola probably didn't date girls anymore. Another thing they no longer had in common. Lola Wilson was a capital-F Famous Hollywood actor and Annie didn't know any of those. She'd known a girl who loved the theater, and the Indigo Girls, and talking earnestly about art and big ideas. Whose lips were eager and soft and couldn't stop smiling when they'd kiss, secretly, during one unforgettable summer.

A summer she should *not* be thinking about! Lola was a completely different person now, probably on a private jet to the kind of rich-person spa they didn't let normies into, where a beet juice cost as much as a small car and they massaged inside your mouth.

Lola left Rhodes. Annie came back. And that's why it was Annie, *not* Lola, whom Jazz had requested to see.

Annie took a left onto Myrtle Street. On the corner, yet another empty shop front. Once upon a time this had been home to Once Upon a Time, a beloved kids' bookstore. Now wild honeysuckle twisted around the wrought iron railing of the unused patio. Annie paused by the smudged windows. She vaguely remembered the whimsical displays from years ago—storybook castles, paper dragons—but now, the interior lay bare, undressed. Without the theater pulling crowds to this end of town, businesses like this didn't stand a chance.

Continuing on, Annie passed a few freestanding houses, an

overgrown lot of unruly, scorched grass, and then, all by itself at the end of the block, there it was.

Rhodes Playhouse. Or, as the misshapen maroon lettering on the sign above the front entrance actually read, *odes P ayho e,* like a permanently paused game of hangman.

The once-pristine cream of its painted weatherboards had faded to a murky gray, peeling and patchy. The windows were filthy, the front lawn overgrown with weeds.

Annie's chest tightened. The Rhodes Playhouse used to be the heartbeat of the neighborhood. Now it felt like visiting a revered old friend, only to find their home in tragic disrepair, milk curdling in the fridge.

She walked up the concrete steps to the overlarge front entrance, took a fortifying breath to calm her nerves, and tried the grimy gold handle, half expecting the enormous door to be locked.

To her surprise, it creaked open.

Inside, the foyer was empty and dim, the late-afternoon light filtering in bruised colors through the unwashed windows.

There was the box office counter with the old-style ticket taker's desk, where if she squinted, Annie could almost see a smiling volunteer selling tickets. On the other side, the concession stand, its shelves now void of chips and candy. The popcorn machine sat empty, sad and neglected. Annie smiled wistfully, remembering how they used to help themselves to buttery popcorn (free for performers!), eating it backstage in the green room, licking greasy fingers.

"Hello?" Annie called, listening. "Jazz?"

Nothing. The playhouse was utterly, and atypically, silent. It was a space meant for noise—the chatter of the preshow audience, the reverent hush as the lights dimmed, the first clear lines of dialogue ringing out from the stage. It was meant for magic, had always felt mythic. The magic was faded now, like music in the far distance, the melody impossible to detect.

The checkerboard parquet floors were gritty underfoot as Annie crossed the foyer, toward the doors leading to the theater itself. On the walls, framed posters of past shows hung askew—*Fun Home* and *Who's Afraid of Virginia Woolf?* and *Love! Valour! Compassion!* and—

"Oh." Her gaze snagged on the original poster for *Rosencrantz and Guildenstern Are Dead,* their play, impossibly twenty years old. It hit like a slap from the past, a hand gloved in velvet, smelling of stage makeup. Annie's breath left her in a soft *ha* at seeing the once-familiar design. Their names were the last ones listed: Vicky Fang, Annie Lightfoot, Dylan Rogers, Lola Wilson.

Back then, the two leads, pictured on the poster, were played by Trixie Hartzog and Ava Kingsley. Trixie was a local legend who used to run an iconic vintage clothing store, Va-Va-Vintage, and who always put aside pieces for people if she felt she'd found a match. Ava was a charismatic flame-haired actor who'd just finished starring in a production of *The Importance of Being Earnest* on (gasp!) Broadway—making her famous, at least to four teenagers from Upstate. Jazz had always treated her casts as equals, no matter their age or experience. It'd felt so cool, so grown-up, to be in rehearsals, and then onstage, with these *adults.* It made Annie feel like she was part of something that really mattered.

Ava, inadvertently, gave Lola her big break. Lola was her understudy, and the one night Ava was out with the flu, Lola's performance was caught by a Broadway producer. He was so impressed by the talented sixteen-year-old, he'd offered her the role of Scout in a touring show of *To Kill a Mockingbird.* And so Lola left. And never came back.

Annie placed a hand on the door leading into the theater itself, the wood warm and dusty beneath her palm. Was the big, bold life Annie had sensed existing without her somehow on the other side?

Only one way to find out.

The doors to the theater whined in protest as Annie pushed them open. The space beyond was pitch-black and musty.

"Hello?" Annie called again, squinting into the darkness. "Is it me you're looking for?"

Nothing.

"Jazz!" Annie called, then shouted, "Jazz! I'm here!"

Still nothing. She tried a few light switches, but none of the overhead lights or sconces turned on. Dragging a trash can in front of the doors to ensure she wasn't trapped in the dark, Annie switched her phone's flashlight app all the way up, then made her way up the central aisle, jumpy with anticipation and nerves.

Her beam illuminated the green and gold crisscross pattern on the carpet, then swept over the rows of faded red velvet seats in the orchestra and then up higher, to the ones on the balcony.

Her light barely touched the crystal chandelier, once sparkling with a thousand tiny lights, now hanging lifeless. Beyond it, she could just make out the gold and rose gilded plasterwork, marred by cracks and peeling paint.

The tall, red curtains that fell from the ceiling were open, revealing the empty stage.

The space was pin-drop silent, but Annie's heart hammered like someone pounding on a door, each beat a memory unlocked.

She remembered peeking out from the edge of the curtains, scanning the audience before a show, looking for friends from school or her grandmother, who came once a week and always sat in the very front row. She remembered watching rehearsals of scenes she wasn't in from the back of the theater, Lola's bare thigh pressed to her own. Most of all she just remembered a *feeling,* the feeling of that time, in this place. A feeling of being young and daring and excited by the world, hopeful for the future. She remembered her friends and the way they were thick as thieves. Riding their bikes without helmets to rehearsal, leaving them unlocked on the lawn, pushing open the front door like they owned the place.

Jumping off the pier into the Hudson River, screaming as the cold hit their sun-warmed skin. Making a bong out of an apple, getting high for the first time and raiding Vicky's candy collection. Playing truth or dare on Dylan's bedroom floor or around a fire pit under a spread of stars, confessing secret things that were accepted as sacred and true. Laughing until she peed her pants. Kissing until her lips were puffy and tender, then being teased about it by Vicky and Dylan, who knew Annie's secret, that she liked girls, specifically, Lola, who liked her right back. A shared, precious secret that only the four of them understood, because Vicky and Dylan were obsessed with each other, too, even if they never acted on it. She remembered catching Lola's gaze, be it alone or with the others or seconds before walking onstage, and feeling like the entire universe—every star, every song, every precious thing—was in her eyes, and how badly she wanted to exist in there forever.

Until Annie destroyed everything with a single, devastating lie that she'd never forgiven herself for.

Annie didn't know how special that summer was until it was over and gone for good. And now, standing in the center aisle, gazing up at the sacred Rhodes Playhouse stage, it was all rushing back.

The theater wasn't supposed to look like this: cast aside and forgotten, like a scruffy rescue dog no one wanted. It was almost too much to bear.

She headed toward the front row, ascending five wooden steps to stand in the center of the stage. She gazed out at the dress circle, and above, barely visible, the empty balcony seats. An audience of none. But art needed an audience.

Impulsively, Annie did a twirl, her flashlight circling her in light. She let out a chuckle. That was silly but fun, so she did it again. Stages were made for performing, after all. Another spin, then without even consciously deciding to, she broke into a little soft shoe shuffle. She could almost feel something grinding loose in the old theater, as if it were a giant, ancient wind-up toy that someone was cranking alive.

"And a bah, dah, ba-ba-ba," Annie sang to herself, tapping and sliding her feet across the stage. "Bah, dah, ba-ba-ba!" Her voice rose, her movements becoming more exaggerated, arms pinwheeling, feet carrying her this way, then that. When was the last time she danced like no one was watching? When was the last time she let go? This was her moment! Better make it count. "*Bah! Dah! Ba-ba-BAAAAH!*"

She spun once more and struck a final pose, arms flung wide, unexpected delight bursting through her chest.

"Brava." A female voice sounded from the audience, clear as a bell.

Annie screamed and dropped her phone. It landed face up, blocking the flashlight and plunging her into near pitch-black. Annie squeaked and dropped to fumble for it, awash with embarrassment that someone had been watching. "Jazz? S-sorry, I thought I was alone."

"I didn't mean to scare you." The low, musical voice sounded closer. Warm and amused.

Annie found her phone, flipping it up to aim it at the voice.

Like an apparition, the beam conjured a woman in the center aisle. She wore a posh, peach-colored dress that hung halter-neck-style off an elegant gold ring circling a swanlike throat. Patent nude heels added a few inches of height, making her almost six feet. Her silvery-blond hair was slicked into a low bun. A bracelet of what looked like diamonds—*legit* diamonds—circled one wrist. Her body looked sculpted and strong and as hairless as a mannequin.

Flawless. Expensive.

The world stilled, pausing on its axis.

Then Annie's stomach plunged through the floorboards. She gasped, stumbling back a step.

"*Lola?*"

4.

LOLA'S BREATH CAUGHT, SHARP AND SHALLOW. HER HEART jolted hard, like a compass snapping north.

She hadn't planned on coming back.

But when Lola woke that morning, a sense of responsibility pressed into her chest. Jazz was the first adult who spoke of the future as something that was Lola's to conquer. She'd booked a car. A quick trip, up and back, before her event tonight: a launch party for a carbon-neutral shoe brand designed by AI. (Important to be "out there," her publicist had emphasized.)

At first, Lola let herself enjoy her return, feeling a swell of pride as the car rolled up familiar old Henry Street. A moment she'd dreamed of ever since she was a kid—returning to her hometown as *someone*. Not just a girl with big dreams, but a working actor. A name.

But then things started feeling more complicated.

Sadly, the shops had thinned at the far end of town, empty lots and deserted storefronts with sun-faded FOR LEASE signs replacing the friendly mom-and-pop shops and services Lola remembered.

She hadn't anticipated the impact of seeing the neglected theater—the peeling paint and empty lobby. The silence where there used to be noise and light. It wasn't just about the playhouse. It wasn't even about Jazz.

It was about the version of herself she'd left behind.

And now that she was here, standing in the dusty theater, watching Annie Lightfoot's eyes widen across the stage, Lola realized how badly she wanted that girl back.

"What are you doing here?" Annie blurted, her whole face blanched of color.

Lola drew on every part of her talent and training to appear unruffled, even as she realized what a self-centered idiot she'd been. Jazz hadn't just invited *her.* "Jazz wrote to me," she replied. "*Something very important to discuss.* You as well?"

Annie gave a dazed nod, the same shocked revelation that Lola was feeling rolling like a summer storm over her face.

In her colorful sundress, cute straw hat, and light blue sandals, Annie looked as simple and pretty as a summer afternoon. Which made Lola feel wildly overdressed. Why was she wearing heels? She hated heels.

Trying not to show her insecurity, Lola gestured lightly at the stage. "That was quite a performance. I didn't realize you'd turned pro."

The old Annie would've grinned and tossed off a pithy reply about being a back-up dancer for Taylor Swift—*it's all in the hips, babe!* But the new Annie walked tight-lipped down the stage steps, pausing at the bottom to fold her arms across her chest. "Well, it's been a while."

"Yes," Lola said. "It has."

Should they hug? Probably not, but, like a sleeper agent, Lola's body activated, and she stop-started forward. They embraced stiffly, more accident, less intent, bodies pressing together.

And yet—Jesus—Annie still fit against her in the same way. Lola's mind flicked back, unbidden, to a different embrace: the night after their last performance of *Rosencrantz,* still in costume, huddled under a scratchy theater blanket in the green room. Annie had pressed her face into Lola's neck. "*You have to leave, and when you do, I'm going to miss you so much I might die.*" Lola had kissed her, promising, "*I'm not going anywhere.*" A promise she had not kept.

Lola's mind screamed to step back, end the hug. But her body betrayed her, softening against the warmth of Annie's bare skin. She smelled like summer in the country—fresh-cut grass, a hint of BBQ smoke, cherries so ripe the juice runs down your chin. The past and the present collided at full speed, and Lola didn't know if she was sixteen or thirty-six or where she lived or what her last name was. Her mind went static while her muscles softened like butter in the midday sun.

Then Annie let go, scooting back as if she'd just been pushed, and Lola remembered the situation.

"Just us?" Lola glanced around the theater, keeping her voice cool. "Where's Jazz?"

"No idea."

"What's all this about?"

"Your guess is as good as mine."

"Huh." Lola frowned. "Mysterious."

The two women looked around the empty theater. Not at each other.

"Jazz?" Annie tried. "Hello?"

Nothing.

It was bizarre to feel so unwelcome in the place that'd once felt like home. So tongue-tied with the girl with whom she used to talk about everything. It was like rewatching her favorite movie and finding an entirely new cast, a completely different plot. The moment lengthened into awkwardness until Lola couldn't take it.

"So, Annie . . . where are you living now? What are you up to?"

Annie recoiled, as if Lola had just asked her how often she masturbated. "Just . . . keeping out of trouble," she replied. "What about you?"

If Annie wasn't answering the question, neither was Lola. "Same," she replied crisply. "Keeping out of trouble."

They lapsed into a silence so uncomfortable that it made Lola's ribs hurt.

"Let's explore," Annie said, abruptly about-facing and heading back up the stage steps.

"Good idea," Lola said, because anything would be better than pretending they barely knew each other.

Switching on her own phone light, Lola followed Annie to the wings, her heels clicking over the stage. Stacks of painted plywood—makeshift sets—lined the dusty walls backstage, alongside bins of old props.

The door to the green room was open.

"Whoa," Annie breathed. "It's all exactly the same."

A few years ago, Lola did a movie that featured a set of her character's childhood room. The production designer used some of Lola's own memories of *her* childhood bedroom, for authenticity. Walking on set the first day of filming, Lola was stunned to see the same posters she had of *Ghost World* and *Mulholland Drive.* A CD collection filled with Sheryl Crow and Norah Jones and the Indigo Girls. That same sense of past-present surreality enveloped her now as she took in the green room.

Their zigzagging phone lights illuminated half a dozen chairs tucked under the long wooden bench that abutted the wall of mirrors, framed by dozens of light bulbs to illuminate performers putting on their makeup, fixing their hair. The ugly orange plaid couch was still pushed against the far wall, scattered with the mismatched cushions Jazz picked up from secondhand stores.

The air was musty but the smell was recognizable: cedar and hairspray and dreams. Lola found her own reflection in the mirror, startled to see an unrecognizable woman in a Stella McCartney dress and heels, not a guileless teenager in cutoffs and kicks. Why was she red-carpet-ready for a casual meeting in an old theater?

"Oh my goodness," Annie said in awe. She was crouched under the wooden bench in front of the mirrors, aiming her phone light at its underside.

Curious, Lola knelt down to follow Annie's gaze.

Annie's chipped lime-green-painted nail pointed at four names scratched in black pen, each in their own distinctive handwriting. *Annie Lightfoot. Lola Wilson. Vicky Fang. Dylan Rogers.*

Lola remembered the way the pen tip had dug into the soft plywood. How had it been twenty years?

Squished this close to each other, Lola could just make out the tiny freckles sprinkled over Annie's ski-jump nose. The faint lines around her powder-blue eyes that weren't there two decades ago. The choppy-chic pink bob that curved around her cheek was both cute and cool, a disorientating combination. Three gold stud piercings curved up her lobe: a croissant, a smiley face, and a heart.

"I can't believe they're all still there," Annie murmured, glancing at Lola. Their eyes locked and the feeling hit Lola's sternum like lightning. She swallowed a gasp. *What was happening*? Why was she *here*, pretending innocent-looking Annie hadn't broken her teenage heart into a million pieces for no good reason at all?

Panic sprang up like a sprinkler on a summer lawn. She had to get out of here.

Lola scooted out from under the bench. "This was fun," she lied, brushing dirt off her now-marked dress, "and it was good to see you." Another lie. "But actually, I have to go."

"Already?" Annie said, following her up. "But Jazz isn't here yet."

Lola backed up, resisting the urge to run. "I'm sorry," she said. "Give Jazz my best. Tell her—"

"Girls!"

They both jumped.

A woman in her seventies stood in the green room doorway. She was wearing oversize Iris Apfel–style glasses, a boldly patterned muumuu, and colorful bracelets stacked up both arms. Her pale skin was flushed with excitement and her short hair was a brilliant snow-white. Her voice was warm, raspy with age but brimming with enthusiasm. Jazz Whitaker still knew how to make an entrance. "You've found each other. Again!"

AFTER EXCHANGING HUGS and hellos, the pair followed Jazz up the circular staircase to the director's colorful, overstuffed office on the second floor. The walls were still crowded with framed posters and black-and-white stills from past shows. The office was windowless, but a few candles and an oil lamp cast the room in warm, yellow light—Jazz assured them she'd get the electricity back on in a jiffy.

"I thought you were still in California," Annie said, as they all got settled.

"My renters gave notice and I couldn't get anyone else in," Jazz said. "As much as I'd loved the Wild West, I decided it was time to come home. I missed the seasons. Missed Rhodes. Even if it has changed a little since I left. Which," she added, "is why I asked you to come." She focused on them each in turn. "The truth is, I don't have many years left."

Annie stiffened. "Oh god." She exhaled in horror. "I knew it."

Panic seized Lola's chest. She kept her tone even. "What's the diagnosis?"

"Good lord, I'm not *dying,*" Jazz said, with an offended laugh. "I'm as healthy as a horse! Just . . . an old one. I'm seventy-eight, my loves. And I want to make sure that when I go, the theater stays open."

"Oh." Annie let out a breath of relief. "The theater. Of course."

"We never reopened after Covid started; the Rhodes Players are defunct. But, I have a plan." Behind her oversize glasses, Jazz's eyes twinkled. "Not just for the theater. For the town as a whole. Look, it's no secret Rhodes isn't *living its best life.*" Jazz addressed Lola. "Young people move elsewhere and we're not on the tourist beat. We need a point of difference. A *draw.* My vision," Jazz declared, "is to rebrand our town as Upstate's number one queer destination! Like Fire Island and P-Town. A safe haven and celebration of the gays!"

Points for the reveal. Not what Lola was expecting.

"Oh-kay . . ." Annie said, sounding bemused. "Based on . . . what?"

Jazz sifted through the collection of books and clippings covering her desk. "Did you know we were the first Upstate town to have a presence at Pride? The first town in the county to pass a nondiscrimination ordinance? That *Oscar Wilde* once summered nearby?"

"I did not." Annie sounded surprised.

"It's mentioned in a biography." Jazz flicked through a dog-eared hardcover. "He called the lake 'a divine little mirror' and scandalized the locals by swimming in 'indecent' silk robes."

Lola chuckled, even as she tried to figure out how she and Annie fit into this plan.

"In the sixties, the old general store was a gay speakeasy, raided at least five times before Stonewall." Jazz went on, "In the seventies, a collective of lesbian artists bought a gallery on Henry—one of their shows was almost shut down for 'obscenity' because of a nude sculpture called *Eve Eats the Apple and Likes It.* A sculpture I proudly own!"

Annie laughed, a genuine, hearty guffaw. The sound softened something hard buried deep in Lola's chest.

Jazz leaned forward over her desk. "Rhodes is already legendary—we just need to remind people."

"How, exactly?" Lola asked.

"A revival!" Jazz's pale eyes gleamed. "Of *Rosencrantz and Guildenstern Are Dead.*" She arced her hand through the air, twinkling her fingers. "A one-night-only fundraiser, last Saturday of August. And you, Lola Wilson, will headline."

Act. Onstage. Back in Rhodes. Lola couldn't keep the incredulity out of her voice. "You mean . . . the—same cast?"

"Sort of!" Jazz's face was alive, jumping on what she seemed to perceive as interest. "But this time, you kids will be in the starring roles."

"I have a prior commitment that week." Lola was relieved for the excuse. "A big premiere for a film I'm in."

"We'll work around it!" Jazz scribbled a note, already moving on. "Annie, you'll be our lighthearted Rosencrantz."

"Me?" Annie sounded horrified.

"Of course! We must have a *queer local* in our *queer local* revival!" Jazz exclaimed. "And Lola, my dear, given you're a *world-famous A-list actress—*"

"I'm absolutely not," Lola swiftly interjected.

"—and Rhodes's best-known export," Jazz went on, "it makes sense you'd be our philosophical Guildenstern. Just like you were the night you were discovered!"

Lola hadn't reread the play since their run, but she recalled the basic plot. The play followed two side characters from *Hamlet,* summoned by King Claudius to unravel their friend Hamlet's famous malaise. Most of the action centered on the bewildered duo fumbling through a story they didn't understand, trapped on the margins of someone else's tragedy. Lots of clever wordplay and philosophical monologues about fate, free will, and the meaning of it all. *Waiting for Godot* meets *The Truman Show* with a dash of *Fleabag*'s fourth-wall flair—artful, imaginative, and darkly hilarious. But reviving it, now, opposite Annie, in just a few weeks, was impossible.

Jazz went on. "If you're still interested in directing, Lola, you can help out there, too."

It'd been twenty years since Lola entertained thoughts of directing. She'd loved it as a teenager, but life as an actor was hard enough. It was so bizarre to have her long-buried passion casually unearthed; Lola felt it like a sock to the stomach. She was speechless.

Jazz checked the time on her wristwatch. "I invited Vicky and Dylan, too, but if they're not available, we'll cast the other roles in open auditions." She examined Annie, then Lola, her gaze heartbreakingly hopeful. "So. What do you think?"

Lola exchanged a dumbstruck look with Annie. The sensation ping-ponged around Lola's ribs, adding to the chaos. "This summer?" Lola hastily tried to shape a sensitive, graceful pass. "Rehearsing, what, for a month?"

Jazz nodded with enthusiasm. "Yes, and that reminds me—I know you're in New York, so you can stay with me. Vicky and Dylan, too, if they show—I have plenty of space."

Jazz owned a rambling five-bedroom Victorian outside town. The original cast had gone there for dinner one night. Under a dusky pink sky, they ate around a long table in an overgrown backyard full of flowering plants. Jazz let each of the quartet have a half glass of wine, which felt unbelievably special and made them all giggly. Lola remembered leopard print carpet and an enormous photograph of two women kissing *with tongue* and a black marble statue of a jaguar *in the kitchen.*

"It'll be wonderful to have a house guest for a few weeks." Jazz clapped her hands, the light from the oil lamp bouncing off her glasses. "I know it's a bit of a wild idea. But you two seem like the type who like wild ideas." Her voice softened, her gaze a plaintive plea. "If we don't act now, everything we built could just vanish. It's not just my legacy, it's the legacy of the town. Something for the future generations." She ticked off her fingers. "We bring back the theater, and that brings back people—tourists, residents, everyone! First for our play, then the next one, and the one after that. They'll go to the bars, the cafés, the gas station." Her eyes were dancing, the vision unfolding in her mind's eye. "Visitors will stay the weekend, maybe buy a little vacation home. Locals will stop heading to the neighboring towns for nights out and realize everything they're looking for is right here!"

Annie frowned, looking a bit bemused. "One show is going to kick off all that?"

"Sure!" Jazz exclaimed. "We've got to start somewhere. This play will be the start of a whole new chapter for Rhodes. That's how we *grow.* So, whaddya say? Help an old broad—and an old town—out?"

Lola had to hand it to her—Jazz was still a dreamer.

This was not going to be easy.

"Jazz." Lola kept her voice as kind as she could. "I admire the enthusiasm and I am so honored to have been asked to do this. I have such fond memories of you, and us, and everything. And honestly, I do think it's such a fun idea."

This wasn't a lie. For a split second, Lola could hear the creak of the floorboards, feel the heat of the spotlight. It was an excellent play, by one of her favorite writers, and a part of Lola wished she could say yes for those reasons alone. Deep down, she was a theater kid, simple as that. But it wasn't as simple as that. Lola had a Jenga tower of a career to consider. *Saturn Rising* to small-town community theater? Her agent would laugh in her face. But of course the most pressing reason was sitting next to her, studiously avoiding eye contact.

"But I must decline," Lola went on, "for . . . personal reasons. I'll be in the front row, I promise. I want this just as much as you do, Jazz. This place means a lot to me, too. But I can't be in a revival."

Jazz looked crushed, letting out a breath of defeat. "Well, what about you?" Lola looked at Annie who shrunk into her seat, color rising in her cheeks.

"Well—it's just—I work," she managed. "Full-time. And Dylan and Vicky didn't even show. I'm not an actor anymore. I won't be any good."

"I've always had a sixth sense about casting." Jazz's reply was sharp. "I know what'll work."

"I'd be happy to make a donation," Lola said, wishing she'd brought a checkbook. "Whatever you need—"

"That's very generous, Lola," Jazz said. "But money alone won't revive the theater. The reopening has to come from love, not money, or what's the point? Community theater relies on the *community.* Our summer show *will* be a fundraiser, just as I planned. And if it's not my four favorite kids up there—" Jazz's voice cracked. Her shoulders slumped, dismay quivering her lips. "Well, that'll be a shame. I was quite looking forward to it."

Sadness, tart as lemon juice, misted up Lola's throat. She'd passed on a hundred shitty projects and terrible offers. But this was far and away the most painful rejection.

"The show must go on." Jazz inhaled, resolute. "Goodbye, girls. Thanks for coming."

She rose to shake their hands, and in that moment, Jazz didn't appear as the creative giant she'd always been in Lola's mind. She looked like a small, old woman who was bitterly disappointed. Lola took Jazz's knobbed hand in both of hers, hoping to convey how truly sorry she was. But Jazz didn't meet Lola's gaze, instead blinking back tears as she turned away.

OUTSIDE, THE LATE-AFTERNOON sun lengthened shadows over the quiet street. The air was warm and smelled like the woods—green and clean and earthy, a world away from the stench of the city in high summer. The only sounds were the twitter of birds and the low rumble of a distant lawn mower.

Annie and Lola stood ten feet apart on the grass in front of the theater. Over the years, Lola occasionally indulged in a fantasy of reconnecting with Annie, typically in a moment when Lola looked and felt effortlessly cool and composed: browsing a bookstore in Paris, maybe, or realizing they were both admiring the same painting at the Met. A spark reigniting over a glass of wine. Their lips meeting under a spray of stars or a waterfall shower. Only now did Lola realize how ridiculous those fantasies were.

Annie had broken up with her. Annie still wasn't interested. They were never going to be friends again, let alone lovers.

Lola shifted her weight, the knife points of her stilettos sinking into the earth. "I guess this is goodbye."

"I guess." Annie's voice was strained.

Lola forced a smile. "Good luck to you." A knot tightened in her throat. "See you in another twenty years."

"Bye, Lola." Annie's voice was soft. "I'm glad everything worked out for you."

God, there was so much Annie didn't understand. So much Lola would never get to tell her. Lola made herself swivel in the direction of her ride. She might just make it before bursting into tears.

The sound of a car gunning up Myrtle Street tore through the quiet afternoon. A shiny black BMW zoomed toward the front of the theater, screeching to a stop. A woman rocketed out of the driver's seat. She wore pleated black slacks and a crisp white button-down. Her lips were coated in glossy red lipstick and her black cat eye-liner was as precise as the crack of a whip.

Vicky Fang slammed her car door with a decisive bang. She was clutching a bright red envelope. "Guys! I *just* opened my mail!"

5.

"SERIOUSLY, WHO SENDS AN INVITE VIA *SNAIL MAIL*?" VICKY DEmanded, brandishing her personalized scarlet letter. "That's like still paying for cable or answering the phone!"

Annie and Lola laughed a little too loudly. They were standing so far apart on the playhouse's overgrown lawn, Vicky felt like she was representing one of them in a divorce settlement. Evidently, the exes had not reconciled since their dramatic decoupling. Love was a bitch, wasn't it?

Vicky assessed the playhouse, noting the peeling paint, the broken-down sign. Sad to see it looking so old and tired and in need of a good power wash. "So. Jazz summoned us all?"

Annie nodded. "Yeah—I got the same letter. Actually thought it was just me," she said, "so I was sort of dancing onstage when Lola came in, like the opposite of *America's Got Talent*. More like *America's Got Problems and Here's One of 'Em.*"

Vicky snorted. Annie was still a cheesy goof. She recalled Lola finding Annie's offbeat sense of humor delightful, but now the striking blonde's gaze stayed unmoved.

"We just met with Jazz," Lola said.

Vicky listened, stunned, as Lola and Annie filled her in on Jazz's pitch—a summer revival of their old play. "Which unfortunately won't be possible," Lola concluded.

Vicky nodded, disappointed but unsurprised—Lola was semi-famous now, and Annie's folded arms did not scream "theater kid for life."

Vicky kept her voice extremely nonchalant. "Where's Rogers?"

Annie lifted her shoulders, her big, blue eyes as sincere as ever. "Dylan didn't show."

Something tight and hopeful collapsed in Vicky's chest. Relief? Disappointment? Both? She shrugged, affecting indifference. "Figures. Okay, I'll say a quick hi to Jazz," she decided, locking her Beamer with a *beep beep.* "Then let's catch up. Dying to hear what you bitches have been up to!"

Annie and Lola traded a hesitant glance.

"I have to . . . get back to work?" Annie said.

"Still a terrible liar," Vicky noted, striking this excuse from the record, then zeroing in on Lola.

"I have an event in the city tonight," Lola said.

"Which means you have time for one drink," Vicky concluded, satisfied. "Oooh! The old diner isn't still open, is it?"

ROCK AROUND THE CLOCK still embraced maximalist fifties cosplay. Mostly.

There'd been some sort of renovation over the past twenty years—the tables and the red vinyl booths all looked newer, and Vicky didn't remember the windows being so large—but the layout was roughly the same. A bar ran along the right wall with about ten round, padded silver stools fixed to the floor. Opposite it, a dozen or so booths lined the windows facing Henry Street, with three more booths tucked up the back.

Above the bar hung framed posters of a hip-swiveling Elvis,

Marilyn licking an ice-cream cone, and Buddy Holly holding a sausage dog. Taped beneath them was a mix of items—a "Wish You Were Here!" postcard from Niagara Falls, a "Welcome, Earthling" *Star Wars* sticker, and a "Pride in the Hudson Valley" flyer. The shelves held collectibles: Vintage Mickey Mouse and Superman lunch boxes shared space with figurines from *Ghostbusters* and *Stranger Things*. It was something Vicky had always liked about the diner: It didn't try too hard. Even the old jukebox was still in the corner. While straight out of an *Archie* comic, a few flips confirmed it still offered only 2000s jams. Playing now was "Mr. Brightside" by The Killers. *It started out with a kiss, how did it end up like this?*

Vicky beelined for "their" booth, the one way in the back, away from the windows. "I totally feel like I'm seventeen again," she said, sliding in. "Like, where is my Motorola Razr and when are we watching *Veronica Mars* and who is going to finger me in the art supply closet?"

"What's the opposite of dibs?" Annie asked.

Lola chuckled. She sat down next to Annie, prompting a look of alarm.

Okay—those two had *definitely* not buried the hatchet.

Vicky had never gotten the full story of Annie and Lola's breakup. While everyone knew why Dylan and Vicky had imploded—the public spectacle at the chaotic closing-night party that Vicky would give anything to rewrite—the reason behind Lola and Annie's breakup didn't have time to surface. They'd all blown apart on that fateful night, respective landlines going silent, MySpace top friends swiftly rearranged. But the past didn't feel dead and buried. It was now surface level, a hand breaking through dirt to claw its way out.

A couple of acned teen girls huddled in a front booth looked between Lola and their phones, wide-eyed and whispering. "Fans," Vicky informed Lola.

Lola nodded, apparently aware of this. "That's why I sat facing away or they'd probably start filming us," she said, slipping Annie an apologetic look.

"I'll make up some shit about privacy laws if that happens," Vicky said, giving the teens her best *don't even think about annoying my friend* eyes.

An uninterested waitress with micro bangs and cat-eye glasses dropped off plastic letter-sized menus. Vicky scanned the menu, her jaw loosening. "Holy shit. I remember when the burgers were five bucks! Now they're *sixteen*. Inflation is a motherfucker." Vicky read on, shuddering. "They've also got the calories listed now. Avert your eyes from my beloved Big Bopper Bacon Burger. Whatever happened to ignorance is bliss?"

"Same thing that happened to mixtapes and Blockbuster," Annie said wistfully.

"Friendster," Lola added. "AIM."

"RIP my youth!" Vicky wailed, tossing the menu aside, and earning herself some giggles. "When did we get so *old*?"

"We're not that old," Lola said diplomatically.

"Speak for yourself: I'll be forty in three years!" Vicky exclaimed. "Walgreens offers senior discounts once you turn fifty-five!"

More giggles. Vicky had forgotten how sisterly it'd always felt with these two. But unlike her actual sisters—who updated each other on every purchase and significant bowel movement—she had no idea about how Annie's and Lola's lives turned out. Vicky reached across the table to tug some of Annie's pastel-pink strands. "Love the hair. You still local?"

Annie nodded, but Vicky didn't miss the flicker of discomfort. Why?

"Yeah. I live above my salon," Annie hedged.

"A hair salon?" Vicky asked, waving to get their waitress's attention.

Annie fiddled nervously with the saltshaker. Even though Vicky had asked the question, it was Lola whose gaze she met with uncertain eyes. "A dog-grooming salon."

"A salon for dogs?" Lola's face lifted in delight. "That's so cute!"

Annie winced.

"I mean, that's impressive," Lola quickly qualified. "How long have you had it?"

"Five years this summer." Annie looked relieved when the waitress approached, asking if they were ready to order.

Vicky forced herself to bypass the Big Bopper Bacon Burger in favor of the Garden Delight Salad—not out of genuine desire, it was just the least unhealthy thing on the menu. "And a Diet Dr Pepper."

"Just an iced tea for me," Lola said.

"Curly fries and a strawberry shake," Annie said, passing back the menu. "With oat milk, please."

"RIP full cream," Vicky said, clutching her heart, before refocusing on Annie. "So, how's business?"

Annie licked her lips, as if doing quick mental math. Then she sat bolt upright, speaking unnaturally loudly. "Really, really . . . *good*," she declared. "We're fully booked, every day. Dawn to dusk—dogs dogs dogs. I'm making so much money, my accountant thinks I should slow down!"

Vicky frowned. "Your accountant thinks you should make *less* money? Babe, that's not how capitalism works."

Annie blinked half a dozen times. "He's . . . a socialist. Just—yadda yadda yadda, living the dream."

Lola nodded supportively, even as she looked a little confused. "Jazz made it sound like Rhodes was in an economic decline. That hasn't affected you?"

Annie shook her head, her reply tumbling out of her mouth like marbles bouncing down a flight of stairs. "No, no, not at all. *Some* small businesses are struggling, a *bit*. But I think Jazz was . . .

exaggerating? For effect? Because business has *never* been better. I guess I'm a success story? A hometown hero? Too blessed to stress?"

Vicky considered her next move. Annie was clearly lying but now might not be the time to cross-examine. She shifted her focus to Lola. "What about you?"

Lola smiled in an automatic sort of way, reminding Vicky of a wind-up doll. "Doing great! I'm working pretty consistently, mostly film. Meeting a lot of . . . talented, interesting people. Tons of travel, but I don't mind that. I bought a loft in Tribeca, which is gorgeous but empty. Just like my exes." A self-deprecating chuckle. "But overall, I'm doing good. Exactly the life I wanted to live."

Annie nodded morosely, as if this was just what she expected.

Vicky wondered how such a good actor could give such a shit performance. To her ear, this sounded as hollow as a freaking Easter egg. "*Exactly* the life you wanted to live?" Vicky tilted her head. "No notes?"

Lola's left eye twitched. She straightened, brushing invisible lint off her dress. "Nope. Just like Annie; living the dream."

Vicky didn't believe any of this, but Annie seemed to buy it and pushing back would likely make them both double down, so Vicky decided to let it go. For now. "Happy for you, superstar."

Lola flicked Vicky's arm. "Your turn."

"It'll surprise no one to learn I'm a lawyer," Vicky said. "Clawed my way up to co-found my own family law firm."

"Sounds like a big job," Annie said. "So, you couldn't have done the show, right? Jazz was talking about a month of rehearsals."

Vicky folded her hands, keeping her expression steely. "I happen to be on sabbatical."

Sort of the truth. At least she could fib a bit more convincingly.

"Sabbatical?" Annie looked intrigued. "Fun!"

Actually, what'd happened last week—in the middle of a *trial*—was less *fun,* more *petrifying wake-up call.* What'd happened last week had changed everything. Vicky understood she had to make some big changes. Doing a no-stakes community show back in Rhodes would've been good for her health. She could've learned to eat better, cut back on coffee, maybe tried a yoga class. Reviving their show might've been perfect.

If Lola and Annie had been up for it.

"Spill," Lola said. "The prosecution calls Ms. Vicky Fang to the stand."

Vicky prepared herself for a boss bitch highlights reel. "Yes, your honor, and I won't be brief as these are billable hours—" She paused, eyes snagging on the front door. "Ooh . . . hello." She fanned herself. "Who ordered the hotcake?"

Lola and Annie twisted around to follow her gaze.

The hotcake was an androgynous, soft butch with flippy hair who'd sidled up to the bar. She—or they?—were in tight, ripped jeans and a loose muscle tee that showed off impressively toned arms and faint wisps of underarm hair. A messenger bag looped over one shoulder and a thin, dog-eared paperback poked out of their jeans' back pocket.

Vicky made a *mmm* noise, ogling Hotcake's biceps. "Welcome to the gun show. Allow me to perform your background check."

Lola and Annie giggled as they all watched the waitress notice Hotcake, transforming from bored to extremely engaged.

"It's like if *The L Word*'s Shane and K Stew in that Rolling Stones video had a perfect little butch baby." Vicky panted like a dog. "Woof. I need to spend more time in Rhodes."

"Well, they're not a local," Annie said. "I hope this doesn't slow down my fries."

"Mascs are my weakness," Vicky confessed, using the mirrored wall next to the booth to apply a fresh coat of shiny red lipstick. "Girl's gotta eat. Should I say hi?"

"You won't need to," Lola said. Hotcake was heading toward them. "Incoming."

Vicky grinned. Paused. Frowned. There was something oddly familiar about the person sauntering over . . .

Fine bone structure. Smirky plush mouth. Striking green eyes.

No way. It couldn't be. Could it?

Hotcake stopped by their table and pushed a hand through their hair, their shirt riding up to expose a pointy hip bone. "Hey, guys. Been a minute."

Stick-and-poke tattoos decorated their buffed arms. Their hair was the same mahogany brown, but now it was tousled and swoopy, like they'd just rolled out of bed after fucking in it all night. All very *Siri, find me a picture of the lead singer of a Le Tigre cover band.*

Vicky stopped breathing. Her vision pin-holed. Every muscle in her body locked, except for her mouth, which opened and shut, searching for words that didn't exist. Her face flushed—bright, hot red, the exact shade of her lipstick.

Lola and Annie spoke at the same time, their voices pitched high in amazement. "*Dylan?*"

6.

DYLAN DIDN'T RETURN TO RHODES FOR CLOSURE OR REVENGE or a meet-cute with fate. They came because Jazz asked—and when Jazz asked, you showed up. No questions. Jazz was the first person who made being queer look like a party they'd want to be invited to. But seeing Vicky again? That was the wild card. Would it undo them? Revert them to the mousy girl they believed they were in high school?

But standing at Rock Around the Clock on Henry Street, Dylan felt grounded. Changed. Pride crept in as their old friends, Annie and Lola, scrambled up to gush. "Dylan, you look *so cool,*" Annie said, disarmingly sincere. "No wonder I couldn't find you online!"

Dylan blushed, hands in their pockets. "Thanks, guys. Yeah—guess I look a bit different than when we knew each other. And I use they/them pronouns now."

Even though they'd come out dozens of times, there was still a wriggle of fear, quelled by the looks of understanding and acceptance on Lola's and Annie's faces.

"Gender's a journey, amiright?" Dylan added.

"Amen," Annie replied. "But not like *amen.* Haven't asked the J-man to take the wheel; still doing all my own driving. And I'm she/her."

"Same," Lola said. "She/her."

For the first time in twenty years, Dylan met Vicky's gaze.

It was, perhaps, the most satisfying moment of their life: watching Vicky Fang freeze like a MacBook with the spinning wheel of death.

Dylan hadn't changed for her. But they hadn't *not* changed for her, either.

"Her/she," Vicky managed to get out. "Hershey."

Dylan almost laughed. This was all better than expected. "Hello, Vicky." Dylan indicated Vicky's white button-down. "Come straight from work?"

It took a moment for the dig to land. Vicky let out an insulted cough. "No," she retorted. "Nothing about me is straight."

So, Vicky Fang embraced the inevitable. Dylan ignored a flare of excitement. "Finally." Dylan gave her an approving nod. "Congratulations."

Vicky looked mildly offended. "I've been out since college. Sophomore year."

"Sophomore?" Dylan couldn't resist; something about Vicky fired up their competitive side. "I came out my first year."

Vicky let out an annoyed huff.

Lola and Annie slid back into the booth. "Take a seat," Annie offered.

Which was next to Vicky. She was wearing a spicy, floral scent, both feminine and a little dangerous, as if a peony was brandishing a knife. Dylan inhaled quietly, liking it.

Bizarre being back in their old booth. Twilight zone shit. Age looked good on everyone. The town had changed, too. Dylan expected gentrification—a Sweetgreen, a natural wine bar pushing small plates. But the top of town was largely frozen in time, and this end was fading away like a half-finished thought. "Sorry I'm late," Dylan said. "Train delay. I went to the theater but couldn't find Jazz. Is the meeting over?"

"Yep," Annie said. "Jazz wants to revive our play—"

"*Rosencrantz and Guildenstern,*" Lola supplied.

"—as a fundraiser," Annie finished, "to reopen the theater, with us four in the leads."

"Cool idea." Dylan glanced at Vicky, catching her gaze tracing their biceps.

"Huh?" Vicky flushed, and Dylan resisted the urge to flex.

Annie and Lola continued explaining Jazz's plan until the waitress dropped off their drinks and curly fries, her eyes glued to Dylan. "Hi again. Can I get you anything?"

Dylan gave the waitress their best lazy smile. Another upside of cultivating self-confidence: learning to flirt. "What's good?"

"The burgers are tasty," their waitress said, nibbling the end of her pen, "but don't snooze on the eggplant parm."

Dylan looked to Vicky. "What'd you get?"

"The Garden Delight Salad," Vicky replied, as if this was what Dylan should strongly consider.

Dylan addressed their waitress. "I'll do the parm."

Vicky frowned. Lola and Annie hid smiles.

"Excellent choice." The waitress scribbled on her notepad. "Anything to drink?"

Booze felt essential. Dylan addressed the group. "Should we split a bottle of wine?"

Vicky and Annie looked to Lola. "Lola has an event . . . ?" Vicky let it dangle.

"That I'm going to skip," Lola said. "It's been too long, and I could really use a glass of sauvignon blanc, if that works?"

"Definitely." Dylan smirked at their waitress. "It's hot tonight."

The waitress blushed, walking backward to the bar.

Vicky sucked down her Diet Dr Pepper so violently she rattled the ice cubes. Dylan grinned, relaxing further into the booth. Annie kept the conversation going. "We didn't think you'd show."

"Anything for Jazz, right?" Dylan popped a curly fry in their mouth. Just as good as they remembered. "And the timing worked out: I'm based in L.A. but needed to be here for work."

"And what is that?" Lola asked.

Dylan met Vicky's eyes. Hopefully, this would be good. "I'm a chocolatier."

Vicky made a noise somewhere between a cough and a gasp. "A chocolatier?" she squeaked. "You make . . . chocolate?"

"Mm-hmm." Dylan nodded, resisting the urge to purr like the Cheshire Cat. Of course, Vicky was still a sugar monster. "A gay Willy Wonka: That's me."

"That's, like, my dream job. If I wasn't a lawyer." Vicky looked either impressed or furious. Maybe both. "You do that full-time?"

"Yup." Dylan gave the pitch, perfected over the past three years. "We're a slow-made, handcrafted chocolate start-up, using natural, organic ingredients. We were just an online business for a few years, but we opened our first retail location in Silver Lake last summer. New York's too expensive but I thought Upstate might work for us. Figured I'd scout some locations and, y'know"—they wiggled their eyebrows—"suss out the vibe."

Annie leaned forward, her sky-blue eyes all lit up. "So you'll be running a chocolate shop, nearby?"

"Not me personally," Dylan said. "I'm just looking for a space, seeing if it makes sense, then heading back to L.A."

"L.A.," Annie repeated in breathless reverence. "I've never been."

Vicky scoffed. "You're not missing much. Desperation, gridlock, way too much sun."

Dylan grinned back, unfazed. "Also tacos, the beach, and sexually curious smokeshows."

Lola chuckled. "L.A. has character," she allowed, reaching for a fry. "What's your start-up called?"

"Marlowe," Dylan replied.

"That was your great-aunt's name!" Vicky sounded like she was making an accusation.

Surprise lifted Dylan's chest. They did not expect Vicky to remember. "That's right. We were close."

"I've heard of Marlowe!" Lola was excited. "It was in a swag bag at an event. Cuffing something . . . ?"

"Cuffing Szn," Dylan said. "We have a core collection of classic flavors, but we also do seasonal drops. All the flavors come from me: my interests, my imagination. Each drop tells a different story. Cuffing Szn was inspired by late-night mistakes and"—they met Vicky's eye—"early-morning cravings."

Vicky looked somewhere between stunned and starving.

"Meow," Annie commented.

Dylan laughed, digging into their bag to unearth three small samples wrapped in shimmery silver.

"The base is dark chocolate," Dylan went on, as the trio peeled open the wrappers, "with espresso nibs—because bad decisions hit different at one A.M.—a salted caramel swirl for some sticky-sweet chaos, and a dusting of cayenne pepper to keep things hot."

"This is *incredible,*" Lola enthused, savoring a bite.

"It's a hookup in chocolate form," Annie moaned.

Vicky's eyes had glazed, her muscles slackening.

"What d'you think?" Dylan prompted her.

Vicky snapped to, cinching herself together. "Yeah, it's—all right."

"All right?" Dylan did not believe this for a second. "Pretty sure I just saw your o-face, Vee."

Vicky blushed, shoving Dylan in a fluster. "You did not just see my o-face! You will never see my o-face!"

Dylan grinned, addressing all three women. "Thanks, guys. It's all a ton of work, but super rewarding. Feels like I'm finally on the right path."

"Sounds wonderful, Dylan," Lola said, more wistfully than Dylan would expect a famous, successful actor to sound.

"Yes." Vicky sounded almost annoyed. "Impressive."

The waitress was back, placing four wineglasses on the table. The quartet had never been old enough to drink when hanging at the diner after shows: The procurement of alcohol was a small but important thrill. The waitress filled each glass, giving Dylan the largest pour, which made Vicky narrow her eyes.

"What are we drinking to?" Dylan asked, as they all raised a glass.

"Old friends," Lola said.

"New adventures," Annie added.

"To the playhouse," Dylan said, then looked to Vicky, prompting her with a raised brow.

Vicky wrenched her gaze away from Dylan's mouth. "To . . . Jazz."

"To Jazz," the others echoed, clinking their glasses.

They all drank, eyes on one another. Dylan could almost see electric sparks zinging between everyone in the group.

Was this quartet situation an open playing field? Not that Dylan was planning on getting sexually messy with anyone. But if they *were* to get *accidentally* sexually messy . . . Who was single? Still doing gay stuff?

Annie couldn't meet Lola's eye without blushing. The air between them seemed spiky. Unfinished business. That answered that. But not this: How was Vicky Fang just as hot, if not hotter, than she was twenty years ago?

THE WINE HELPED ease the friction. Lola stepped out to speak with her driver—someone she'd booked for the whole night—to make sure he could wait. She returned to the dish Annie had ordered for her, gasping at the sight of the Rockin' Roast Chicken Salad Sandwich. "You remembered! The perfect meal." She unfolded the napkin across her lap. "It's roast chicken—

And here the others joined in with her, reciting, "*It's salad, and it's a sandwich.*"

"Hey, she said what she said." Dylan slouched back against the leather booth, holding a fry as if it was a cigarette.

They all told stories from the past twenty years: the time Annie found herself with four rescue dogs, three rescue cats, and a rescue *parrot.* "I was basically Doctor Dolittle, with boobs," she reminisced. "Bird on one shoulder, cat under one arm, and dog leashes tangled around my legs. A cry for help or just a Tuesday?"

Dylan told them about being in New York during the Occupy Wall Street protests, helping run the makeshift kitchen. "We served three meals a day, all from donated food. I'd always been into cooking but that taught me how to make a meal out of anything, and the power of community." They paused, eyes sliding to Vicky's. "But sex in a tent—very hard on the knees."

Oh so satisfying to make Vicky Fang blush.

Lola recalled meeting Meryl Streep at an awards show: "I was standing by her table, babbling about what an inspiration she was and after minutes of this, she just looks up at me, very graciously, and says, *I'll have the squid and a glass of merlot.* So I said, *Absolutely,* and found a waiter and put in her order. Meryl needed her merlot!"

Vicky recounted the time she bled through her white pantsuit midway through cross-examining a witness and decided to keep going instead of requesting a recess: "Menstruation is a natural process and nothing to be ashamed of!" she insisted, while they were all cracking up. "But seriously, you guys, it looked like I'd just slaughtered a pig."

Dylan laughed hardest of all, feeling bright and switched all the way on. "If only Chip Chadwick could see you now!"

The name of Riverstone Prep's blond football king—and Vicky's onetime ex—ricocheted around the table like a gunshot.

Lola's eyes pulsed wide. Annie choked on her wine.

Vicky looked as if she'd just taken a bullet.

Dylan instantly regretted throwing Chip back in the mix. "Oh, whatever." They winced, pushing a hand through their hair. "Like, I don't care. Sorry, that was dumb."

For a moment, it felt like the good mood might sputter out. Dylan looked to Annie and Lola, worried.

"I think we need more wine," Lola said smoothly, waving the waitress over. "We all in?"

They all were.

"Remember when we did a late show after getting wasted on that Midori I nicked from your dad's liquor cabinet?" Vicky said to Dylan, after they all had fresh glasses.

"Still can't drink Midori," Dylan admitted.

"I was so drunk, I couldn't juggle," Annie said with a groan, "which is also the name of my memoir."

Lola laughed, bright-eyed with nostalgia. "That was my first real hangover."

"That was all our first hangovers!" Dylan exclaimed, nudging Vicky. "You corrupted us."

"You wanted me to corrupt you." Vicky tossed her hair over one shoulder. "That's why we were friends."

Dylan paused. Were they really "just friends" that summer? True, they'd never hooked up. But when Annie and Lola started doing exactly that—squirreled away in some secret nook at Dylan's parents' house—Vicky and Dylan started spending a lot more time one-on-one. In between their nonstop bickering, their conversations became more profound. More personal. More flirtatious. But Vicky never let it happen. Never gave an inch. Until the closing-night party. When everything fell apart.

They weren't "just friends" that summer. Friends don't inspire other friends to google "am I gay?" every night for weeks on end.

Was history repeating itself—or was Dylan already writing a different ending?

It was almost ten P.M. by the time the waitress dropped off the check. After a good-natured tussle over who would pay, each of them dropped a credit card in a clatter of plastic. "So." Dylan stretched, fighting a yawn. "When do rehearsals start?"

The iconic opening riff of the White Stripes's "Seven Nation Army" thumped out of the old jukebox, minimal and tense. Vicky, Lola, and Annie exchanged glances. "Oh, we're not actually doing the play," Vicky said.

"*What?*" Dylan pitched forward across the table, incredulous. "Why not?"

On the surface, a dumb question—everyone had jobs, reputations, commitments, including Dylan. But in this moment, none of that mattered. This impromptu diner dinner party had been the most fun they'd had in years. Like being with comfy old friends who were also fascinating new friends. A long, hot August rehearsing for a brilliant old play in a little country town sort of sounded like heaven.

Especially if Vicky stuck around.

"Look, I'm in," Dylan spoke before anyone could back out. "This feels right."

Vicky spoke next, short and sharp. "I'm in, too."

All eyes swung to Lola. "Oh no—I can't," she said, shrinking back. "I love Jazz, obviously, but it doesn't make sense for me. My agent would have a fit."

"Exactly," Annie jumped in. "We're too small-town for *Lola Wilson.* This is just one of Jazz's wild ideas."

"Wild ideas are the best kind," Dylan said. "And community theater isn't about being *a real actor.* It's about having fun and giving back."

"I run a dog salon!" Annie exclaimed. "I haven't done a show in twenty years. I probably can't remember lines anymore, let alone do it with"—her eyes flickered to Lola—"a professional."

Dylan turned their sights on Lola. "What about you? You used to love doing plays."

"I still do," Lola said, almost offended.

"And who's *ultimately* in charge of your schedule." Vicky picked it up. "You, or your agent?"

"Well, I am . . ." Lola hesitated, thinking. "And Jazz did offer for all three of us to stay with her." She slowly swiveled to Annie. Her voice was light, almost casual—but something in her expression wasn't. "What do you say?"

Annie didn't answer. Instead, she went almost preternaturally still. The kind of stillness Dylan had only seen in actors right before they stepped onstage. Right before they became someone else. Annie looked at each of them in turn—first Dylan, then Vicky, then Lola. Behind her eyes, a blustery push-pull of a decision so much bigger than the sum of its parts.

C'mon, Pink Lady, Dylan found themself silently begging. *Say yes.*

Annie lifted her chin. A flash of defiance lit her blue eyes. Her fingers relaxed around the stem of her wineglass. She looked like someone choosing to jump even though the landing might break her. "Okay," she said, "I'm in."

Lola let out a surprised breath. Then her mouth curved up into an excited, nervous smile. "Then I am, too."

The quartet all looked at one another, alert and a little on edge, as if they were playing a group game of chicken, wondering who was going to swerve first.

But no one did.

OUTSIDE, THE NIGHT air was warm enough not to need a jacket. They all tumbled out, all talking at once, and it felt like another rip in the fabric of time. Dylan wouldn't be surprised to see their bikes leaning unlocked against the side of the diner, baskets stuffed with damp swimsuits and poorly rolled joints. But it wasn't the past, it was the present and Lola was pointing to her waiting car, offering Dylan a ride back to the city.

"Sweet," Dylan said. "Thanks."

Vicky's gaze zipped between Dylan and the idling Suburban. "I'm definitely a Lohan level of drunk," she said. "I'll ride, too; get a Taskrabbit to pick up my car or something."

Electricity sparkled in Dylan's belly even as they made a show of rolling their eyes. "A Taskrabbit? God, Vee, you're *so* bourgeois."

"Shut up!" Vicky pushed Dylan's shoulder. "How are you even *more* annoying?!"

"Same way you're even more of a brat." Dylan flipped back with a smirk.

Annie shouldered her bag. "I'm going to walk."

They all glanced up darkened Henry Street.

"But I can drop you all the way home," Lola said.

Annie bristled. "I'm fine."

"But I don't think I'll be." Lola's smile was pleading. "I'd just sleep better knowing you were safe."

"I appreciate the offer, Lola." Annie's tone was cool. "But I'd rather walk."

She waved and headed up Henry Street.

Lola looked somewhere between crestfallen and annoyed.

Dylan arched an intrigued brow at Vicky. Christ, she looked *exactly the same.* Same smooth olive skin stretched over the high slope of her cheeks and the decisive point of her chin. Same lustrous black hair falling down her back, parted down the center with military precision. It was all so surreal: a teenage past reliving itself as a spicy, modern reboot starring this new-old person who still made them sweat.

Dylan wasn't sure if they'd said yes to the play to fix something, break it, or just prove that they could walk away unscathed. But being around Vicky again—smug, beautiful, just as infuriating—they weren't sure walking away was even an option.

Vicky elbowed her way in front of Dylan, angling to get into the back seat first. "Mind if I cut in?"

Dylan chuckled, following Vicky to settle into the buttery soft leather of the back seat. Their gaze caught on Vicky's mouth. "Oh, you have . . ." They gestured at Vicky's lips.

Vicky frowned. "I have . . . ?"

Dylan leaned across the back seat, slow and deliberate, to wipe away a smudge of red from the corner of Vicky's warm, glossed mouth. And all at once, they were fifteen and horny and hopelessly besotted but also thirty-five and horny and a bit more in control. A bit less willing to let Vicky Fang stomp all over them. A bit more interested in seeing what happened if they stood their ground.

Vicky inhaled—barely, but Dylan noticed. Her body softened, the suggestion of a smile skating fast over her mouth. Then she reanimated, swatting Dylan away. "Excuse me! I'm not a freaking child!"

Lola slid into one of the captain seats, making small talk with the driver as he pulled onto Henry Street. Dylan sat back, wired, the night streaking past outside. Even in the dark, they could feel Vicky's presence—bright, hot, impossible to ignore.

"No," Dylan replied. "You're grown. We both are."

Vicky cut her eyes at Dylan in a challenge, her voice low. "Just don't fall in love with me, Rogers."

Love. The very idea of it made Dylan edge back. Lust, they understood. But love? Love had a shelf life. "That," Dylan said, with confidence, "will not be a problem."

PART TWO

Exit, Pursued by Feelings

7.

Six weeks till show day

THE NEXT WEEKEND, ANNIE TOOK SOCKS FOR A WALK PAST THE open auditions for the remaining roles in *Rosencrantz and Guildenstern.* She expected a modest turnout. To her surprise—and a guilty dash of dismay—the line ribboned all the way up Myrtle Street, ending outside the empty shop front formerly known as Once Upon a Time. Folks of all ages stood in groups or alone, studying script pages.

The prospect of the play being revealed as an elaborate practical joke was rapidly diminishing. Saying yes was easier than disappointing Jazz, who'd been thrilled—though not remotely surprised—when Annie called. ("I had a feeling," she'd said, maddeningly smug.) And saying yes meant doing something good—for the town, for Jazz, for the version of herself that still craved a bigger, bolder life.

Sure, a one-night-only production wasn't going to single-handedly save Rhodes. But if it sold out, if they got good press, if the next show did just as well . . . it could spark something. Jazz's plan might work. It'd take some time, but Annie could see how Rhodes could become an actual destination, known for being queer-friendly, artsy, a little weird. Visitors could become regulars. Word would spread. People might even move here, looking for what she'd found: A slower pace of life and meaningful work. A community. A home.

Saying yes was also about pride. Annie didn't want to look like a coward in front of Lola or the others. She wanted to prove that she could be brave—not just to them, but to herself.

But now? She was regretting it in high-definition, surround sound, possibly smell-o-vision.

"Annie! *Annie!*" Deborah Buttrose waved her down. The nail salon matriarch was sporting frosted pistachio eye shadow and the confidence of someone who'd seen *Cabaret* on Broadway while wearing a top hat. "Are you sitting in on auditions? Ooh, can you put in a good word for me with Jazz?"

"You're trying out?" Annie couldn't keep the surprise out of her voice. "Which part?"

"Polonius," Deborah replied, making a vampy cat-claw motion. Her nail art was tiny comedy-tragedy masks. "Adviser to the King."

"Certainly the sexiest one in the cast," Annie noted, as Socks sniffed the overgrown front lawn. "If you like conniving bad dads with control issues."

"I keep an open mind," Deborah said. "My husband and I used to swing, before he died."

Annie's mouth fell open. "Oh, I—didn't know . . ."

"Tractor accident," Deborah said. "Years ago."

"I knew he'd passed—I meant the swinging," Annie said. "Not that I want any details or future acknowledgment of this conversation."

"Lube is *key,*" Deborah said firmly, before swiveling to address those waiting behind her in the line. "Folks, this is Annie Lightfoot! She's playing one of the leads. Opposite *Lola Wilson*!"

The small group animated, appraising Annie with fascination and respect. "Lola Wilson?" an older woman asked, awestruck. "Tom Hanks's wife?"

"No, Mom, that's Rita Wilson." A genderqueer teenager with a white-blond shag and double eyebrow piercings didn't look up from their phone. In their baggy streetwear and scuffed Doc Martens, they were the human equivalent of an eye roll. "Lola Wilson's a B-list actress who's in movies no one watches. No offense," they added, flicking Annie an unapologetic side-eye.

"I think some people watch her movies . . ." Annie hedged, already regretting engaging a terrifying teen. "I didn't know you were a performer, Deb."

"Neither did I!" Deborah beamed, her oversize rhinestone clip-ons glinting in the morning light. "But then I saw the audition flyer in your window, and thought, why not? We all have the capacity to surprise ourselves. It's never too late to try something new." Then, dropping her voice to a stage whisper, "I should know—I was forty when I discovered I'm into butt stuff."

Annie wished briefly for death. Any death, really, just a fast and immediate one. She wasn't a prude—butt stuff for prez, vote one butt stuff—but the minor luxury of her occasional gel manicure didn't include imagining the person buffing her nails biting the pillow.

Deborah went on, "I can tell you that because you're a performer, an artist. You're open-minded."

"To play devil's advocate, maybe not all artists are open-minded," Annie suggested. "Maybe that's like saying all lesbians like, I dunno, Birkenstocks and carabiners."

Deborah looked pointedly at Annie's bright blue Birkenstocks. And then at her carabiner key ring attached to her belt loop.

The line inched forward. Annie let Socks tug her along, struggling to stay ahead of a growing sense of panic. The play was really happening. With Vicky, and Dylan, and *Lola.*

Who was a glamorous, successful movie star, and to whom, twenty years ago, Annie had told a life-altering lie.

A lie that had broken both of their hearts.

A wrong she had never, could never, right.

ANNIE HAD ALWAYS had a skill for memorizing lines—it was one of the talents that made doing community theater possible. And her role of Rosencrantz was the one she'd understudied as a teen. She meant to reread the play. But every time she got more than a few pages in, she suddenly remembered something she needed to do for someone else. Get ahead with bookkeeping so Sal wouldn't have to. Send personalized emails to each regular explaining she was taking August off. Bake a month's worth of peanut butter treats. She didn't mean *not* to read the play. But all at once it was the first Saturday in August, the day of the table read, and Annie hadn't made it past page four.

Reading it meant thinking about it. And thinking about it was panic-inducing.

"What if I fake a seizure?" Annie trailed Sal around the Groom Room. "I don't think I'm that far off." She paused, feeling her pulse. Bouncing like a kid on a goddamn trampoline. "Why do I smell toast? Isn't that a sign of a stroke?"

"It's your toast," Sal said, pointing to the plate she'd forgotten she'd brought down from her apartment upstairs.

"Oh. Phew." Annie took a bite. "Okay, scrap the seizure. I'll just tell Jazz that while I love her to bits, this whole idea is on par with green-lighting *The Apprentice* or bringing back the dinosaurs." She flapped her hands, quoting *Jurassic Park,* their shared fave. "We were so preoccupied with whether or not we could, that we didn't stop to think if we should. And we should not!"

Sal tapped on the salon's iPad, confirming the day's three appointments. "Jeff Goldblum is such a zaddy."

"I worship at the altar of Laura Dern's legs." Annie glanced around for something to do. "Maybe I can come up with some wacky new summer specials."

"What's wacky," Sal said, looking at her over his glasses, "is how nervous you are."

He was right. Despite the fact it was only community theater, her insides felt like they were being tossed around by an amateur juggler. "Honestly?" Annie admitted. "It's Lola."

"Why, because she's *a movie star*?" Sal vamped, fluttering his eyelashes.

"Not just that." Annie blew out a breath, double-checking the sign on the salon door was still flipped to CLOSED—BUT STILL OPEN TO COMPLIMENTS. "When we were kids, Lola and I were . . . together. Scene partners, with benefits."

Sal's deep brown eyes widened, his lips curling up in charmed delight. "You *were*? Baby gays?"

Annie nodded, her cheeks warming. "Big time. We were in love. Or, thought we were, at sixteen." Annie allowed herself the forbidden pleasure of remembering what it felt like to fall for Lola Wilson. "I'd never met a girl like her, ever. She knew all about film. Had big dreams of being onstage. Everyone else was gravel; Lola was rose quartz. She made me feel so *alive,* like I was seeing clearly for the first time. And when we kissed . . ." Annie's entire body shivered. She could still recall, with delicious, painful clarity, the feel of Lola's mouth on hers. "I'd never felt that way about anyone. In a way, I haven't since. Do you ever love as hard as you do at sixteen?"

Sal nodded in understanding. "Robbie Brayer broke my heart with his faux-hawk." He poked his glasses up his nose, intrigued. "So, what happened?"

Annie was in no way ready to tell Sal about the lie she'd told. Even though he'd never explicitly said it, Sal thought Annie was a good person. He'd be horrified if he knew the ugly truth.

"She got a role in a touring show and left," Annie abridged. "I stayed with Gran to finish high school."

Pearl's health declined gradually. She refused to leave her house, so Annie stayed living with her during her last years—helping with day-to-day things while nurses handled medical care. Sal came by for weekly home visits in that final year, always managing to get Pearl laughing when nothing else could. Pearl died from heart failure when Annie was twenty-two.

"Seeing Lola again makes me feel weirdly insecure," Annie went on. "I didn't let her drop me home because she'd see the salon, and the size of my apartment. Things I'm usually so proud of."

"Because she's a massive snob now?" Sal asked, ready to hate Lola on principle.

"Maybe?" Annie guessed. "But I don't think so. It's me, it's all in my head."

Sal hooked an eyebrow, somehow looking both empathetic and judgy. "You have *nothing* to be insecure about, Annie. Twenty years is a long time, babe. Even if it was a bad breakup: you were just kids. I'm sure Lola has forgiven you." He grasped her shoulders, speaking with atypical earnestness. "You've created a beautiful life in Rhodes and you're gonna *crush it* today. The Annie I know isn't afraid to take a risk or show up for the people she loves."

"She sounds amazing. When do I get to meet her?"

Sal tutted, smoothing the lapel of his pink jumpsuit. "Can you please go and have fun? Too much sincerity gives me the runs."

Annie smiled, forcing down one more bite of peanut butter toast.

It was either face the day or fake her own death, and frankly, the latter felt like too much effort.

A FEW MINUTES later, Annie parked her yellow Bug in front of the playhouse. New York might have its minutes and moments, but you could always get a parking spot out front of wherever you were going in Rhodes. Surveying her reflection in the side mirror, Annie wiped cherry lip balm off her teeth and checked her breath, which smelled like peanut butter toast (ugh, great). After a hung-jury level of deliberation, she'd decided on a squiggly print romper and white sneakers, and had shaved the bottom half of her legs, but not her thighs as Vicky used to insist the hair would grow back thicker if she did.

The past was over. But somehow, it still had a say.

A guy who looked about her age headed up the steps to the playhouse. Clean-cut, on the shorter side, with a pleasant, open face. Someone you might see advertising an Apple Watch. One of the other actors? Annie watched as he paused at the front entrance. He took a few deep breaths before shaking himself out and pulling the front door open with a smile fixed to his face.

At least she wasn't the only one feeling first-day nerves.

THE FOYER WAS brighter and cleaner than last time, the windows all open to let in much-needed fresh air. Annie's sneakers squeaked over the mopped parquet floors as she made her way toward the chatter bubbling out from the theater itself.

Inside, the wall sconces were lit up, the grand chandelier aglow. Four long tables forming a square had been set up on the stage, with a dozen or so chairs. Vicky sat in one corner, intently highlighting her script and scribbling notes into a separate notebook. Her thick, black hair was pulled into a high pony and she was wearing a boxy, blue-and-white-striped button-down, rolled at the sleeves. Her crisp cat eyeliner remained flawless.

Across from Vicky, the bleached blond teen with the double eyebrow piercings whom Annie had seen outside the auditions was slouched over their phone. At the far end of the table, another teenager in Wayfarer glasses and blunt brown bangs sat absorbed in a book. The bag at her feet was covered in patches and pins.

Apple Watch guy was taking a seat next to—oh boy—Deborah Buttrose, who, spotting Annie, waved and called hello.

Annie was just about to call back when a warm hand grazed her bare arm from behind. “Morning.”

A zingy charge raced through Annie as she met Lola’s gaze. Which only deepened as Annie took in Lola’s outfit. A two-piece summer suit in expensive-looking linen the color of wheat, paired with strappy wedge sandals and an alarming amount of gold jewelry. Her silvery-blond hair was parted dead center, ironed straight. Lola had always been pretty, but the truly legendary beauty she’d become made Annie feel like a knockoff. Annie’s ex looked ready for a meeting in L.A., not a ragtag table read in a small-town theater.

Impossible that they were the same age.

“Hey.” Annie did not open her arms for a hug. “How are you?”

“Really good.” Lola’s face was as lit up as the chandelier overhead. “I’d forgotten how brilliant this play is! And so *funny.* Isn’t it crazy rereading it? So much went over my head as a kid, but all the existential questions about fate versus free will are so interesting. *Look on every exit being an entrance somewhere else.* That’s just so clever!”

Annie stared back, feeling a creeping sense of worry. “Uh, yeah. So clever.”

“I don’t think I fully grasped the feminist implications of gender-swapping the cast,” Lola went on, pulling a copy of the play from her fancy leather tote. Unlike Annie’s still-crisp printout, Lola’s was filled with multicolored stickies. “It makes the questions of power and agency so nuanced, don’t you think? Like when Guildenstern tries to comfort Rosencrantz in act one by suggesting they don’t have free will or agency—*There’s a logic at work—it’s all done for you.* Or when Rosencrantz says, *We drift down time, clutching at straws*? From a female character, both of those lines become about how little control we have in a male-dominated world, don’t you think?”

Annie had no idea what Lola was talking about. "Sounds like you've already done a deep dive."

"Oh, not really, I just read it a few times," Lola said, flipping through her script. All of Guildenstern's lines were highlighted neon orange. "Maybe five or six."

Lola had read the play *five or six times*? Annie's creeping worry was now fully upright and wringing its hands.

"So, do you think Jazz was serious when she said I could help direct?" Lola went on, looking hopeful. "I haven't done it since high school but I can't stop thinking about it. Anyway." She gave Annie an encouraging smile. "How'd you find rereading it?"

Annie swallowed hard. "Haven't finished it."

Lola looked alarmed. "You haven't read the play yet?"

Annie's pulse jackknifed. "No," she snapped, "because I run a dog salon and you're a professional actor. Our lives are very different now."

The air between them turned crispy. Lola blinked a few times, her mouth opening and shutting.

Annie regretted letting her insecurity take the mic.

"Hey, party people." Thankfully, Dylan loped toward them, hair tousled and falling over one eye, limbs loose in low-slung jeans. Their black muscle tee was emblazoned with *Rick's Garage, Indiana: You break 'em, we fix 'em.* Silver chains of various thicknesses circled their throat. "What's good?"

Annie trailed a chatting Lola and Dylan up to the tables onstage, sitting next to Lola, who sat next to Vicky. Dylan dropped into the open seat on Vicky's other side. Scanning the other performers' scripts in front of them, Annie quickly realized she was the founding and solo member of the Did Not Read the Play in Advance Club.

"Annie!"

She jumped. Clyde of Clyde's Grocery was, inexplicably, taking a seat.

"Clyde?" Annie tried not to look as shocked as she felt. "You're in the show?"

"I'm Gertrude!" Her first boss pulled the script from a Clyde's Grocery reusable bag. "Already memorized all my lines!"

Okay, that was it. She was screwed. "You're as conscientious as your commitment to organic produce! As prepared as your to-go sandwiches!" Annie crowed, wondering if this was what a mental breakdown felt like and did she have enough time to speed-read the entire play before Jazz arrived?

Vicky tossed a granola bar on the table with a huff. "Why does everything healthy taste like an old shoe?"

"I don't remember you being healthy," Lola commented. "Your idea of breakfast was a Snickers and six cups of coffee."

"I seriously miss that." Vicky sipped a bottled green juice then made a face. "Ugh. Like licking a cat. And unfortunately for me, I mean that literally."

"Vicky." Amused, Lola nudged her, nodding at the kids seated opposite.

"Check out the Breakfast Club," Vicky murmured back.

Two more had joined the young pair. One was a thoughtful-looking teen with a heart-shaped face and glossy black hair streaked with lavender, wearing a floaty aquamarine top and silver rings on nearly every finger.

Next to her, an energetic strawberry blonde wore a crop top and hoop earrings. She gazed out hungrily at the theater's empty seats before stealing a curious, reverent peek at Lola. Annie would put money on the strawberry blonde being an Aspiring Actor with a subscription to *Deadline* who'd seen every single one of Lola's films.

Another young woman, very short, maybe in her late twenties, took a seat near Apple Watch. She looked tired and a little flustered, immediately getting her phone out to type something, blowing feathery blond bangs out of her eyes.

Walking hesitantly up the aisle toward the stage was a nervous-looking woman in her sixties, whom Annie didn't recognize. She was wearing minimal makeup and what Annie's own grandmother would've referred to as "church clothes": a floral-print blouse, long dark skirt, sensible shoes.

Annie scanned the opening stage directions—*Two Elizabethans passing the time in a place without any visible character. They are well-dressed—hats, cloaks, sticks, and all.* Her hope that the entire play would magically reemerge from muscle memory alone proved futile.

Dylan peeled back the foil from a burrito. The savory smell of eggs and cheese wafted.

Vicky inhaled, her eyes turning desperate. "What is that?"

"Egg-white breakfast burrito," Dylan said. "With bell peppers and feta cheese." They took a luxurious, theatrical bite, making a satisfied *mmmm.*

Vicky groaned. "I'm a plane-crash-in-the-Alps-eating-my-seatmate level of starving. Can I have a bite?"

Dylan took their time chewing, swallowing, and smacking their lips before answering. "No."

"What?" Vicky asked in outrage, as Dylan took another massive bite. "Why not?"

Once again, Vicky had to wait, dying, until Dylan swallowed. "Because, Vicky. You might have cooties."

Vicky whacked them. "I don't have cooties. Please? I'll give you five bucks."

"Five?" Dylan looked offended.

"Ten. *Fifteen.*"

Dylan took another bite.

Vicky made a strangled noise. "Twenty. *Thirty.*"

Dylan chewed and pointed *up* with their index finger.

Lola and Annie giggled.

"Greedy much?" Vicky huffed. "Fifty. *Fifty* dollars for *one* bite and that is my *final* offer."

Dylan swallowed, wiping a fleck of hot sauce but not the amused smirk from their mouth. They handed what was left of the burrito to Vicky. "Seeing you beg was payment enough."

"Fuck you," Vicky mumbled, already inhaling the burrito and groaning with relief.

"This might be a good time to tell you," Dylan spoke seriously, "that I, in fact, have cooties. Chronic condition—doctors are baffled."

"Shut up." Vicky was half laughing, half chewing. "God, you are so—"

A hearty, if raspy, voice bellowed from the theater entrance. *"Good morning, thespians!"*

It felt like falling through layers of time seeing Jazz, in a bright pink muumuu and oversize glasses, ascend the steps to the stage, not bouncing up as she had twenty years ago, but holding the rail. What hadn't changed was her enthusiasm, evidenced by the clap of her hands as soon as she sat down.

Enthusiasm Annie desperately wished she shared.

Jazz began a rousing welcome speech. Annie stared at the script in front of her.

How. Had. She. Let. This. Happen?

She was one of two leads in a production that was all but a two-hander. She badly wanted to ask Clyde if spontaneous combustion was real and how one might facilitate it.

"But we are here for the *most* important reason of all."

Annie forced herself to tune in to Jazz's opening remarks.

"*We are storytellers,*" Jazz emphasized every word. "Through stories we learn the experience of others. And we more deeply understand the story of *ourselves.* We are the stories we tell ourselves, about ourselves. But here's the best part, folks—a story is never finished. We can always rewrite it, add another act, or tear up the ending and start again."

Next to her, Lola made a thoughtful *hmm* noise. Her posture was impeccable. She smelled like the expensive perfume they sold in department stores Annie couldn't afford to shop in. When they were teenagers, Lola wore lemongrass.

"The story we are telling in four short weeks' time is a very special one." Jazz held her script aloft. "*Rosencrantz and Guildenstern Are Dead,* by the celebrated playwright Tom Stoppard, and still relevant today as we present it, sixty years after its first staging at the Edinburgh Fringe, and twenty years after the Rhodes Players presented it on this very stage, starring these four wonderful performers," Jazz said as she swept a hand at Annie, Lola, Vicky, and Dylan, "who've generously returned to breathe life into these pages, and by extension, the playhouse itself."

Deborah, and several of the other adults, broke into applause.

"Before we begin," Jazz went on, "let's introduce ourselves, and the part we're playing."

The encouraging smile she directed at Annie felt like a shove she wasn't expecting. "Me? Oh, sure." Annie superglued a smile in place. "I'm Annie. Lightfoot." For some reason, she put on an old-timey voice and mimed taking off a hat. "Annie Elizabeth Lightfoot, if you please."

The twelve other actors stared back with expressions ranging from bemusement to the secondhand embarrassment Annie was already feeling.

She went on in her regular voice, trying not to show how on edge she was. "I'm from Rhodes and I run the Groom Room, up the street? Which isn't a question as I definitely do. That, or I'm clipping a *lot* of dogs for free."

Annie's anxiety ballooned into panic at the vision of every seat in the nearby audience being filled by people watching *her* as a *lead* in just *four weeks* opposite Lola Wilson, *her first love* who was also *a professional actor.* And so Annie did what she always did when she felt out of her element. She began to babble.

"I'm a Pisces and I'd like to learn to roller-skate. I love banana splits but I haven't had one in years, come to think of it. Bananas, ice cream, whipped cream . . . fudge? Do banana splits have fudge? Once, in middle school, I wore a shirt that smelled like soup and one of the boys started calling me Stinky Soupy Annie, which stuck for the rest of the year—*Stinky Soupy Annie!*—it was so embarrassing, and I'm not sure why I'm bringing it up as I really don't want that nickname again but I guess I haven't found a natural deodorant that totally works so I'm open to any recommendations on that. I'm not stinky. I like cheese." She stopped abruptly.

For a painfully long moment, no one said a word. Her entire face flamed. She knew she looked like a chaotic tomato in a romper.

Jazz's voice was gentle, with a mortifying undercurrent of concern. "And what part are you playing, Annie?"

Annie resisted the urge to stand up, leave the stage, and begin a new life in Switzerland as a goat herder named Svetlana. "Rosencrantz." Her voice was the size of a teacup Chihuahua. "I'm one of the leads."

8.

I'M A PISCES AND I'D LIKE TO LEARN TO ROLLER-SKATE WAS hands down the most memorable introduction in the history of table reads. Lola wanted to laugh in delight, but Annie looked miserable. Lola tried to catch her eye, offer a supportive smile, but Annie's gaze was fixed on the table.

Discomfort flickered through Lola. Typically, she'd brush it off. But being back in Rhodes made everything feel sharper. More present. Like a fog she hadn't realized she'd been living in was beginning to dissipate. She wanted to understand her unease, not ignore it.

"Lola?" Jazz indicated she go next.

Lola met the circle of curious gazes with her most generous smile. "Hi, everyone, I'm Lola Wilson. I'm playing Guildenstern, and Jazz has invited me to be her assistant director. I'm looking forward to supporting all of you in bringing this exceptional play to life."

The words came easily, as they always did. But to her surprise, they didn't feel like a script. They felt . . . real. Like she actually meant them. When was the last time she'd said something with total certainty?

"Like Annie, I also grew up here and was a member of the

Rhodes Players," Lola went on, "which prepared me for a career as an actor. I live in New York City now, but I'm grateful and excited to be back, with my old friends, helping make this meaningful show happen, for both Jazz and the community as a whole."

Lola smiled at Annie, who was watching her warily. "I, too, like banana splits, and I believe they *are* made with fudge."

Everyone laughed lightly, except Annie, who watched the rest of the introductions with the expression of someone awaiting their execution.

Vicky went next, then Dylan. Jazz always cast a mix of theater kids and quirky locals, the latter represented by nail salon owner Deborah Buttrose, who self-defined as a "childless MILF," and Clyde, the longtime grocer, who worked in his hypothesis that "aliens may walk among us" because "how else can we explain Comic-Con?"

The clean-cut thirty-something man introduced himself as Jamie. "Ophelia," he added, "but Ophie to my friends."

This won some chuckles.

Buoyed, Jamie went on. "I'm in Kingston, so not that far. I just moved up, after six years in Brooklyn."

"Looking for a change of pace from city life?" Deborah asked.

"Not exactly." Jamie paused, took a breath. "I moved up after . . . well, after my fiancée broke off our engagement because she was sleeping with my best friend."

"Jamie." Dylan pressed a hand to their heart, as everyone made sympathetic noises.

"Yeah. Turns out no one goes to *that* many hot yoga classes," Jamie said with a rueful smile, fingering the collar of his polo shirt. "Anyway, I did theater in high school and college but not since. I love this play—big Stoppard fan—and gender swapping it is genius. Really looking forward to meeting some new friends and trying something different."

"Thank you, Jamie," Jazz said. "Happy you're here. Mikaela?"

The short young woman with choppy blond hair waved at the group. "Hey, y'all. I'm Mikaela, but most people call me Mikki." She had a higher-pitched voice and a sweet, clear energy. "I'm also in Kingston. Shout-out to Rough Draft."

"Great bookstore," Jamie said with a nod and a smile.

"I'm playing Horatio, and I'm tickled pink to be here," Mikki went on. "Also a former theater kid who gave it up when I graduated college to work in experiential marketing in New York. Did that for almost four years before accidentally getting pregnant when I was twenty-five." She waggled a finger at the teens. "Kids, wear a condom."

The teens stared back, mortified.

"I quit my job and moved back in with my mom." Mikki smiled, a dimple popping in each cheek. "My daughter, Flora, is three now, and she is my entire world. This play is the first thing I've done just for me, since she was born. I'm so excited to talk with adults about topics other than *Bluey* and Elmo and pooping."

"You're in luck," Jazz declared. "Very little of all three in this play. Next?"

This was the woman in her sixties dressed conservatively. "I'm Maria." Two spots of color rose in her cheeks as she fiddled with the purse in her lap. "I live just outside Rhinebeck. I retired last year after working in the local library for twenty-five years. Now I spend my time with my grandkids and I'm in a women's choir," Maria all but whispered, "which is how I met Jazz and heard about this show. Jazz's email said I was playing King Claudius?"

Lola could not picture this soft-spoken former librarian embodying the powerful and manipulative king of Denmark, uncle to Hamlet and head of the royal court. She risked a glance at Annie, expecting a flicker of relief—finally, someone more out of their depth than she was. But Annie's shoulders were tense, her gaze directed straight ahead.

Maria looked to Jazz, as if certain Jazz would correct her.

But Jazz just nodded, looking nonplussed. "Welcome, Maria. That brings us to our four Tragedians." Jazz indicated the teenagers. "While our band of down-on-their-luck traveling actors have next to no lines, they're still a vital part of the show, performing clowning and other physical theater. Plus, they're our understudies. Emery?"

The white-blond teen with double eyebrow piercings. Emery lifted a hand in a limp half wave. "What's up, I'm Emery. They/them."

Emery cut their eyes at Dylan, who'd not only introduced their pronouns but explained what those meant for those who needed the debrief (Clyde and Maria). Dylan gave Emery an encouraging smile.

"I'm a sophomore at Hudson High, which I kind of hate. Everyone there is, like, so boring. I'm vegan and I have ADHD. Ritalin girlie, represent. Understudy for Hamlet and Horatio." Emery flashed a peace sign then slouched back down.

Next was the pretty teen in an artsy aquamarine top. This was Orchid, a "proudly bisexual Vietnamese Dutch senior at Riverstone Prep" who was an "actress, filmmaker, writer," and at least three more things Lola lost track of. "Understudy for Ophelia and the Player," she added, smiling brightly at Vicky.

Kat was a self-described libertarian socialist with short sharp bangs who embraced community theater as an anti-capitalist form of resistance. "Understudy for Polonius and Guildenstern. She-slash-her," she said, seeming to accidentally direct her entire introduction at Orchid.

Which left the strawberry blonde in the crop top, who looked the most eager out of the entire cast. "I'm Zoë Lark," she said, her gaze lingering on Lola. "Understudy for Rosencrantz and Gertrude. And the craziest thing just happened to me."

Zoë's voice was so rich and confident, Lola assumed she'd had vocal training.

"Last week, I was on my stepfather's yacht in the Caribbean,"

Zoë said, "and we were rolling *deep*. My stepdad's a big-time entertainment lawyer and a bunch of his clients were there—Miley, Olivia, Sabrina. Just like, a *crew*."

"Okay, money," Emery murmured.

"Whatever, it was chill. But then," Zoë said as her eyes widened, "we were attacked by *pirates*."

Kat gasped. "For real?"

"For real!" Zoë nodded vigorously. "Like, they came on board the yacht with *guns* and *swords* and it was *so* scary. Because the captain was blackout drunk! So then *I* had to fight them!" Zoë was fighting a smile. "I grab one of the swords"—she mimed a sword fight—"and I'm going at it, like *hah! Hah! Hah!*—" At this, Zoë broke into uncontrolled laughter. "Sorry, sorry. I'm totally messing with you."

Orchid was wide-eyed. "Wait, did any of that happen?"

Zoë shook her head, still laughing. "My stepfather's an accountant. I live with my parents in Westchester, and I like to tell stories." She mock bowed in her seat. "Triple threat, at your service."

Lola chuckled, amused. She'd missed those theater kid antics more than she'd realized.

"Whoa, I totally believed you!" Emery laughed, no longer looking bored.

"Same here, I was like, *Bitch, when are we going on that yacht?*" Orchid said.

"Pirates of the Caribbean," Kat said, putting it together. "Good one. Though I bet most pirates are disenfranchised minorities who do it as means of surviving global inequity."

Orchid swung to Kat. "I think you're going to teach me things."

Kat blinked, looking unsure. "Only if you want me to."

Orchid gave a coquettish shrug. "I'm up for it."

Lola leaned over to Annie, whispering, "*Pirates could happen to anyone.*"

Annie returned Lola's grin with a shaky, "Huh?"

Lola's smile dropped, realizing her error. "Oh—it's from the play."

The play Annie had not read. Poor thing looked spooked.

"Tragedians." Jazz tried to get their attention.

"How do you define yourself politically?" Kat asked Orchid, sounding shyer than before.

Orchid tapped a fingertip against her lips. "Open to ideas."

"Tragedians!" Jazz quietened the teens. Their director indicated the script. "Shall we begin?"

The cast turned their attention to their pages. Despite still feeling worried on Annie's behalf, Lola felt a fresh bubble of excitement expand in her chest. Table reads were sacred, the critical first step of the rehearsal process. They could never happen twice.

Jazz began reading the opening stage directions, "*Two Elizabethans passing the time in a place without any visible character.*"

The play began with Rosencrantz and Guildenstern betting on coin tosses, which had landed on heads seventy-six times in a row, and counting. The implausibility of it was a source of contention. Annie's Rosencrantz accepted the situation while Lola's Guildenstern was more concerned. The play's defining characteristics surfaced quickly—wordplay, circular logic, the confusion between reality and illusion.

The table read wasn't technically a performance, but it was the first chance the actors had to bring their characters to life—to show their take on what the production could be. Lola prided herself on being a team player. She was prepared for the read not just as a performer, but as the assistant director, too. But as they got into it, something shifted. The words on the page weren't just dialogue; they were music, a melody she hadn't sung in years but somehow still knew by heart. Rather than stay safe with a performance designed to please, Lola took risks. She experimented. She had fun. She'd never been cast in a comedy before, but the play was funny and her comic timing worked. People laughed. That sound, warm and intimate, hit her like sunlight breaking through clouds.

Oh, she realized, *I'd forgotten how much I love this.*

As they all got into it, she found herself listening differently, too—making mental notes on how the others could nudge, calibrate, build on their tentative first steps.

The rest of the cast was raw but game. Vicky was bold and wily as the Player. Dylan played watchful Hamlet with quiet intensity. Deborah's Polonius oozed with self-serving charm, and Clyde, true to his word, had memorized every one of Gertrude's lines. Jamie and Mikki were both solid, and more important, they were having a blast.

But Annie . . . Annie was floundering.

She missed her cues. She stumbled over her lines, butchering the delicate rhythm. Each mistake made her shrink in her seat, as if she were trying to disappear inside her own skin.

Lola knew what Annie was feeling—the panic of failure. She tried to catch her eye. *It's okay,* she wanted to telegraph. *We've got this.* But Annie wouldn't look at anyone. By the final act, she'd given up any pretense of effort, speed-reading her way through in a dull monotone.

"*The play fades out,*" Jazz read the final stage direction aloud, and then, at last, it was done.

No one said a word. The air in the theater felt strained and lightly traumatized.

Lola sat breathless, caught between exhilaration and sympathy.

Annie's breath had gone shallow. She pushed back her chair. The screech of metal on wood made everyone flinch. "Excuse me."

And then she was moving, crossing the stage, running up the aisle.

Jazz's voice rang out behind her in surprise. "Annie—"

But she was already gone.

Lola exhaled sharply, rising from her seat. "I'll go."

• • •

OUTSIDE, AN AVALANCHE of blinding sun dazzled Lola before her eyes adjusted and she spotted Annie hurrying for a yellow Volkswagen Beetle parked out front. "Annie!" she called after her. "Wait!"

Wedge sandals wobbling, Lola dashed across the lawn to where Annie was desperately trying to unlock her car with a trembling hand, swearing under her breath.

"Hey," Lola said, catching up to her. "Wait a sec."

Annie spun on her, both cheeks splotchy, her blue eyes glittering with tears. "Why? So you can tell me *it doesn't matter* and *we'll get there*? Well, it *does* matter and we *won't* get there."

Lola held out a placating hand. "Annie, no one expects perfection on the first read."

"Says the girl who did it *perfectly.* God!" Annie threw her arms up. "What was I thinking saying yes to this? Why did I think this'd be *fun*?"

"It can be," Lola said, "if we work at it. If we keep trying."

"*We?*" Annie gave a short, manic laugh, a tear streaking down her cheek. "We are not a *we,* Lola. You and I will never again be a *we.*" Her voice rose, impassioned and pained. "For fuck's sake: You won. Okay? *You won.* You left Rhodes in search of your dream life and you got it. And that's why you, and Vicky and Dylan, are out there leading big, bold lives and I'm still in a *small* apartment in my *small* town running a *small* business. That's why you're living the dream, and I work six days a week *washing dogs.* I should obviously just stay in my lane. My *small* lane."

Lola was momentarily speechless. Nothing about Annie's life seemed small. It seemed meaningful and manageable. Idyllic. "So—what? You're quitting?"

"Oh, you'd love that, wouldn't you?" Annie wrenched her car door open.

Lola caught it before she could slam it shut. "I absolutely would not," she said, unable to keep an edge out of her voice. "I'm putting myself out there, too, Annie. I'm only doing this because we're all doing it—Vicky, Dylan, and *you.*"

Annie stared back at her, wet eyes full of pain. Behind that, shame. "Well, I'm doing this for Jazz and the town, so no, sorry, Lola: I'm not quitting. I'm going home to eat a month's worth of ice cream and read the fucking play. Okay? *Okay?*"

She tugged on the door. This time, Lola let it slam. Without another word, Annie peeled off, the sound of screeching tires tearing through the peaceful afternoon.

Lola stared after her, stunned. Her pulse was still pounding from the argument, her brain trying to catch up to what had just happened.

You won. You're living the dream.

Annie believed that, and why wouldn't she? That's what Lola had said. *Exactly the life I wanted to live.*

It fit the story. The one where Lola got everything and Annie got left behind. Because admitting the truth would mean what? That she'd made a decades-long mistake? That the dream she'd chased wasn't what she thought? That it hadn't been worth leaving?

Panic reared inside Lola. No. *No.* She was not conceding that. Her life may not be perfect but it was perfectly fine.

She squared her shoulders, bristling, feeling a familiar hardening of her exterior.

Annie Lightfoot did not get to hurt her again.

9.

After the table read wrapped up, everyone gamely pretending one of the leads had not fled the scene, Vicky spent the rest of the afternoon reacquainting herself with Rhodes. Clyde's Grocery, with its hand-painted signs and rows of glass jars filled with colorful candies. The criminally delicious smell of butter and sugar wafting out of a new bakery called French Kiss. You Nailed It was still in business, but now, there was a surprising number of muscled men thirst traps plastered to the walls. Vicky waved hello to Deborah as she passed.

She bought some gold hoop earrings in a new, tiny jewelry store, chatting with the woman behind the counter who was also Asian—a rare moment of relief for Vicky in this mostly white town. The town did seem a little more diverse than before, though still largely homogenous, as much of Upstate tended to be. Vicky hadn't been the only Chinese girl in her grade at Riverstone Prep, but she was the only person of color in her friend group, which wasn't something they'd ever discussed. Her school friends seemed to think Vicky didn't want to acknowledge her ethnicity or that she, being smart, pretty, and popular, somehow existed outside her race. She remembered them doing impressions of Mr. Yunioshi, a shockingly racist Japanese character played by a white actor in

Breakfast at Tiffany's, which they'd all watched at Kayleigh Kessell's sleepover. When she didn't join in the impressions, Kayleigh tossed off, "Oh, but you're not like *Asian* Asian."

Vicky had gone home that day with the phrase looping in her head. *Asian* Asian. Because she was born in America? Because she didn't use chopsticks in front of her friends? Both her parents were Chinese. She was Asian American. Did that mean she wasn't Asian Asian?

Things were different with Lola, Annie, and Dylan. In rehearsals, Jazz would emphasize the importance of "radical honesty" and "wild curiosity." Rather than difference being something to hide or ignore, in the theater, as artists, difference was to be explored and celebrated. Deep into one of their first exhilarating hangs at Dylan's house, Dylan asked her what it was like being American-born Chinese. At first, Vicky didn't know how to answer—she'd never been asked so directly. She tentatively offered that it was hard seeing racist characters in movies that her white friends weren't bothered by; conversely, they were entertained or titillated. She braced for dismissal; the implication she was overreacting. Instead, her trio of new theater friends all listened, wide-eyed and attentive.

All sorts of things started spilling out. At first it was small—like how her mom always bought rice in giant fifty-pound bags. "Fifty?" Dylan had repeated, eyes wide, which made Vicky laugh and keep going. She told them how her family made mooncakes and tangyuan instead of the cookies or cakes her white friends had. "That sounds amazing," Annie had said, sounding so sincere, and Vicky felt herself relax a little more. She shared the intense emphasis her family placed on academic success, and how her parents showed their love through actions rather than words. Lola had asked what sort of actions, and Vicky told them things like cooking her favorite meals or making sure she had everything she needed for school, but sometimes she wished they would just say how they felt. "You want them to say 'I love you'?" Dylan had guessed, and

Vicky nodded, surprised at how much that felt true. She explained the traditions around Lunar New Year—red envelopes, dragon dances, dumplings—and finally admitted how often she'd felt different, like she had to hide her real self just to blend in. Her voice caught, but her friends didn't flinch. They just kept listening, interested and patient, and she found herself telling them more than she'd ever told anyone before. It was chaotic but cathartic, and the whole time her new friends asked questions that felt like a door opening. They didn't pretend to fully understand—how could they?—but their willingness to listen made Vicky feel like all of her, not just the parts that fit in, was welcome at the table.

That night, back home in her bedroom, Vicky remembered crying into her pillow. Not out of sadness. More like relief. She'd finally found friends who wanted to see her, all of her—even if they couldn't know exactly what it felt like.

She'd forgotten about all that until coming back here to Rhodes.

ROCK AROUND THE CLOCK was just as quiet as last time she was there. "Maps" by the Yeah Yeah Yeahs wailed from the jukebox. *Wait. They don't love you like I love you.* Karen O's plaintive cry still ripped Vicky's heart out.

She reflexively pulled out her phone, thumb hovering over her work inbox for a quick check. She caught herself with an irritated grunt. *Sabbatical, remember?*

She felt a tap of disappointment at seeing someone in "their" booth in the back, before realizing the person with the artfully messy hair frowning at their phone with a toothpick clenched between their teeth was none other than Dylan freaking Rogers. Annoyance and something like excitement crashed into her chest. Would she ever recover from the plot twist that Dylan Rogers was hot? Not just "the years have been kind." More like the years have produced a genderqueer Adonis.

Vicky marched over. Without meaning to, her words came out haughty. "I hope you weren't planning on 'me time,' Rogers."

Dylan started. On registering Vicky, a smile dashed over their lips before they shook it away with a theatrical scowl. "You again."

Vicky slid opposite them. "Miss me?"

"Like the deserts miss the rain," Dylan replied dryly. Their brows might be darker now, and a little more sculptured, but Dylan's eyes were the same beautiful sea-glass green.

Their phone buzzed. Dylan checked it, muttered, "Jesus," and flipped it face down.

"What's wrong?" Vicky asked.

"My mom heard I'm back. Wants to meet," Dylan said.

"Didn't your folks move?"

"Dad's in Seattle but Celine's in the same place."

Vicky pitched forward in surprise. "Wait, they split?" Vicky recalled Dylan's tech entrepreneur father as charismatic and charming, but always away for work. "What happened?"

Dylan shrugged. "Dunno. File it under Things That Ruined Valentine's Day Forever."

Vicky raised an eyebrow. Clearly, Dylan was no romantic. "Are you going to see her?"

"We've barely spoken in five years—I'm too busy," Dylan said, in a *case closed* way.

Perhaps a lie, but Dylan *was* busy.

Dylan, Lola, and Vicky were all staying with Jazz for the month, arriving on her doorstep over the course of yesterday evening. Vicky had anticipated a group dinner, which may or may not have explained her three outfit changes, each a little cuter than the last. But Lola spent all night studying the play while Dylan worked in their room, then *meditated* in the downstairs library.

Vicky then spent her night reading every word of Marlowe's beautifully designed website. Research, after all, was Vicky's primary love language.

> Welcome to Marlowe, where every bite of our sustainable, small-batch chocolate tells a story. Inspired by the daring spirit of creators who forge their own paths, Marlowe reinvents tradition, creating delicious artisanal chocolates that are as unique as you.

The About page explained that Dylan's journey was "as rich and nuanced as the chocolates they create." Marlowe was inspired by Dylan's travels to Belgium, Ecuador, and Italy (what were those like?); their experience working in the food industry (which was?); and passion for inclusivity and thinking beyond the binary (um, when did Dylan get so cool?). Marlowe was focused around Dylan as the face of the brand—founder and visionary, whose life and stories inspired the flavors. Dylan had also completed an MBA.

So it was a little amusing to see how ice queen Celine had reverted boss babe Dylan Rogers back into a grumpy teenager, slouching low in the booth at Rock Around the Clock.

Vicky picked up the menu. "How long have you been here?"

"An hour or so."

"Lucky I arrived," Vicky said with a cheeky smile.

"Actually, I like being alone," Dylan volleyed back, relaxing into their down-for-whatever vibe. "Time to think. Indulge my own preferences. Use the power of my imagination."

Vicky rolled her eyes. "What are you imagining, Rogers? Adding to your unhealthy collection of low-rise jeans?"

Dylan's gaze dropped to Vicky's mouth before zigzagging away. "Don't diss the jeans."

Vicky felt a kick of *something*, right in the center of her chest. Heat stormed her cheeks as she glared at the menu, hoping Dylan didn't notice. She'd probably imagined Dylan looking at her mouth. The reason why there was still simmering tension was because Dylan had not forgiven Vicky. Maybe even hated her.

Her antics at the closing-night party, twenty years ago, had been the height of mean girl shit. No matter what good Vicky did in the world, the image of baby Dylan, holding that sad bouquet of paper daisies, tragically dapper in a suit, would forever remind Vicky that she was not a good person, at all.

Sure, they didn't *seem* resentful. Maybe forgive and forget was a tenant of their *Queer Eye* makeover. Or maybe Dylan was hiding how they *really* felt. After all, Dylan brought up Chip Chadwick during their very first dinner together, didn't they?

Rock Around the Clock wasn't the place to right a wrong that'd been torturing Vicky for two decades. But she could start with reconnecting with Dylan. They'd be living together for the next month, after all.

"Vicky?" Dylan spoke as if they'd already said it once. "Yo."

The same waitress with the micro bangs was back, notepad in hand.

"Want anything?" Dylan prompted.

Vicky tried not to look at the soft yet assertive shape of Dylan's mouth. She wanted a beer but knew she should be cutting back on alcohol. "Uh . . . the . . . Groovy Grilled Veggie Wrap."

Dylan looked bemused. "Still no Big Bopper Bacon Burger?"

Vicky hesitated. "I'm on a . . . health kick."

Dylan narrowed their eyes.

Vicky didn't want to lie, but she also felt too ashamed about what'd happened last month to explain further. So she just stared back, not giving an inch.

Dylan gave up, addressing the waitress with a lazy smile. "I'll do another beer and some curly fries."

"Excellent choice." The waitress twirled a lock of hair. "The fries are amazing."

"Oh, you like them?" Dylan leaned forward, chin resting on one hand, voice low and sexy.

"I do," their waitress simpered, and Vicky was surprised she didn't just pour herself into Dylan's lap.

Vicky decided to step in before someone, who wasn't her, ended up wrist deep. "Fries, beer, veggie wrap," she snapped. "Thank you!"

The waitress gave Vicky a bitchy smile and left.

Vicky huffed, giving Dylan a look of derision. "Save your fuck-boy antics for some other time, Rogers."

Dylan blinked, looking surprised. Then almost flattered. "You think I'm a fuck boy?"

Vicky was no fool. "I know you're a fuck boy. Everything about you screams *I'll text back two days later with a winky face.*"

Dylan didn't seem offended. They seemed pleased. "Okay."

Well, that confirmed it. Rogers was a player. A certified panty dropper. A licensed hardbody. Vicky's jaw tensed. "Where the hell's my veggie wrap?"

"You only just ordered it." Dylan regarded Vicky as if she was a particularly tricky Wordle. "I remember you as the unhealthiest person I'd ever met. Twizzlers was one of your five food groups. Your idea of an apéritif was a hoagie."

"People change."

"Do they?" Far from it being rhetorical, Dylan sounded genuinely curious.

"Yes." Vicky jutted her chin.

She could smell Dylan. Incense and leather and very ripe plums. Not quite feminine, not quite masculine. Alluring. Intoxicating. Annoying! Vicky tried to ignore it.

"So. When did all this happen?" She indicated Dylan's overall existence. "The gay glow-up."

Dylan chuckled. "In stages, I guess. Started in college, when I came out."

"College." Vicky narrowed her eyes. "Somewhere progressive. Probably the West Coast, to get away from your mom."

Dylan's eyebrow ticked up. They nodded. "Berkeley."

"Berkeley," Vicky repeated. "You joined the poetry club to meet girls, fell in love with your straight roommate, discovered hallucinogens, wore a lot of . . . plaid?"

Dylan blinked, looking taken aback. "Maybe a bit?"

"How much is a bit?"

"You're four for four, freak." Dylan's ocean eyes did not leave Vicky's, their gaze intrigued.

Vicky grinned, now fully engaged. "Okay. You went to your first Pride parade and stayed up late talking about Judith Butler with the drummer in an all-girl punk band, who you were too scared to make a move on, but luckily she kissed you and you came with your pants still on. You got a lip piercing sophomore year, but it got annoying so you took it out. Tried veganism until you couldn't live without eggs. Skipped *Twilight,* read *Harry Potter,* lied about loving *Breaking Bad,* but were actually obsessed with *Glee.* Door-knocked for Obama. Cried when he won." Vicky cocked her head. "Or something?"

Dylan's mouth was ajar. The waitress dropped off the fries and beer, and Dylan all but lunged for the glass, downing a third of it. Finally, they spoke. "It was a tongue piercing."

Vicky cackled. It was a reliable party trick, thanks to her professional skill set and the fact that she'd spent a lot of time around a lot of queers.

But Dylan didn't laugh. They just kept watching her. Something opened up behind those pale green eyes. "How did you know all that?" they asked, softer, curious. The teasing edge was gone.

Vicky smiled, a tiny bit charmed at Dylan's lack of pretense. "Guess I just know you." It was and wasn't the truth. "What about coming out as nonbinary?"

"You don't want to take another disturbingly accurate guess?"

"I'd prefer not getting canceled today, thanks."

Dylan winced. "I know what you mean, but I kind of hate how awkward everyone gets about it. Like, I can tell when people get so afraid of messing up my pronouns that they can't relax around me. I can see them getting in their heads, like, panicked."

"Well, they don't want to misgender you," Vicky said. "They don't want to offend you."

"I know. I appreciate that. It's just hard." Dylan ran both hands through their dark brown hair, messing it up, then smoothing it back down. "Long story short, I just never felt like a girl. It was a shoe that didn't fit, but I couldn't figure out why. Then, about five years ago, I went on this group trip to Joshua Tree, and there was this nonbinary person with us, Kai. We all did shrooms and Kai and I talked for hours and suddenly, all the pieces fell into place."

"Of course you had your big gender mic drop moment high as fuck in the desert," Vicky snickered. "That's perfect."

"Shut up." Dylan grinned, tossing a fry at her, which Vicky ducked with a giggle.

"I'm happy for you, Dyls," Vicky said, meaning it. "Really."

"Thanks." Dylan reached for some fries, their expression curious. "What about you? How was Harvard?"

Vicky explained how she threw herself into undergrad, majoring in political science with a minor in sociology. "I was always at the library or in debate club meetings. Prelaw track, so tons of law-related courses and internships. I'd study until ten, party until two, get up at seven for a spin class, and be back in a lecture by nine. Went straight to Harvard Law School after that, graduated with honors, and the rest is herstory."

Dylan whistled, cheekbones popping. "Impressive."

"I know." Vicky couldn't help tossing her hair back and grinning.

Dylan stretched, the hem of their threadbare muscle tee riding up. "Family law—that's like divorce and custody battles, right?"

Vicky nodded. "Exactly. And I run a free legal clinic through the firm."

"Fair Fight Legal Aid," Dylan said.

Vicky felt a sweet tickle of surprise at the knowledge that Dylan had done some digging of their own. Ensuring the wives of shady billionaires got a fair deal was satisfying, and lucrative, but it was worlds more meaningful to work pro bono for disadvantaged people who couldn't afford a good lawyer. "But it's not easy balancing both," she admitted. "Sabbatical's the first time I've stepped back in . . . god. Ever, I think."

Every time her body screamed at her to take a break, another heartbreaking case would land on her desk. She ignored all the signs of burnout and fatigue and stress until it was too late. Which, in a way, was why she was back here in Rhodes. Her sabbatical was, quite literally, what the doctor ordered.

"Jesus, Vee." Dylan's gaze stayed curious. "So, not much time for relationships then?"

The question plunged into Vicky's chest like an arrow hitting a bull's-eye. All her exes had the same complaint. She loved work more than she loved them. Well, duh. Hard work was what she knew.

"Nope," Vicky replied. "Too busy fixing the fallout of failed marriages."

"New Slang" by the Shins started on the jukebox, melancholic and wistful.

"How did you end up in family law?" Dylan asked.

Vicky squirmed. "Personal, um, reasons."

"Meaning?"

Micro Bangs dropped off Vicky's veggie wrap, lingering in an attempt to make eye contact with Dylan. But Dylan was looking only at Vicky.

"Honestly it was because of my parents' divorce," Vicky began slowly. "How it all went down. My dad really screwed my mom over. Financially, legally—everything."

"I remember them fighting." Dylan leaned forward, their expression empathetic. "What happened?"

Vicky rarely opened up about those years. But with Dylan,

things felt different. Safe, somehow. "You know my dad made bank in the import-export business, right?" she began. "My mom made a lot of that possible. She spoke fluent Mandarin; Dad didn't. Mom never had a clue about the legal side of anything—she trusted my dad. And in Chinese culture, women are expected to be modest and not question their husbands. But when they decided to divorce, my dad hired lawyers—good ones. Like, scarily good."

She paused, feeling the old anger and frustration bubbling up. "I found out later that he hid assets, created fake debts, underreported his income. My mom ended up with a fraction of what she was entitled to. He kept the house while she struggled to pay the rent. It was so freaking unfair."

Dylan nodded, putting it all together. "So that's why you became a divorce lawyer."

"Pretty much," Vicky said. "I didn't want other people going through what my mom did. I wanted to make sure they understood their rights and got a fair deal." She picked up a curly fry, twisting it between her fingers. "I remember, that summer, sitting in court and watching Mom sob. Dad's lawyers made her seem like a gold digger. I decided to be just as cutthroat—but for the right reasons."

"That's so admirable, Vee." Dylan reached across the table to squeeze Vicky's forearm. It echoed throughout her body like a wind chime in a storm: a sudden jangle of heat. Inside her bra, her nipples pinched into tight points.

Oh, that's right. She had a body. A body that liked to be touched. It'd been a minute since anyone had reminded her of that.

"Thanks." It came out a little breathier than she intended. Vicky prayed she wasn't blushing. "It's just . . . it's what I had to do. For my mom."

Dylan nodded soberly, not looking away.

They'd had deep conversations as teenagers—that was part of what made their friendship feel so important—but it felt different discussing things like this as adults. More serious. More exposing. More meaningful.

Dylan frowned. "You said 'that summer.' The summer we did the play?"

Vicky nodded. "Whenever I said I had a *family meeting*? That was court."

"You never said anything about that." Dylan looked confused, shaking their head. "I knew they were getting divorced but I didn't know you were, like, watching it happen." Dylan sat back, looking devastated. "Shit, Vicky. You were just a kid."

"Why do you think I was such a bitch all the time?" Vicky joked weakly. "I liked you guys so much. What we had saved me that summer. I didn't want to make it all about me."

"So, then . . . that means . . ." And for a second, Vicky was terrified that Dylan was going to bring up closing night, but thankfully Dylan just finished it with, "Huh."

"Let's talk about something else," Vicky said quickly. "The cast. Is every teenager these days a bisexual vegan with ADHD or what?"

Dylan let out a laugh and the conversation moved on.

But all Vicky could think about was what she was keeping secret and what Dylan wasn't saying. And how, for the first time in forever, she wasn't thinking about work.

Just Dylan.

And the side of their leg pressing against hers under the table. Their bodies were touching, but neither of them was acknowledging it, or pulling away.

10.

Twenty-seven days till the show

DYLAN FIRST MET VICKY AT THE OPEN AUDITIONS FOR THE Rhodes Playhouse summer production of *Our Town,* the year before *Rosencrantz and Guildenstern Are Dead.* It was a fresh May morning and the line stretched all the way up Myrtle Street, ending outside the charming kids' bookstore, Once Upon a Time.

Dylan was by the theater's front entrance, one of the first ones dropped off, partly because their mom wanted to get to a step aerobics class in Hudson, and partly because Dylan preferred to read alone than endure Celine and her barely veiled criticisms.

The theater world intrigued Dylan. It was a chance to unzip the girl suit and try on something else.

"Mind if I cut in?" were the first words Vicky Fang ever spoke to Dylan.

Dylan looked up from *The Bell Jar* to see a breathless girl assessing them with sharp eyes. Dylan recognized her instantly—junior, queen bee, intimidatingly polished.

"Uh, sure . . ." Dylan had replied, but it wasn't really a question, as Vicky was already doing it.

Dylan watched, mesmerized, as Vicky pulled out a lip gloss and compact mirror, applying with the precision of someone who expected to be looked at. Dylan didn't wear makeup—it made them feel like a circus clown and as comfortable as the dresses and long hair their mother insisted on. But there was something hypnotic, even addicting, about watching Vicky Fang dab her pillowy lips with the sticky glaze. Another puzzle piece sliding into place. Dylan didn't like wearing makeup but they liked that Vicky wore it. They liked it a lot.

Vicky caught them staring and snapped the mirror shut. "What?"

Dylan backed up. They tried to speak without showing their braces. "Nothing."

Vicky fluffed her hair, which was moonless black with the slightest wave. "How do I look?"

Dylan couldn't say what they really thought: *Terrifying and hot and like I would let you kidnap me if it meant we could spend a little time together.* "Good," they said. "But you have . . ." They gestured at Vicky's mouth. A stray smudge of gloss.

Vicky frowned. "I have . . . ?"

Dylan surprised them both by reaching up, gently wiping the gloss from the corner of Vicky's mouth. The feeling of touching a pretty girl like this quickened Dylan's breath, making them even more sure of something they'd long suspected: that they liked girls, and not in the way other girls did.

There were a lot of ways in which Dylan didn't feel like other girls at all.

Dylan's gaze flickered to Vicky's, holding it for a heartbeat. Vicky stared back with a mix of defiance and something less certain. As if they both shared a secret. Vicky's hot gaze throbbed throughout Dylan, intoxicating their bloodstream and making them light-headed.

Then Vicky stepped back, and Dylan remembered where they were. Open auditions in a small town. Caution cooled the heat under their skin. Whatever had just happened, Dylan suspected their mother would think it was wrong, even if it felt very, very right.

"Thanks," Vicky said briskly, opening her bag. "Good luck in there."

Jazz had thrown open the playhouse doors, greeting the line of hopefuls with a lusty, "Good morning, thespians!" The theater's artistic director wore a matching set patterned with pop art-style speech bubbles in bright primary colors. Her glasses were shaped like two giant stars.

"I go to your school." Dylan spoke in a rush.

"Radical," Vicky tossed off, not looking back.

That summer, Dylan didn't get cast. Nor did Annie. But Vicky did. And Lola, who played Emily Webb.

Over the next year, Dylan started saying hello to Vicky when they passed each other in the corridors of Riverstone Prep. Vicky was in the group understood as the popular girls: pretty teenagers who tweezed their eyebrows into twigs and treated those beneath them with gentle disdain. Vicky only returned Dylan's hellos if she wasn't with her pride of lionesses.

Vicky didn't seem to have a steady boyfriend like some of the other girls, but their school was co-ed, and plenty of boys displayed their interest by roughhousing in front of her. Dylan saw Chip Chadwick, the towheaded football star, crush a Coke can to his forehead in an attempt to impress Vicky. Dylan began referring to him as "Chimp," describing his behavior as zoo-like to their mother. "Boys will be boys," Celine had chuckled in response.

The next year, Dylan was once again front of the line at the open auditions for *Rosencrantz and Guildenstern*. Once again, Vicky was pushing her luck.

"Hey!" Vicky's greeting was a pant. "Mind if I cut in?"

Dylan looked up from *Oranges Are Not the Only Fruit*. They smiled at Vicky, but unlike before, the smile had an edge. Dylan was trying something new. Guts. "Yes, I do. So no, you can't."

"Please?" Vicky tossed her hair back and tried an even bigger smile. "There are so many people here."

It was fun, seeing her beg. "People who got here on time."

Vicky huffed. "I'm cutting in."

They stood nose-to-nose. Dylan had two inches on her. "No," Dylan said calmly, "you're not."

Anger and delight sprang onto Vicky's face. Her hands balled into fists even as her gaze flashed to Dylan's lips, before slicing back up. "People are watching."

Dylan smiled, unfazed. "Radical."

That summer, all four of them—Vicky, Dylan, Annie, Lola—were cast, quickly becoming inseparable. But after Vicky rejected Dylan at the closing night after-party, they'd never spoken again.

Until now.

THE NEXT MORNING, Sunday, Dylan awoke in Jazz's guest bedroom on the second floor feeling hot and bothered. Not just because it was already sweltering and Jazz did not have central air. Because right across the hall from them, in the exact same queen bed as Dylan had, lay one Victoria Mei Fang.

How had this happened?

Oh, that's right. Dylan had made it happen. Dylan had returned to Rhodes. Dylan had opted in.

Scooting up a little, Dylan surveyed their bedroom for the next month. Colorful, whimsical, and a little slapdash. The comforter was royal purple, trimmed in black lace. The largest framed poster read *Buy Weed from Women!* French doors opened to a balconette overlooking the green gulp of the garden.

Dylan fell back against the pillow, trying to summon the momentum to get out of this very comfortable bed.

Years of therapy and self-growth had helped Dylan develop perspective and self-protection. Rolling into Rhodes on that first afternoon, Dylan had felt good—Dylan had felt in control. But Dylan had not adequately accounted for the extended impact of Vicky Fang.

What'd she called them last night at the diner? A fuck boy? It wasn't true—not really—but Dylan was thrilled at the misconception. Fuck boys were sexually in-demand scoundrels with massive dicks. Dylan did not hate that Vicky thought that about them.

Their teen obsession was a *woman* now. A woman with full breasts and a round ass. A sharp, hot tongue. Closing their eyes, Dylan relaxed, imagining that tongue pressed against various parts of their body. Licking. Sucking. Taking orders. Obeying.

Dylan reminded themself they should definitely *not* be masturbating to Vicky—again. Vicky had long been an investment in Dylan's spank bank but fantasizing about her here, now, was probably a bad idea. But not bad enough to stop Dylan from reaching inside their boxer briefs. Jesus, they were already wet. This would take seconds, not minutes.

Dylan should *not* be imagining Vicky, naked on her hands and knees, begging for it.

Dylan should *not* be imagining grabbing a fistful of Vicky's tit as they fucked, squeezing a dark brown nipple until Vicky cried out, her glossy red lipstick smeared and messy.

Dylan should *not* be imagining reaching a climax with Vicky, about to come together, sweaty and delirious and—

Someone banged on their bedroom door. "Hey!"

Dylan landed back in reality with a gasp, then a groan. So close. They were panting, and sweating, and *so close.*

"Rogers!" Outside the bedroom door, Vicky knocked again. "You in here?"

"Just a sec!" Dylan threw the sweat-soaked sheet aside, feeling half-deranged with unmet need as they stumbled over the fuchsia-pink carpet to yank open the door. "*What?*"

Vicky swayed back in alarm. She was dressed in blue-striped seersucker shorts and a cropped white tank showing off a sliver of olive skin. Her eyeliner was flawless. Her lips were, distressingly, sticky with gloss. "Lola and I are ready. You're . . . not dressed."

Her gaze slid to Dylan's loose black tank and TomboyX boxers. Vicky's eyes pulsed wide. She sucked in her lower lip.

Dylan didn't typically answer the door in something you could basically see their nipples in, but they were too flustered to care. They swiped hair out of their eyes, trying to focus. "Okay, okay, I'll just jump in the shower." A very, *very* cold shower.

Vicky clucked in annoyance. "We don't have time for—"

"I need a shower! I'll ride with Jazz!" Dylan said hotly, shutting the door in Vicky's face.

TWENTY MINUTES LATER, Jazz's Mustang lingered at a stop sign. Definitely best to ride with Jazz in her ancient convertible, even if she did drive at approximately ten miles per hour and stopped for a full ten seconds at every stop sign. Today, their director was dressed in a flowy, emerald-green jumpsuit. The top part was emblazoned with the words *Drama Queen* in the same bright pink as her oversize glasses.

Sweat pooled under Dylan's thighs as the sun beat down. High summer.

Hot & Sweaty. The words dropped into their brain like a surprise gift. Hot & Sweaty captured something about not just summer, but *this* summer: the tension, the playfulness, the heat. The salt of sweat on skin, the pop of nerves seeing a crush, the sticky sweetness of a kiss . . .

Having developed dozens of unique, story-driven flavors in the three years Marlowe had been operating, Dylan knew an idea when they had it.

They swiped open their Notes app, brain starting to buzz. What made those sticky teenage summers so alive? What could they *taste* like, in chocolate form?

Bare thighs on vinyl (diner booths). Sweat, salt, the taste of summer skin. Longing and heat. Something nostalgic? Teenage candy?

Jazz eased the Mustang forward, setting off down the empty country road. Dylan barely noticed. They were in the zone, ideas flowing like a chocolate fountain.

The sticky red of V's lipstick . . . sweet, sexy, with heat. A glossy raspberry compote with something spiced and warm: cloves?

Summer tasted like buttery popcorn from the theater's concession stand. Summer felt fizzy, almost chaotic, like soda bubbles against your tongue.

Popcorn, Dylan typed, for crunch!!

By the time Jazz parked outside the playhouse, Dylan knew they had something.

The pair crossed the front lawn, heading for the playhouse entrance.

"So, how's the plan to rebrand the town as Upstate's answer to the Castro going?" Dylan asked. It was such a good idea to make Rhodes a queer destination.

"Fabulous!" Jazz declared, adding she'd pitched the idea at a town meeting (actually just half a dozen locals in Clyde's backyard) and the reception had been positive. "Assuming the show does well." Jazz hesitated before admitting, "The bank gave me until the end of the month. It's now or never."

Dylan's stomach dipped. "The bank?"

Jazz sighed. "If I don't come up with the money, they'll foreclose. Take the building, turn it into a damn Dollar General."

Dylan stopped walking. "*What?*"

Jazz lifted one shoulder in a half shrug. "I'm a little behind on the mortgage."

"How little?"

Jazz didn't smile this time. "Little enough that if the show doesn't sell out, I'll have to."

Dylan's chest pulled tight. They knew the play was meant to save the theater, and the town, but they *didn't* know the theater was on the brink of foreclosure. It was easy to forget that Jazz hadn't just gotten the quartet together for kicks. "The show will be great," Dylan assured her. "We'll get the money."

"I know. I have faith." Jazz's voice was fond as she regarded them. "I'm just so glad my four best girls are back together."

Dylan felt a crunch of disappointment, chased by a surge of nerves that knocked at their ribs. Correcting their beloved mentor hurt more than they expected. Still, their voice came out steady: "I'm glad we're here, too. But I don't identify as a girl anymore. I did, in high school. I don't now."

Jazz pressed a hand to her orange-lipsticked mouth. "Of course you don't. I knew that. I'm sorry."

"It's okay," Dylan said automatically. They took a breath. *Was* it okay? Or did they just want it to be? They cleared their throat and tried to say something that felt honest. "It takes a bit of practice to, like, make the mental shift. The effort's what's important to me. I don't expect anyone to be perfect."

"Me neither," Jazz said.

"Keep that in mind as I butcher Hamlet," Dylan joked. Because *Rosencrantz and Guildenstern* was set inside the original *Hamlet,* intertwined with the plot, Hamlet's lines were mostly ye olde Shakespeare. *Nymph, in thy orisons be all my sins remembered.*

"You've got yourself a deal." Jazz regarded Dylan with a mix of gratitude and sincerity. "Thank you for giving up the rest of your summer for this. I know you're busy. It means so much."

"You mean so much," Dylan said. "Do you remember what you said to us before our first rehearsal, back in the day?"

Jazz shook her head, her white hair glowing in the already blazing sun.

"You told us the Tragedians didn't have a gender: They could be played as women or men or 'someone in-between.' That stayed with me. That . . . permission. I don't think I ever thanked you." Dylan tapped the script in their book bag. "This is me, saying thank you."

"Thank *you,*" Jazz said. "For continuing to educate *me*. The greatest gift you can give me is your honesty. To let me in on who you really are."

Dylan socked Jazz's arm softly, blinking away the push of tears. "You got it, boss."

Dylan rode a wave of warmth for their old mentor as they pulled open the playhouse's front door.

This whole process felt like history repeating in the weirdest way, except now, Dylan wasn't an oblivious teenager oscillating between feeling smugly convinced they'd figured the whole world out, and desperately trying to, painfully clueless. They were an adult, somehow. Even at thirty-five, Dylan didn't always feel like a capital-A Adult. Why was that, when they had the markers of adulthood: a master's degree, a start-up, a concern about cholesterol, an opinion about vacuum cleaners? Perhaps because, despite being in their fourth decade of life, their capacity for human emotion remained the same. Jealousy, insecurity, shame, regret—these powerful feelings were able to level them back to their high school self. Even as an Adult, Dylan's high school crush could still rock their hard-won equilibrium.

After their very cold shower, Dylan was thinking more clearly.

Feelings, of any kind, for Vicky Fang were a let's-travel-on-that-spiffy-new-ship-called-the-*Titanic* level of terrible idea. Dylan reminded themself that Vicky was still an annoying bossy brat, and Dylan didn't want or need to complicate their full, well-balanced life. Their focus needed to be Marlowe and the play and *boundaries.* Nothing else. Best to avoid the open seat next to Vicky, and instead take the one next to their new old pal Clyde.

Dylan gave him a nod. "Morning, Clyde."

"Ah, good morning, young Dylan," Clyde replied. He took off his glasses, his expression intrigued. "Now, where are you on whether or not the moon landing was faked?"

"All right," Jazz announced, from her position at the head of the table. "Are we all here?"

Dylan scanned the individuals seated around the U-shape of tables—the new Rhodes Players. Vicky and Lola were seated together, both looking fresh and pretty. Deborah Buttrose's earrings were even bigger than the ones from yesterday, some sort of feathered Etsy disaster; she was chatting with Maria, who still looked terrified. Ophelia and Horatio, aka baby-faced Jamie and sweet, tiny Mikki, were on Dylan's other side, both finishing up cream cheese bagels.

The teens were bunched together but each locked into their own universe: Emery, white-blond and moody, slouched over their phone in a baggy T-shirt repping a band Dylan was far too old and uncool to recognize. Zoë, all earnest theater kid energy, softly sang what sounded like "My Shot" from *Hamilton,* no doubt manifesting a Broadway debut—or at least TikTok virality—by the end of summer. Kat—plaid pants and a *No Gods No Masters* tee—flipped through *Resistance* magazine like she was personally prepping to eat the rich at lunch. And then there was Orchid: a walking art installation mid-selfie, angles dialed to maximum slay. Influence or be influenced, baby.

The new generation. Dylan could feel themself aging in real time.

"Where's Annie?" Jazz directed this at Lola.

Lola shrugged, looking worried. "I don't know," she said. "She hasn't replied to my texts."

The cast members' gazes flickered toward the theater aisle that Annie had escaped up after yesterday's table read.

Jazz let out a disappointed sigh before forcing a resilient smile. "Well. That's okay. We'll just have to—"

The doors to the theater banged open. Annie burst in, juggling two large doughnut boxes, pushing a pair of heart-shaped sunglasses into her hair. "Sorry!" She hurried up the aisle. She was wearing another colorful sundress, a strap falling off one shoulder. "I had the brilliant idea to get doughnuts for everyone," she explained breathlessly, "but French Kiss isn't open till eleven, so I went to that truck stop that used to sell Vicky cigarettes but has surprisingly good doughnuts, and sorry but I'm here, I'm here."

"Wonderful to see you, Annie." Jazz spoke as if she'd never had any doubts. "We were just about to get started."

"Sorry," Annie said again, taking a seat and passing the boxes around. "Also, kids, cigarettes are *not* cool even if they *look* cool in the movies. Danny Zuko has a *lot* to answer for."

Emery took a bear claw. "Who?"

"RIP my cultural references," Vicky said with a sigh, which made Dylan snort laughter. Over the past twenty years, Vicky had become even funnier, in addition to smarter and hotter.

Nope: Dylan was *not* supposed to be thinking things like that.

"Focus please," Jazz instructed, clapping her hands. "Let's begin."

Jazz explained that today was part of the "understanding" phase of rehearsal, when the entire cast would discuss the play and what it meant to be staging it. "In addition to answering what is this story about," Jazz told the thirteen listening actors, "we must answer the question, 'Why are we telling it *now*?' What do we want the audience to walk away with? What connection do we personally feel to the work as a whole?"

Jazz was bright-eyed as she went on, surveying the group. "I want to hear from everyone!"

The cast exchanged tentative looks: No one wanted to go first. Clyde sat back in his seat like a spectator on game day: happy to be there but in no way kicking it off himself. The teens looked at the adults as if to say, *you're the grown-ups.* Deborah looked expectantly to Lola, who was looking at Annie. Annie took an enormous bite of a cream custard doughnut, getting granulated sugar on her nose.

Dylan glanced at Vicky, catching Vicky looking at them. A pulse of energy arrowed directly between Dylan's legs. Dylan reminded their body that Vicky was off-limits, especially *during a table read.* Unfortunately that just made their body more interested.

"Well, it's just so richly written." Mikki was the first to speak, hesitantly. "The word play, all the banter. Wow."

Jamie nodded supportively. "Yeah, it's like . . . modern Shakespeare. So many big ideas."

"Honestly, I thought it was weird," Deborah said. "No offense."

"There were a lot of words in it," Clyde said, as if making a powerful observation. "A lot."

Another pause so awkward, Dylan could feel *it* cringing.

"I agree: *Rosencrantz and Guildenstern Are Dead* is wordy, weird, clever, and complex." Lola spoke clearly, with warmth and enthusiasm. "Still a relevant and engaging story for a modern audience."

Everyone let out a relieved breath, swiveling to face the only professional actor among them, eager to hear what the group's natural leader and assistant director had to say.

"First, the failure to communicate," Lola began. "Rosencrantz and Guildenstern spend so much of the play confused by what's going on because they misinterpret or misunderstand things. Language and communication are supposed to lead *to* understanding. But in this play, words and language do the opposite: They *obfus-*

cate the truth, in a way that isolates the characters and makes them feel alienated. That's often played for comic effect, but there's real poignancy there."

Zoë spoke up. "Right, so when Guildenstern says that line about *Words, words. They're all we have to go on,* that's ironic, isn't it?"

"I think so," Lola said, smiling at Zoë. "Not only is it ironic—drawing attention to the play as a play, performed by actors who only have the script and its words to go on—but in this day and age, showing how words and language lead us *away* from truth, into confusion and loneliness, is more relevant than ever."

"Do you mean, like, deepfakes and fake news and everyone living in their own separate reality bubbles?" Orchid asked Lola.

"Yes," Lola said. "None of that existed when Stoppard wrote the play. But whether you see truth as an absolute or a mutable concept that means different things to different people, our inability to communicate is more relevant than ever."

Dylan vaguely remembered a similar discussion twenty years ago. Back then, they were barely brave enough to say two words. Now, in addition to feeling a degree of responsibility to help kick things off, they were looking forward to diving in.

An insight bubbled into their brain: the concept of truth as a theme of the play, that called into question the very nature of existence. They started forward, half raising a hand.

"Yes, Dylan?" Jazz prompted.

Dylan accidentally caught Vicky's eye.

When they were a teenager, Dylan's parents had taken them on safari. Their group came across a jaguar, drinking from a water hole. Its shoulder blades moved beneath taut fur as if well oiled. Its paws were the size of dinner plates. That same mix of surprise, fear, and wonder all collided in Dylan's rib cage now, undershot with something they had not felt while looking at that phenomenal jungle cat.

Attraction. Lust.

Electricity zinged across the stage. The power of it blinded them, obliterating their complex web of thoughts.

"Dylan?" Jazz repeated.

"I was just thinking about—truth?" Their fully formed insight slipped away, replaced by the neon-bright image of a sticky, glossed mouth, lips parted in invitation. "And, uh . . . art?"

Lola picked up the thread, making a salient point about the leads' constant questioning. Dylan slid back into their chair, eyes trained on the table.

So. Vicky Fang was still their sexual Achilles' heel.

So much for playing it cool.

11.

Twenty-six days till the show

REHEARSALS STARTED AT TEN A.M. SHARP THE FOLLOWING morning.

The first four days were just Lola and Annie. No full cast, no stage manager, not until Friday. Just the two leads and an empty theater. Which, in theory, should've made things easier. Given Lola and Annie space to find their rhythm, rediscover the easy chemistry that had made them such natural performers as kids.

Instead, it made everything ten times worse.

Lola hadn't done theater since her late twenties when she'd been in a production of *Funny Girl* starring Hollywood legend Babs Belvedere, who—after a few drinks—had memorably given Lola the timeless showbiz advice of "Fuck 'em before they fuck you." But despite her absence from it, the Rhodes Playhouse stage felt comfortable and familiar. Walking onto the worn wooden floorboards on Monday morning, Lola felt a surge of expectant energy, like a jet plane taking off. First days brimmed with promise. They were Christmas morning and Memorial Day weekend and the inhale of breath to blow out a birthday candle.

And then Annie entered the theater, and the jet plane Lola had been coasting in plummeted straight into turbulence.

Despite her funky knee-length skirt and sun-yellow tee printed with *I'm Here, I'm Queer, Have a Great Day!*, Annie's expression was tight as she climbed the stage steps. Not angry, exactly. Just . . . careful. A closed door with the lock turned twice.

You won. You're living the dream. Annie's tear-choked words replayed in Lola's head even as she gave Annie a smile. "Morning," Lola said, keeping her voice light. "Ready for today?"

"Yup." Annie pulled her script from her tote, flicking through its pages. Unlike at the table read, it was frilled with multicolored stickies. Her lines were highlighted neon pink. She met Lola's eye. "Look, I'm sorry. About . . . the other day. I was really rude and that wasn't fair. We're all grateful you're doing this. It means a lot."

Lola felt a swell of surprise. She hadn't expected an apology. "That's okay. It was a hard day. And I'm sure me being back is . . . disruptive."

A flash flood of emotion twitched across Annie's face. She let out a soft laugh. "Just a bit." She toed the stage with her sneaker, hesitating. Then drew a breath, bracing herself. "The thing is, Lola . . ."

The rawness in her voice made Lola lean closer. She could feel it—*something* hovering between them. "Yes?"

Annie's gaze became more intense. "The thing *is* . . ."

Lola ached with wanting to know. "What?" She instinctively raised a hand, fingers skimming Annie's arm—but Annie flinched. Looked away.

The moment broke like glass.

"The thing is we really need the play to go well," Annie said briskly, stepping back. "For the town, and Jazz, and the rest of the cast."

Lola wilted. They both knew the theater was in danger of

foreclosure—Dylan had dropped that bomb yesterday. "I know," she said carefully.

"So, I'm here for that."

Not, it seemed, for Lola herself. Before Lola could process the sharp pang of that realization, the theater doors swung open.

"Good morning, thespians!" Jazz's jubilant voice shook the chandelier. "Are we ready to work?"

They were out of time.

Lola expected Annie to shake off the tension once they got going. Surely, once they stepped into the rhythm of the play, she'd thaw out.

They started with act one, scene one—betting on a coin toss. A deceptively simple moment, Jazz explained, but one that established the world of the play—absurd, improbable, playful. In the beat, Lola as Guildenstern grew increasingly agitated over the impossibility of flipping heads over and over, while Annie as Rosencrantz remained cheerfully unbothered.

It should've been a lighthearted opening that built rhythm and a growing sense of the impossible made real. But Annie wasn't reacting to the absurdity of what was happening. She stayed closed when Lola needed her open.

Lola tried to inject some life into the scene, delivering her very first line in a tone rich with mock gravitas: "*There is an art to the building up of suspense.*"

Annie responded instantly. "*Heads.*"

Too fast. Too flat.

Lola clocked it instantly—part of her instinctively reaching for a redirect, a note, something she might have said as assistant director *if* she weren't in the scene herself. But she wasn't just observing. She was floundering alongside her co-star.

Lola threw another two coins, catching them one by one. Her voice dipped lower, like a magician leading an audience into a trick. "*The law of probability, it has been oddly asserted, is something to do with the proposition that if six monkeys . . .*" Lola let the idea intrigue her character, snapping her fingers theatrically. "*If six monkeys were—*"

Annie rushed in. "*Game?*"

Lola blinked. Wrong timing. She adjusted, trying to save it. "*Were they?*"

Annie looked panicked and Lola could tell she wasn't acting. "*Are you?*"

Jazz called for a pause from the house seats.

Annie's gaze dropped to the floor.

Jazz pulled off her glasses, pinching the bridge of her nose. "This scene is a microcosm of the whole play," she said. "Where we establish tone, and stakes, and personality. The coin toss isn't just a game. It's the universe behaving in a way it shouldn't. That should make you question everything. But Annie, my dear, it feels like you're just trying to get through it."

Annie's throat bobbed. For half a second, her lips parted like she wanted to argue. Then, instead, she bit it back.

"Try it again." Jazz waved a hand. "From the top."

Lola swallowed. She could already feel that it wasn't going to get better. Still, she flipped the coin.

Annie let it fall without looking at it. "*Heads?*" A question when it should've been a statement.

Lola's stomach twisted. She was losing her. Again.

By the end of the first day, Lola hoped things would click on the second.

The following day, Lola tried everything: emphasizing different words, throwing in new gestures, even tossing Jazz a desperate "maybe I fall to the floor here?" suggestion. Nothing landed. Annie still felt miles away.

By the third day, Wednesday, Lola's hope had curdled into dread.

At the end of the day, Jazz sat them both down for notes. "What I'm sensing," she said carefully, "is a lack of *honesty.*"

Lola straightened. She thought she'd been holding her own. But Jazz's gaze was too sharp.

"Great performances come from a willingness to open up," Jazz went on. "To let yourself be seen. Even when it's uncomfortable."

Lola's pulse stuttered. She flicked a glance at Annie, who'd gone still, her hands knotted in her lap.

Jazz looked at them both. "*Especially* when it's uncomfortable. We're still at the beginning, but I will need you both to find that honesty. Truth is the spine of a great performance," she declared. "Without it, the whole thing collapses."

For Lola, wearing a mask was second nature—onstage, in interviews, even in her own life. But now, under Jazz's knowing gaze and in this hallowed space, that mask was cracking. She had no idea if she was ready to see what was underneath.

"No pressure," added Jazz, "but the whole town's counting on you both."

THE NEXT DAY, rehearsals did not improve: if anything, they were even more tense. Late that afternoon, back at Jazz's, Lola worked on a response to her stylist, to nail down her look for the *Saturn Rising* premiere at the end of the month. She clicked robotically through endless collages of skintight dresses and sky-high heels, her mind tangled elsewhere.

Did Jazz *know*? Had she somehow intuited that Lola's life wasn't as perfect as she made out? The version Lola presented—glamorous, confident, successful—was so automatic that even she barely registered the omissions. But rather than making things easier, the lie felt like a burden.

She tossed her laptop onto the bed with a sigh. She wasn't making any progress anyway.

The attic had been converted into a guest room since the last time she was here, but its bones were the same: pitched ceilings, exposed beams, a row of arched windows along one wall that let in golden light at this time of day. A gauzy canopy framed the queen-size bed, and the mismatched furniture—antique desk, velvet arm-chair, a battered trunk—gave the space Jazz's signature maximalist charm. A dresser was cluttered with jewelry and vintage perfume bottles, and the farthest corner still had an old clothing rack crammed with costume pieces from long-forgotten shows.

Lola remembered sneaking up here with Annie as teenagers, back when it was a dusty attic full of props and abandoned set pieces. They'd rummaged through the trunks, draped themselves in gauzy gowns and pirate hats, spinning through the dim space in mock duels and grand declarations. They'd also made out up here. Pressed against the splintering wooden walls, their bodies buzzing with adrenaline, hands uncertain but eager. Even then, their love had felt like forever.

So why had Annie ended it? Had there been something Lola didn't know about? Some*one* she didn't know about?

The questions rattled through Lola's chest as she blinked herself back into the present. Her pulse ticked higher, the answer always just out of reach.

She could really use a glass of wine.

Padding downstairs to the second-floor landing, she ran into Vicky emerging from her own bedroom.

"Hey!" Vicky gave her a sisterly squeeze. "How'd it go today?"

"Great!" The lie came so easily, Lola barely registered it as the opposite of truth. Professional hazard—Hollywood thrived on a constant projection of success and good news. But Vicky wasn't a colleague. She was a friend.

And she wasn't fooled. "Really?" Vicky said, eyes sharp. "Being back onstage with your ex after twenty years of no contact—that's a breeze?"

Lola let out a wry chuckle, leaning against the hallway wall. "Okay, you caught me. It's been tough. I don't think Annie trusts me."

Before Vicky could respond, a door creaked open down the hall.

"I heard tea being spilled." Dylan poked their head out of their room, hair falling over one eye. "And baby, I'm thirsty."

Lola giggled despite herself. "No tea, really, it's just . . ." She hesitated, trying to arrange her thoughts. "Jazz thinks Annie and I are not being honest."

Vicky tilted her head. "Interesting."

A question dropped into Lola's mind, unprompted but suddenly urgent. "Can I ask you guys something? I'm trying to figure out why Annie and I broke up, and this is a weird long shot, but when we were kids, did either of you . . . hook up with her?"

Vicky's jaw nearly hit the carpet. "What? *No!* Are you crazy?"

"You were the only one kissing Annie," Dylan said. "Why are you asking about this?"

"I'm just wondering why she dumped me," Lola admitted.

Dylan leaned against their doorframe, frowning. "Really? I always assumed *you* broke up with *her*—because you were leaving to go on tour with *Mockingbird.*"

"No, I hadn't committed yet," Lola said slowly, piecing the memory together. "I wanted to stay. Be with Annie, finish high school, help out with Pearl. But then . . . she broke up with me. Said she didn't love me, never had. So I left."

"Ouch," Dylan murmured.

Lola exhaled heavily. "I thought coming back was a good idea. That we could smooth things over or I'd get some closure. Figure out what I did wrong. But the way rehearsals are going . . ." She shrugged. "Maybe I was wrong. Maybe I should've let sleeping dogs lie."

Vicky and Dylan exchanged a glance.

"Nah," Dylan said, wandering over to give Lola's arm a light punch. "Dogs are way more fun when they're awake."

Vicky nodded. "And the energy will shift once we start full cast rehearsals tomorrow. For now, maybe spend tonight *not* thinking about the play. Or Annie."

Lola hummed in agreement as the front door opened downstairs. Jazz appeared at the bottom of the staircase, weighed down by bags of groceries. "Taco night?"

Dylan and Vicky spoke as one. "Hell yeah."

Vicky poked Dylan's ribs. "Jinx, buy me a Coke."

Lola called down to Jazz. "Sounds lovely."

"Excellent," Jazz said, turning toward the kitchen. "Oh, and I invited Annie."

Vicky's mouth pressed into a smirk.

Dylan chuckled, low and amused. "Oh boy."

Lola's gut clenched. She gave a bright, breezy nod. "Great!"

What else was she supposed to say? Please don't? That would make it a thing. And Lola wasn't about to make it a thing.

Even if it already was.

12.

Twenty-three days till the show

JAZZ'S HOUSE WAS JUST AS IMPRESSIVE AS ANNIE REMEMBERED: a turreted three-story Victorian painted in sun-faded pink and purple, with a gable roof, wrap-around porch, and decorative woodwork curling around the windows. The grounds had surrendered to wild, beautiful chaos—ivy tangled around the porch railings, jasmine curled up broken trellises, rosebushes spilled over a mossy stone path. An abandoned swing hung from a sugar maple, swaying gently in the early-evening breeze. The lawn was a meadow of tall grass and wildflowers, unruly but vibrant. Even a little weathered, the house wore its eccentricity like a crown.

Annie walked up the creaking porch steps, pausing on the doormat to take a grounding breath. Find the courage to knock.

Okay, so rehearsals weren't going swimmingly. They were going drowningly. It wasn't just the rust of not having acted in decades. It was Lola. Playing opposite her meant unsheathing herself. Letting the feelings and deception Annie had buried rise to the surface. She was trying, she really was. But *honesty*? Complete, ruthless honesty? Was that possible?

Annie imagined revealing it. Confessing the truth about what really happened, and why, to Lola.

She pictured the stunned silence. Lola's tears. Then her anger. Cruel words, a cold goodbye, tires screeching as she left. Well before opening night. The show could definitely *not* go on without its only headliner. The show that was the central tenet of the plan to save a town on the brink.

No. Annie shook her head. Honesty wasn't possible. And it wasn't exactly a lie—it was a strategic omission. The kind you make when the truth could ruin a life.

She just needed to muddle through, survive the show, and let this whole summer fade into a fever dream of costumes and coin tosses and stage makeup. And right now that meant enjoying a casual taco night while pretending things weren't extremely awkward with her movie star ex.

Annie knocked on Jazz's front door. No one answered. It was unlocked, so she let herself in, stepping into the front room.

And almost laughed out loud in delight.

Three sofas, two settees, and a worn leather armchair were arranged haphazardly around two coffee tables: a seventies-style funky shape made from mint-green glass, and a refurbished wagon wheel. On the coffee tables: a stack of feminist zines, salt and pepper shakers of two mustached leather daddies, an ashtray shaped like a pair of breasts, a hunk of sparkling amethyst. One, two, three bookcases, all overflowing: *Sister Outsider* and *The Beauty Myth* sandwiched next to the collected works of Lynn Nottage and William Shakespeare. A curiosity cabinet full of china plates and more colorful tchotchkes sat next to an old-fashioned writing desk stacked with handwritten letters and a crystal ball on a faux-gold stand. In the corner, a mannequin was draped in a jeweled and feathered iridescent-green gown that Annie recognized as Titania's, from the Rhodes Players' production of *A Midsummer Night's Dream*.

Each wall was crowded with artwork: black-and-white photography of a student street protest; an energetic, expressionist painting of two women making out; a poster from the Hilma af Klint retrospective at the Guggenheim. A funky 1998 Wigstock poster was signed in red lipstick by Lady Bunny.

Even though it was cluttered, the room still felt homey. Like Gloria Steinem and RuPaul shared a lease and zero storage solutions.

"Hello!" she called.

"In here!" someone yelled back.

Annie followed the sound of chatter and jaunty jazz, passing a formal dining room dominated by a polished-wood, twelve-seat table piled with half-melted candles and tins of vintage silver cutlery. The light fixture overhead was a birdcage filled with fairy lights and paper cranes. Then a library with leopard-print carpet and even more books, more play scripts, more armchairs and floor cushions, all evidence of Jazz's expansive heart and curious brain.

The kitchen was painted a bold sunshine-yellow, the backsplash a crooked display of decorative Spanish tiles. Hanging plants tumbled from hooks on the ceiling. The counters were cluttered with spice jars, vintage canisters, and open packets of coffee and tea. A black marble statue of a jaguar still arched a paw in one corner.

Dylan was at the stove, cooking something sizzling in a cast-iron pan.

Vicky chopped a tomato with the force of someone who considered murder a form of stress relief.

Lola sat at the kitchen island, a glass of white wine in front of her. She was the first to see Annie in the doorway. They locked eyes and Annie's heart did a swan dive. For a second, the sounds of the others grew faint and it was just the two of them, staring.

Some people just settle into your bones and feel like home. Despite everything, Lola was still one of those people.

"Annie, hiiiii!" Vicky's screech popped the moment like a pin to a balloon and Annie dropped back into the busy kitchen with a thud.

"We're making tacos," Dylan announced.

"With fake meat." Vicky made a face.

"I told you we could get beef!" Dylan exclaimed.

"I told you I'm fine with seitan!" Vicky insisted.

"Are you on a diet?" Dylan asked this as if it was an impossibility.

Vicky gasped in offense. "Excuse me?"

"Ho*ney.*" Dylan slung an arm around Vicky, which she elbowed off with an eye roll. "I'm not saying you should be on a diet, I'm just trying to figure you and your fake meat out."

"Well, stop," Vicky said with a huff. "There's nothing to figure out!"

"Methinks the lady doth protest too much," drawled Dylan, eyeing Vicky with suspicion before turning back to the pan.

"Let the lady have her secrets," Jazz told Dylan, bustling by to retrieve five mismatched plates from a cabinet.

"Oooh." Dylan ground pepper into the pan. "There's a secret?"

"No!" Vicky exclaimed. "There's not!"

Lola met Annie's gaze as she held a bottle of sauvignon blanc poised over a glass. A pink rose was tucked behind one ear. The hem of her hippie-ish white maxi dress brushed the floor, like a barefoot summer bride. "Wine?"

"Please." Annie put the bottle she'd bought on the counter, hoping the others wouldn't identify it as one of the cheaper brands and feel sorry for her. Or, even more humiliating, try to help. Being broke was bad enough—being a burden was unbearable.

Annie gratefully accepted the glass Lola handed her. "Cheers, queers."

"Cheers!" Lola and Dylan chorused, raising their glasses.

Dylan looked to Jazz, then Vicky. "You want some?"

"When we eat," Jazz said, filling a wicker basket with tableware and tapered candles, like a woodland witch preparing for a midsummer supper-slash-séance. "Off to set the table!" Their hostess headed for the back door.

"None for me." Vicky massacred lettuce with vengeance. "I really shouldn't be drinking so much."

Dylan lifted their hands. "Why not?"

"None of your business!" Vicky shot back.

"They've been like this for hours," Lola whispered to Annie, her hazel eyes shimmering with amusement.

"Decades," Annie countered, hopping up on the stool next to Lola. The kitchen island was cluttered with dog-eared cookbooks, mini potted succulents, and jars of dried herbs. She addressed Dylan and Vicky. "How's your week been?"

"Awesome," Dylan enthused. "Set up a bunch of site visits for Marlowe."

"And I've gone to *two* yoga classes," Vicky bragged.

"You did *yoga*?" Dylan spun to stare at Vicky. "The woman who once told me that yoga is to exercise what karaoke is to Broadway?"

Vicky tossed a defiant handful of nuts into the salad bowl. "People change!"

Dylan raised their palms in surrender, then switched off the burner. "Help me carry the food outside, Lols?"

Lola and Dylan balanced bowls of seasoned ground seitan and sour cream and plump black beans, disappearing out the back door and leaving Vicky and Annie alone in the kitchen.

Squeezing lemon over the salad, Vicky flicked Annie a casual look. "So, how are rehearsals?"

"Yeah, good . . ." Annie lied, pretending to be absorbed with a hunt for the hot sauce.

"No lingering sexual tension?"

Vicky spoke jokingly but Annie could tell her friend was fishing. "Nope."

Vicky spun to face her, eyes glittering like the lawyer she was. "But you guys were *so close* back in the day. What happened?"

Annie froze. Of course Vicky just *asked.* "We, uh, drifted apart?"

Vicky scoffed. "No, you didn't. You spent every waking second together. You were disgustingly in love."

Annie's insides tightened, a warning without words. She gave a weak laugh. "We thought we were."

Vicky raised a disbelieving brow.

Annie exhaled, feeling trapped. "Lola and I—we just . . . didn't make sense. We couldn't."

"Why not?"

"There were . . . other factors." Even to her own ears, she sounded shady. "Something I can't explain."

"Try," Vicky said softly. "Just try."

Annie stared back. Opened her mouth, the truth right on the tip of her tongue.

A sound at the doorway.

Lola. Standing still, one hand braced on the frame. "Just grabbing the salsa," she said, voice quiet as she picked up the jar.

Annie's pulse misfired, then began to gallop. By the time she caught her breath, Lola was already gone.

IN THE SOFT purple dusk, Annie and the others sat around the backyard's weathered wooden dining table in an odd assortment of primary-colored plastic chairs. They built their tacos and ate with their hands. Jazz told stories about riding out the pandemic on her ex-wife's ranch in Northern California. Days spent under a stretched blue sky, mucking out the stables and tossing grain to fat chickens.

Terry was tough and outdoorsy, a stone butch in Blundstones who was a secret softy without much interest in the arts. Back then, to the teens, she'd been a curiosity; she was an adult they didn't have permission to ask about. Now Jazz spoke more openly about their life together, and why it ended.

They'd gotten together young, lived as "roommates" until both sets of parents passed, and, Jazz recalled with a laugh, Ellen DeGeneres told the world *Yep, I'm gay,* which changed everything. They never legally married, but in their fifties, they'd held a ceremony for friends. Terry, raised in Arizona, struggled with East Coast winters and longed to return West, to the heat and silence of the desert. She did, just after she and Jazz split, over a decade ago.

But despite the breakup, they remained close, speaking weekly until Jazz went to live with her during lockdown—and ended up staying through all of it, and then some.

"So, I don't think of it as a failed relationship," Jazz said, her elbows propped up on the table. "We were together for forty-five years, and we'll always be family. That's not a failure in my book."

Everyone agreed it wasn't.

Annie's eyes slid to Lola, who didn't meet her gaze. Love could shape you, break you, and save you all at once. Annie ached with how much she wanted all that. With how much she couldn't say.

"So, no regrets?" Dylan asked, shaking some hot sauce onto their taco.

Jazz exhaled, thoughtful. "I would've loved to be a parent. But it wasn't in the cards. Back then, we were fighting for the most basic rights. Gay marriage was a fantasy, let alone donor sperm or adoption." She shook her head, both amused and wistful. "Things have changed so much, so fast."

"A bittersweet victory," Vicky suggested softly, "to see the generation behind you enjoy the spoils. What's left of them."

"It's complicated," Jazz allowed. "For everyone. Some things are better for the younger generation, and some are much worse. But I did like hearing all the kids in our play share their identities." She chuckled. "I would've put my mother in an early grave if I'd announced I was a bisexual socialist vegan."

"Same," Dylan said with a laugh. "The kids these days are dope."

"I often think how it would've been different for us," Lola said, a little abruptly. She'd been silent until now, listening without sharing. Everyone shifted to face her. "If we'd all been out, back then," she went on, her gaze alighting on Annie. "If it wasn't a secret."

Her words gave Annie full-body chills. That sentence opened a door she'd spent twenty years trying to bolt shut. If it wasn't a secret, she and Lola might've been high school sweethearts, freed from the pressure and uncertainty of sneaking around, wondering what people would say. What her gran would think. Pearl had been kindhearted but she was still of her era. The few times Annie nudged sexuality into a conversation, Pearl became uneasy, reacting as if all gay people were stricken with a terminal disease, deserving of sympathy but only from a distance. Teenage Annie wanted to safeguard against any danger. Adult Annie wondered if that'd been the right decision.

It was another world to imagine the freedom the teens in the play didn't even realize they had. It made Annie feel old, at thirty-six. Old and a little sad.

If she'd been brave enough, back then, to tell the truth—to herself, to Lola—maybe things would've been different.

Maybe they still could be.

AFTER DINNER, JAZZ went to bed while the quartet did the dishes.

"You know what's crazy?" Vicky said, hands in the sudsy sink. "I was at least twenty-five by the time I realized that Jazz had masterminded our friendships like a gay fairy godmother."

Annie frowned as she dried a glass. "What d'you mean?"

"I mean casting all the queer girls and theys in a one-hundred-mile radius," Vicky said, like it was obvious.

Annie and Dylan stared back uncomprehendingly.

Vicky looked alarmed. "You thought it was a coincidence we were all gayer than Christmas?"

Yes, that was exactly what Annie had thought. "I was today years old when I figured that out."

A look of understanding dawned across Dylan's face. "Wait, so it wasn't just . . ."

"Fate?" Vicky barked an amazed laugh and swung to Lola. "Tell me you knew."

"I'd guessed something like that," Lola said, "but I wasn't twenty-five. More like seventeen."

"When you were on tour with *To Kill a Mockingbird*," Vicky deduced. "After you left Rhodes."

Lola's gaze stutter-stepped over Annie, before bouncing off. "Yeah. Back then." She scraped leftovers into the compost. "So, do you miss work, Vicky?"

"Like a phantom limb," Vicky replied wistfully, scrubbing a plate. "But the sabbatical's growing on me."

Dylan flipped a dish towel over one shoulder and faced Vicky. "Y'know, I mentioned this so-called sabbatical of yours to a lawyer friend and *he* said a partner in a law firm of your size taking an entire *month* off was basically unheard of."

Annie expected Vicky to tell Dylan they didn't know shit. But instead, Vicky narrowed her eyes and began to blush.

Annie stood up straighter. Was Dylan right? This wasn't a sabbatical?

"You don't have to tell us," Dylan said, taking a few steps toward Vicky. "But if you want to tell us, because secrets will drive you cuckoo for Cocoa Puffs, you know you can trust us."

Vicky blew out a breath. She grabbed the dish towel from Dylan's shoulder to wipe her hands clean. "Okay, whatever. Just don't tell anyone."

"Of course," Annie said, as Lola and Dylan nodded in agreement.

"It's not a big deal," Vicky said, "and it's my own stupid fault. Ugh, this is going to sound so dramatic."

An odd feeling of past and present commingled in the yellow-tiled kitchen. The four of them huddled around, whispering secrets. But they weren't gossiping teenagers elevating the everyday into breaking news. They were adults. Annie braced herself for the worst.

"Right before I got Jazz's message," Vicky said, "there was an . . . incident. I was in court, representing the wife of this sleazy billionaire tech guy—they're always the worst—making my closing arguments in front of the judge and jury, and all of a sudden, I had . . . a . . ." Vicky cringed, trailing off.

"You had a . . . past life experience," Lola volunteered.

"Realization you hate the law and want to be a small-town actor," Annie tried.

"Baby?" Dylan guessed.

Vicky gave them a scornful look. "Yep, that's it. I had a baby, in a courtroom, and now I'm up here, rehearsing for a play all month. Mother of the Year."

"Okay, okay." Dylan made a *go on* motion, twirling their fingers.

"All right, don't overreact," Vicky said, "but I sort of had a minor . . . well, not that minor . . . heart attack."

The trio's mouths fell open. Annie went ice-cold. "*What?*" she squeaked.

"You had a *heart attack*?" Lola's eyes were the size of boulders. "But you're only thirty-seven!"

All of the color drained from Dylan's face. They looked like they'd not just seen a ghost, but become one. "Vee," they choked out. "*Fuck.*"

"I know, I know!" Vicky spoke quickly. "I'd always gone hard, but this year was especially bad. I was sleeping four hours a night, living on Taco Bell and espresso. My stress levels were through the fricking roof. I'd felt some chest pains and stuff, but just ignored it all, kept powering through. Then all of a sudden, I pass out in court and wake up in a hospital bed in Mount Sinai. *The next day.* I'd been asleep for twenty-four hours."

"Holy shit." Dylan clutched Vicky's arm.

"Yeah, I know," Vicky said, looking chagrined. "My doctor put me on blood pressure meds and said take the summer off—no stress, *at all*, eat better, start sleeping—or I'd be back in the hospital, in a freaking body bag. So technically I *am* on sabbatical because if I wasn't, I'd be, like, dead."

For a long moment, no one said anything.

Annie felt numb. Stricken. What if Vicky hadn't woken up in that hospital bed? What if Jazz's message wasn't about a revival, but an invitation to a funeral? She wanted to go back in time and sit Vicky down. Tell her to sleep. Eat. Breathe. Tell her she was loved. That she didn't have to earn her right to rest.

Next to her, Lola shifted closer, putting a hand on Annie's shoulder. Annie clamped her own hand over it, holding it tight.

Dylan grasped Vicky's arm, their eyes dark with something between concern and longing. "Jesus, Vicky. I can't believe you came so close to . . ." They broke off, shaking their head. "I could've—we could've lost you."

"You guys, I'm fine," Vicky insisted. "I'm already feeling way better. I'm not working like that anymore so I'm getting a semi-normal amount of sleep and trying to eat healthy, obviously. I'm seeing a good cardiologist—I have an appointment with her next week, actually. Stop looking at me like I'm dead!" She shooed them all back.

Dylan let go of Vicky's arm reluctantly. "Why didn't you tell us sooner?"

"I didn't want to make things weird," Vicky said. "I was embarrassed. But telling you guys actually feels really good."

Annie could see it—the weight lifting off Vicky's shoulders the moment she stopped hiding. A little lightness in her expression that hadn't been there before.

"The scary part is over," Vicky went on. "Now I just want to do the play and have a fun month with you all. Okay?"

"Okay," Annie and Lola agreed.

"Okay," Dylan said, sounding less sure.

"Okay, Rogers?" Vicky prompted them, poking Dylan in the ribs. "Can you be normal or is that beyond your very limited skill set?"

"Fuck off," Dylan said with a wobbly grin. "No more limited than the cool part of your wardrobe."

"Oh, *burn,*" Vicky said with a relieved giggle.

Lola and Dylan returned to cleaning up. Annie went to Vicky, pulling her into a long hug. "I am *not* okay with almost losing you," she whispered. "I love you, Vee."

For a moment, Vicky went rigid. Then she softened, meeting Annie's eyes with a sheepish, grateful smile. "Thanks," she mumbled, hugging Annie back.

LATER, LOLA WALKED Annie to the front porch. "See you tomorrow?"

"Yes, ma'am." Annie nodded. "Gonna be great. Or mediocre. Or truly terrible but ruh-roh, we've already committed."

Lola chuckled, and the sound winged its way up, through the tree branches. She really did have such a pretty laugh. If only Annie could tell her that.

If only she could tell her a lot of things.

"Night." Annie instinctively opened her arms, second-guessed herself, then decided to go for it, which, regrettably, ended in patting Lola's back like a benevolent uncle. "And the award for the world's most awkward hug goes to . . . us! We did it. Huge thanks to my poor spatial awareness and the Academy of Making Things Weird."

Lola laughed again, eyes bright, and Annie was struck by how much she wanted to keep doing that. Keep making Lola Wilson laugh.

Lola's smile was soft and a little dreamy. It was late and they'd both drunk their fair share of wine, but nonetheless something about her gaze felt newly intimate. "Still the funniest girl I've ever met."

Annie flushed with the compliment. "C'mon. I'm sure you've met, like, actual comedians."

"And they don't have anything on Annie Elizabeth Lightfoot."

Something about the way Lola said her name—low, a little teasing, almost sexy—made Annie's skin prickle. "Well, you still win Best Hair."

Lola rolled her eyes.

That wasn't a good compliment. Lola was so much more than her looks. "And Best Attitude," Annie added. "Hardest Worker. Biggest Heart."

This won a nod of appreciation. "Well, thanks."

They smiled at each other, and for the first time since Lola Wilson returned, it didn't feel weird or forced. It felt warm and good. They didn't look away.

God, Annie wanted more. To touch Lola's hand. Step close enough to smell her skin, her hair.

A ping of electricity zipped between them. Annie inhaled, but it was already gone.

She edged back. "Better go before I turn into a pumpkin. Orange is not my color."

Finally breaking their gaze, she turned and trotted down the stairs.

"What other factors?"

Lola's question caught her mid-step. Annie spun around, staring up at her.

Lola *had* heard the conversation in the kitchen.

"What other factors were there?" Lola repeated with quiet insistence. "In our breakup?"

Annie's mouth opened, but no sound came. Her pulse fluttered like a moth pinned under glass. "I—uh—have to go."

She could feel Lola's eyes on her back—steady, unblinking.

Annie had no idea what Lola suspected. Only that the wall Annie had built around herself—around the past—was starting to crack. And that the urge to tear it all down was getting stronger.

13.

Twenty-two days till the show

ON FRIDAY MORNING, VICKY WAS STUNNED TO REALIZE SHE'D slept in. Seven thirty A.M. might not be considered sleeping in by most people's standards, but for someone used to a punishing five A.M. spin class—if she'd even slept at all—it might as well have been noon. No night terrors, no three A.M. insomnia. She stretched, feeling lighter. Unburdened. Had opening up to her friends about her heart attack actually . . . worked?

Yawning big, Vicky padded downstairs to the kitchen.

Sunlight flooded the ground floor windows, the hot engine of the day revving into gear. She didn't expect anyone else to be up, so it was a surprise to see Dylan, in boxer shorts and their worn Sleater-Kinney tee, chopping a pineapple in the kitchen. The sticky sweetness perfumed the air.

Vicky stopped short. "Hi."

Dylan looked up in surprise, knife paused mid-cut. Their gaze dropped to Vicky's pj's. A pale blue silk teddy. Short and sexy and clinging to her curves. Not something Vicky would typically parade around in, but she thought she was alone.

Dylan's jaw dropped. The knife slipped, and they winced. A spot of red oozed from their fingertip. "Ow."

Vicky grabbed a dish towel and pressed it to Dylan's finger. "Here."

"I'm fine." Dylan tried to pull back but only succeeded in smearing blood on Vicky's teddy. "Oh shit."

"Does it hurt?" Vicky wrangled Dylan's hand back into her grasp, applying light pressure.

"No, I mean, your . . . outfit." Dylan's eyes skittered downward. "It looks expensive."

"Thank you." Vicky tossed her hair back, feeling the delicious slide of silk over her skin. "Stay still."

Vicky had built a career around helping vulnerable people in the biggest-picture way: winning custody, upholding restraining orders, splitting assets. It felt surprisingly sweet to help in this way: the gentle act of healing a wound.

The bleeding had stopped but Dylan still couldn't look at the cut. Vicky was surprised. "Are you squeamish, Rogers?"

Dylan's gaze flicked toward the wall. "Not good with . . . blood."

"Lucky I'm here." Vicky smirked. "But next time, the nurse fantasy will cost you."

Dylan's breath hitched. For a long, charged second, they both stared at each other.

Time slowed, like honey drizzling from a spoon. The air between them shimmered, daring them both to move closer.

Instead, Dylan jerked back. "Fruit salad."

Vicky blinked, thrown. "Huh?"

"I made a fruit salad," Dylan said, voice weirdly strangled. "For you. For everyone. Help yourself."

"How wholesome," Vicky said, as Dylan backed toward the kitchen entrance. "Are we riding together?"

Dylan spun around so fast they almost tripped. "What?"

"Are we riding to rehearsals together?" Vicky repeated. "Or are you getting a lift with Jazz?"

"I'll ride with Jazz!" Dylan called back, all but running up the stairs.

Vicky made herself a bowl of fruit salad and took it outside.

Jazz's back garden was gloriously overgrown. Life burst from every pot and patch of soil. Potted herbs crowded the back steps: fragrant basil in a terra-cotta pot, thyme in a San Marzano tomato tin. Dark green mint grew in a blue teapot affixed with googly eyes.

Vicky picked her way through the cool grass to sink into one of the Adirondack chairs positioned under the oak tree, spearing a wedge of juicy pineapple.

Okay. There was definitely a vibe between her and Dylan. But how could Rogers *not* still resent her for what happened twenty years ago?

She'd had countless tough conversations in her life—as an attorney, if Vicky didn't witness someone crying or screaming in a day, was she even at work? But this would be different. Personal. Raw. The hardest conversation of her life—if she had the guts to start it.

FRIDAY WAS THE first day all the actors were in attendance, as well as their stage manager, Garrett. Garrett was in his thirties, slight but charismatic, with sharp gray eyes and a pronounced chin dimple. He wore chipped navy nail polish and a baseball cap embroidered with *Cole Escola*. "All right, baby dolls: your attention, please," he announced at exactly ten A.M. "Lola, Annie, Vicky, Dylan, Deborah, Clyde, Jamie, Mikki, Maria, Emery, Kat, Orchid, and Zoë: Circle up!"

"Bend me over and spank me silly—*I* don't even know everyone's names yet," Deborah whispered to Vicky, as they all formed a horseshoe around him.

"I'm here to keep things running smoothly," Garrett began, clipboard in front of him. "If you need anything—props, blocking notes, a passionate defense of Britney's *Glory* era—I'm your girl. I hope you're all ready to work. By the end of today, Jazz wants a first pass of act one."

"Rough is fine," Jazz assured them, shuffling through her notes, a dozen colorful bangles clanking. "Rough is good!"

Deborah coughed and raised a disturbingly knowing eyebrow.

But things weren't just rough. They were a train wreck.

Maria was too soft-spoken for King Claudius. Emery was visibly out of sync with the other Tragedians. Deborah kept making Polonius sound like a horny bartender.

But the real problem was Annie and Lola. Annie seemed allergic to eye contact while Lola was about as relaxed as a hostage. The awkwardness evident between them both at Jazz's taco night was getting worse, not better.

At the end of the day, they all bravely attempted a run-through of act one. It reminded Vicky of a rickety car careening down a bumpy road as bits fell off—a window, a door—until the driver was left holding nothing but the wheel.

Dylan as Hamlet spoke the final line of the act, an arm slung convivially over Lola's and Annie's shoulders. "*My excellent good friends! How dost thou, Guildenstern? Ah, Rosencrantz! Good lads, how do you both?*"

"Not great," murmured Emery, sitting a few rows behind Vicky in the audience.

They weren't wrong.

The unease in the theater was palpable as everyone gathered up their things, darting nervous looks at the three hundred empty seats. It seemed impossible they'd be ready to put on a show here in just twenty-two days' time.

Dylan leaned against the side of the stage, arms crossed, examining Annie and Lola with narrowed eyes, before meeting Vicky's gaze. No smirk. Just concern.

Concern Vicky shared. If Annie couldn't pull it together, if Lola bailed, if the whole thing crumbled? Jazz's big plan—maybe even the entire town—would go up in rainbow-colored smoke.

14.

BACK AT JAZZ'S LATER THAT EVENING, DYLAN'S RENTAL JEEP was parked out front, but when Vicky called out, no one answered. Her stomach rumbled. Dinner for one, just like every night back in Manhattan. She opened the fridge, eyeing the kale and frozen wild blueberries she'd bought in an attempt at healthiness. Cooking had never been a strength.

Giving up, Vicky trudged upstairs toward her bedroom. Dylan had whipped up quite a few delicious healthy meals since they'd arrived, turning a handful of limp vegetables and some rice into a mouthwatering risotto or a few eggs and some salmon into a savory fish pie. They just had a knack for it. If only they could magically appear now, bearing some form of life-giving dinner, Vicky thought wistfully as she passed the open door of Dylan's bedroom.

"Hey." Dylan sat cross-legged on the floor next to their laptop, surrounded by sushi and two cans of Diet Dr Pepper. They slipped off some headphones. "You eaten?"

Vicky almost passed out in delight.

Their bedroom was a similar layout to Vicky's—four-poster queen bed, bulky wardrobe, eclectic artwork, and knickknacks galore—but where Vicky's tiny balcony faced the front yard, Dylan's looked onto the garden. Warm golden hour sunlight poured like syrup into the room.

"Sorry about the mess." Dylan's belongings were strewn around haphazardly, just like they had been two decades ago. Clothes, half a dozen novels. The weights in the corner were new.

Vicky joined Dylan to sit cross-legged on the fuchsia-pink carpet, wiping her lip gloss off with a paper napkin in preparation. "Hello, I'm in heaven."

"Deb recommended this place," Dylan said, mixing wasabi and soy sauce together with the tip of their chopstick. "She thinks the guy who runs it is a 'stone-cold fox.'"

Dylan chuckled, offering Vicky a spicy tuna roll.

She bit into it and moaned. The salty flavor of the fish and taste of fragrant white rice was beyond comforting. "Sorry," she laughed, through a mouthful. "As always, I am starving."

They chatted about the day's rehearsal as they ate, sharing the food in easy companionship. Dylan didn't want their pickled ginger, which was perfect, as Vicky loved it. Vicky wasn't a fan of sea urchin, which was great, as Dylan was.

When they were done, Dylan let their head fall back against the end of the bed, eyes closed, a contented smile on their frustratingly perfect face. "I could eat that every day of my life."

Vicky ignored the intrusive thought of *same,* referring not to the food, but Dylan themself. "I'll Venmo you."

Dylan waved this off, arching their back to stretch, the edge of their threadbare tee riding up. "You get the next one."

Such a generous act. They had every right to freeze Vicky out, to not buy her dinner.

Vicky inhaled a deep breath. It was time. "I want to talk to you about something."

Dylan opened their eyes, focusing on Vicky. That impossible sea green. "Okay."

Vicky wiped her hands on her bare legs. "I, um, don't know

where to start," she confessed, her previously sated stomach now twisting like a bucket of eels.

Dylan cocked their head. Soft, tousled hair fell across their forehead. "The beginning?"

Vicky nodded.

The beginning.

"I'd never met anyone like you before," Vicky started slowly.

Understanding flickered in Dylan's eyes. "The *beginning* beginning."

"I remember the day we met," Vicky said. "In line for *Our Town* auditions. You probably don't remember this, but you wiped away some lip gloss. From my mouth." Even now, Vicky shivered, recalling the way Dylan had touched her. Gently but assertively and in a way no one else had. "I got full-body chills."

Dylan's light green eyes didn't leave Vicky's. They nodded, voice low. "I remember."

"Part of me knew, right then, that I was, well, gay," Vicky said. "And maybe you were, too. But another part wouldn't admit that. Couldn't admit it." She grabbed a paper napkin, balled it up, just to have something to do with her hands. "It's so crazy to meet these kids, in the play, and see how comfortable they all are with their sexuality. That just didn't exist for me. I mean, no one was out at our school, right?"

"I think maybe one guy, in the grade above you?" Dylan said. "But yeah—things were different, for sure."

"It just didn't seem like an option," Vicky said helplessly. "To admit the truth. To myself. Let alone anyone else."

"And what truth was that?"

Vicky tossed the balled-up napkin at Dylan. It bounced off their knee. She was blushing. "That I had a giant crush on you."

Dylan's face split into a vindicated grin. "Twenty years! It only took you twenty years to admit it. Well done, Fang."

Vicky's cheeks were burning. She felt seventeen years old all over again—confused and certain, excited and terrified. "You just . . . got me. And you were the only person to ever tell me *no,* to push back. Which was"—Vicky huffed an embarrassed chuckle—"a turn-on, I guess."

Dylan's lips twitched even as their gaze stayed unblinking.

Vicky went on. "I just felt so switched on around you. I didn't care what most people thought of me but I cared what you thought. I liked fighting with you, I liked performing with you. I liked talking with you." Her heartbeat was loud enough to be illegal in a library. "I just liked you. And I knew you liked me."

"Yeah, didn't have much of a poker face back then," Dylan said, adding under their breath, "still don't."

Vicky had the urge to swerve off the road they were going down. She forced herself to stay the course. "And then when you asked me to be your date for the closing-night party." An invitation made on a steamy August night, sitting on the edge of Dylan's pool, their feet dangling in the neon-blue water. "And basically," Vicky went on, "we'd both . . . come out."

"That was the plan." Dylan's knee bounced. "I couldn't sleep. Or eat. It was all I could think about."

"I know. Me too. And I wanted to. I remember Annie and Lola were so excited for us. And you got a suit made." Remorse exploded in Vicky's cheeks in hot starbursts.

"My suit." Dylan let out a pained half laugh, half whimper. "I thought my mom was going to kick me out. I think that was the first time she knew I wasn't going to be the girl she always wanted. But, fuck. I felt good in that suit. The first time I felt like *me.* And then . . ."

"And then I ruined everything." Her pulse ricocheted around her rib cage, like it was trying to find an exit. Every ounce of self-protection screamed at her to shut up, stop talking. But she couldn't. Vicky dropped her head into her hands. "I can't believe I showed up with Chimp freaking Chadwick. I'm a monster."

She explained it'd been a last-minute decision. She'd confessed her and Dylan's plan to her sisters, expecting surprise, but ultimately, support. Her middle sister, the peacemaker, was sympathetic and encouraging. But her younger sister was scared and annoyed that Vicky had been keeping such a big secret from them all. She told Vicky that her life would be over before it began, that it would break their mother, anger their father.

Panicked, Vicky had pivoted. Tried to play it all off as theater kid antics. And to prove exactly how straight she was . . .

"You picked up the phone and gave old Chimp a ringle dingle," Dylan concluded with a grimace. "Then made out with him all night. In front of me."

That was the worst part. It would've been one thing to show up with a guy. But Vicky's sisters were at the party, and everyone was speculating as to why Annie and Lola both left in tears. A rumor spread about a lovers' quarrel. Seeing Annie and Lola—an OTP, the closest couple Vicky had ever known—implode that night made Vicky doubt anything with Dylan would ever work, outside the insular world of the theater. She convinced herself that their romance was all in her head, and Chip was who she should be with, proving it with an egregious display of PDA.

"It was so dumb." Vicky was on the edge of tears. "Cruel and cowardly and dumb."

"I wish you could've given me a heads-up. I bought you flowers, dude," Dylan said with a sad laugh. "Flowers!"

Vicky's throat cinched shut. "Paper daisies." Red ones.

"Yeah." Dylan let out a sober sigh. "You smashed my gay little heart into a million pieces that night."

"I did. I did do that." Vicky leaned forward to grab both of Dylan's hands. "Dylan. I am so, *so* sorry for bringing Chip as my date instead of you. It is my greatest regret. My biggest mistake. I *really* liked you. I *really* hurt you. What I did was *not* okay." A hot tear spilled down her cheek, blurring the image of an alarmed

Dylan sitting across from her. “You don’t have to forgive me but just know that that night has haunted me forever and”—sobs rose in her throat, choking her words—“I’ll never—forgive myself—for hurting you.” All at once, she was crying.

“Vicky, hey.” Dylan’s arms were around her, stroking her back. “Babe, it’s okay.”

“No, it’s not,” Vicky sobbed. “We were supposed to *come out*. Instead I kept you *in the closet.*” She cried harder. “I’m *such* a bitch.”

“Vicky.” Dylan sounded stunned. “Seriously, it’s cool.”

Vicky kept sobbing, letting out twenty years of bottled-up shame and guilt and regret. And Dylan just kept stroking her back and murmuring soft, soothing things. Eventually, Vicky felt the peak of her emotion pass, like a storm moving on, thunder and lightning softening into rain. She grabbed for some stray napkins, blowing her nose. “I’m such a mess.”

Dylan squeezed her shoulder. “Everyone’s messy, every now and then.” They peered at her, expression still baffled. “Wow, you’ve really been carrying that around, haven’t you?”

Vicky nodded, wiping her face. “Haven’t you?”

“Honestly?” Dylan shook their head. “No.”

Vicky blinked in confusion. “But—I broke your heart.”

“You did,” Dylan said, nodding. “At the time it was definitely the worst thing that’d ever happened to me, and that includes every dress my mother forced me into. But then, time passed. I got perspective. Yes,” Dylan admitted, “you hurt me, and humiliated me, and delayed my coming out. But we were so young. And your parents were in the middle of a crazy divorce, like, *in court.* And ultimately it was my responsibility to come out, not anyone else’s. I forgave you. Years ago, really.”

Vicky couldn’t believe what she was hearing. She stared at Dylan in disbelief. “Wow. I’m sort of shocked. I thought you still resented me.”

“What?” Dylan laughed in confusion. “Vee. I don’t resent you.

Yes, you're still very annoying," they allowed, "and occasionally bratty and you're the only person I know who wears pleated slacks unironically, but I don't resent you. We're buds."

"Buds?" Vicky repeated.

Dylan's gaze flicked to Vicky's mouth before they cleared their throat. "Yeah. Buds."

Vicky felt a tingle in her low belly. She was suddenly aware of how close they were to each other. Their knees were touching. "Buds," she said again, softer. "Okay. Good."

Dylan's gaze found its way back to Vicky's. For a long moment, they just looked at each other.

Joy seeped into Vicky's veins. Dylan didn't resent her. Dylan had even forgiven her. What a gift that was. The best gift of Vicky's life. Vicky wanted to hug them.

Okay, truthfully, she wanted to kiss them. She wanted to pick up where they left off and do all the things they hadn't done when they were teenage virgins. She wanted to show Dylan *exactly* how sorry she was.

Vicky tested the waters. "Guess I should go . . . ?"

"Yeah, I should get back to work." Dylan gestured at their laptop. The tips of their ears were pink.

Vicky reapplied her lip gloss using the ever-present tube in her pocket, buying herself a few seconds and, maybe, making herself a little cuter. (Was it her imagination or was Dylan always staring at her mouth?)

"Thanks for dinner," Vicky said, getting to her feet. "And, y'know, saving my soul from eternal damnation."

Dylan chuckled awkwardly, following Vicky to the door. "Not sure if I did that, but no worries."

They both lingered in the doorway.

Dylan's gaze was glued to Vicky's freshly glossed mouth. Still, they didn't make a move.

"Night." Vicky backed reluctantly into the hall.

"Night," Dylan echoed, giving the door a little push until it closed.

Vicky stood in the middle of the hallway, every inch of her skin flushed.

Was that—a moment? A moment they somehow both missed?

She knew she should go back to her own room, but a pulsating one-track need kept her rooted to the spot.

The door whipped back open. Dylan took a decisive step into the hallway, registered Vicky still standing there, and pulled up short. "Oh."

For a second that felt as long as a lifetime, the pair stood there, the air between them sparkling with enough electricity to power the entire town.

The corner of Dylan's mouth kicked up. Their voice was a low rasp. "I was coming to find you."

Vicky was jittery with a fever pitch of need to touch the person in front of her. "I wanted you to," she whispered.

That was it. The final vestiges of self-protection and denial burned up like tissue paper in a roaring blaze.

Dylan surged forward, until Vicky could grab two fistfuls of Dylan's tee. She tugged them to her with a gasp. Their lips met, mouths hot, and Vicky's body was no longer a body: It was molten lava, it was liquid heat. This kiss was fresh water after being lost in the desert. Medicine on a deathbed. It was a kiss twenty years in the making, and it was worth every fucking second.

Dylan's mouth was salty from the sushi and sweet from the soda, and even as Vicky tasted it, she craved more. Her hands slid to Dylan's arms, feeling the warm swell of their biceps, bulging as Dylan's hand moved, fisting the back of Vicky's head, holding her in place. God, these *arms*. Teenage Dylan did not have these arms. A desperate moan escaped Vicky's mouth, disappearing into Dylan's.

Dylan pulled back first. Their mouth was a sexy mess of sticky red gloss. Their pupils were the size of the moon. "Fuck, Vee," they said with a choke, "are you trying to kill me?"

"If I was, you'd already be dead." Vicky tried to swallow, feeling lightheaded. "I really thought you hated me."

"Oh, I do," Dylan panted, flustered, "in an I-also-want-to-fillet-you-like-a-fish-and-serve-you-for-Sunday-supper sorta way."

Vicky was momentarily thrown. "What the hell does that mean?"

"I have no idea." Dylan looked up and down the empty hallway. Their voice was low and a little uncertain. "This is a good idea, right?"

Vicky hooked her fingers into Dylan's belt loop, pulling them step-by-step back into the bedroom. "Probably not. But guess what?"

Dylan shut the door after them. The air was an unlit Molotov cocktail. One match and everything would explode. "What?"

Vicky tipped her mouth up, lips parted. "We're gonna do it anyway."

Dylan let out a low growl, tousled hair falling over one eye, and then their mouth was back onto Vicky's, kissing her deeply. Vicky felt like she was being split open—her heart, her lungs, the very center of her being. She moaned, impatient for more even as Dylan gave it to her. Dylan's lips were driving and insistent, pushing Vicky's mouth wider, their tongue licking hungrily into the kiss, again and again and again.

"God," Vicky panted, in between kisses, "I can't believe how hot you are."

Dylan's hands dropped to Vicky's waist, squeezing the curve of her hip. "I can't believe how the same you are."

Vicky shoved them, laughing, until Dylan's mouth reclaimed hers, hot and possessive.

Without breaking the kiss, Dylan spun them both around one hundred and eighty degrees and backed her across the carpet, stumbling over a stray pair of sneakers until she landed against the wall with a thud that surprised them both. Vicky caught Dylan's eye and exhaled half a laugh, half a groan. Her hands were in Dylan's hair, so full of snapping desire she wanted to rip it out at the roots, pulling too hard.

"Ow," Dylan broke off, laughing.

"Sorry." Vicky dropped her hands, panting.

"Bad girl." Their bodies still agonizingly flush, Dylan held Vicky's gaze. Without breaking eye contact, they circled both of Vicky's wrists with one strong hand.

Thrilled, Vicky let them.

Dylan lifted Vicky's hands up, pinning them to the wall above her head. The feeling of Dylan holding her in place, in charge and able to do whatever the fuck they wanted with their free hand, was almost too much. Vicky's underwear was soaked. She'd never been more turned on.

Dylan ducked their head close, lips meeting in another scorching kiss. Vicky shut her eyes to savor the wild heat, the addictive taste of Dylan's confident mouth. Dylan's lips slid down Vicky's jaw, to the sensitive curve of her neck, biting and sucking her skin. Vicky groaned, tipping her head farther to the side to give Dylan more access.

Then Dylan pulled back. One hand still held Vicky's wrists, while the other dropped slowly down her chin, tracing an agonizingly slow line over the soft dip of her throat. Down her décolletage. Into the dip of her cleavage. Vicky needed Dylan to touch her nipples, squeeze her boobs. But instead, Dylan's finger kept moving south, between Vicky's breasts, over her tank top, toward the soft mound of her stomach. Vicky moaned, every inch of her skin on fire. If Dylan made it all the way between her thighs, she'd come right here against the bedroom wall. "Touch me," Vicky pleaded. "*Please.*"

Dylan's fingertip reached the top of Vicky's shorts. *Take them off,* Vicky wanted to scream. *Burn my clothes: I won't need them anymore!* Instead, Dylan paused, finger idling at the button. Their fingers tightened around Vicky's wrist.

Then, a noise. Downstairs. The front door opening. The sound of chatter and laughter spilled in. "We're home!" Jazz sang.

"Vicky?" Lola's voice floated up. "Dyls?"

Vicky whipped to find Dylan's gaze, feeling like she'd just been shaken awake. Every nerve ending was on fire. "That . . . wasn't in the script."

Dylan let go of Vicky, the sexy spell of the kiss fading like the sunlight leaving the bedroom. "I mean, we could . . ." Dylan tipped their head at the closed bedroom door.

"Stay in here?" Vicky guessed. "Hide?"

Energetic disco-funk blasted from the kitchen. "Got to Be Real" by Cheryl Lynn, one of Jazz's faves. "*What you find-ah. What you feel, now . . .*"

"Yeah." Dylan crooked an eyebrow. "Live in the now."

But Vicky shook her head. "No more hiding."

She leaned forward to touch her lips to Dylan's in a warm, slow kiss that made her whole body hum. Then, reluctantly, she slipped toward the door, peeking over her shoulder. "Coming?"

Dylan looked tortured. "Hard yes. I'll meet you downstairs."

Vicky giggled, her bloodstream still as fizzy as the Diet Dr Pepper they'd had with dinner. With a nudge of her hip, the bedroom door swung shut.

Alone in the hall, Vicky had to steady herself against the wall. She touched her lips, her hair.

Had that really just happened? And, equally important, what happened now?

15.

Twenty days till the show

"LINE!" ANNIE'S VOICE SHOT UPWARD, PINGING OFF THE CHANDELIER overhead.

Lola suppressed a groan as a ripple of irritation flickered through the cast, watching from the house seats.

Jazz strode onstage, muumuu flapping. "Annie, you knew this yesterday."

"Sorry!" Annie flipped frantically through her script. "What's the—what's the line?"

"*I remember when there were no questions,*" Lola recited softly.

Annie's eyes snapped to her.

"That's the line." Lola hesitated, then added, "Maybe try it a little wistful."

"Wistful?"

Lola nodded. "Nostalgic. Like . . . when we were younger, and there weren't as many questions." When adulthood was a distant irrelevance and they'd never, ever get old.

Annie stared back with an expression as layered as the line

itself—understanding mixed with something more vulnerable. "Okay. Thank you."

Lola warmed with pleasure. Jazz had told her she was free to jump in with performance notes—and it felt surprisingly good, this balancing act of playing a role and shaping one. As challenging as this whole process was, as stilted as things were with Annie, directing gave Lola a sense of purpose.

Jazz clapped her hands. "Okay, five-minute break. Remember what I keep saying, kids. Use your lived experience. Keep it *real.*"

The chatter in the theater rose, but Annie was still looking at Lola. She licked her lips, like she was steeling herself. "Hey . . . do you have plans tonight?"

Tonight, Vicky was staying at her condo in Midtown for a doctor's appointment first thing tomorrow. Dylan had plans to whip up a test batch of a new flavor for Marlowe in Jazz's kitchen. Lola shrugged, curious. "Not really."

Annie's gaze flicked down, then, cautiously, back up. "Come over for dinner." She lowered her voice, so only Lola could hear. "There's something we really need to talk about."

Annie asking to talk could mean only one thing: The tension between them was about to be named, dissected, discussed. It was both a relief and unbearably nerve-racking. For the rest of rehearsal, Lola could barely focus. Her mind kept spiraling ahead to dinner—imagining every version of how it might go, from awkward to intimate to catastrophic. She wanted clarity. She also wasn't sure she could handle it.

Back at Jazz's, Lola tried on five different outfits before deciding on tan trousers, a simple black tank, sneakers. Something she felt good in, without feeling overdressed or overly feminine. It was unnerving to think she didn't fully know her own style. That, at thirty-six and possessing so many trappings of external success, she was still figuring out who Lola Wilson actually was.

• • •

RAIN BEGAN TO drizzle as Lola parked her rental car out front of the Groom Room. Even though it was closed and empty, the cozy, colorful interior felt instantly familiar as an extension of Annie herself.

On a humid Sunday evening, Henry Street was quiet, with just a few people under umbrellas walking their dogs. Lola flipped down the sun visor mirror to diligently dab on some lipstick before reconsidering. She didn't really like wearing it; it'd only end up all over the wineglass. She'd skip lipstick tonight. Annie knew what her face looked like.

She had ten minutes to kill. She tapped over to Instagram on her phone.

The first post on her feed was from Clay Russo, the actor playing Robin Hood in the reboot Lola hadn't gotten, whom Lola had followed after meeting him in the last audition. In the candid snap, handsome Clay grinned next to a curvy redhead in a quasi-medieval dress. Sabina Waters, the actor playing Maid Marian.

The photo inspired no emotion—no jealousy that Sabina had won the role over her, no regret that Lola was here and not there.

Odd.

The next few photos were of Clay enjoying a sunny day by the Thames, a raised pint at an outdoor pub, a decadent high tea at the Ritz. Lola smiled, feeling faintly nostalgic for the magic of London in full bloom.

The last picture was of the film's director, Kris Mack, a veteran action filmmaker who she'd also met in that final audition. Kris wasn't posing; he was working, examining a monitor, brows furrowed in concentration. A few crew members hovered in the background, ready to obey his next command.

Something cracked open inside Lola: a bruised, breathless thing made of jealousy, wonder, and a longing to be someone else. A marrow-deep hunger to redraw the map of her own life.

Acting on sheer instinct, Lola called her agent.

Kevin picked up. "Wilson, hey. How's the play?" A hint of condescension, which she ignored.

"Fine." Lola licked her lips. She hadn't planned this. "Look, I've been thinking." Her heartbeat picked up, anxious. "What if—I mean, is there any world where I can . . . It's just, I've been thinking about my career, and . . ."

"You've been thinking about your career and . . . ?" Kevin prompted.

Lola forced herself to speak. "Is there any way I can . . . direct?"

"Direct?" Kevin asked. "Direct what?"

"Films. Stories. Actually, I'd love to direct theater," Lola admitted.

There was a supremely awkward pause. "I'm sorry—you're asking me, your film agent, if there's any way you can go back to theater. As a director? Dude, are you on shrooms?"

"Sadly not," Lola said wryly. "It's just . . . I'm not sure if I'm on the right path, Kev. I was just on Instagram and—" She cut herself off. The details didn't matter. "Should I—could I—pivot to directing?"

"*Instagram.*" Kevin said this as if now everything made sense. "The source of everyone's existential dread. Look, Wilson, I get it. You want to move to Hawaii."

Lola felt very unsure about who she was and what she wanted but relocating to Honolulu was not on the list. "I—what?"

"You're *on vacation,*" Kevin emphasized. "Doing some no-stakes community theater, with your old pal Chazz—"

"Jazz."

"—and you're like, *This is fun. This is easy. Maybe I could live here forever.* But you don't move to Hawaii, Wilson. You drink a few mai tais, you get a tan, and then you come back to real life."

Was her agent right? Was all this just vacation goggles?

Or was she finally seeing things clearly?

"This isn't just a vacation. It's the first time I've felt like an artist in years." Lola made her voice firm. "What does a move into directing look like?"

Kevin hissed out a breath. "Well, Kris made his first short at age seven, went to the best film school in the country, then worked every job in the camera department for two decades. Oh, and he has family money. So, unless you want to pivot to being a camera assistant making twenty bucks an hour, we continue to build you as an actress—which is what you're *known for* and *good at*—until you're landing things like *Hood,* then try to parlay that into something. But I'm telling you now, that path won't be easy or quick."

Kevin continued, listing obstacles and warnings. Lola peppered in thoughtful *mmm* noises, her mind wandering.

It was one thing to know your life had to change—that walls needed to be torn down and rebuilt from scratch. It was another to figure out exactly how to do that. Exactly what to build.

Still, the impulse for rebirth lingered. She remembered standing onstage, gazing out into the dark, knowing the audience was with her, completely still, completely hers. Not because of how she looked or who she was. Because the story was good, and it was hers to tell.

No two shows were ever the same. That's what made them feel so alive. Theater had never been glamorous. But it had always felt like home.

Thunder rumbled overhead. The call dropped out. Some things never changed, like Rhodes's lack of cell service at the suggestion of a storm. Lola put her phone away, gazing out onto rainy Henry Street.

Still no script. Still no blocking. But for the first time in a long time, Lola felt the stir of a curtain ready to rise.

ANNIE'S HOME WAS as colorful and charming as the woman who lived in it. Unlike Lola's blank, white-washed Tribeca loft, Annie's cozy apartment felt like a home. The two-bedroom was spread out over the top floor of the building, with large windows in every room. A cute, open-plan kitchen looked over a living room with a plush deep blue L-shaped sofa and a pale pink love seat. The hardwood floors were softened by a patchwork rug. A candle flickered on the coffee table. Most of the furniture looked thrifted, and Lola got the sense that every object had a story, down to the resin fruit-slice coasters and hand-knitted rug. And everywhere, on shelves and sills and hanging from the ceiling: plants. Healthy and green. Succulents, ferns, a fiddle-leaf fig. A vine trailed gracefully along the windowsill, beyond which rain pattered against the glass. It reminded Lola of Jazz's house, but neater, simpler, less chaotic, more contained. Lola wanted to curl up on the sofa and never leave.

A tiny black-and-tan Yorkie trotted in, nose twitching.

"Is this the famous Socks?" Lola asked, kneeling down to scratch his chin.

Annie, who was in the kitchen opening the wine Lola brought, called back, "Yup. He's pretty cute, right?"

"As adorable as your place." Lola gave Socks one more pat before he trotted off to a dog bed in the corner.

"Thanks." Annie came over, handing Lola a glass of white wine. She was wearing a simple slip dress the color of the gray-lavender dusk outside. "I really like it, but one day I'd love to have an actual house. Big backyard, rambling garden, guest bedrooms galore. But home ownership seems as likely as finding vintage jeans that fit."

Lola chuckled while mentally tucking away Annie's ideal.

A series of framed photographs lined a shelf. Lola looked closer. Annie with three cool-looking friends Lola didn't recognize, grinning in a sun-spangled pool. Annie sitting on a sofa with her grandmother, in Pearl's later years. And a sun-faded one of a smiling man and woman in their thirties, holding a chubby toddler in pigtails. Lola picked up the frame. "Are these your parents?"

"Yeah." Her smile was forlorn. "Wish I could remember them a bit better."

It still surprised Lola that kind, optimistic Annie had a childhood defined by such loss. That kind of trauma could have made her closed and distrustful. Instead, Annie seemed to love even more deeply—as if she'd decided that opening her heart was the only way to keep it whole.

"You have your mom's nose," Lola realized, glancing from the photo back to Annie.

They were standing close. The warmth from Annie's body rolled over Lola's skin, and it felt like sinking into a deliciously warm bath.

She caught herself with a start. She was here for an important conversation, not to fantasize about bubble baths. Lola put the photo back, attempting a neutral tone. "So. What did you want to talk about?"

Annie's gaze skittered to the rug, her fingers tightening around her glass. For a second, it seemed like she might back out: change the topic, announce that dinner was ready. But then Annie exhaled slowly and met Lola's gaze. "Us," she said. "And what really happened."

Lola's heart kicked against her ribs. She wasn't sure what Annie meant but her expression was alarmingly intense. "What really happened when?"

"When we were kids," Annie said. "I know it's been ages, but I don't think I can do the play—or, like, sleep at night—until you know the truth."

"Are you talking about . . . our breakup?" Lola steeled herself. It was still so hard to reconcile that her first love hadn't loved her back.

Things had started to become tense between her and Annie during the final week of the original show, especially anytime Lola brought up the future or anything to do with Pearl's health. Annie seemed anxious during their final show and moody on the short walk to the closing night after-party, held in Trixie Hartzog's backyard; their fellow cast member lived a few minutes from the theater.

Lola recalled little white lights strung up in the backyard, a bluegrass band playing by folding tables piled with food and drink. A self-serve bar. No one was monitoring the teens. They'd both gotten stupid drunk after stealing a bottle of something clear that tasted like gasoline.

Annie had pulled Lola into an unfamiliar bedroom, her cheeks already tearstained. A messy, jagged fight spewed between them, peaking when Annie finally cried the words that Lola would never forget. *I don't love you! I never have!*

Even now, decades later, the words were an axe swinging right into Lola's heart. "It was . . . how you felt," she said. "I wasn't enough—"

"But it *wasn't* how I felt!" Annie's grip tightened around her wineglass.

A low thrum of anxiety curled through Lola's chest. "What do you mean?"

Annie stared up at Lola. Something enormous shifted behind her eyes. She let out a long breath, sounding steady and sure. "Let's sit."

Outside, the rain got a little heavier, drumming against the windows. They sat a few feet apart on the blue sofa. Lola couldn't move, each muscle tight with anticipatory tension.

Annie began, her voice thin. "The summer we did the play, Gran's health was starting to decline. I knew I had a long road ahead of me and I'd be putting off anything after high school to look after her."

Lola frowned. "I remember." More specifically, she remembered Annie refusing every offer of help.

Annie squeezed her eyes shut for half a second, then forced herself to look at Lola. "Everyone knew you could make it. You were talented and beautiful, but you were tough, too. When that

Broadway producer offered you *Mockingbird,* it just . . . felt inevitable. *Of course* you were going to leave. *Of course* you were going to be someone."

Lola's heart kicked hard, like it was trying to break through bone. Where the hell was Annie going with all this?

Annie's voice took on a desperate edge. "But you'd started talking about staying in Rhodes. To help me. You were going to turn down the audition. For me."

"Well, I loved you," Lola said bluntly, almost offended. "Your family was my family."

"I couldn't let you do it." Annie's eyes were wide. "I had to get you to leave. It was what was best for you." Her voice became a hoarse whisper. "That's why I told you I didn't love you."

Lola's breath snagged in her throat. Her chest started to burn, her mind scrambling to catch up.

Annie sounded tortured. "It was all a giant lie. I *did* love you, Lola. So much. Too much to make you stay with me and deal with—everything."

The heat in Lola's chest started to infect her limbs. "So . . . you lied to me?" Her voice was knife-sharp. "*You?*" Annie—the most honest person Lola had ever known. The person who never hid anything.

"I knew things with Gran would get tough," Annie went on, tears filling her eyes. "And I couldn't be the one keeping you small, in this town, with me. *That's what I did to Gran.*"

Lola let out a hard, confused breath. "What?"

"Lola, my parents died when Gran was only fifty-five." Annie's words were a plea. "I found out that summer that she had all these plans for her second act. She wanted to take art classes, and date, and travel. Maybe even do community theater! But instead, she was back to playdates and potty training. She was trapped."

"That wasn't your fault," Lola said.

"It still kept her here," Annie pushed back. "So I wasn't going to keep you here, too. And you would've left, eventually. Lola Wilson wasn't going to stay in Rhodes for the rest of her life. I think I figured, by ending it, I had some control over the inevitable."

Annie's words were choked, each one sticking in her throat. "I lied about not loving you. I did love you, Lola. I loved you so much, I couldn't make you throw away your future to stay in your tiny hometown, looking after my *dying grandmother* with me."

Lola was having trouble breathing. The whole world seemed to contract around her. Blood roared in her ears. Every instinct told her to run. She pushed up off the couch, backing away over the rug. "But—my whole life—all my—trust issues." The past twenty years rewound jerkily in her mind's eye. The way she'd pushed people away. Second-guessed their declarations. Cut things off before they got too serious.

For nothing. For a lie.

"I didn't know that'd happen," Annie whispered miserably. "I thought you'd forget about me."

"Forget about you?" Lola spun on her, voice rising to almost a shout. "I loved you. I loved you and *you broke my heart.*"

Annie's eyes widened, scared.

Lola's breath was shallow. "I can't—I can't believe this."

Annie got up, reaching for her, but Lola slapped it away. "Don't touch me."

"I'm sorry." Annie began to cry. "Lola, I'm so sorry. I didn't know . . . I didn't know how much it'd hurt you."

"Then you don't know me at all!" Emotion reared in Lola's chest. She was about to cry or have a panic attack or break something. Maybe all three. "I need a minute."

She moved blindly down the hallway, yanking open two closet doors before finding the bathroom and locking herself in. Finally alone, she sank to the tiles, put her head between her legs, and started to cry.

16.

Annie cried until her insides felt scooped out, hollowed out by an uncaring hand. Tears of guilt, of shame, of regret. And a sadness with jaws the size of a mountain that swallowed her whole.

She'd made a choice and it'd been the wrong one. She wanted to be a good person, but she was just a person.

Eventually, her tears subsided. Annie washed her face in the kitchen sink before returning to the couch to wait for Lola.

Finally, the bathroom door creaked back open. Annie scrambled to her feet, fresh adrenaline in her veins.

Would Lola leave? Never speak to her again? Scream at her for an hour?

On seeing Annie, Lola pulled up short in the hallway. For a long beat, they regarded each other. Annie had the strange sense she was meeting Lola for the very first time.

"Can I have"—Lola inhaled a heart-stopping breath—"some water?"

Annie almost broke a sweat fetching it. Lola downed it in three quick pulls, handing back an empty glass.

The pause between them lengthened.

"So . . ." Annie said. "Where do we go from here?"

"Part of me wants to run away," she said slowly. "But I think I should probably stay."

"Why?" Annie couldn't help asking.

Lola's hazel eyes looked darker than usual: the color of syrup held to the light. "I guess . . . when I'm with you, I feel like myself. And I don't want to lose that."

Relief cascaded through Annie. She could finally breathe.

They returned to Annie's couch. In the corner, Socks snored softly. Outside, the rain was easing. Inside, things were shifting.

Lola sipped from the fresh pour of wine in her glass. "So I'm trying to be optimistic about this new film I'm in, but I'm pretty sure it's garbage."

Annie blinked, the confession catching her totally off guard. "Sorry, what?"

Lola sighed, looking down at her glass. "Forget it."

"No," Annie said, nudging Lola with her foot. "Say it."

A beat. Then Lola let the air leave her lungs. "Basically, my big break is a feminist nightmare in zero gravity. I'm a blue-skinned bimbo with a complex backstory no one asked for. Honestly? I'm not that proud of anything I've been in recently."

Annie felt surprised. Sure, Lola's films weren't winning Oscars. But she was usually good in them. And they were actual *movies.* "Really?"

"Yeah." Lola looked right at Annie, her expression rueful. "I'm not living the dream, Annie. That was also a lie."

Annie shook her head, unable to accept this. "But you're a *movie star.* You're living the life you always dreamed of."

"I'm someone who's paid less than the men around me, and while they're stuffing their faces at craft services, I'm in six-inch heels and forced to indulge brainless interviews and sexist directors. People who've never met me trash-talk me online. My schedule makes it impossible to date or have a work-life balance. So yeah, sure, I'm a movie star."

It hit like a small, electric shock: the truth behind Lola's words. Annie had the sense of puzzle pieces rearranging themselves, making a new, previously undetected pattern. "Oh."

"You're right that this is what I worked for," Lola said. "But I'm scared I'm living a life that suits everyone except me. I've worked so hard, for so long, but I never really pause to check in with myself."

Annie shifted closer. "Check in with yourself how?"

"Like asking, does this make me happy?" Lola took another gulp of wine. "It's easy to delude yourself when everyone's saying you're doing a great job. When you're too overworked to think about your own feelings. When you put yourself last on the list of people to keep happy." She exhaled sharply. "I'm in a position a million actors would kill for. It doesn't feel like I have permission to say, maybe I don't want it."

Annie's heart throbbed with empathy. "That sounds so hard."

Lola rubbed at her eyes. "Everyone said moving to film was the right call. And it was, professionally. But deep down, I knew it wasn't what I wanted." She let out a strained laugh. "I don't want to blow up my life, but I don't know how much longer I can keep pretending that everything's great."

Annie kept her eye contact steady, while inwardly reeling. "Oh, Lollie."

Lola's old nickname—the one only Annie used—fell out of her mouth. Lola softened, a smile flickering over her lips.

Annie sipped a nervous breath. "Can you handle it if I reveal we have a trio of lies on our hands?" She braced herself. "My salon isn't doing well. It's not dawn to dusk dogs dogs dogs. It's barely a dog a day. I'm not a hometown hero and I'm not too blessed to stress."

For the first time since she came out of the bathroom, Lola looked amused. "I figured."

"What? Who told you?"

"You're still a terrible liar, Annie," Lola teased, adding quickly, "which is a good thing."

Annie blushed. "Incorrect. I lied to you. I told a twenty-year lie."

"You did." Lola's smile faded into something sadder. "I sort of see why you did. But I wish that you hadn't."

"I know. Me too." Annie reached over to squeeze Lola's arm. "I'm so sorry I lied."

"I'm sorry I wasn't honest, too," Lola said. "Moving forward, let's always tell each other the truth, okay?"

"Definitely," Annie promised, meaning it. "One thousand percent."

They stayed holding eye contact for another few seconds. Then a few more, and it felt like realizing you couldn't touch the bottom at the deep end of a pool. Disorientating, a little scary, but also exhilarating.

Lola broke contact first, returning to the metaphorical shallow end. "So . . . you going to feed me or what?"

That she was still staying for dinner felt like a huge win. Annie lit up, even as she remembered she'd been too nervous about this conversation to plan anything. "Yes! On the menu . . . Spaghetti à la Spontaneity. The trick is there is no trick, or plan, or method of any kind. Prepare to be amazed."

Lola smiled. "You're a goof."

"Fun fact: Only natural-born goofs use the word *goof*." Annie got to her feet, extending a hand. "I heard that on NPR."

Lola laughed.

The night relaxed into improvising some pasta, taking turns playing DJ, opening another bottle of wine. Annie remembered how easy spending time with Lola was, like they were attuned to the same frequency. They never ran out of things to say. They found the same things funny. And now, nothing was off-limits. The air between them felt pliable and honest, as washed clean as the streets outside.

And then, it was midnight. Dishes were done, wine bottles were in the recycling. Lola lingered by the front door. "Of all the dinner dates I've spent crying in the bathroom, this was by far my favorite."

Annie laughed. "You are very generous, Lola Wilson."

"And you're a good host, Annie Lightfoot. And a good friend." Lola touched Annie's bare arm. "Look, we can't change the past. We can only move forward with what's happening right now. A fresh start. The play."

Annie groaned. "Don't remind me. You're Dame Judi Dench, I'm Judi Bench—sitting this one out."

Lola giggled. "I love that you can make me laugh." Her hand slid slowly down Annie's arm to her hand, folding their fingers together. "We can do this, Annie. Together. You and me."

Annie felt cautiously hopeful. She squeezed back, their fingers lacing together. Familiar and entirely new. "You and me . . ."

Time became slippery. Annie knew she should step back, mention being tired, call it a night—but she couldn't let go. Her thumb stroked the back of Lola's hand, swirling slow circles over her warm skin. She could feel her pulse in places she didn't usually feel things. Their hands were still touching, fingers sliding together.

Lola sipped some air, her gaze bright, on high alert. Pupils and possibilities expanding.

Annie wasn't looking away. Her entire body warmed with a bright golden feeling. Every cell in her body urged her to lift her mouth to Lola's parted lips. On instinct, she did, just a millimeter.

Lola moved closer, too.

A dog barked, sharp and close.

Annie jumped, startled.

Socks was awake, tail wagging with enthusiasm.

Annie dropped back into the present. The reality of what'd almost happened widened her eyes. She let out a shaky laugh, looking confused. "Sorry—I didn't mean to . . ."

"Right—me neither." Lola's hand flew to the doorknob, cheeks flushed. "Too much wine. I should . . . good night."

"Good night," Annie called after her, heart pounding in rhythm with Lola's retreating footsteps.

What. The hell. Was that?

17.

Eighteen days till the show

DYLAN ROGERS WAS NOT OKAY. THEY'D HAD CRUSHES BEfore. They'd even been in love—twice, in fact. And they'd definitely fucked a lot, particularly in the last few years. But this—this felt different. More dangerous. More permanent. Vicky Fang was *doing* something to them, like, on a *genetic* level. Their kiss was playing in Dylan's brain like a YouTube clip on loop, and yeah, they'd most definitely liked and subscribed.

They'd long held a candle for Vicky, one that burned quietly but steadily through the zigs and zags of life. But now that they knew Vicky was equally into it, that little candle was an out-of-control wildfire, growing hotter and hungrier with every second. Seriously, the townsfolk needed to evacuate.

The idea of Vicky Fang becoming the one who mattered most was as thrilling as it was terrifying. But okay, they were also imagining getting that sticky red gloss all over their face as they humped like horny bunnies. In the green room of the Rhodes Playhouse. Tangled up in Vicky's sheets. Or—in one particularly nostalgic fantasy—facing the mirrors in the pink-tiled bathroom of Rock Around the Clock while Chip Chadwick was forced to watch.

And on top of their one-kiss-to-rule-them-all, Dylan was also processing that Vicky had had *a fucking heart attack.* What if she hadn't woken up? What if she wasn't here, bossing Dylan around in those seersucker shorts? Now that she was back in it, it was impossible to imagine Vicky not being in their life . . .

"Ugh." They thumped the side of their head. "Focus!"

It was Tuesday at lunchtime during the one-hour break between morning and afternoon rehearsals. Dylan sat outside on the Rhodes Playhouse lawn waiting for a call from the real estate agent who was lining up viewings of potential retail spaces for Marlowe's Upstate location.

The sun blazed in the blue summer sky, heating Dylan's bare arms and legs. They slipped on a pair of aviator sunglasses, partly to reduce the glare but mostly to disguise what they were pretty sure was a look of raw-yearning-slash-extreme-horniness. *Focus.*

As they waited for the call, Dylan nibbled the first test batch of Hot & Sweaty. They'd spent Vicky's two-day absence—a doctor's appointments in the city—distracting themself in Jazz's kitchen. It . . . wasn't good. The raspberry compote was too sweet, the cloves overpowered the whole flavor profile. The popcorn was fun but not enough.

What would make it work? Where was the balance?

"Hey, Dyls!" It was Mikki, who was with Clyde, Zoë, and Jamie. "Want anything from the diner?" she called.

"Thanks, I'm good," Dylan called back.

"'Kay!" Mikki waved as the group headed in the direction of Henry Street.

Dylan felt a wave of warmth at the easy way the oddball group was chatting. Theater bonds were so real.

Across the lawn, Orchid and Kat sat together in the shade, Kat's combat boots scuffing a lazy rhythm in the grass while Orchid, all graphic eyeliner and trending gloss, listened intently, twirling a lavender-streaked strand around her finger. Emery emerged from the theater, white-blond hair flopping into their eyes, oversize tee swallowing their frame. They clocked Orchid and Kat, took one cautious step their way, then stopped, pulled out their phone, and slumped onto the theater steps—every inch of them broadcasting *don't notice me but maybe do?*

Dylan got up, wandering over. "Hey, Emery."

Emery sounded more guarded than Fort Knox. "Hey."

Dylan leaned against the railing, trying not to sound like a camp counselor. "Having fun?"

Emery shrugged, their attention on their phone.

Dylan remembered Emery was their understudy. Zoë was already attending most of Lola and Annie's rehearsals, devoted to learning Annie's part. "Need any help with Hamlet's lines?"

"I'm okay."

How did one converse with a teenager? Dylan had no idea. It'd be easy to peace out, but they felt a tug of responsibility to a fellow enby. "I think it's so cool you're out, like, with your pronouns," they tried. "I was way more clueless when I was your age."

Emery looked up again, the tiniest flicker of interest visible beneath their white-blond shag. "Yeah?"

"Yeah." Dylan took the chance to sit a few feet away. "Didn't figure it out till I was almost thirty."

"Thirty?" Spoken with unchecked horror.

Dylan chuckled, remembering feeling that thirty was ancient. They nodded in the direction of Kat and Orchid. "Those guys seem cool."

Emery glanced over, watching Kat and Orchid laugh at something. They made a noncommittal noise and pulled their knees to their chest.

"I met Vicky and Annie and Lola through the theater," Dylan tried. "And they're, uh, low-key iconic?" How did the kids talk these days? "High-key serve. Big rizz. No cap."

Emery didn't look up. "Never say any of that again."

"Noted." Dylan didn't want to be the annoying adult who didn't understand when to quit. "Okay, well . . . If you ever, like, need to talk—"

"I don't really have any friends," Emery said quietly. "Not who know all my shit."

"Oh," Dylan said, trying to parse their words. "Like . . . you're not out at your school?"

Emery shook their head.

"*Oh,*" Dylan said, getting it. "Wow. Well, it's awesome you're out here. That took a lot of guts. Theater's always been a refuge for the gays," they added. "A place to meet like-minded people."

They both looked over at Kat and Orchid who were looking back, expressions open. Orchid waved, smiling.

"I'm not gonna tell you how to live your life," Dylan said, "but I'll tell you that my life got way better when I made friends. Friends matter, especially for us queers."

Their phone rang. The real estate agent.

"Sorry—work call," Dylan said, standing back up. "Go hang with Kat and Orchid. They seem dope."

Emery hesitated. "What'll we talk about?"

"Start with the play," Dylan said, "and take it from there." They gave Emery a final, reassuring smile before hitting Accept and focusing on the call. "This is Dylan."

There was a pause. Then the caller spoke in a slightly enunciated feminine voice. "Dylan, hello."

Not the real estate agent. Dylan frowned in confusion. "Sorry, who's this?"

Another pause. "Dylan. It's your mother."

Celine? Dylan's stomach dropped like a rock flung into the Hudson. They hadn't heard their mother's voice in five years. "What— Why aren't you calling from your number?" *Which I never would've answered,* Dylan silently added.

"Oh, I got my phone wet while gardening." Celine chuckled.

"With all this heat, I'm just constantly watering, covered in mud."

Celine was many things—Pilates devotee, wine club member, floral print obsessive—but muddy gardener was not one of them. "You gardening? I don't see it."

Celine's tone stayed light. "So you're the only one who's allowed to change, is that it?"

Dylan swayed back, feeling as if they'd just been shoved. Impossible to read their mother's tone. Lighthearted and observant? Or combative and judgmental? Teenage annoyance boiled up from their gut, fisting their hands. Dylan worked hard to stay even. "Why are you calling me?"

"To invite you to lunch," Celine replied smoothly. "As I've said in my texts."

Dylan pictured their mother, blond hair tightly coiffed, makeup thickly applied, standing in her large, light-drenched kitchen holding the phone with a manicured hand. *Appearances sound important to her,* a therapist once accurately observed.

"So, lunch?" Celine went on. "Let me know when you're free."

Dylan's pulse ticked up, a wallop of irritation tightening every muscle. "I'm pretty busy."

"I know—the play, and, of course, Marlowe. But surely you can spare an hour. Text me. I'll make my meatloaf."

She hung up.

Dylan coughed an outraged laugh. They sank to the grass, running a bewildered hand through their hair. It was a shock to hear that Celine knew about Marlowe, something she'd surely find as frivolous as Dylan's love of acting. God, she just *assumed* Dylan still ate meat, which they did, and the thought of Celine's one-and-only specialty had their stomach rumbling, but still. The audacity! The nerve!

"Hey." Vicky picked her way through the tall grass toward them, carrying a brown-bagged lunch. The sight of her cut through

Dylan's irritation, their heart now throbbing for an entirely different reason.

Dylan hadn't been alone with Vicky since the kiss. This morning she'd been friendly but not flirtatious, which was to be expected in public, but still—the kiss was burned onto Vicky's hippocampus for all time, too, right?

Vicky plopped down, tossing her black hair over one far-too-kissable shoulder. "What's up, Rogers?"

Dylan briefly considered lying—offering an easy-breezy-everything's-chill response. But this was Vicky. She'd probably call bullshit, and besides, Dylan wanted to offload to someone they trusted.

They groaned and flopped onto their back, speaking to the cloudless sky. "My mother just ambushed me. Asked me to lunch."

"Whoa." Vicky settled alongside Dylan in the grass, head propped on one hand. "You gonna go?"

"I don't think so." Just the thought of seeing the woman who spent their entire young life pressuring them to dress, act, even think in a way antithetical to their authentic self made Dylan nervous. "Because trauma, and stuff?"

Vicky pulled a sad cheese sandwich out of her brown bag and took a half-hearted bite. "I get that. Kinda nice she asked though. Literally never hear from my dad."

"I'm sorry, babe." Dylan rolled onto their side so they were facing each other. Lying in the long grass made Dylan feel fifteen.

Fifteen in an adult's body.

They pulled out a blade of grass and traced it down Vicky's bare arm. "How could anyone not want to spend time with you?"

Vicky let out a soft *mmm,* her eyes sharp and bright. Her skin shivered into goosebumps. "Ooh, that tickles . . ."

Definitely flirtatious. Heat seeped up from Dylan's belly. They were lying so close to Vicky, they could smell the summery tang of her sunscreen. They kept their voice low. "Are you ticklish?"

Vicky arched a brow. "In some places."

Dylan almost groaned. The idea of stroking a quivering Vicky made them giddy. "Jesus, Vicky." They glanced around. Lola and Annie were by the front entrance, talking with Jazz. Emery was with Kat and Orchid—yay!—all posing for a selfie. Dylan looked back to Vicky. "You're bad."

Vicky licked her lower lip. "I can't stop thinking about our kiss."

Thank god. That kiss had been the hottest minute and a half of Dylan's entire life. The way they'd attacked each other like hungry dogs. The feel of Vicky in their arms. The sound of her moans. The *taste* of her. The sweat on Dylan's brow had nothing to do with the heat. "Me neither."

Vicky's eyes traced Dylan's mouth, their arms, their flop of hair. "You're sort of insanely sexy."

Dylan's mouth opened. Closed. A fizzy-hot sensation flared in their chest. "You're, uh, sort of insanely sexy, too, Vicky."

Vicky didn't break eye contact. "I kind of want you to . . . do things to me."

Dylan's jaw loosened. That they were talking like this, out in public, was a massive turn-on. Dylan pushed their aviators off their face and wiggled closer to Vicky in the grass. Their question was urgent. "What sort of things?"

Vicky inhaled a breath. Through the stretch of Vicky's white tank top, Dylan could see her nipples had tightened into two sensitive points. Her breasts were a wedding cake Dylan wanted to bury their face in. "Dirty things," Vicky whispered.

Dylan's mouth went dry. A flash flood of filthy fantasies careened into their head. The two of them sucking, thrusting, begging, gasping. Bare, sweaty flesh. Vicky tied to a bed. A thumb in someone's mouth. "Dirty things?" Dylan's voice was a desperate croak. "Holy shit. Like what?" They inched even closer. "Vee. You *have* to tell me—"

"Shh." Vicky instructed. "The others." She shifted to sit up, calling brightly to Lola and Annie, already on their way over. "Hi! Come sit."

Lola and Annie were next to them before Dylan was able to right themself, fumbling their aviators back onto their face.

"Dylan, you look a bit sunburned," Annie said in concern. "Need to borrow my sunscreen?"

"Yeah, Rogers," Vicky said with a smirk. "You're all red."

"I'm fine." Dylan willed themself to cool off. "How are you guys?"

Lola and Annie exchanged an oddly loaded glance. "Fine," they chorused, both busying themselves with their lunches.

"Look at us," Vicky said, eyes flashing with amusement. "All fine."

Dylan shot her a *cool it* look. "You guys did good this morning," they managed, jerking their chin at the playhouse. "In rehearsal."

It was true: The previous awkwardness that'd plagued the two leads since the get-go had disappeared, replaced by a new light-footed ease.

Lola and Annie exchanged another layered glance. "Things are feeling . . . clearer," Lola said.

"Honest," Annie added.

Vicky stretched, every inch of her tight top obedient to her curves.

Dylan tried not to drool. "I know what you mean."

IN THE AFTERNOON, Lola and Jazz blocked out the clowning and physical comedy of the four Tragedians that occurred in act one, each beat of which Vicky was present as the Player. Dylan watched from the darkened seats of the audience.

Vicky began the monologue about the Tragedians' summary of services for a watching Rosencrantz and Guildenstern.

"*Tragedy, sir,*" Vicky began with a flourish, as the four teens, playing the band of traveling actors, play-acted their leader's words. "*Deaths and disclosures, universal and particular—*"

The teens succumbed to exaggerated stage deaths—Orchid stabbing Emery, Emery aiming to stab back but instead plunging her invisible blade into Zoë, who, miming outrage, accidentally stabbed Kat.

"*—denouements both unexpected and inexorable—*"

A marriage scene between Emery and Kat became a farce as Emery swooned over the priest (Zoë, in a robe) and Kat mimed kissing the best man, Orchid.

Vicky continued, "*—transvestite melodrama on all levels, including the suggestive—*"

"Hold up." Kat broke the fourth wall, addressing Jazz, who was seated near Dylan in the house seats. "*Transvestite* melodrama. *Transvestite?* That's not cool."

"Kat, the play was written in 1966," Jazz said.

"The text reflects the era," Lola added, "even if it may be politically incorrect today. But the vast majority holds up, and our gender-swapped version opens up room for discussion."

Jazz nodded. "Exactly. Let's pick it up with *We transport you into a world—*"

"Wait." Kat shook her head. "That's not good enough."

It was interesting, Dylan thought, seeing a young adult push back, ask for more. When they did this play twenty years ago, the dated nature of certain ideas didn't come up. Maybe they just didn't feel as confident as the kids today seemed to be.

"Transvestite is insensitive and outdated," Kat declared.

"She's right," Orchid said, stepping forward.

"That term's harmful," Emery added, moving to stand next to Orchid.

Zoë hesitated for a beat before stepping forward, too. "Yeah. We should probably change it."

Kat squared her shoulders. "What if we say *gender-bending melodrama* instead?"

Lola's gaze swept over the four teens standing in solidarity. "Altering the text could be seen as changing the play's artistic integrity." Her voice softened. "But what about a talkback? The day after the show, we host a discussion about the language and how it reflects the era. We keep the text intact but give the audience context."

"I like it," Dylan called. "Good compromise."

Vicky nodded. "Yeah. That way, the text stays true to the play, but we make room to challenge it."

Kat's gaze swept over her friends. Orchid, Emery, and Zoë all shrugged and nodded. Kat exhaled. "Okay. A talkback works."

"Great," Jazz said in relief. "Let's pick it up from *We transport you . . .*"

Vicky was already on her mark, seamlessly shifting back into character. "*We transport you into a world of intrigue and illusion,*" she recited, her words reaching the chandelier overhead. "*Clowns, if you like . . .*"

Dylan couldn't take their eyes off her, a potent mix of pride, admiration, and something deeper than lust simmering in their chest.

It was fascinating what happened when everything was out in the open.

DYLAN GOT VICKY alone only during a five-minute break in the final hours of the day, when Vicky refilled her water bottle from the tap behind the still-grimy concession stand. "Hey!" Dylan came behind the counter. "Amazing job up there—you're killing it."

Vicky turned off the tap. "Thanks."

"So, what are you doing tonight?" Dylan asked, trying not to sound too eager.

"Rewatching *Killing Eve* and masturbating," Vicky replied, twisting the lid back on her water bottle. "Why? What are you doing?"

Dylan coughed a laugh, uncharacteristically flustered. "Just, um, the latter."

"Fun." Vicky winked, just as Garrett called out that break was over. "See ya."

Dylan rubbed their jaw as Vicky sauntered back into the theater with a wiggle in her hips.

Maybe it was the kiss, or the way Vicky's apology had cleared the air; either way, Fang was not here to play, and Dylan did not have a plan for handling it beyond getting her alone as fast as humanly possible. Just like Dylan themself, the end of the day could not come fast enough.

The Rhodes Players emerged from the theater when the burnt orange sun was halfway below the horizon, the late-afternoon air silky warm on their skin.

"So, what's everyone up to tonight?" Clyde asked jovially.

"Oh, probably an early night." Dylan tried to sound tired.

"Boring!" Deborah scoffed, her beaded martini earrings swinging.

Maria was babysitting her grandkids. Garrett had tickets to a sing-along of *The Rocky Horror Picture Show* in Woodstock.

"We could get a drink," Lola said somewhat experimentally to Annie.

"That sounds fun," Annie said, smiling back.

"There's plenty of food and drink at mine," Jazz announced, locking the playhouse doors. "Come over! The more the merrier. You lot, too," she added, addressing the teens. "I'll call your parents."

"Tonight?" Dylan fumbled for a reason why this was not a brilliant idea. Tonight was alone time with Vicky. "But it's . . . Tuesday."

"It's *summer,*" Jazz corrected.

"Could be cool," Emery said with a shrug.

"Could it, though?" Dylan made their voice doubtful.

"I'm in for sure!" said Zoë, her gaze flicking to Lola, then back to Jazz. "I'll talk to my dad. He was gonna drive us all home." She ran over to where a bearded man waited by a minivan.

"I'm in, too." Jamie, who'd been quietly orbiting sweet blond Mikki since rehearsals started, looked to her hopefully. "I can drop you home after. Be your designated driver."

"A dinner party where no one will throw food on the floor that I have to clean up?" Mikki sounded excited. "I'll see if my mom can watch my kid."

"No, no, not tonight." Dylan looked desperately to Vicky. "Don't we all need a night in?"

"*No,*" Jazz declared. "We need a night *out.* Dinner under the stars in my backyard. A mini-mingle! Pizza on me!"

A cheer went up around the actors.

"Woo-hoo," Dylan said miserably. "Yay."

Everyone split up to head for their cars or sort out rides to the mini-mingle. Dylan slung their bag over one shoulder, their hope for uninterrupted time with their teenage-and-current crush fading like the dying rays of the sun.

"Cheer up." Vicky sidled up next to them. "If you're good, I'll let you play footsie with me under the table."

"I want to do a lot more than just play footsie," Dylan told Vicky.

"Oh really?" Vicky lifted an eyebrow.

Dylan let their fingertips rest on Vicky's forearm and leaned closer, speaking directly into her ear. "I want to make you come so hard you forget every one of your lines. I want to make you come so hard you forget who I am and what you're doing back in Rhodes. In fact, I want to make you come so hard that I ruin you for every future lover, for the rest of your life." Dylan pulled back and gave Vicky a blithe smile, as if they'd just been talking about who'd drive. "Cool?"

Vicky's mouth was slightly ajar. Oh so satisfying to see those pretty lips lost for words. This sexual one-upping was quickly becoming Dylan's favorite game.

"Clyde, my man!" Dylan jogged after him. "Did you hear about that UFO sighting in Queens?"

"I did!" The grocer sounded thrilled. "And I've been eager to talk about it with young Dylan!"

"Love that you think I'm young," Dylan replied, before calling over their shoulder to Vicky. "Coming?"

"Count on it," Vicky muttered, fanning her bright red cheeks and following after them.

18.

BACK AT JAZZ'S, DYLAN BEGAN MAKING A TOMATO, WATERmelon, and feta salad while Lola, Vicky, and Annie assembled the backyard for guests, ferrying bottles of wine and cans of seltzer and stringing up little white lights. Jazz phoned in an order for pizza, bustling around with joyful anticipation, declaring things like, "Mini-mingles offer maximum chances for fun!"

Dylan was alone in the kitchen slicing tomatoes when Vicky came in, bending over to dig for cloth napkins in a bottom drawer. She'd changed into a summery red satin slip dress that slid over her curves. Not something she'd worn before.

Dylan didn't bother hiding their open ogling, wolf whistling low.

Vicky smirked over her shoulder. "Like what you see, Rogers?"

"Always. Can I follow you? Do you have a Substack?"

Vicky started folding the napkins. "Only for paid subscribers."

"Sign me up." Dylan slid the tomatoes into a bowl. "Founding member."

"Fair warning: I post daily."

"Make it hourly. I'm *begging* you."

Vicky giggled as Jazz and Lola passed through, debating if they had enough wine.

Vicky moved next to Dylan, reaching to a high shelf for a serving platter. "I love seeing you beg," she whispered. The curve of her breast brushed Dylan's upper arm.

Dylan almost groaned. It took all their strength not to position Vicky against the counter and kiss that sticky gloss off her cheeky mouth. Heat boiled beneath their legs. "Jesus, Fang. You should come with a health warning."

Vicky grabbed the platter without putting any distance between them. Their mouths were only inches apart. "Buyer beware. Think you can handle me?"

"I do." Dylan inched even closer, their hips now flush. "I'm going to devour you like Thanksgiving dinner, Vicky." Dylan was so horny, they'd officially lost control of their mouth. "When I'm done, you'll never be able to look at a turkey again."

Vicky half laughed, half whimpered. "What about cranberry sauce?"

"Cranberry sauce?" Panting, Dylan ran their fingers through Vicky's luxuriously thick hair, tangling a decadent fistful and tugging. "You won't even remember what it is—"

"Hello?" Their neighborhood grocer's voice sounded down the hall.

Startled, Dylan and Vicky went to jerk apart, but Dylan's hand was still twisted in Vicky's hair. "Ow!" Vicky yelped.

"There you are!" Clyde beamed in the kitchen doorway, looking surprisingly put together in a button-down.

"Oh, I see," Dylan desperately improvised, pretending to peer at Vicky's ear while extracting their fingers from her hair, "yes, yes—you're right. Incredible."

"What's that?" Clyde asked, setting a bottle of red wine and some flowers on the counter.

"Well, Vicky was just showing me . . ." Dylan gestured at Vicky's ear, looking to Vicky like *help me.*

"How one of my earlobes . . ." Vicky continued uncertainly.

"Is bigger. Than the other," Dylan finished.

"That's right," Vicky said, folding her arms. "It's a family thing. Same for both my sisters. We all have one earlobe that's bigger than the other."

Clyde looked fascinated. "Really?"

"That must make shopping for earrings hard," Dylan offered, trying to keep a straight face.

"Oh." Vicky lifted her gaze skyward. "You have *no* idea."

Clyde leaned closer, examining Vicky's ears. "They look the same to me."

"Bless your heart!" Vicky wailed. "Where were you during middle school? The teasing was *relentless.*" She hooked her arm into his. "Backyard's this way. Almost done with that salad, Rogers?" she added over one shoulder, winking at Dylan as she hustled Clyde out.

Deborah, Mikki, Jamie, and all four teens arrived, walking wide-eyed into the eccentric home. The house filled with lively chatter, punctuated with bursts of laughter.

Dylan had just finished up in the kitchen when the doorbell rang. "Must be the pizza," they said to Deborah, handing her a glass of the zinfandel she'd brought. "'Scuse me."

Dylan headed for the front door, just in time to hear the long-haired pizza guy tell Jazz, "Sorry, ma'am—your card's been declined."

Ten white pizza boxes were stacked on the porch behind him. Jazz sounded tense. "Try it again."

The delivery guy ran the card, prompting a low, decisive *beep* from the handheld card reader.

"Damn," Jazz muttered. "What's the total?"

"Two hundred and sixty-eight dollars," he said.

Jazz gaped. "For pizza?"

"I got it." Dylan stepped in, extracting a credit card from the slim wallet in their back pocket.

"Absolutely not," Jazz said, trying to bat Dylan's hand away. "This is my treat. I can take care of my own cast!"

With a maxed-out credit card? Was Jazz proud or delusional?

"Course you can," Dylan said, pushing the card into the pizza guy's hand. "This is a thank-you for doing just that."

"I don't need charity," Jazz insisted. "I think I have some emergency cash in a shoebox upstairs—"

Thankfully, the card reader began spitting out a receipt. "Save it for a rainy day," Dylan said, moving to collect the boxes.

They'd forgotten that the play was important not just emotionally but practically.

Jazz was broke. The theater was on the brink. The play had to work.

THE CAST ATE around the long wooden table in the backyard, passing pizza boxes and serving one another salad.

Despite the fact that Dylan hadn't snagged a seat next to Vicky, they were having fun. In no other world would they be breaking bread with this eclectic group of humans. Community theater wasn't just about putting on a show. It was about strengthening a town. It gave folks from all walks of life a chance to step into a different role for themselves: expand the definition of their own identity and more clearly understand the identities of others.

Love thy neighbor had never meant that much to Dylan, especially living in a city where people didn't know who lived next door. But now, watching all these lovable oddballs chat and laugh, the phrase glimmered anew in their mind. Especially as Dylan's gaze landed—once again—on Vicky, who was indulging Clyde's theory that Gertrude was actually a spy sent by a rival kingdom to gather intelligence on Denmark.

"Interesting," Vicky allowed.

Dylan smiled and tuned into the conversation at the other end of the table, where the talk had turned to the play. "It seems to me," Annie was saying, "that the characters are aware they have no free will, but they don't really try to fight it. Rosencrantz is quite passive, even about death."

"Maybe because it's such a hard thing to get your head around," Deborah said. "I always laugh at that line about eternity being a terrible thought and *where's it going to end* because it *is* sort of impossible to comprehend. The longest thing I usually have to get through is tax season."

All the adults chuckled, except Annie, who looked a little pensive. "I guess Rosencrantz's passivity makes me think about my own, in some way."

"What do you mean?" Deborah asked.

"Well, Rosencrantz and Guildenstern waste a lot of their time questioning and philosophizing instead of deciding and doing," Annie said. "Questioning things can be easier than *doing* something." Her gaze slipped to Lola, who ducked her eyes and blushed.

Now, *that* was interesting.

"And isn't Stoppard saying questioning things is pointless?" Mikki asked, swiping her long blond bangs out of her eyes. "Because people can never truly understand the world and their place in it? The Player literally says, *You can't go through life questioning your situation at every turn.*" The entire table was tuned into the discussion now, all looking at Mikki. She licked her lips, seeming to summon some courage. "When I found out I was pregnant, I spent weeks—months—just asking why me? How had this happened? What if I'd just said, *Sorry, pal, no glove, no love*? Then, one day, I caught sight of my bump in the bathroom mirror and realized all that questioning was totally pointless. I was having a baby. That was the day I called my mom and asked if I could come home. I didn't have time for questions. I *had* to act."

The table nodded thoughtfully. A sweep of country-bright stars twinkled overhead. The air smelled faintly like the citronella candles keeping the mosquitoes at bay.

"I felt that way when my husband died," Deborah said. "At first, there were so many questions—why, why, why? But then, after the funeral, I got a mortgage bill. I realized, *Oh shit. I need a job.* That's when I started working part-time at You Nailed It. Now I own it. Funny how things work out."

Jamie nodded, leaning forward on the table. "I definitely felt the existential dread when Sara—that's my ex—broke off our engagement. In my case, I think I was too focused on doing, and not enough on questioning. I was doing what was expected of me—grow up, get married—but after it all fell apart, I realized there were signs. I just ignored them. Too busy living the life I thought I should lead."

"*Mmm.*" Across the table, Lola nodded intently. This, evidently, resonated.

"What else?" Jazz looked to the teenagers. "Let's hear from someone who hasn't spoken yet."

"I have a question." Emery looked at Lola. "When the Player says, *We're actors. We're the opposite of people*, does that, like, offend you?"

This invoked a titter of laughter, including from Lola. "Does it offend me?" she asked with a smile. "No. It's a very funny line, especially as it's given by an actor: an example of meta-theater. To me, this line can be interpreted several ways. Actors play roles and adopt personas that aren't real. People experience real emotions, real events. Actors create illusions. Real life is not an illusion. Actors are bound by the script. People can say anything they like."

Annie reached for her glass, taking a big sip of wine.

Lola went on. "There's a point in the play when the Player gets angry that Rosencrantz and Guildenstern left when the Tragedians were performing, leaving the actors with no one to watch them. He—or I guess she," Lola amended, acknowledging Vicky, "has a line about the humiliation of being tricked out of the single assumption that makes their existence viable—that somebody is watching. To me, that raises questions about whether we have a fixed identity or are we shaped by the ways that others view us? Are our words and actions still meaningful if no one is there to be affected by them?"

The table lapsed into thoughtful silence.

Zoë was the first to speak, half teasing, half earnest. "I feel so lucky to be here." She lifted her glass of seltzer, splashed with the parent-approved half cup of wine. "To Lola and Jazz. Our fearless leaders."

"To Lola and Jazz." The table chorused, glasses raised.

Dylan held Vicky's gaze as they all sipped. She smiled at Dylan, tugging her left earlobe.

Dylan grinned back, tugging their own in response, their chest billowing with a needy, greedy sort of warmth.

Across the table, Jazz, Clyde, and Deb began discussing the town's approval of a new rainbow crosswalk. Jamie refilled Mikki's drink, their fingers brushing. The teens hunched over a phone, debating which songs "slapped" and which were "cringe" for the cast party playlist: *Hamlet, but Make It Hot.*

Dylan leaned back in their chair, soaking it all in.

Love thy neighbor. This was the kind of love they trusted. Big, messy, collective. Built through shared time and effort. The kind that wasn't likely to fizzle out for no good reason at all.

They could build a business. Build a play. Even build a moment like this—light-strung, wine-soaked.

But build a life with someone? That felt like trying to balance glassware on a trampoline. One wrong move and everything shattered.

Wait, why were they even thinking about this? Dylan blanched, shooing off the thoughts like an errant mosquito.

This glorious night, full of weirdos and warmth, was what they wanted to be paying attention to.

This, and the curve of Vicky Fang's neck.

19.

Seventeen days till the show

THE NEXT MORNING, LOLA DRAGGED HERSELF INTO THE THEater at just after ten—late, but not the latest. Her body felt boneless, slack with the afterglow of too much dancing, too little sleep.

"Rough night?" An unimpressed Garrett looked pointedly at his watch.

"The mini-mingle . . ." Lola paused to chug half a gallon of ice water. "Became a major dance party."

"Clyde has serious moves." Dylan lay spread-eagle on the stage, aviators tilted at a drunken angle, muscle tee crumpled and inside out. "I threw my back out trying to keep up."

"What about Deborah's twerking?" Vicky sounded a little raspy. Despite looking underslept, her cat-eye makeup was still impeccable. "Almost lost my voice screaming like a teenage girl."

"The teenagers were the first to arrive." Garrett indicated the quartet, who was huddled on the other side of the stage.

"I miss not having hangovers," Dylan moaned, reaching feebly in the Tragedians' direction. "Give me your youth."

Vicky giggled, looking just a bit totally smitten.

The teens glanced between Dylan and Vicky, whispering. Those two had been all over each other last night, periodically disappearing for long stretches of time. Lola was looking forward to finding out more, even if a part of her wished it was her and a certain dog groomer the cast were gossiping about.

Last night had been the most fun she'd had in—maybe ever? Annie had ripped up the dance floor, jumping and spinning with unselfconscious joy, which made Lola want to dance like that, too. She'd felt sixteen, but also, somehow, exactly her age. In her professional life, she was old. Here, in Rhodes, she wasn't old or young. She was just alive.

The theater doors opened, spilling daylight from the foyer.

Lola snapped awake.

Even hungover—pink hair mussed, socks mismatched—Annie looked distractingly, painfully cute. Lola's brain replayed for the one-thousandth time the almost-kiss at Annie's front door. The way it felt holding hands, the way Lola's body became as charged as the air between their mouths. And then last night, at the mini-mingle, they kept catching each other's eye in a way that seemed . . . *meaningful.* Every time they did, Lola's stomach bottomed out.

"Good morrow." Annie held two iced coffees, extending one to Lola. "Thought you might need this. Extra shot."

Of course, Annie remembered her hangover coffee order. "You're a saint." Lola took it, and their hands brushed. *Meaningfully.*

Annie swallowed a gasp even as she began to babble. "No problem. Just coffee. Not that I'm minimizing coffee. Justice for coffee!"

Lola sipped through a smile, the caffeine not the only thing making her pulse jump.

As rehearsals began, things became even more awkward.

"For the part when Rosencrantz remembers being summoned," Jazz instructed, gesturing from her perch by the stage lights, "the lines *It was urgent—a matter of extreme urgency, a royal summons, his very words*—you should be inches apart, looking right at each other. Raw, edge-of-your-seat desperation!"

Lola made herself hold Annie's gaze. Her soft, sweet lips were parted and smelled like cherries.

"Closer!" Jazz hollered. "This is existential theater, not middle school prom! *Inches apart!*"

Did Jazz have any idea what an inch could do? The havoc it could wreak? Still, Lola obeyed, stepping forward until she could count the freckles scattered across Annie's nose. Close enough to smell Annie's skin. Lola's hands twitched at her sides. She was overcome with an urge to tug Annie backstage. Cup her flushed cheeks with both hands and press their mouths together. She imagined how Annie might kiss her back. Might whimper in pleasure. Might taste.

Lola gave her head a panicky shake, blinking under the stage lights. "Uh, line?" she croaked, as she stumbled backward, tripping over her own existential crisis.

Annie was holding it together much better. Ever since confessing the truth about their breakup, she'd gotten more and more confident. The truth, evidently, had set her free, or at least, freed her up to step into her role with more ease.

Yet the most notable moment of the day came from Maria.

The older woman was only a few soft-spoken lines in when Jazz called for a pause. "Maria," Jazz said, coming onto the stage. "Remind me: What was it I saw you perform last summer, in your choir? The Aretha Franklin cover?"

" 'A Natural Woman'?" Maria said tentatively.

"Exactly," Jazz enthused. "Stirring stuff. Can you give us a few bars of that now, my love?"

Maria glanced around at the other actors, rigid with nerves. "Alone? I'm not warmed up."

"Oh, come on." Jazz smiled with encouragement. "Just give it a try."

Lola winced, already feeling empathetic for Maria's potential embarrassment.

"Trust yourself," Jazz added softly. "I have faith in you."

Lola wondered if she should step in, offer Maria an out. Before she could, Maria opened her mouth.

A rich and powerful voice poured out of her, a waterfall of pitch-perfect notes vibrating with feeling. "*You make me feel, you make me feel . . .*" Maria's voice swelled, raw and soulful. By the time she hit the final "*woman,*" the chandelier itself seemed to be shaking, overcome with emotion.

Everyone broke into applause.

"Holy shit, Maria," Emery said, impressed.

"I stan," Garrett said, snapping his fingers.

"That," Jazz said in an airy voice. "Do it like that."

This unlocked the role for Maria. As they all started up again, Maria stepped into the role of King Claudius with a newfound confidence.

Sometimes, things just needed a little time to be ready for the spotlight.

WHEN THEY WERE done with a run-through of act two, Garrett called a ten-minute recess. As the rest of the cast chatted or wandered toward the foyer, Lola noticed Zoë tucked into a corner of the stage, quietly mouthing to herself. She caught Lola watching and froze. "Sorry."

"You don't need to apologize," Lola said, coming closer. "Just curious what you're working on."

"Practicing Rosencrantz's lines." The young actor gave a sheepish smile. "I'm Annie's understudy. I'm almost off book."

"You nearly know the whole part?" Lola asked, surprised.

Zoë nodded, tucking a lock of strawberry blond hair behind

one ear. "Pretty much. I've been practicing at home, in the mirror. Like a total theater nerd."

Lola nodded. "Respect."

Zoë chuckled, before her expression sharpened into conviction. "Thing is . . . I *get* her. Rosencrantz. She's not dumb, she's just scared. She wants to do the right thing but she doesn't know what that is, and it's like—the more confused she gets, the more she panics. But she's still trying."

Lola blinked, struck by the insight. "That's a really smart read."

Zoë's expression brightened. Lola remembered how vital these words of affirmation were to a young actor. What an impact she could make.

"Wanna run a few scenes with me?" Lola asked. "I'll play Guildenstern, you play Rosencrantz?"

Zoë's eyes went wide, like Lola had just offered her an Oscar. "Seriously?"

"Sure." Lola flipped to act one. "Let's pick it up from the coin toss."

They began. At first, Zoë was tentative—her voice too quiet, her gestures unsure. But Lola slowed the scene, letting Zoë settle in, offering warmth instead of pressure.

"Hey, pause for a sec," Lola said, focusing on Zoë. "I think you're making her too apologetic. What if she's . . . pissed? Like, what if this whole cosmic confusion is actually driving her nuts and this moment is the first time she lets it show?"

Zoë blinked. "Like . . . she's cracking?"

"Exactly. Try it with some bite."

They started again. Zoë raised her voice, infused her lines with frustrated urgency. It worked.

"Whoa." Zoë laughed, a little breathless. "That felt . . . great."

Lola felt it, too—that tingle when a scene found its rhythm. When something clicked. "You've got good instincts, Zoë. You're a natural."

Zoë stared at her, eyes full of awe and gratitude. "No one's ever made me feel like I could actually act. Thank you."

Lola smiled, caught off guard by the warmth blooming in her chest. No performance. No fanfare. Just . . . connection. Mentorship. Art.

This. This was what she'd missed.

"You're going to be great," Lola said. "Don't give up."

Zoë beamed, glowing. Lola felt like a light had switched on inside her, illuminating the parts of herself she'd been ignoring for far too long.

ON FRIDAY AFTERNOON, Garrett and Jazz wrapped everyone an hour early. They'd all done excellent work, Jazz said. Plus, she had an appointment with a journalist from *Out* magazine, intrigued by whispers of Rhodes's queer renaissance.

"All right, Jazz!" Vicky called from the stage, where she and Dylan sat, legs tangled. The couple had been flirting outrageously all week, when they weren't making out in the green room or feeling each other up in the back booth at Rock Around the Clock.

Lola felt a twinge of longing. She and Annie had been inching closer for days, a slow burn she didn't want to rush—but with rehearsals nearly halfway through, maybe it was time to pick up the pace.

As the cast packed up their things, a few people tossed out ideas for a post-show hang. Shakes and fries at the diner? Beers by the river? Mani-pedis at You Nailed It?

"How about afternoon tea?" Lola suggested quietly to Annie, "in Jazz's backyard?"

"Sure," Annie said, "with the others?"

"No," Lola said, affecting supreme casualness. "Just us."

• • •

LOLA HADN'T SPENT many daylight hours in the back garden, but as soon as she came out the side door, balancing a lacquered bamboo tray overloaded with tea and treats, she realized what she'd been missing.

The afternoon air was warm and fragrant with nectar. The only sounds were birdsong and the buzz of drowsy bumblebees floating around the flowering plants, which grew higgledy-piggledy by the three back fences. Lola imagined Jazz tossing handfuls of seeds unperturbed by when and how they bloomed, but bloom they had.

Decadent peonies, floofy as a wedding dress. Yellow-striped snapdragons and burnt orange dahlias, monarch butterflies fluttering between them. Hardy purple lavender swayed next to vivid blue delphiniums. Behind the plants, climbing wild roses in various shades of pink and red claimed the fences. Jazz's untamed garden was a rainbow of flowers.

Annie sat in one of two red Adirondack chairs beneath an enormous oak tree. She was gazing up at the cloudless sky, so blue it was almost purple, twirling a clover between her thumb and forefinger.

Lola threaded through the grass, the earth soft under her bare feet. "Postmates delivery," she announced, placing the tray on a little side table between the two sloping chairs.

"Holy mac." Annie sat up, her gaze roving around the tray, then up to Lola. "Have I told you I like eating my feelings or is that just my vibe?"

Lola laughed and took a seat. "Apple cake." She pointed to the two fat, sticky wedges of it. "Homemade, from the farmers market. Local cherries, which are incredible. Plums. Olives. Spiced nuts. And some Brie, to have with the baguette."

They piled their plates and dug in.

"So," Annie said, after a few mouthfuls, "whatever should we talk about?"

There was still so much Lola didn't know. "Everything."

They swapped stories. Annie explained how, after her grandmother died, she sold the house to pay off her medical bills. There wasn't much left; college wasn't an option. "Did the vagabond thing for a bit—Brooklyn, for a year. Fun, but hectic, and I couldn't really afford it." Then, she followed a girl to Portland, Maine. After they broke up, she decided to move to Austin. "I liked the food, the people, the size of the city. Got a part-time gig in a dog-grooming salon, which I absolutely loved." The memory brought a smile to Annie's face. "I ended up as the manager, but then the pandemic hit and it felt like time to come home."

Lola envied the ease with which Annie had moved through the world, following whims and women. She wanted to know more—every detail.

Most pressingly about the girl Annie followed to Portland.

Under a single plum tree, a blue jay was cooling off from the afternoon heat in an old stone birdbath. If only she were a bird, something small and nimble, able to change course with the flick of a wing. Her own path didn't feel anywhere near as easy. Living simply was underrated.

In turn, Lola told Annie more about her last two decades in the business of show—the guest spot on a police procedural where everyone was lovely, and a very popular sitcom where everyone was not. The commercials that paid well but were mildly humiliating and definitely bizarre: "*A spinach shake so silky, it's simply sublime* is unfortunately a sentence not even death will take from me."

Lola told Annie about fun style teams and laidback grips and fascinating co-stars. About how casts and crew grow so close over a shoot that everyone feels like family, and then, poof, the film wraps and the family disbands, and how it took years to develop the emotional resilience to handle that ride.

But also the much harder parts. Having a public profile meant living in a fishbowl, every move potentially monitored. She couldn't spontaneously dye her hair pink or move to a different city on a whim. "I love acting," Lola said. "But most of what I do now isn't acting. It's reading terrible scripts. Waiting alone in a trailer. Keeping my body camera-ready. Acting for film doesn't feel freeing or artistic—it's a grind. But ever since we started rehearsals, I'm remembering how much I *love* performing. Creating something; *collaborating.* Even when it's hard, it's fun. Being back here"—she gestured expansively at the back garden, at their snacks, at Annie herself—"it's all just reminding me how many different ways there are to live. Maybe I just need fewer."

"That's funny," Annie said. "Because you being back makes me wonder if I should want more. I love Rhodes," she added, "I do. But sometimes I get lonely. Sometimes I want a bigger life." Annie's gaze settled on Lola. "When you first came back, I felt insanely insecure. About everything, but especially my job and where I lived. I felt like it must pale in comparison to your life. I wanted to impress you, which is ironic, as I just repeatedly embarrassed myself in front of you. *I'm a Pisces and I'd like to learn to roller-skate.* Kill me."

Lola giggled. Wit was the quality Lola found most attractive in another person. Some people were drawn to money or power or physicality. As a flamboyant hair stylist once observed, Lola went gaga for a ha ha. "Ah, the infamous table read." She reached for a sun-warmed cherry and took a bite. "It wasn't that bad."

"Lollie, I made preschoolers doing *The Nutcracker* look like the Rockettes."

Lola laughed. God, it felt good. Being around Annie just felt *good.* "Well, you've made up for it since. Rehearsals are going well."

"Yeah," Annie said, sounding a little surprised. "They are."

They exchanged a smile. And didn't look away.

Despite their bumpy start, being around Annie still felt deeply comforting and unexpectedly electrifying. Lola was relaxed but not mindlessly so. She felt the same sort of presence she did during a take; a switched-on hyper-focus. But with Annie, she wasn't performing or being someone else. She just felt wholly, even urgently, in a moment she didn't want to end. Lola didn't want Annie Lightfoot to disappear from her life for another twenty years.

The sun was dipping toward the horizon. Golden hour. All that remained on the tray were cherry pits and olive seeds.

"You know," Lola said, "we haven't caught up properly on . . . relationships."

Annie flicked Lola a loaded look. "We haven't."

"Not that you asked," Lola said, "but I still identify as bisexual."

"Oh." Annie looked surprised, then a little sly. "I was curious about that, actually."

Lola smiled. It'd been freeing to say those words out loud. "I don't talk about it much because I've never had a serious girlfriend or dated a woman publicly. I know that I can be queer without a relationship, and that I can still be queer while dating a man. But, y'know"—she twirled her wrist—"the internet can be brutal. I don't want to take space away from someone who needs it more."

"So is Brett Burns really your celebrity crush?" Annie asked delicately.

"Oh god," Lola groaned, vaguely recalling saying that in an interview—one that felt very long ago. "*No.* I don't even like him. I said it to keep my publicist happy. So stupid."

"You're not stupid. You're just navigating a lot." Annie's cheeks were the color of cut grapefruit, her lips curved in a pleased smile. "But I'm glad you're still on Team Gay."

"Put me in, coach," Lola quipped. "I'm ready."

They both chuckled, the air between them warm and lightly charged.

"I admire how out you are," Lola added. "With the business, and just in your own life."

Annie nodded, looking a bit surprised. "Well, I love being queer. Love being part of the queer community. It's the tits, literally."

"But I'm sure sometimes you get . . . pushback?"

"Like the time someone threw a rock through our window?" Annie said. "Or started hassling my ex and me when we were making out on the train? Yeah. But, fuck 'em. I'm not, like, dimming my light to appease a bunch of homophobes."

"I like that you stand your ground. That's"—Lola searched for the word—"rare. Especially in my world."

The sun was a glowing orange orb in the west, kissing the horizon.

"What about you?" Lola asked, shifting to face Annie. "Deborah mentioned you'd been through a breakup?"

"Yeah, that was Harriet, my ex. We were together for a couple years—she moved in with me, above the salon—but by the end, we were more like roommates. And she didn't want kids. By the time we were peeing with the bathroom door open and calling each other 'bro,' I knew it was over." Annie sighed. "She left me for some chick who makes ceramics shaped like her own vagina."

"Yikes." Lola made a sympathetic face, waiting the right amount of time before asking, "So you want kids?"

"Yeah," Annie said, lightly. "One day. You?"

"Yeah," Lola said, just as lightly. "One day."

Lola felt her neck get hot. They both looked out at the darkening backyard. Beyond the fence, the sky was purpling. The moon was overhead, a pale disc all alone in the sky.

"Oh look," Annie said softly, pointing. "A firefly." Floating in the twilight, like a tiny fallen star.

As they watched, more lightning bugs appeared, hovering above the peonies, drifting over the wild roses. Beyond the back fence, Lola could see more in the distant fields, high up in the trees.

"They only live for a few weeks," Annie murmured. "They light up to find a mate."

They watched the fireflies pulse, tiny green spells blinking against the dark.

A memory slid into place, the way a long-lost key finds its lock. The two of them, starry-eyed and moonstruck, kissing under a blanket on an evening just like this. Back when they were both foals, gangly and inexperienced. Back when life was a blank page, waiting for them both to make their mark.

The whole evening shimmered with magic—Lola could feel it in the humid air, clinging to her skin. But the magic was predicated on one thing. The girl next to her. Lola swiveled to face her. "You're still so important to me, Annie."

Annie's mouth fell open in soft surprise. "I am?"

Lola nodded, her heart thudding in her chest. A slow breathless warmth spilled through her limbs at the spontaneous admission. "Yeah. You feel like home."

Slowly, Lola shifted her hand toward where Annie's lay on her armrest, longing to close the distance—skin to skin.

"Hey, bitches!" Vicky's voice cut through the quiet like a firework. "Movie night?"

20.

Movie night? Annie looked to Lola, who was smiling back hopefully, fireflies drifting around her like a living constellation.

Annie hadn't intended on staying this late. Of course she wanted to reconnect with her ex. Smooth over their messy past, maybe even end up as friends. They were queer after all—being friends with your ex was de rigueur. But there seemed to be more than just friendship growing between them. They'd definitely had *a moment* at her apartment at the end of their dual lesbian confessional, until canine interruptus, aka Socks, cut it short.

Annie flushed, reminding herself that falling for Lola again, only to bid her farewell as she jetted off, *again,* was an incredibly dangerous idea. She wiggled her toes in the grass. "It's late . . ."

"Yeah, but we're only young once," Lola said.

"Are we young?" Annie asked. "I thought we were old."

Lola shook her head with a smile. "Forever young," she said. "It's a mindset."

THE TV ROOM was past the kitchen. There, a long paisley-print sofa slouched between two armchairs—one velvet, one scuffed leather—all facing a boxy TV. The coffee table was already set up with dessert. Vanilla ice cream, a bowl of maraschino cherries, a can of whipped cream, some chopped nuts. . . . Annie frowned. Wait. Was all this for—

"Banana splits. We hear you're a fan," Lola said warmly, as she and Vicky set down four bowls, each with a peeled banana sliced down the middle. "And, of course . . ."

"Fudge," Annie finished, abashed, as Dylan placed a bottle of it down with a flourish.

The trio grinned at her, their expressions expectant and hopeful.

Annie's table read debacle replayed in her mind—*I love banana splits but I haven't had one in years.* The memory still made her cringe. Made her want to sink into the paisley couch and vanish. She almost did. Almost. But then she remembered what she and Lola had talked about—wanting more. A bigger, bolder life wasn't always easy. It came with risk. With red cheeks. So, she could flee . . . or she could laugh.

So she laughed. A full, unfiltered belly laugh. "At last!" she declared, grinning.

Relieved, the trio exchanged the smiles of successful co-conspirators. "I knew you'd love it," Lola said, giving Annie's arm a squeeze.

Dylan winked at Vicky. Annie had watched the whole flirty circus at the mini-mingle—shared drinks, whispered jokes. They'd both vanished mid conga line and reappeared looking suspiciously . . . tousled. Equally cute, scandalous, and envy-inducing.

"So, what are we watching?" Dylan asked, making up their bowl. "Something scary? For old time's sake?"

Annie remembered horror movie marathons in Dylan's parents' home theater. Vicky and Dylan were obsessed with scary movies while she and Lola endured them, shrieking as the others shushed them. *The Blair Witch Project, Scream, A Nightmare on*

Elm Street . . . Annie recalled the brushed velvet of the seats sliding back and forth against her bare thighs as she clung to Lola in a way that made her feel giddy.

"I haven't seen the new *Scream* yet," Vicky bounced with excitement. "Or we could do the first one!"

"Is that okay for your blood pressure?" Dylan asked Vicky, sliding to the floor to lean against the leather armchair.

"You're asking the person whose comfort watch is *Twin Peaks,*" Vicky said scornfully. "I can handle a mid-nineties slasher."

"If you're cool with it then, yeah, a throwback!" Dylan nodded with enthusiasm. They dropped their voice into a creepy rasp, "*Do you like scary movies?*"

"Yes!" Vicky squealed as Lola and Annie chorused, "No!"

"We don't," Annie said, shaking the can of whipped cream. "I like movies where the scariest thing is the prospect of someone not falling in love with their fated mate but always doing exactly that."

"Seconded," Lola said, reaching for the fudge.

"Rom-coms." Vicky groaned performatively, plopping onto the leather armchair with her bowl. "Nooo."

"Rom-coms are great—right up until the credits roll," Dylan said. "Then it's just reservations for one and unresolved emotional trauma."

"Cynical much?" Vicky gave Dylan a look before adding, "My beef is you always know how they're going to end."

"Same with horror movies," Lola pointed out. "The final girl is basically the grand gesture."

"Interesting," Dylan mused. "Is the first murder the meet-cute?"

"*I'll explore this basement alone* is pretty much *let's fuck to get it out of our systems,*" Lola said. "A fool's errand."

Annie chuckled, feeling warm at hearing Lola mention fucking. Extremely tempting to imagine it. "Rom-coms aren't about the ending, they're about the journey," she said to Vicky, popping a sticky red cherry atop her perfect split. "Just like in the play!" The idea arrived as she spoke it aloud. "Rosencrantz and Guildenstern are fated to die—it's right there in the title—but what's interesting is the twists and turns along the way. The banter, the big ideas. The rest of the cast! Their story is *also* about the journey."

"Not just a pretty face over here." Dylan leaned over to tap their wineglass to Annie's, who blushed, pleased. She'd never been the "smart one." But things had changed since high school. Things were changing all the time.

Annie hopped up onto the paisley sofa next to Lola, their thighs touching. She tried to ignore how nice it felt. Familiar. Dangerous.

"We could do an indie," Lola suggested, licking whipped cream off her spoon. "There's this brilliant new French film about sex workers, filmed on location in a housing estate. It's three hours long and subtitled and I think it's pretty heavy but—"

"Pass." Vicky chomped a piece of banana. "Sorry, Lols, I know you like all that underground stuff, but I'd seriously rather have a lobotomy."

Annie swallowed a laugh, secretly relieved. She made up her first bite of banana split, with a careful ratio of banana-to-ice-cream-to-whipped-cream-to-fudge-to-nuts. Soft, sweet heaven on a spoon. Annie let out a satisfied groan. "This is *perfect.*"

The others all agreed. Vicky's bowl was notably less decadent than everyone else's. Annie understood why.

In the past, the line between private and public, what's mine and yours, felt less defined. Back then, Annie liked that it didn't matter whose house she might sleep at. Now they were adults, and that meant having boundaries, even if these three people made her want to dissolve the ones around her. Sleep in the same bed every night.

Or, more accurately, sleep in Lola's bed, with her. Naked. After hours of making each other—

"What about a lezzie throwback," Annie spoke quickly. "From our youth?"

"*D.E.B.S.*," Dylan listed. "*High Art, Imagine Me & You, Better than Chocolate, Loving Annabelle.*"

"*Loving Annabelle*!" Vicky cackled. "God, it was *so* bad and I watched it one hundred times."

"Same," Annie said with a laugh.

"Before I met you guys, the only lesbian moments I remember were in hetero films," Lola said. "Like *Empire Records*."

"Yes!" the trio half yelled, half groaned.

"The chokehold young Liv Tyler had on me!" Dylan moaned.

"That blue cropped sweater and plaid miniskirt are burned on my brain," Annie said.

"*Cruel Intentions*," Lola listed.

Vicky crossed herself. "Sarah Michelle Gellar and Selma Blair's kiss is sixty-seven percent why I'm gay."

Lola laughed. "Let's not forget *Wild Things*."

"Stop." Dylan grinned, raking a hand through their hair. "That's actually one of my Netflix-and-chill films."

"Ooooh," Lola and Annie chorused.

"That gets 'em in the mood?" Annie teased.

"One hundred percent success rate," Dylan shot back with a smirk. "What's your guys' movie move?"

"*Show Me Love*," Annie said, truthfully. A subtle, smart late nineties indie about two girls, one popular, one shy, who fall in love in small-town Sweden. She'd related, given the similarities with her own life, as a shy small-town teen who fell hard for a bright, shining star of a girl. Only as she said it aloud did she remember it was a film she'd first watched with Lola. Many times. First as friends. Then, intertwined. Never making it to the end. A sudden rush of heat flared under Annie's skin. She hurried the conversation along. "What about you, Vee?"

Vicky shrugged, slicing off some banana. "*Hereditary. It Follows* is good. *The Shining* is cool."

"Dude." Dylan's mouth hung open in shock and awe. "Those are all so intense."

"Maybe that's why I'm still single," Vicky fired back, a little crossly. "Lola?"

Annie met Lola's gaze, feeling a zip of energy. Lola looked caught out, glancing to the others. Her voice was light. "Same, actually."

"*The Shining*?" Dylan groaned theatrically, their face in their hands. "Please don't tell me you also don't know how to date?"

"No," Lola said, brushing off her hands. The skin on her neck flushed red. "*Show Me Love.* Once or twice."

"Ooooh," Dylan and Vicky singsong chorused, then giggled. The pair resumed bickering over movie picks.

But Annie was looking at Lola. And Lola was staring right back. The moment lengthened, growing bigger and louder with every passing second. Annie knew she should look away. Rejoin the conversation. But she didn't. She held Lola's gaze, and it felt even scarier than the table read, even more momentous than agreeing to the play.

Something shifted between them. A rise in pressure. A question. Or maybe, a statement.

"By George, I've got it!" Dylan declared. "*But I'm a Cheerleader.* It's a rom-com, and a throwback, and it holds up."

"Also Clea DuVall is so sexy in that movie," Vicky groaned. "*I'm Graham, and I like girls. A lot.* Ugh, tattoo me!"

Lola blinked, finally looking away from Annie, back to the others. "Sounds good."

"Yeah, bring on Adam and Steve not Adam and Eve." Annie managed to reference the film despite feeling slightly fevered.

Vicky jumped to her feet, eyes sliding unsubtly to Dylan. "I'm just gonna . . . pee."

Dylan scrambled up, practically panting. "Yeah, me too. You guys figure out how to stream it?"

Lola gave them both a knowing look. "You're not fooling anyone."

Vicky blushed, looking pleased, while Dylan gave a guilty-as-charged shrug.

Annie nearly clapped. "The rumors are true!"

"Rumors?" Vicky squinted. "What rumors?"

"Please," Lola said. "You spent most of the mini-mingle only mingling with each other."

"The town grapevine has already exploded," Annie informed them. "So obviously the next step is ship names. We have Vylan—sounds like villain, maybe not ideal; Dylvee—could be a new line of sex toys; or my personal favorite, Dicky."

"Dicky?" Vicky cackled.

Dylan blushed. "What can I say? Mouthy lawyers in seersucker does it for me." They grabbed Vicky's hand, tugging her away. "And I'd put money on you two hooking up first!"

The pair hurried out, leaving Annie and Lola alone, Dylan's parting shot vibrating between them.

For a long moment, neither woman moved. Spoke.

The air in the room felt so bracingly alive it practically had a pulse. Annie was overly aware of her body and its proximity to Lola's.

"I haven't seen *But I'm a Cheerleader* in years." Lola's hazel eyes were the color of firelight. Her voice was low. Unguarded. "I still love it, though."

Annie's breath caught in her throat. Her chest felt tight with the force of it—the wanting, the ache. She wanted to tell Lola everything. Give her everything. Not lose her a second time.

Why was she fighting this? It was time to lay down arms. There was simply no way she couldn't.

"Same," Annie whispered back. "I still love it, too."

21.

Fourteen days till the show

THE NEW DYLAN ROGERS WAS MANY THINGS. AN ANNOYING flirt. A low-slung jeans devotee. A very, *very* good kisser.

And, apparently, president of the quinoa appreciation society. "You can use it in soups, or salads, or even in a breakfast bowl!" Dylan rinsed a handful of fine, brown grains in a sieve under the tap in Jazz's school-bus-yellow kitchen. "*Quinoa is life.*"

"I know what quinoa is," Vicky said witheringly, before reconsidering this. "Wait, what is it?"

"Quinoa," Dylan spoke with utmost seriousness, "is a superfood."

They were a few minutes into an afternoon cooking lesson. Dylan was helping Vicky learn to cook for herself.

Vicky frowned at the reddish-brown grains in the silver sieve. "A superfood? Like, mild-mannered reporter by day, masked avenger by night?"

Dylan chuckled, switching off the tap. Today's muscle tee featured a Mexican wrestler called Cassandro. "Exactly. Fighting crime, and high blood pressure."

"Be still my clogged arteries." Vicky scooped some wet grains on her fingertip and popped them in her mouth.

"No, Vee!"

"*Ugh.*" Vicky flinched. "That's disgusting."

"They need to be cooked first," Dylan reminded Vicky, handing her a wet paper towel. "Like pasta."

"Pasta is one of the five food groups," Vicky countered, scrubbing her tongue clean. "Quinoa is now part of my villain origin story."

"Sorry, honey." Dylan's grin was lazy and amused. "Should've warned you."

Honey. The word invoked a push-pull of delight and apprehension.

That she was finally hooking up with her high school obsession was like something out of a rom-com that other people enjoyed.

Of course this couldn't *be anything.* Dylan was basically their generation's answer to Leonardo DiCaprio. They lived thousands of miles away, and Vicky would never do long distance. Not that it would even be appropriate to bring up that sort of future-worry in what was clearly a summer fling. In the effort to self-protect, Vicky made her voice haughty. "Your seduction strategy needs work, Rogers."

Dylan paused in surprise, knife poised above a tomato. "I'm not trying to seduce you, Vicky. I'm trying to make sure you make it to ninety."

A little thrill fizzed through Vicky at Dylan's mix of earnestness and charm. They seemed to be taking Vicky's health seriously. She tossed her hair over one shoulder. "Why do you care what happens to me?"

Dylan put the knife down, their eyes not leaving Vicky's own. "I don't know. I guess I have a crush on you, Vicky."

The words landed like a bomb in her belly, making Vicky falter, suck in a breath. *Goddamnit.* Vicky had no idea if Dylan was being serious or flirtatious or just trying to get a rise out of her, something they could pretty much give a masterclass on. It was a struggle to toss off a pithy reply. "Don't you mean you *still* have a crush on me?"

Dylan didn't flinch. A tiny smile kicked up the left side of their mouth. "Okay. I still have a crush on you."

Vicky felt herself getting wound up, huffing out a petulant breath. "Don't be ridiculous, Rogers. We're too old to have crushes."

"Oh really?" Dylan slunk forward, each step increasing the temperature in the kitchen, speaking low and deliberate. "So the fact that we keep mauling each other like hungry dogs—that's just . . . ?"

"Biology," Vicky managed, her head getting swimmy at Dylan's ever-closer presence. At the way their gaze was burning a hole right in her heart. "Dumb—physical—need."

Dylan was close enough to scoop Vicky around the waist and pull her close, "For a lawyer, you're a terrible liar."

"For a foodie," Vicky panted, "your quinoa is shit."

With a growl, Dylan pressed their mouth to the sensitive skin of Vicky's neck. The heat of their breath, the touch of their tongue, made Vicky woozy. She groaned, her head falling back as Dylan's lips traced down to her collarbone. Her words came in gasps. "This—doesn't mean—anything."

Dylan paused, breathless, mouth wet. "Huh?"

"*This*"—Vicky sawed the air between them—"doesn't mean *anything.*"

Dylan cocked their head, a flop of dark brown hair sliding over their annoyingly dreamy green eyes. Their mouth twisted into an amused smirk. "Oh, Vicky. Vicky, Vicky, Vicky."

"What?" Vicky snapped, even as she reached greedily for Dylan's belt loops.

"Just admit it, babe," Dylan drawled. "You're already falling in love with me."

Vicky's breath stuttered. Her heart missed its next beat. She gave a brittle laugh. "Uh, *no*! I'm *not*! I'm just taking advantage of your proximity by taking advantage of *you*. I have *needs*. You're meeting those needs. This isn't emotional and I'm definitely not falling in love with you, you delusional narcissist!"

"Really?" Dylan grinned, twisting out of Vicky's grasp to grab a toothpick from the canister that Jazz kept on the counter, popping it between their teeth. "Allow me to present evidence to the contrary, your honor."

Her own stupid fault for putting a stop to things. Vicky rolled her eyes. "What are you talking about, Rogers?"

"I'm saying you have feelings for me and I have enough evidence to go to trial."

"Then I'll see you in court!" Always fun to have a reason to say that. Vicky hopped up onto the kitchen counter and waved her hand, judicious. "Court is now in session. The defense may proceed."

Hands behind their back, Dylan assumed a mock-serious stance. "Madame Judge—"

"Just 'your honor,' counsel." Vicky arched her brow. "I will not have my courtroom made a mockery and, in this case more than most, language matters. Especially as I appear to be both the judge," Vicky said with a frown, "and the defendant."

"We live in strange times. Your Honor," Dylan amended. "The defendant, Ms. Vicky Fang, claims that the very satisfying and undeniably hot physical relationship between her and myself, quote, *doesn't mean anything* and that she isn't, quote, *falling in love* with me."

"Sounds like a practical woman who understands her own mind."

"This may be true," Dylan allowed, beginning to pace Jazz's yellow kitchen. "But consider this: midway through a *mini-mingle dance party,* Vicky was the one who dragged me into the kitchen pantry, stating that she'd been, and again I quote, *waiting all night to jump my bones.* She then stuck her alarmingly strong tongue into my mouth, in a manner not unlike *this.*" Dylan picked up a nearby ketchup bottle and jar of mustard. "The defendant's alleged embrace!" they declared, play-acting the condiments getting it on. "In this very kitchen, on the night in question!"

Vicky's pulse sped at the memory of exactly how spicy things had gotten while backed against the spice rack. If sex was defined by an orgasm with another person, then *technically,* she'd fucked in that pantry. "Is this a courtroom or a cooking show?" Vicky quipped. "Everyone knows kitchen pantries are highly erotic locations, and this seems circumstantial at best and not at all related to your claims."

"Your honor, I contend that this encounter was no one-off, but one of several passionate exchanges." Dylan gave Vicky a crooked grin that made her heart send up a flare. "Last week, the defendant cornered me in the green room, locked the door, and told me in a tone I'd describe as breathless that she couldn't stop thinking about—and my apologies to the court for vulgarity—my ass in those jeans."

Vicky narrowed her eyes even as a blush flared in her cheeks. "And is it true you encouraged said behavior by wearing those jeans?"

"I plead the Fifth." Dylan smiled blithely, before continuing. "Furthermore, the defendant then placed my hands on her very beautiful breasts and asked me if I liked that."

Vicky pressed her lips together. Things had also gotten a bit out of hand in the green room. "And, um, how did you respond?"

"In the affirmative." Dylan cocked a brow. "Quite enthusiastically, if I recall."

Heat built between Vicky's thighs. She squirmed on the kitchen counter, resisting the twin urge to giggle and moan. "Objection.

Counsel is getting flirty." Vicky cleared her throat. "This is all very entertaining, but I fail to see the evidence you claim you have."

"Then, the other night, after Lola went to bed and Annie went home, leaving Victoria and I to watch the original *Scream*—"

"The best *Scream*."

"Agreed. We ended up, I believe the technical term is *humping*, on the couch. Over the course of that evening, and, for full disclosure, a bottle of very good wine, the defendant admitted, and I quote"—Dylan paused for effect, raising a finger—" 'You're annoyingly hot.' " They ticked off their fingers. "Exhibit B: 'sort of funny.' Exhibit C: 'a bit impressive.' And, dare I say, Exhibit D: 'a total freaking catch.' All of this is conclusive proof that the defendant is having *feelings*. Feelings, Your Honor, of love." Dylan let out a breath, bowing slightly. "I rest my case."

It was a struggle to maintain composure.

It was true that things had heated up very quickly with Dylan. But love? That wasn't a good idea. Vicky reminded herself for the one-millionth time that Dylan was a fuck boy. A player, a clit tease, Don fricking Juan. They probably had a whole bed full of girls waiting for them back in L.A. Dylan was just trying to get under her skin, when Vicky would prefer they get into her pants. Love could not be in the fine print.

For that, and for a much more embarrassing reason that Vicky would prefer not to think about. A reason that very few people in her life even knew about. Not even her sisters.

Vicky refused to think about *that*. She didn't want to waste any more of their time off not getting off.

"I've reached my verdict." Vicky hopped off the kitchen counter, padding closer to Dylan. "After careful consideration of the facts, I'm sentencing you"—she wound her fingers into Dylan's belt loops, tugging them close—"to more making out."

Dylan grinned, tipping Vicky's chin up with their fingertip. For a moment, their gaze softened—something warm and unguarded behind the teasing smile. "Sustained."

THE NEXT MORNING, Vicky was back on her bullshit—aka being a Responsible Adult. She pushed open the door to the Rhodes Playhouse, ready to work.

On one side of the stage, Kat and Emery mimed swordplay, parrying back and forth so effectively, Vicky could almost hear the clang of metal. On the other side of the stage, Annie was practicing her blocking, speaking her lines softly as she ran through a scene, script in hand, expression inward and focused. Today only called for Rosencrantz, Guildenstern, the Player, and the teen Tragedians. Dylan's call time wasn't till midafternoon, so they were planning on making yet another test batch of their new chocolate for Marlowe, the details of which were mysteriously under wraps.

"Kat, Emery, remember to keep your shoulders back, heads high—less flailing, more fencing!" Lola called from the stage. "Annie, you'll be crossing downstage *left* when you deliver the line *We must be born with an intuition of mortality*—it's going to look crowded if you linger too long in the center. Vicky, hi: Our costume designer requests your measurements by end of day, please."

"No problem, Lols," Vicky called back, saluting.

There was something wonderfully otherworldly about spending a sunny Sunday inside a grand old playhouse. Vicky loved how theater let adults treat make-believe as meaningful and important. It was the opposite of her work as a lawyer, which affected real people's lives. And yet, there were similarities—both were about telling a story with conviction and guiding an audience—be it jury or crowd—to feel something true.

Vicky took a seat near Orchid, who was slurping a smoothie while scrolling on her phone. "Hey." Vicky waved. "Cool shirt."

"Thanks." Orchid brushed a piece of lint off the puffy sleeve of her shimmery blue top. "I made it."

"You did?" Vicky was impressed. "The extent of my sewing abilities is dropping things off to be tailored."

Orchid chuckled, putting her phone down. "I just like making things."

"Right, you wear a lot of hats." Vicky recalled the teenager's introduction—actress, filmmaker, writer.

"I guess I have a lot of interests and I don't want to limit myself." Orchid shifted to face Vicky more directly. "How did you decide to become a lawyer? Was it, like, hard to whittle it down?"

"Not really—I guess I didn't have a lot of interests," Vicky said. "But you don't need to make any forever choices now. You're so young."

"I'm the oldest student in the cast—I'll be *seventeen* this fall."

Vicky remembered feeling this way—hopelessly old, well before she actually was. "The thing about feeling old," Vicky said, "is you never get any younger. As soon as you think you're old—you are. So if you think you're old now, at seventeen, you're gonna be old for the next, like, *seventy years.* And that's if you're lucky!"

Orchid blinked. "I've never thought of it that way."

Neither had Vicky. This was a new concept for her, too.

"You're not even old enough to vote," Vicky said. "You literally have your whole life ahead of you. You can make a million mistakes, change your mind a million times."

Orchid looked doubtful. "That's not what my mom says. She's riding my ass over my senior year, putting all this pressure on me to do well, so I get into a good college, so I get a good job, so I have a good life. It feels like one wrong move and I'm destined for failure."

Vicky remembered that pressure intimately—the weight of her parents' expectations not just to succeed, but to succeed in a way that validated the sacrifices they'd made moving to the United States.

Being good wasn't enough; Vicky had to be exceptional. There was no road map for that, especially as one of the only Chinese girls at Riverstone Prep. Back then, she equated invisibility with safety. She laughed when her white friends laughed, ate what they ate, and never corrected any mispronunciation. But the pain of not being seen didn't go away just because she was good at hiding.

She hated how much she'd let slide—how long it had taken her to name things for what they were.

Back then, she hadn't had anyone like Orchid to talk to. She hadn't even realized she needed someone.

"I can one hundred percent relate," Vicky told Orchid. "My parents were strict, too. They were acting out of care and didn't get that their pressure made things harder. And that not everything is about good test scores or getting what they think is a good job."

"So, what's it about then?" Orchid asked.

Vicky had been asked this sort of thing before—hell, she'd given keynotes on climbing the law ladder. Of course she had—she was a textbook example of someone who'd made it. And where had it landed her? First, in a hospital bed, then here in Rhodes, in a community theater production. So what was it all about?

"Honestly? I'm still figuring that out." Vicky thought about Dylan, and Lola, and Annie, all, in their own way, muddling through. "I think everyone is always figuring it out. But what I'm working toward now is a balance. A life that allows for work and play. Healthy eating and Taco Bell. That has room for discovery and adventure and taking the long way home."

The words coming out of Vicky's mouth surprised her—she'd never taken the long way home in her life.

"I love my job," Vicky went on, "but I don't want it to be my whole life anymore. Because doing this play has been the most fun thing I've done in ages. And fun should not be underrated. Joy should not be underrated. The joy you make and the joy you take really matters. So, choose joy. I guess that's my advice."

"Choose joy," Orchid repeated, her eyes shimmering. "I like that."

"And keep in touch," Vicky said, "after all this is over. I can be a resource."

"Thanks," Orchid said, sounding moved. "I will."

"Okay, kids!" Garrett called from the stage. "It's ten A.M. Circle up!"

"Let's hit it." Vicky got up, extending the teenager a hand.

Smiling, Orchid took it, rising up.

22.

AFTER REHEARSALS ENDED, VICKY FIGURED SHE AND DYLAN would ride back to Jazz's together, but Dylan had other plans. They were heading to Hudson to hang up show flyers in a few local businesses and check out another retail space for Marlowe. None of the locations so far had *the right vibe*.

Vicky leaned against Dylan's Jeep as they unlocked it, shielding her eyes from the blazing afternoon sun. "I can come with you," she offered. "Two heads are better than one."

"Mmmm—say *head* again." Dylan tugged Vicky close with a grin. "And *come*."

Vicky giggled, letting Dylan nip at her neck for a few seconds before pushing them back—no need to go overboard. "Keep it in your pants, Rogers." She cleared her throat, heading around the passenger side to open the door. "Let's check it out together, then grab a drink. My treat."

Dylan shrugged, all loose limbs and give-no-fucks. "Whatever you want, babe."

Babe. Hmm. Sounded a bit couply. But then again, Dylan was an equal opportunity flirt. They probably called Deborah "babe." They probably called *Clyde* "babe."

"Let's motor," Vicky said, getting in and shutting the door.

• • •

THE PAIR STUCK up a dozen show flyers in and around Hudson's noticeably busier cafés and shops. While local interest was vital, everyone knew it was equally important that nonlocals knew about the fundraiser—nonlocals who might spread the word about Rhodes, and come back again and again.

When Vicky and Dylan were done, they drove to the retail space, which was a few blocks back from Hudson's main street. Dylan parked in front of what looked like a small, abandoned church. No stores in sight. "Where is it?" Vicky asked, climbing out.

"You're looking at it." Dylan gazed at the church, interest glimmering in their eyes. "The landlord'll meet us—he said it's unlocked."

Vicky followed Dylan up the steps to a wooden door that creaked open when Dylan gave it a push.

Inside, dust motes floated in the multicolored light streaming through the stained glass windows, creating a muted, ethereal glow across the old floorboards, which groaned beneath their feet. The space was mostly cleared, with a few old pews stacked in one corner, next to a collection of wrought iron candleholders and a pile of old hymn books. The smell of damp wood and smoky incense hung in the air.

Dylan spun in a slow circle, transfixed, their gaze drinking in every detail: The faded frescos on the stone walls. The vaulted ceiling crossed with ancient wood beams. The solemn, forgotten beauty.

Dylan's voice was reverent. "This is *incredible.* I can literally see the whole space! Displays here, and here." They began pointing, practically skipping around the old church. "Register here. We'd have room for a little coffee bar! Maybe keep the pews as seating? And we could use the stage for poetry readings and live music! Like a real community space!"

The front door creaked open again. Dylan hurried to introduce themself to the landlord, a gruff, older man in a tweed newsboy cap. "Needs a spit-polish," he rasped, "but there's nothing else like it in the neighborhood. Built in 1901."

"Wow." Dylan was brimming with excitement. "Back when they were built to last. What d'you think, Vee? Um, Vee?"

Vicky was busy examining a jagged crack snaking down from a window.

"What do you think?" Dylan called. "Amazing, right?"

Vicky strode back. Where to start? "There's mold up there." Vicky pointed to a patch of it near the ceiling.

The landlord looked surprised, at both the patch and Vicky's mention of it. "That's nothing. I'll paint over it myself."

"Totally." Dylan waved off Vicky's concern. "No big deal. I mean, look at this place! It has character. The kind of place that people will be psyched to discover, don't you think?"

"Will they discover it?" Vicky asked. "You're not on the main street. Less foot traffic means less walk-ins."

"That's what makes it cool. The right people will find us." Dylan admired the admittedly beautiful stained glass windows. "This is a *vibe.*"

Vicky raised a disbelieving brow. "They teach you that in your MBA?"

Dylan scoffed. "Don't be so cynical." They started pacing again, describing the vintage chairs they'd put in the corner, how they'd repurpose the candlesticks, the smell of fresh chocolate in the air.

Maybe she shouldn't say anything just yet. Dylan was having a moment. Vicky didn't want to burst their bubble.

The landlord looked her up and down, his tone dismissive. "What do you think, little lady?"

Vicky burst the bubble. She pointed again to the mold. "Well, old man, mold isn't something you can just paint over—it's a health and safety violation under New York State law. You're legally required to correct any conditions hazardous to health—including mold."

The landlord met Vicky's gaze with a huff. "Well, that's the first I'm hearing of that."

Vicky went on, striding toward the back of the building. "Also, under Section 1109 of the New York State Building Code, every public business requires accessible restrooms, clear path-of-travel signage, and compliant entryways. You don't have any of that, right?"

The landlord's face began to darken. He pulled his cap off his head, looking around with a mixture of annoyance and confusion. "It's an older building."

Vicky gave him a patient, steely smile. "Which is not exempt from safety codes just because it hasn't been updated. You're leasing to a new business, which means you're obligated to meet those standards, regardless of prior use."

Dylan's shoulders drooped. "Maybe it's worth fixing? I could split the costs . . . ?" They glanced uncertainly at the landlord.

"As long as you have a budget in the tens of thousands to get everything up to code," Vicky said, pointing to some peeling paint. "Including that lead paint. New York State Law mandates that any chipping paint in pre-1978 buildings be tested for lead. Plus, under the state's Lead Poisoning Prevention Act—"

"Okay, okay," Dylan interrupted, sounding bewildered. Then, to the red-faced landlord, "We'll think about it."

The landlord mumbled something about them "seeing themselves out," shutting the front door behind him.

Vicky inhaled a careful breath, preparing herself for Dylan's disappointment, even annoyance. After all, she'd invited herself along on this inspection, and in her experience, not everyone responded with gratitude to bad news, even if it was, objectively, helpful and important. "It's just, you deserve a space that's legally secure, not a liability waiting to—"

She was cut off by the warm, urgent feeling of Dylan's lips, kissing her square on the mouth for a long, luscious beat.

"—happen," Vicky finished, after Dylan pulled back. She blushed a little, not used to this sort of thanks in this sort of situation. "I thought you might be pissed."

"Pissed? Dude. That was hot." Dylan ran their hands up and down Vicky's arms, gazing at her with a new sort of wonder. "I've never seen you in action before. You probably just saved my butt."

"I definitely saved your butt," Vicky said, snaking her hands around Dylan's waist. "It's a butt worth saving."

Dylan grinned, eyes flashing like tossed emeralds. They cupped Vicky's face to kiss her again, then gazed into her eyes with a surprising depth of emotion. "I like having someone to look after, who also looks after me." They nibbled her earlobe, speaking low and warm. "Me and you and your differently sized earlobes. We're sort of a good team, don't you think?"

Vicky froze. A hard knot of fear tightened in her chest. Deep down, Vicky *did* think they made a good team but that was a feeling she could *not* afford. She was *not* leaving Rhodes hung up on Dylan Rogers *again.* She made her voice light but firm. "Sorry to disappoint, but I don't team up with fuck boys."

Now it was Dylan's turn to stiffen. They let out a low, frustrated laugh, swearing under their breath. "Okay," they muttered, "this has gone on long enough." They stepped back, looking Vicky right in the eye, dead serious. "Vee. I'm *not* a fuck boy. I don't sleep around. I'm too busy building a business! Yeah, I hook up sometimes, but not like it's my job. And not with anyone else since you. Because you're not just . . . anyone."

Vicky's cheeks warmed even as she shook her head. "What? No, you basically said it yourself."

"No, *you* said it, and I didn't correct you." Dylan gave an embarrassed shrug, combing a hand through their hair. "I was kind of flattered."

A strange swell of emotion caught Vicky by surprise. Relief chased by something deeper. Darker. She resisted the urge to snap off a snarky reply. Instead, Vicky summoned her courage. "Then, we need to have an honest conversation," she said, "about what we're actually doing here."

Dylan nodded, apprehension tightening their face. It took them a long beat to speak. "Agreed."

VICKY AND DYLAN sat across from each other at Rock Around the Clock, both nursing sodas that were becoming lukewarm. The drive over had been quiet and quick, like trying to outrun a coming summer storm.

Dylan slouched way down in the vinyl booth, turning their glass in a slow, endless circle.

Vicky tried to tap into her professional skill set—to organize the facts, prepare a logical argument, keep emotion out of it. A Sisyphean effort. This was Dylan, after all.

Which was exactly why she needed to be honest.

"Look," she began, "we both know this isn't just"—she fluttered her hand—"a hookup. We have history."

Dylan nodded. "Yeah," they said softly. "We do."

"But we also know," Vicky went on carefully, "that this can't go anywhere. Be anything."

Dylan tipped their head, their tone not defensive, more questioning. "Because?"

Vicky ignored the quick thrill of their pushback, focusing on staying practical. "Because we live on different coasts. And I'm not doing some long-distance thing destined to fail."

"Long distance?" Dylan ran an uneasy hand through their hair.

Vicky could tell Dylan had not gotten that far in their thinking. "I guess you're right," they murmured.

"I'm not moving to L.A., and unless you've been busy cooking up some plan to relocate to New York . . . ?" Vicky dangled the question.

For one wild, unfiltered moment, she imagined Dylan casually making a grand romantic reveal: a canceled flight. A lease on a one-bedroom apartment. A plan.

But Dylan live-in-the-now Rogers just looked caught off guard. "Uh, no. Just been cooking . . . chocolate."

Vicky ignored her childish crush of disappointment. "Exactly. So this is . . . a summer fling," she said, testing the idea. "Right?"

Dylan flinched. Their brows drew down. "Yeah," they said in a teenage monotone. "Cool."

Vicky huffed annoyance, pushing both drinks out of the way and leaning across the table. "Hey," she said, "I don't want to feel like one of those annoying couples in movies where you're like, 'Jeez, all this drama would just be resolved by one honest conversation.' So, tell me how you're really feeling. What you're really thinking. We're not dumb teenagers anymore. You owe me that."

Dylan looked briefly shocked. "Yeah, you're right." They sat up a little, pushing their hair out of their eyes. "What I'm thinking is, this doesn't feel like a fling. This feels like something more." Dylan's expression became unguarded, their voice earnest. "I *like* you, Vee. I always have."

A dangerous amount of joy bubbled in Vicky's chest. The door to a new future cracked open. Dylan, waking up next to her in Manhattan, stark naked and sleepy-hot, the contents of their overnight bag strewn across the bedroom floor . . .

"But," Dylan went on, "if you want me to be honest . . ."

"I do," Vicky said, even as a warning flare went off in her stomach.

Dylan let out a very long breath. "I guess I don't think we'd actually make it."

The words hit like a sucker punch. Vicky worked hard to keep her voice neutral. "Why not?"

Dylan hesitated. "It's not that I don't believe in love. I've been in love. But in my experience, love doesn't last. Even true love, even big love. Maybe it's not supposed to." Dylan paused, gaze flicking toward the window. "Or maybe people don't know how to make it work."

Vicky sat back in the booth, stunned. "What—why—do you think that?"

"Apart from the fact that I'm still single?" Dylan puffed out a breath, leaning forward across the booth. "Okay, so, my dad used to have this old cuckoo clock. German, I think. Red and brown with these little green shutters, and a tiny painted bird that popped out every hour. He loved that thing. Like, *weirdly* loved it. Said it reminded him to be present or some shit."

Vicky listened, every muscle tense.

Dylan went on. "But then one day, the bird stopped coming out. It jammed; the chime got messed up. Started going off at all the wrong times. Dad kept it, though. Refused to get rid of it. He'd wind it every night, even though it didn't work. Then one day my mom threw it out. Tossed it. No warning. Like it was nothing. He was so upset." Dylan looked up at Vicky with a raw expression. "Maybe love is like a busted clock we keep winding, because we're too scared to admit it's already broken. Or that someone else might throw it away before we're ready to let go."

Vicky stared down at her soda, her throat tightening. She had the urge to say something—to tell Dylan that maybe love was fragile, but that didn't make it worthless. That maybe we still wind the clock because hope matters.

But what the hell did she know?

Dylan went on. "Sex with you is"—they let out a short laugh—"literally the best. I *really* like you." Dylan's gaze softened. "And some dumb romantic part of me wonders . . . if maybe . . ."

What? Vicky wanted to scream. *Some dumb romantic part of you wonders what?*

But then Dylan looked back, their expression firming up. "You're right. This is a fling. Summer fun. We don't let things get too emotional. That'll only make leaving harder. And it's already going to be hard."

Vicky went cold. This was exactly what she'd expected. Exactly what she didn't want to hear.

"What about you?" Dylan asked. "What's your take on love?"

Vicky blinked, feeling exposed. "What do you mean?"

"How did love end for you in the past?" Dylan asked.

Vicky chugged half her soda. "Love?"

Dylan frowned. "You have been in love, right? I mean, you're thirty-seven." They flicked her arm. "*So old,* remember?"

Vicky braced herself. This conversation may have been a terrible mistake. "I've had girlfriends. But, the truth is . . ." She glanced down at the space between them, her heart pounding with nerves. "Shit, not even my sisters know this."

"Know what?"

"I've never said 'I love you' to anyone," Vicky admitted. "Except once. To a cat."

Dylan's mouth fell all the way open. "You've never been in love?"

"I don't know! Maybe?" Vicky let out a strained, embarrassed laugh. "You don't get it—growing up, my parents *never* said 'I love you.' Not to each other, not to me, not to my sisters. They did love us, I think . . . but they showed it by doing things for us. Like, giving us food and rides and money. But words?" Vicky let out a dry laugh. "Nope. So, I guess that's why. I mean, if no one's ever said it to you, how do you know how, or when, or why, to say it yourself?"

Dylan was still wide-eyed. "But has anyone ever said it to you? Like an ex?"

Vicky nodded miserably.

"What'd you say back?" Dylan asked.

Vicky made a *sheesh* face. "That I needed to pee. Which I did. Too much sangria."

Dylan laughed, a shocked, charmed laugh. They reached across the table to take Vicky's hand with an affectionate smile. "Oh, *honey.*"

"Shut up!" Vicky shot back, even as she folded her fingers into Dylan's, squeezing tight.

"Sounds like neither of us are very good at love," Dylan said.

Far from it being upsetting, the idea felt oddly generous. Vicky was expecting fuck-boy Dylan to mock her romantic inexperience. Instead, Dylan seemed not just to understand, but to feel a little kinship. "Yeah," Vicky agreed. "We suck."

Dylan laughed. "Maybe that'll make this easier—we're on the same page. We fuck like dirty little sluts for the rest of the month, then after the show, shake hands like gentlemen and bid each other adieu."

Deep down, Vicky knew it wouldn't be that simple. That feelings were already involved—neither was even pretending otherwise. But she truly was so inexperienced in this whole love thing—maybe she could compartmentalize. Keep emotion out of it, like she did at work. "Sounds like a plan," Vicky said. "But maybe you shouldn't call me honey. That might be confusing."

Dylan smiled, their thumb sliding over the back of Vicky's hand. "Deal. I won't call you honey."

Instantly, the potential absence of this pet name made Vicky feel like she'd lost something. No one ever called her honey. "I said *maybe* you shouldn't," she backtracked. "Maybe it's okay. But only until you leave. And all this sexual insanity is . . . over."

Dylan let out a short sigh. Their eyes became a little sad as they gazed at Vicky. "Whatever you want, honey."

Vicky knew she should pull her hand back, move the conversation on. Or just go home and fuck until she couldn't think at all. But she just stayed there, in their booth, holding hands with Dylan Rogers. Pretending she wasn't absolutely terrified of the crushing loss to come.

23.

Thirteen days till the show

WHEN THEIR ALL-CAST REHEARSAL WRAPPED LATE ON SUNDAY afternoon, Annie hurried out of the theater to go meet Sal for an overdue catch-up. Kat was at the far end of the foyer, taping up a poster.

Annie hesitated. Lola, Vicky, and Dylan had all taken on mentor roles with the teens, helping them learn lines or offer advice. Annie hadn't.

She had the urge to sneak out—happy hour with Sal was calling—but that seemed spineless. So Annie made her feet walk over, aiming for casual. "Kat."

Kat glanced up. "Stinky Soupy Annie."

"Ha!" Annie squirmed. She scanned Kat's handmade flyer.

⚠ JOIN US FOR A
POST-SHOW POLITICAL DIALOGUE ⚠

TOPIC: Decoding Gender, Power, and Capitalism in *Rosencrantz and Guildenstern Are Dead*

🧠 Hamlet as Late-Stage Capitalism's
Most Exhausted Employee

🪶 No Hetero: A Bi-Curious Reading of Act Two

🎭 The Role of Clowning
in Resisting Neoliberalism

💀 Death as Metaphor for Corporate Burnout

PLUS: Q&A on problematic language in the
original 1966 text, with optional zine swap.

"The personal is political. The dramaturgical is political. Honestly, everything's *political."*
-Kat Goldman

"Wow," Annie said. "That's . . . a lot of big ideas."

"Well, theater has a long history of being a meaningful form of anti-capitalist praxis." Kat squinted at Annie. "How do you resist?"

Annie blinked. She wasn't sure Kat would be impressed by voting and composting. "Um. Well, I did once protest a twelve-dollar smoothie."

Kat looked interested. "You organized a rally?"

"No. I just . . . never went back."

"Oh." Kat zipped up her bag with a soft snort. "Gotta run. Mr. Pickles awaits."

"Mr. Pickles is your . . ."

"Pit mix." Kat held up a hand. "And before you ask, no, he's not 'aggressive.' Pit mixes are actually—"

"One of the most misunderstood breeds!" Annie finished, excited.

Kat paused. "Wait, you like dogs?"

"Dude!" Annie exclaimed, "I own a dog-grooming salon! *Dogs* are *life*!"

Kat thumped her forehead. "That's right! Sorry, I forgot. I love dogs, too. I'm obsessed with that TikTok account where they dress them up like historical figures."

"Shut up! Have you seen Napoleon? The corgi in a velvet cape?"

"Yes! And the Frida Kahlo Frenchie? I cried actual tears."

They both cracked up laughing.

"That's it," Annie declared. "After I'm back at work, you have to come by the salon to meet my favorite regular. Harvey's a pit mix who thinks he's a show dog. You'll die."

"I'd love that." Kat gave her an approving nod. "It's cool you have your own business. Less mediocre white men at the top, y'know?"

Annie nodded back in agreement. "Absolutely."

Stepping out into the balmy late afternoon, Annie felt lighter. Self-assured. Proud.

She might not have a manifesto or an anti-capitalist zine collection. But she cared. She showed up. She tried to make a difference.

And after years of wondering if that was enough—if she was enough—she was finally starting to believe she could be.

OVER A ROUND of happy hour margaritas at the town's only Mexican joint, The Spicy Cactus, Annie told Sal everything: the Big Lie of the past, the unveiling of said lie last week, and the sexy, simmering tension between her and Lola.

"Maybe it's not totally over between us." A bubbly, giddy excitement filled Annie's chest at the confession. She expected Sal to squeal or beg for more details. Encourage Annie to make a move.

But instead, her best friend's expression became frighteningly . . . delicate. "What are you hoping happens?"

"Honestly? I'm hoping she sticks her tongue down my throat."

Sal didn't laugh. His concern deepened. "Is that a good idea? From the sounds of it, Lola means a lot to you."

Annie frowned, licking margarita salt off her fingertip. "Are you saying I should stick my tongue down the throat of someone who means nothing to me?"

"I'm saying you should stick your tongue down the throat of someone you can actually date."

A flicker of annoyance sparked in Annie's chest. "With the caveat that it's ridiculously early to even be talking about this since we haven't even hooked up yet—"

"*Yet?*" Sal arched a brow.

"—Lola and I live in the same state," Annie finished. "New York City's only a train ride away."

"But do your lives actually fit together?"

The annoyance sharpened. Annie wasn't prepared to defend her crush. "They're fitting pretty well now. We're together all the time."

"On summer vacation," Sal pointed out. "Doing the play. But after that's over . . . then what? And *technically,* she's fitting into your life, here, where you live. Do you think you can fit into hers? Do you even know what that life is?"

A server checked to see if they wanted another round, but happy hour was over, and Annie couldn't afford a full-price cocktail.

Not something she wanted to think about when defending her crush on able-to-afford-anything-on-the-menu Lola.

Her response came out sharper than she intended. "Are you saying I'm not good enough for her?"

"I'm saying I don't want you to get hurt." Sal's eyes didn't leave Annie's. "It's obvious you have real feelings for her. Before you take things further, just be sure there's a world where this works long-term and you have a future. Not a future heartbreak."

Annie left The Spicy Cactus in an irritated funk. It sounded like Sal *did* think Annie wasn't a match for Lola, and that Annie *wasn't* good enough for her. But striding up Henry Street toward the small business *she* built, in a town she had *real and meaningful* roots in, Annie felt a surge of self-confidence. Why couldn't she and Lola work? Why wouldn't Lola pick her? She sent hilarious handmade birthday cards. Baked a legendary pumpkin bread for her neighbors every fall. Was the sort of plus-one who didn't need to be taken care of at parties—she could handle herself! She, Annie Elizabeth Lightfoot, *was awesome.*

What Annie realized last week at the mini-mingle had stuck—questioning things was easier than doing something. She'd spent so much time processing and pondering and debating. It was time to *do.*

Lola picked up on the fourth ring, sounding close and slightly breathless. "Hi!"

"Do you wanna go on a hike with me?" Annie blurted into the phone. "Short hike—more like a stroll. Nature stroll. To a water hole. Swim optional. Tomorrow, on our day off."

A pause. Annie held her breath.

Maybe she'd misinterpreted things. Maybe this was a mistake. Maybe Lola was suddenly realizing Brett Burns *was* her celebrity crush, and, given they were both celebrities, why didn't she just call him right now, invite *him* on a celebrities-only nature stroll—

"I'd love that," Lola replied. Then, with certainty, "It's a date."

Annie imagined her heart putting a DO NOT DISTURB sign on each of its four chambers and taking the rest of the night to recover.

Sal didn't know what he was talking about.

THE NEXT MORNING, Annie picked Lola up from Jazz's at just after eleven. It was already eighty-five degrees when Lola climbed into the passenger seat of Annie's yellow Bug. Her outfit was the most casual Annie had seen all month: blue cutoffs, white tank, and a baseball cap embroidered with *Tell Me Your Story.* The smell of lemongrass and sunscreen filled the car.

Lola pulled the door shut and smiled at Annie. "Hi."

"Hi." Annie smiled back, bewitched.

They found an oldies station and hummed along to some throwbacks. When "Bennie and the Jets" came on, Annie turned it up. They both belted along—*Bennie! Bennie! Bennie and the Jets*—as sunlight flickered through the trees.

The drive didn't take long. Annie parked near a gate, hung with a sign that read THE MCCORMACKS: PRIVATE PROPERTY. "It's my friends' land," she explained, hauling a backpack from the trunk. "And they're away this week. So we should have it all to ourselves."

"Perfect." Lola arched her back, stretching, and Annie tried not to notice the outline of her equally perfect breasts, straining under the white tank top. "Cute sunglasses," Lola added, nodding at Annie's heart-shaped ones. "Well—you always look cute."

It wasn't spoken in a platonic, girls-complimenting-girls way. There was a sizzle underneath that heated the already sticky August air. "Thanks for noticing," Annie replied, coquettish, pulling the trunk shut.

"Oh, I've noticed." Lola came closer, then closer still. For a brief, head-spinny moment, Annie thought she was leaning in for a kiss, before Lola scooped up the backpack at Annie's feet. "I'll get this."

"It's heavy," Annie protested.

Lola waved her off, swinging it easily onto her back. Her biceps and several other muscles Annie could not name rippled beneath taut golden skin. Lola looked impressively strong.

"If you're going to insist on packing everything, I'm going to insist on carrying everything," Lola said, with no room for argument.

"Okay." Pleased, Annie fished out the gate's key from under a rock and pushed it open. "You are super ripped right now. Not letting you show it off would be a crime unto itself."

Lola chuckled. "From *Saturn Rising,*" she said, following Annie through the open gate. The scent of pine and earth filled the air as they stepped onto the trail, the gate clinking softly shut behind them. They set off up a path that snaked alongside a trickling stream. Lola went on, "And I sort of like . . ." She flicked her gaze to Annie, looking a little abashed.

"Sort of like what?" Annie asked.

"Is it terribly 1950s of me to admit that I sort of like carrying the heavy bags?" Lola asked. "Although, if you wanted to carry them," she added, "I have no problem with that."

Annie's cheeks warmed. She knew she was smiling more than the moment called for. "Interest in carrying a heavy bag is a zero," she said. "And, I didn't know that about you. You like a more masc role?"

"To be honest, I don't really know," Lola said, her sneakers snapping some twigs underfoot. "But I guess it was something I always struggled with in my straight relationships. I never liked 'being the girl.' I hated feeling like that meant I could and couldn't do certain things. Even just the way a waiter would offer tasting wine to a male date or assume that he's going to pay, when I might know more about wine or make more money. It didn't make sense to me."

"I think that's it exactly," Annie said. "When I'm dating someone, it's more about our preferences and strengths, as far as who does what. Like, with Harriet, my ex, she knew about wine, so she did the taste. I'm more a *yup, tastes like wine, put it in my mouth* girl."

"I like the idea that, in a queer relationship, you get to reinvent so many things," Lola said a touch wistfully, pausing to lift a low branch for Annie to duck under, the air thick with the scent of wildflowers and a chorus of cicadas. "You get to write your own script, to use a very on-brand metaphor."

Annie's laugh was a little breathless. It was thrilling to be talking in this way, so openly and honestly about dating and preferences. It didn't feel like there were any walls between her and Lola anymore; rather, it felt like they were circling each other, wondering who was going to make the first move.

Annie decided to be bold. "So, *theoretically*, if you *were* dating a woman," she said, "who'd take out the trash, you or her?"

Lola glanced over, an excited smile flashing onto her face. "I do the trash, you do the recycling? I mean, *she* takes out the recycling," Lola amended quickly, her cheeks flushing pink. "And, uh, I take out the trash."

A trickle of sweat slipped down Annie's back. "What about vacations—are you the here's-a-link-to-our-full-itinerary-I-have-the-passports-snacks-and-compression-socks or the one who jumps in the car asking where we're going?"

Lola laughed. "Spreadsheet fiend, guilty as charged. You?"

"Spontaneous girlie slash terrible planner, equally guilty," Annie admitted. "But fun in the moment! And I can roll with anything."

"I'm sure," Lola said. "Ooh, I have one: dishwasher. Do you stack it like a Swedish scientist or just chuck everything in and hope for the best?"

Annie considered this. "Probably a pinch more chuck-it-in reckless, but I'm not a monster. You?"

"A pinch more Swedish scientist," Lola said, "but also not a monster."

"Then hey, this just might work," Annie joked.

Lola glanced over, her smile turning inquisitive. "Yeah," she said, "it might."

Annie's heart thumped so loudly it drowned out the cicadas. She couldn't parse the exact tenor of Lola's last line; if Annie had taken it too far by suggesting, albeit accidentally, that they *date*. On their first date. If this was a date. Lola was still going back to her big, bold New York life at the end of all this. The point was just to enjoy the moment, not start planning an impossible future.

Annie pointed to the clearing coming up ahead. "We're almost there."

The stream next to them fed into a sunny water hole, fringed by lush trees and plants, the underbrush dense with ferns and wildflowers. The water sparkled like liquid glass. A lone dragonfly skimmed the surface, breaking the stillness. It was the sort of idyllic Upstate swimming hole that'd typically be teeming, but today, luxuriously, they had it all to themselves.

They climbed up onto a flat, sun-dappled rock that jutted out over the water. Annie spread out two colorful, mismatched towels. "Eat or swim first?" she asked.

Lola was already unbuttoning her cutoffs. "Swim."

Annie watched, mesmerized, as Lola shucked off her tank top and cutoffs, revealing a skimpy white bikini. Lola's body was insane—powerful, lean.

"You look like . . . a sports car," were the words that fell out of Annie's mouth.

Lola laughed, moving with grace to the lip of the rock. "Oh yeah?" She raised a cheeky brow. "Wanna go for a ride?"

Before Annie could muster a response, Lola dived in, arrowing elegantly into the water. She resurfaced, her platinum blond hair slicked to her skull. "C'mon." She gestured with a grin, water droplets arcing off her hand like scattered jewels. "Come in!"

Annie yanked off her clothes so quickly, she got tangled in her T-shirt. Her own two-piece was less cover-of-*Sports-Illustrated*—she didn't think they typically featured funky graphic prints and full butt coverage—but she felt cute enough, and the halter neck top made her boobs look good. Holding her nose, Annie jumped.

The water was a delicious cold shock. Annie let herself sink for a few weightless moments before kicking up to the surface, emerging into the warm air. The sun was right in her eyes, blinding her. When Annie refocused, Lola was treading water, six feet away. A bobbing, beautiful blond head. "Amazing, right?" Lola called.

Annie nodded, every cell in her body shining bright. "Perfect."

The only other sound was birds twittering in the treetops. They splashed around, ducking and diving. Beneath the surface, Annie watched Lola's body move with the fluidity of a sea creature, poetic and otherworldly.

They ended up on their backs, floating on the surface, limbs starfished, eyes half closed. But rather than feel relaxed, Annie's entire body was pulsing, invisible forces urging her toward Lola. She wanted to roll on top of her, pressing their mouths together as they sunk to the murky bottom, because what was death but another great adventure?

Annie climbed out first, drying off then setting out the epic picnic lunch she'd spent all morning preparing: a tomato and caramelized onion galette; whipped feta dip with crunchy homemade crackers; green goddess salad; quick pickled cucumbers; fresh lemon bars from *The Moosewood Cookbook;* two bottles of beer, still cold.

She picked her way over to the sun-warmed rocks to their towels, easing down to lie on her belly. Moments later, Lola was kneeling down beside her, droplets of water falling onto Annie's back. "Cold!" Annie squealed, giggling, as Lola flicked a few extra drops.

Lola lay on her side next to Annie on the other towel, head propped up to face her. It felt like being in bed together, side by side, close enough to touch. Their afternoon stretched out before them, endless in time and in possibilities.

For the first time since Lola Wilson had returned to Rhodes, Annie let herself stare, falling without a safety net into Lola's dark gold eyes. She'd never thought much about eyes being the window to one's soul, but now, the old phrase took on new meaning. Annie imagined climbing through that window, left open just for her, to explore at leisure the inner workings of Lola's being. An exploration she would never tire of.

A smile flickered dreamily over Lola's mouth. Her gaze moved down Annie's body, pausing in surprise on her side. "You have a tattoo."

Four delicate words inked in old-fashioned cursive. *Always with you, darling.*

"Gran's handwriting," Annie said. "From my last birthday card."

Lola traced the words with her fingertip. The touch made Annie shiver in pleasure, the sensation gushing hot inside her. "It's beautiful," Lola said. Her fingers slid slowly up, tracing up Annie's side, skating over her décolletage, to land on the side of her face, one thumb touching Annie's cheek. Lola's words were soft but certain, her gaze awed. "You're beautiful, Annie."

All thoughts of the picnic, the play, the rest of the world—everything vanished. There was only this: Lola Wilson's fingers cupping her face, sweet words on her breath, her body agonizingly too far away.

Annie tipped her chin up, filled with a sudden urgency. It had all been leading to this. "If you don't kiss me right now, I think I might die."

A wondrous smile bloomed on Lola's face. She inched closer until their bodies were touching, damp, warm flesh pressing together.

Annie slid her hand into Lola's wet hair, pulling her close. Their breath intermingled, mouths a millimeter apart. Then Lola's lips touched Annie's own, soft and insistent, and it felt like coming home to a place Annie had never been before. A sun-spangled sensation of strange and familiar, of entirely new and something beloved rediscovered. Lola was half on top of Annie, miles of skin rubbing and sliding. Lola's mouth moved with certainty against Annie's, kissing her deeply, their tongues brushing. Annie let out a soft, needy moan. Lola responded with authority, one hand braced by Annie's head, the other tugging her chin down for an even deeper kiss that made Annie feel like a spotlight switching to full power. It was the giddy high of stepping onstage, the gratifying sound of an audience laughing, the brief and wonderful pleasure of accepting applause.

"Oh, Lollie." The gasp slipped out of its own accord.

Lola lifted her head, panting, her hazel eyes a brilliant gold. "God, I love it when you call me that."

"You do?" Annie was desperate both for their mouths to be back on each other and for every word Lola wanted to dole out.

"I do," Lola said, her voice a low rasp. "Because only you call me that."

Lola's lips moved down the curve of Annie's neck, her teeth scraping the sensitive skin of her throat. Annie groaned, unable and unwilling to stop her noises of need. Lola's breasts slid against Annie's arms, her nipples hard and tight beneath the scrap of her luscious white bikini. That Lola was turned on made Annie feel even more wild.

"I've wanted you for so long." Annie was delirious, unaware if she was whispering or shouting the words. "I've never not wanted to kiss you."

Lola's tongue was on her ear, sucking an earlobe. "Me too," she panted, catching Annie's gaze for a searing heartbeat before kissing Annie, long and deep, again and again and again.

They rolled around on the rocks, getting caught up in the towels, laughing and kissing until Annie felt like every part of her was flung wide open. Why had she ever resisted this? What was there to be afraid of?

Kissing Lola was like chugging ice-cold lemonade in the dead heat of summer. It was the slippery, sexy feeling of beads of salty sweat sliding down her back. It was the moment you step out of a darkened cinema into a sun-drenched afternoon, disorientated but happy, crossing the threshold between worlds like a carefree god.

But Annie wasn't crossing a threshold anymore. She was already on the other side.

24.

Eleven days till the show

FOR LOLA WILSON, IT COULDN'T BE CLEARER: LOVE WAS ON-stage at the Rhodes Playhouse.

It was in the way Jazz called *Good morning, thespians!* when she pushed open the theater doors, her enthusiasm and faith in the cast kicking off another day under hot stage lights.

It was in the way everyone listened to Lola's ideas and offered their own suggestions, never once dismissing proceedings as *just community theater,* but elevating their discussions into something of utmost importance.

It was in the way they did silly warm-up exercises with gusto, passing focus with Zip Zap Zop or embodying animals on Jazz's commands—roaring lions, swinging monkeys, gamboling puppies. Clyde, on all fours, earnestly mooing like a cow was a sight Lola would treasure forever.

Most pressingly, though, love was Annie Elizabeth Lightfoot.

The girl who Lola was inexorably, uncontrollably, unrestrainedly falling for. Again.

Lola barely slept a wink after their water hole date.

The next day, she'd arrived at the theater a bundle of nerves. Sitting alone in the green room, Lola spiraled into worry.

Maybe Annie regretted crossing the line. Maybe things would be awkward or noticeably weird. Lola had never had a crush on a co-star, let alone spent an entire afternoon rolling around with them in a swimsuit. What had she done?

She flinched when someone touched her shoulder. Annie, in a brightly patterned playsuit, holding a yellow wildflower. "Penny for your thoughts," she said with a cautious smile. "Or, this?" She held out the flower.

"For me?" Lola got to her feet, charmed. Companies sometimes sent her arrangements, some worth hundreds, even thousands of dollars. None meant as much as this simple flower.

"It's yellow, which I'm just remembering means friendship," Annie began to babble, "but don't read anything into that, like, *Oh, Annie just wants to be friends.* I mean, I *do* want to be friends, but I also want to do this." Stretching on her tiptoes, she brushed her lips against Lola's, warm and eager.

Lola closed her eyes in relief, sinking blissfully into the kiss. The worries in her head calmed. Her hands slid down Annie's back, pressing them closer. Annie's fingers curled around the nape of Lola's neck. A low, hungry sound escaped the back of Annie's throat, making Lola feel a little bit crazed. The theater slid away and there was only Annie—her soft mouth, her pulsing need, her sweet, summer smell.

Was there anything hotter than kissing a girl?

Annie's eyes shone in the low light, lips lifted in a smile. "So, Lollie. It appears we are kissing."

"It appears we are."

Annie stayed close, her fingers curling around a lock of Lola's hair. She smelled like ripe cherries, sweet and just a little tart. "I wasn't sure if yesterday was a one-off."

The honesty in Annie's voice undid her. No curated aloofness, no games—just Annie, speaking her heart out loud. It wasn't just attractive. It was rare.

"I don't want it to be a one-off," Lola said, skimming a hand down Annie's cheek.

Annie smiled at the touch. "Me neither."

Noise from the main space—laughter and chatter. The rest of the cast. The play.

Annie edged back. "We should probably . . . y'know."

Lola understood. Broadcasting their brand-new romance wasn't how either of them rolled. And Lola couldn't afford to let her growing feelings spill onto the stage—not when the whole production depended on her and Annie's focus.

AS THE THIRD week of rehearsals kicked into gear, Lola tried not to melt when the characters held each other's gaze. Swoon when Annie as Rosencrantz touched her. Giggle too much at Annie's comic timing. But as soon as the final note for the day was given, the last stage light turned off, Lola couldn't get to Annie's apartment fast enough.

They kissed in doorways. On the soft L-shaped sofa. Pressed against windows, against walls—legs hooked around hips, fingers twisted in hair, whispering stupefied, sweet things. *How are you so pretty? You feel so good. I can't stop kissing you.*

On Wednesday night, it rained. Not a polite summer sprinkle, a raucous booming downpour. Rehearsals let out early, and they ran, squealing, through the parking lot, soaked before they hit the car. At Annie's apartment, they peeled off wet clothes, skin warm from laughter and something more electric. Annie fetched mismatched pajamas—Lola got a threadbare tee with a faded Groom Room logo. They ate microwave popcorn in bed, legs tangling under the covers, *Show Me Love* playing on the laptop. They kissed lazily throughout, the softest kind of kissing. The kind that could go on forever.

Lola had acted in two films with sex scenes, where her characters stormed into bedrooms, clothes flying off. But this first week back with Annie wasn't about urgency—it was about savoring every single second.

ON THURSDAY EVENING, Lola met with Jazz in her office to finalize the lighting design. "I want that cold, moonlit feel for the graveyard scene," Jazz said. "Sort of surreal, like the characters are trapped in limbo."

"What about some deep blue gels," Lola suggested, seeing it clearly in her mind's eye. "And if we throw in a harsh white from upstage, we'll get some long, eerie shadows. Like the light's trying to pull the characters forward, but they're stuck where they are."

Jazz nodded with enthusiasm and Lola was reminded, again, of how much she loved directing. She typically felt like window dressing. Now she wasn't just decorating a house, she was helping build it.

The quartet was meeting for dinner at Rock Around the Clock. Lola wanted to change at Jazz's before they did.

Hurrying into her bedroom in the attic, Lola found a FedEx box sitting on her bed. Inside it, a dress bag.

At first Lola assumed it was her costume for the play, delivered in a surprisingly formal way.

Unzipping the bag, Lola held up what amounted to a few scraps of slinky black material and a pair of vicious heels. Her outfit for the *Saturn Rising* premiere. Her other life. Her real life. The thought landed like a stone, sinking deep in her guts.

Stepping into the dress felt like returning to a job she'd spectacularly, unequivocally quit. The blonde in the mirror looked svelte, deadly—an assassin with a gun strapped to her thigh. The blonde in the mirror was on magazine covers in Japan and ate carbs only every other Sunday. The blonde in the mirror was a stranger whose name Lola could not place.

How had she survived so long in a life that looked so perfect but felt so hollow? How had she spent so long being admired by many but touched by no one?

Lola hated the dress.

Shoving it in the back of her closet, she yanked on her regular clothes. And yes, *there* was someone she knew. There was someone she liked. The girl in the mirror wore jeans and a baseball cap. No heels. No gloss. No armor. For the first time in years, Lola liked what she saw.

Not a movie star. Just a girl who wanted to keep kissing Annie Lightfoot and find out what might happen if she risked everything.

NOT LONG LATER, the quartet was back at Rock Around the Clock, electing to wait a few minutes for their booth to be free rather than take any of the other open tables.

Lola posed for a few selfies with eager locals while the others loaded up the jukebox with aughts throwbacks. After they sat and put in their orders, "Take Me Out" by Franz Ferdinand came on. "*I want you to take me out,*" all four sang along, enthusiastic and—with the exception of Vicky—tuneless.

"Oof." A slouchy Dylan pretended to wince, touching their ear. "Lucky we're not doing a musical."

"Nope. Straight plays for us," Lola said, hearing the expression for nonmusical theater anew as she said it. "I mean, straight plays, starring a gaggle of gays."

Next to her, Annie giggled. "A gaggle of gays," she repeated, gazing at Lola, chin on one hand. "You're funny, Lollie."

The way she said it—like she meant it, like it mattered—made

Lola feel seen. As if the person she was in Rhodes, the one who laughed freely and ate carbs whenever she wanted, might be the real her.

Lola wanted to tell Annie that *she* was the funny one. The cute one. The adorably goofy and extremely kissable—

"Okay," Vicky announced from the other side of the booth. "I'll say it." She waggled a fingertip between them. "*Obviously,* you guys are smushing."

Lola froze, surprised to be sprung. Then, not. She glanced at Annie, ready to take her lead.

Annie blushed, a smile on her lips. She gave Lola an *I'm game if you are* shrug. "Guess so," Annie hedged.

"Yes," Lola said, folding her fingers into Annie's. "We are."

"Welcome to the second chance romance club." Dylan slung a lazy arm around Vicky's shoulder, their dark brown hair flopping over one eye. "Vicky is already back in love with me."

Vicky's eyes popped wide. She elbowed them off with a shocked laugh. "Shut up! This is a *fling,* remember?"

Dylan's jaw tightened, their grin becoming a grimace. Then they rolled their eyes with a theatrical groan. "How can I forget?"

Lola could see the effort behind the pretense—the way Dylan's hand lingered on Vicky's shoulder before pulling it away, the way Vicky's gaze went soft. They were both playing it a bit too cool.

Lola glanced at Annie. Is that what she thought this was, too—a fling? With an expiration date?

It didn't feel like a fling. It felt deliberate. Like they were building something—not just for the summer, but for the long haul.

"I am *not* in love," Vicky said, still protesting. "She's fucking with me! Sorry, *they're,* um, fucking with me."

Even though she'd recovered quickly, no one missed Vicky misgendering Dylan.

"Sorry," Vicky said, sheepish. "I truly don't think of you as a girl, in my head. It just slipped out."

Dylan's smile was pained. "I get it. Don't love it, but I get it."

"I really am sorry," Vicky repeated, softer this time.

Dylan blew out a breath. "Well, no one's perfect. Except eighties-era Susan Sarandon." They nudged her. "I know you're trying."

Relief flooded Vicky's face. "Thanks, babe." She tugged her left earlobe. Dylan tugged theirs in return.

An inside joke. Lola and Annie exchanged a smile, but there was something uncertain about it. Even though Vicky and Dylan were claiming this was a fling, they acted like an old married couple. Maybe, Lola thought, Annie was also aware of how fast the pair was moving. How, by comparison, she and Lola weren't.

Vicky reached for her soda. "So, when did it start?"

When did it start? Was it the moment Lola saw Annie soft-shoe shuffling over the Rhodes Playhouse stage? Lingering in Annie's doorway after Spaghetti à la Spontaneity and an almost kiss? Fireflies in the backyard? Flirting at movie night?

Or twenty years prior, in this very booth, after rehearsals of the same show they were doing right now?

"Right." Vicky intuited. "It's sort of been happening the whole time."

"Monday was a game changer," Annie offered, stirring her oat-milk shake.

Lola started in mild alarm. "I don't think we need to get into details."

"Really?" Annie looked surprised. "We used to go into details."

"As teenagers," Lola said, "with no boundaries."

"Dylan fingered me in the kitchen pantry during the mini-mingle," Vicky offered.

"*What?*" Lola and Annie both gasped.

Dylan groaned, red-faced, dropping their head into their hands. "Vee! Why'd you tell them that?"

"Annie wanted details," Vicky protested. "It was superhot; I got off."

"Vicky!" Dylan shouted.

"What?" Vicky shot back, giggly. "You're not the only one who gets to shock-jock. My sex drive is back, which is honestly a miracle because I was pretty much dead inside before coming back to Rhodes."

Well, Lola could relate to that.

Annie cleared her throat. "While we're spilling secrets, I have another: the real reason why Lola and I broke up, back in the day."

Lola listened as Annie explained the truth to Dylan and Vicky—the lie meant to save her, that drove her away.

Dylan whistled low. "Teenage heartbreak and moral sacrifice?"

Vicky raised her glass. "God bless queer chaos."

Lola smiled. "New policy. No more lies."

"No more lies," Annie repeated, smiling gratefully at her. "Starting right now, I will never again enter a pantry during a mini-mingle."

Their food arrived: burgers for Annie and Dylan, roast chicken salad sandwich for Lola, quinoa bowl for Vicky.

Lola took a bite of her sandwich, letting out a groan of satisfaction. "This is truly the perfect meal. It's roast chicken—"

On cue, the others joined in. "*It's salad, and it's a sandwich!*"

Lola laughed, savoring everything about this familiar-but-new Thursday night.

This time next month, she'd be back in Tribeca, in her empty loft. Dylan would be back in L.A., Vicky in a courtroom. And Annie . . . Annie would still be here, one hundred miles away. Separate lives. Separate worlds. The thought curled, cold and sharp, around her ribs.

When they were teenagers, the future was frustratingly beyond their fingertips. Growing up couldn't happen fast enough. Now Lola wanted to slow time down. Freeze it altogether. Suspend this flirty weeknight in the back booth of Rock Around the Clock for all time. Because now, the future was far too close and far too unknown. Lola wasn't just afraid of what she might lose—her momentum, her carefully curated path. She was afraid of what she might want.

Something lasting. Something rooted. Someone like Annie.

Far from it being the solution to her problems, Lola worried that the future might ruin everything.

25.

Eight days till the show

THE NEXT MORNING, DYLAN AWOKE TO AN ACHINGLY FAMILIAR spicy, floral scent. Vicky, in bed next to them. In her sexy silky teddy, she looked like a just-roused Disney princess. Dylan propped themself up on one elbow, skimming their fingers down her bare arm. "Hi."

Vicky gazed back. The typically sharp glint in her eyes was as soft as the morning light. "Hi," she whispered back.

Dylan dropped their mouth to kiss her, and it felt so sweet. So easy. A beloved recipe that always satisfied: banana pancakes sizzled in butter, served with warm maple syrup.

Kissing Vicky just felt right.

"I have morning breath," Vicky protested between kisses.

Dylan ignored this, dipping their tongue into Vicky's open mouth, feeling a flare of excitement at the way Vicky moaned softly, her hands tangling in their hair.

"We both have the day off," Dylan reminded her, trailing kisses along Vicky's jaw, "so let's do it like they do on the Discovery Channel."

Vicky giggled, running her fingertips up and down Dylan's biceps. "We have been doing it quite a bit." She ticked off her fingers. "The pantry. Your bed. My bed. Back seat of my car."

Dylan smiled at the recent memory of being on their knees in the passenger seat, eating Vicky out while blasting Chappell Roan. A fantasy fulfilled, even if the baiting refrain of *Is it casual now?* hadn't just been living rent-free in their head, it was threatening squatter rights.

This *was* casual, they reminded themself. Summer fling. No strings. Right?

Dylan stroked Vicky's arm. "Yeah, our list is solid but I wanna make you come with this." They reached into the bedside table drawer, pulling out their rainbow strap-on and leather harness, dangling it all with a curved eyebrow.

Vicky coughed a surprised laugh then narrowed her eyes playfully. "Sure you're not a fuck boy, Rogers?"

The heat of the moment cooled. Dylan dropped their gear back in the drawer, trying not to feel hurt.

What was happening this summer was special. Vicky was special.

Dylan decided to keep it light. "I like to be prepared. Fingers can only get you so far, y'know? But if dicks aren't your jam . . ."

"They are," Vicky said slowly. "But, I don't know."

"Why not?" Dylan asked. "And I don't mean that in a pushy way, I just mean, I wanna know what you want. What you like. How I can service you." They waggled their brows.

Vicky smiled back but there was something uncertain about it.

"What?" Dylan asked softly.

Vicky shrugged, fiddling with her teddy. "Fucking like that, literally letting someone inside me, is just—intense. Like, emotionally. I don't want to . . . get confused."

Dylan's pulse jumped even as they played clueless. "Confused how?"

Vicky exhaled sharply, eyes bright with emotion. "Isn't it obvious?"

Dylan froze. Was Vicky about to confess . . . feelings?

Vicky shook her head, the intensity of the moment deflating like a popped balloon. "Isn't it obvious, Rogers? I'm trying to protect myself . . . from . . . herpes. I'm negative and obviously you're not."

"Hey! I already told you I'm good to go!" Dylan protested, but Vicky was already sliding out of bed, saying she needed to pee.

Bummed, Dylan reached for their phone, scrolling through their work inbox. The first draft of the branding for Hot & Sweaty landed. Tapping open the PDF, Dylan felt a wave of excitement. The design's bright pops of red looked slick and sexy. Dylan was still tinkering with the final recipe, but it was close and once that was done, they couldn't wait to show everyone the final product. Especially Vicky.

Truthfully, it was all just for her.

A text slid in. From their mom. Looking forward to lunch! 1pm. Don't be late.

Dylan let out an annoyed sigh as Vicky came back into the room, scooping up her clothes from the fuchsia-pink carpet.

"What?" Vicky asked.

"Just Celine." Dylan tossed their phone back on the bedside table. "We're having lunch today."

Vicky looked surprised. "I thought you weren't gonna see her."

"She wore me down," Dylan said with a sigh. "My mother can be very . . . persuasive."

Vicky sat on the edge of the bed. "If you want, I can come with."

Dylan blinked, taken aback. "Why would you wanna do that?"

Vicky shrugged. "Because family is important, even if they suck. If it's bad, we'll bail."

Dylan was touched. And a tiny bit confused. Didn't Vicky want this to be a fling? Or was she offering as a friend? And did Dylan really want Vicky to see them devolve into a moody brat as they somehow always did around their mother? "I don't know, babe."

"Don't overthink it—it's just lunch. I'll bring wine." Vicky hooked a cheeky brow. "And I'll let you finger me in your childhood bedroom."

The thought lit Dylan up like a just-struck match. Their loins actually quivered. Game-changing suggestion. Dylan tugged Vicky back into bed, straddling her greedily. "I do want that. I want that *a lot.*"

"Thought you might." Vicky looked pleased with herself. "I'll drive."

"Sounds chill," Dylan said, though nothing about this felt chill. Especially not the hot girl under them, offering wine, a ride, and something dangerously close to love.

A FEW HOURS later, Dylan shifted uneasily next to Vicky on the doorstep of the Rogers family manor. Well, technically just Celine's manor—it was her family money; she'd kept the house. The estate loomed—a sprawling, three-story Georgian monstrosity. Sunlight gleamed off its pristine white columns and huge, dark windows, like a place too perfect to house anything human.

Dylan glanced at the wrought iron gate they'd passed through moments earlier, debating an escape route. "Is it too late to call everything off?" Dylan asked.

"It is," Vicky said, tossing her hair over one shoulder. She was in her blue-and-white seersucker shorts and a preppy matching jacket, her smooth legs elongated in wedge sandals. In her hands, flowers from Jazz's garden and, crucially, a bottle of white wine. "Just ring the damn bell."

Dylan fussed with their hair, their insides clenching so hard they might be sick. "It's so weird that I have to ring the doorbell to the home I grew up in. Like, *let me in to my own life.*"

"But this isn't your life anymore." Vicky swung to look Dylan in the eye. "You have a full, impressive life all your own. Your own business. Your own home. Your own hot fuck buddy, here for emotional and sexual support."

Dylan softened, reaching over to squeeze Vicky's arm. "C'mon, Vee. You know you're more than a fuck buddy." They stared deeply into Vicky's cat eye–lined eyes. "You're a friend, with *benefits*."

Vicky scoffed. "Fuck off."

"My side chick. My boo thang."

"Okay."

"My meal, with wheels." Dylan inclined their head. "Get it? Because you drove."

"Watch me die laughing," Vicky said dryly, reaching over to ring the doorbell.

Dylan sobered at the sound of the familiar three-chime bell. "Should we make a run for it?"

"Your maturity is astounding."

"Can you run in those shoes or should I throw you over my shoulder?"

"I'd love to see you try."

Before anyone could make a run for it, a humorless older woman in a starched blouse and skirt opened the front door.

"Uh, hi," Dylan said, momentarily caught off guard by who was most likely a new house manager. "I'm Dylan. The great disappointment of Celine Rogers's life."

Vicky elbowed them with *cool it* eyes, but the house manager just stepped aside, receiving Vicky's flowers and wine in a way that made Dylan suspect they'd see neither of them again.

The foyer was as grand and impressive as ever, all cold marble and elegant objets d'art. Small, modern sculptures sat in lit niches along the walls. The sweeping staircase, with its wrought iron balustrade and glossy wood handrail, spiraled upward toward Dylan's old bedroom, where they were already plotting to drag Vicky later. Some of the artwork was new, Dylan noted, as they followed the house manager past the formal dining room toward the kitchen.

Perhaps a bit more color and dynamism on the white walls, but maybe they were misremembering things.

The large, open-plan kitchen was at the rear of the property. It was separated from the backyard by a series of sliding doors, all of which could be opened in sunny weather. Dylan recalled Celine rarely making use of this functionality, claiming it let in too many bugs. Today, however, all the doors were opened, the afternoon's warmth and a few drowsy flies circling in the sunlit space.

A tall woman with a gray grown-out pixie cut stood by the kitchen island, arranging freshly cut flowers into a vase. Dylan assumed this woman in loose linen pants and a floral cotton blouse was the new gardener. So it was a jaw-dropping shock when the woman turned around and Dylan found themself looking into their mother's green eyes.

"Celine?" The greeting was a cough of surprise. They'd been expecting formal wear, not something out of *Home & Gardens*. Celine was *gray*. She was *barefoot*. Had Dylan ever seen their mother's feet?

"Darling. You came. I'm so glad." At least her voice was the same, that slightly enunciated posh-girl warble drummed in by years of boarding school. Celine moved closer, pausing a few feet away.

She looked, well, *her age*. Sixty-two, with lines around her eyes and sunspots on her cheeks. Was it possible she wasn't wearing any makeup? Celine always wore makeup. She wore it in the bath.

Dylan caught themself staring, getting flustered. "Yeah, well . . . I'll do pretty much anything for meatloaf." They thrust an awkward hand in Vicky's direction. "This is—"

"Vicky Fang, yes, of course I remember," Celine said, smiling with what appeared to be warmth. "How are you, Vicky? I believe you're a lawyer now?"

Vicky nodded. "Family law, in Manhattan. Your home is as lovely as ever, Mrs. Rogers."

"Oh, please, it's just Celine. And thank you for the flowers," she said, accepting them from the house manager with a "thank you, Louisa." Celine held the blooms to her nose. "Peonies—my favorite. Oh, and look at these gorgeous delphiniums."

When Dylan was growing up, the only flowers Celine permitted were austere lilies from the region's most expensive florist.

Celine began adding the colorful blooms to the larger bouquet, seeming to garner actual pleasure from doing so. "There's refreshments outside. Make yourselves comfortable and I'll be out in a tick."

ON THE SHADED back patio, Dylan chugged half a glass of white wine, eyes darting to take in even more changes. The manicured garden and symmetrical hedges of their youth had overgrown into something more natural—a wilder, lived-in beauty. The patio furniture was comfortable. There was a smudge on a fork. "Who is that woman and what has she done with my mother?" Dylan squinted suspiciously at the hors d'oeuvres and salad that didn't appear to be catered. "Do you think she's going to ask me for a kidney? Or reveal that Louisa is my sister?"

Vicky chuckled, sampling a tiny tart. "You said you haven't spoken in five years, right? That's a long time."

Dylan had changed a lot in the last five years: new start-up, new gender identity, newfound appreciation of pleated slacks. Slightly embarrassing to realize they'd assumed their mother would be exactly the same.

"Still," Vicky added. "Must be disorienting. My mom's still, like, in her factory settings."

Dylan chuckled and squeezed Vicky's knee. "I'm glad you're here, Vee. You're good in a crisis and you're incredibly hot."

Vicky gave Dylan a comforting smile. "And you're very sexy and incredibly needy."

Dylan laughed as Celine came out, carrying a ceramic pan with oven gloves. "Mom's Marvelous Meatloaf," she announced, placing it in the center of the table. "Careful, the pan's hot."

Vicky kept up polite chatter as Celine served them all a fat wedge of the savory loaf. It was almost disconcertingly good: perfectly seasoned, juicy ground meat and a tangy-sweet glaze that melted into the crispy edges. Delicious, as always, but also a sense-memory of being fifteen and furious to be forced into a dress.

Dylan chewed tensely, watching the two women discuss the play.

"I don't know if you remember Jazz Whitaker, our director," Vicky said to Celine, "but she has this whole plan to rebrand Rhodes as, like, a queer hotspot."

Dylan tensed, anticipating Celine's disapproval. But Celine nodded with interest. "Sounds like a great idea. If she needs any help, I'd be happy to roll up my sleeves." She gestured laughingly at a streak of soil on her arm. "As you can see, I don't mind getting dirty."

That was the final straw. Dylan let their fork clatter to the table. "What the hell is going on?"

"Rogers," Vicky warned them.

"No, really, what is happening?" Dylan pushed back a few inches, chair legs scraping over the flagstone. "You're not wearing shoes. You're gardening. You're not wearing makeup! You wear makeup to bed. You make the Marvelous Mrs. Maisel look like a homeless woman!"

"Dylan," Vicky said more sharply.

"It's okay, Vicky," Celine said. "Dylan's right. I've made a lot of changes." She let out a breath, looking calm and clear-eyed. "A cancer scare will do that to you."

Dylan froze. A chill raced through them. "A . . . what?"

Celine didn't flinch. "Stage one breast cancer. Sounded like a death sentence at first, even though my doctor assured me it wasn't.

They caught it early; I was incredibly lucky. Only one round of chemo, but even that knocked me off my feet."

"Chemo," Dylan repeated in horror. "You had *chemo*?"

Celine nodded. "I'd always thought of myself as strong—someone who could push through anything—but the fatigue, the nausea, the fear . . . It was humbling. And then there was the waiting. Waiting for scans, results, assurances that yes, the treatment worked. It felt like my whole life had been put on pause. But somehow, I came through it. I still do. Every day."

Dylan was speechless. Did their mother go through all that *alone*?

Vicky leaned forward to touch Celine's hand. "I'm so sorry."

"I was lucky," Celine repeated firmly. "Not everyone makes it back from the kingdom of the sick to the kingdom of the well. Certainly the worst year of my life. But, in another way, also the best."

"How so?" Vicky asked.

"Well, I realized every product I was using contained carcinogens." Celine gave a wry laugh before sobering and looking at Dylan directly. "It was a wake-up call. It made me want to be honest. Take *full responsibility* for everything in my life."

This sounded strangely loaded. Dylan frowned, unsure. "Meaning . . . ?"

Celine inhaled a breath. "Like being honest about why your father and I divorced."

"Huh?" Dylan blinked five times in a row, thrown. "Didn't it just, like . . . fizzle out?"

"No. I know that's what I implied, but that makes it sound like there was no one to blame," Celine said. "But there was someone to blame. Us." Her gaze stayed unblinking. "Your father and I stopped showing up for each other. Stopped asking what the other person needed. Stopped listening when the answers changed. Stopped being honest about our own needs. So eventually . . . we just stopped."

Their mother's words hit like a slap—sudden, sharp. Dylan had always thought there was no real reason why their parents' marriage ended. But now, Celine was laying out a perfectly logical one.

"I was only twenty-three when I met your father," Celine said. "Twenty-seven when I had you. I was so inexperienced, I didn't know what I could ask for. What I needed. But in the end, I think I fell back on that inexperience as a sort of . . . excuse. Then, when I went back to work, we both used our jobs as an excuse." Celine went on, "We made ourselves too busy to be present, meet the other's needs."

Next to them, Vicky let out a soft breath. Dylan met her gaze. Between them, a million unspoken words that Dylan was desperate to hear.

Celine's gaze stayed steady. "Love is a living thing. It needs light and air and attention."

Dylan's pulse was a tectonic rumble. It felt like something massive inside them was cracking apart. "Why are you telling me all this?"

"I suppose," Celine said, "that I wanted you to know the truth. So that you could have love in your life, too."

Was it possible they'd built their entire understanding of love on a lie? They'd always internalized the idea that love didn't last because the very concept of it was flawed and doomed to die on the vine. Not that love was something that existed because of commitment. Because of honesty. Because two people decided to be brave and show up.

"I'm sorry," Celine said quietly. "For not listening. For so many things. I thought I was protecting you, but . . . I wasn't." She exhaled, her words tentative and careful. "I hope we can start fresh. Or at least . . . move forward in a better way."

Dylan's heart gave a violent lurch. It was a struggle to assimilate all the information. "Well—one plate of meatloaf isn't going to, like, magically fix everything."

"I know," Celine said. "But if you're open, I'd like to try to rebuild our relationship. I'd like to know you, Dylan. Starting with being nonbinary." The word was spoken a little awkwardly, but their mother's expression seemed genuine. "I'd love to hear about who you are now."

Dylan looked at Vicky. She wasn't smiling—just watching, as steady as the horizon.

"I think," Dylan said, "I'm still becoming that person."

Under the table, Vicky's hand brushed their thigh. Just once. Just enough.

26.

Seven days till the show

ANNIE HAD BARELY OPENED HER FRONT DOOR BEFORE LOLA kissed her. "I've been waiting to do this all day," she declared dramatically, stepping over the threshold to capture Annie's mouth with hers.

It was Saturday night, and they had big plans to stay in.

They'd spent the day running the show in full for the first time—once in the morning, then two more times after lunch. Endurance theater. The stage felt like an extension of Annie's own body, the smell of it more familiar than her own salon. Annie wasn't just scaling the mountain she never thought she'd scale. She was running up and down it. She was summiting daily.

Annie kissed Lola back quickly before extracting herself and gesturing awkwardly at the sofa. "I don't think you two have officially met. Sal, this is Lola. Lola, Sal."

Given that Annie had stayed over at Jazz's twice already this week, and Sal had seen Lola leaving with Annie several more times than that, Lola wasn't a secret. But the Sal × Lola collab hadn't taken place until now.

"No smooches for me, please," Sal said, rising from the sofa. "I'm getting over a cold, and I'm very gay."

"S-sorry," Lola stuttered, putting down the bag of Thai takeout she'd brought. In her cream cutoffs and tight cream tank, she looked both fresh and unbearably sexy. "Didn't realize you had company."

"Sal isn't 'company,'" Annie said, hooking her arm into his. "More like family. The kind who knows you a bit too well."

"Ask her about her unholy obsession with stray socks." Sal aimed a teasing look at the mismatched pair on Annie's feet. One red-and-white stripe, one checkered with a frill. "Anyway, I'm not staying—we were just having a chat."

"About the Groom Room," Lola surmised, gesturing at Sal's light pink jumpsuit.

"Nope." Sal poked his tortoiseshell glasses up his nose. "We were having a chat about you."

Annie elbowed him. "I'd offer for you to stay," she said through a *shut the hell up* smile, "but we're planning on a lot more smooching."

"You're already a *we*?" Sal grimaced. "Lesbians are weird."

"Wait till you see our hers-and-hers Birkenstocks," Annie said, "and matching tattoos of anatomically correct vulvas."

"Thank you for relieving me of my appetite permanently," Sal said smoothly. His gaze slid back and forth between the pair. "I'm excited for the show. Can't believe it's in—what—a week? Then I guess you're back to New York, right, Lola?"

His tone was light but the subtext was deafening.

Lola blinked, looking taken aback.

Mortified, Annie hustled Sal to the door. "And that's your cue."

"Nice to meet you, Lola!" he called, before giving Annie a hug and a meaningful look, speaking too low for Lola to hear. "Just . . . be careful, okay?"

Annie smiled, playing dumb. "We can't actually get pregnant, dude. One day I'll explain it to you in full, but basically—"

"I'm serious. I know you're happy. Just . . . make sure you don't get left behind."

Annie blinked, caught off guard.

"Okay, bye!" Sal added in his usual chirp, clomping down the stairs.

Sal's warning replayed as the door clicked shut behind him. *Make sure you don't get left behind.* It wasn't like she was planning on it. It was just too early to actually be making plans, so Annie shook it off—mostly.

Lola was here. All night. Even though they were doing sleepovers, they hadn't yet had sex, as in Annie had not yet come with Lola in the room (climaxing on her own while *thinking* of Lola, well, that'd happened a record number of times).

The idea of letting Lola see all of her was exciting but also a little bit scary.

What if intimacy just complicated something already uncertain?

She stole a peek at herself in the hallway mirror. Funky midi floral-print skirt and a cropped boxy tee exposing a pink satin bra strap. Her underwear was a matching set. The girl equivalent of a starter gun.

What if everything worked out?

Lola emerged from the kitchen, placing bowls of drunken noodles and red curry on the coffee table. "Sal seems cool," she said, brushing Annie's lips with a kiss. "Straightforward."

"You don't have to worry," Annie said with a laugh, sliding to the carpet and reaching for her noodles. "We mostly talked about *Hood*—he's a huge Clay Russo fan." Sal had made her watch a *lot* of behind-the-scenes TikToks of the *Robin Hood* reboot. "He cannot *believe* you were almost in that film! Neither can I."

Lola half shrugged, seeming more interested in her curry than a sliding doors moment. "That's the life of an actor. A lot of near misses and working lunches. That anything gets made is a miracle."

"Sounds hard," Annie said, twirling noodles around her chopsticks. "But there's no part of you that's bummed about it?" The film was shooting in London with an all-star cast. It seemed so glamorous and exciting.

Lola dabbed her mouth with a paper napkin, considering. "The exposure would've opened doors, and I do love England. The money was . . ." She squirmed a little. "Let's just say I could've bought Jazz ten new theaters. But honestly, Annie, I'd choose being here."

Annie fixed Lola with a disbelieving stare. "Come on. That can't be true."

"It is, I swear!"

"Lollie!" Annie exclaimed. "I appreciate the gratitude, and yeah, this is meaningful for me, too. But you can't tell me you'd have picked community theater over your shot at the A-list! Way more fame, and power, and dollar dollar bills!" She tapped her chest. "I love Jazz more than anyone, and I don't think *I* would've picked that!"

"Fame, money, power," Lola listed. "What's missing? Art. Passion. The bigger picture." She let out a breath. "I want to prioritize what's purposeful for me, no matter how big or glamorous it is or isn't. I know it might sound silly, but doing this play *is* purposeful for me." Determination flashed in her eyes. "I'm not out here spouting a substandard script that wouldn't pass the Bechdel test—I'm performing a masterpiece by one of our greatest playwrights. I'm not being belittled or made to feel like a pretty face—I'm listened to and shown respect. I'm helping save the town with a cast I like and admire. And I get to do it all *in sneakers.*" Lola's gaze fixed intensely on Annie as she took Annie's hand, folding their fingers together. "But of course, the most important part of all of this is you."

Admiration, desire, and wonder pinballed in her chest as Annie's heart surged. "Me?"

Lola nodded slowly, her golden-hour eyes not leaving Annie's own. "Yes. You."

Annie edged closer, one hand touching the curve of Lola's cheek. She smelled like lemongrass; citrus, with a kick.

"It's always been you," Lola murmured, tilting her chin to press her lips to Annie's.

Lola's kiss was slow and deep and sweet as honey. It wasn't just a kiss of passion or of lust, although Annie felt both those things running like quicksilver through her veins. It was a kiss of care and commitment. A kiss of honesty and trust. It was a kiss as big as tomorrow, containing every unspoken wish, every secret dream, every impatient, hungry desire.

Lola let out a groan, shifting to kiss Annie more deeply. Annie moved willingly, rolling her hips to grind against Lola, every second of contact revving her up more and more. She needed to feel Lola's bare skin on her own. To cross the line from controlled to crazed. To leap into oblivion together.

Breaking the kiss, she tugged at Lola's cream tank top, her words a pant. "Why are all these clothes still on?"

Lola didn't need to be told twice. She pulled her top off, revealing a sheer cream bra that cupped the generous swell of her perfect breasts. Her pink nipples were stiff inside the delicate fabric. The sight pin-holed Annie's focus. Breasts had long been her number one turn-on in a woman. The weight of them. The shape. The way pleasure could narrow to such a small, powerful point.

Annie pushed Lola to the carpet, her head on a floor cushion. Still straddling her, Annie bent to run her tongue over Lola's left breast, relishing the sensation of the bra's slightly scratchy material, the shape of Lola's full breast, the feel of tight nipple under her tongue.

She'd wanted to do this for twenty years.

Lola moaned, arching her back to give Annie better access. Her hands tangling in Annie's hair. Writhing on the carpet, her moans became commands. "Yes, baby," Lola panted. "Suck me. Lick me."

The orders from Lola's usually controlled mouth made Annie's mind go static. She began licking Lola's other breast, her tongue moving over and around Lola's erect, sensitive nipples, soaking the sheer material.

Lola's moans became pants. "Oh Jesus. Oh fuck." Her head was thrown back, the skin on her neck splotchy. "Fuck, that feels good."

Annie reached for the clasp at the back, popping it open. The cream lace slackened. Annie helped tug it off, exposing a sight Annie had long craved: Lola's full, bare breasts. There was a faint tan line from her bikini, the skin that the swimsuit covered a milkier white. The idea that she could touch what not even the sun could made Annie even wetter than she already was.

"Lollie. You're perfect." Annie breathed, taking a long moment to stare at the topless girl underneath her. Commit the size and shape of her flawless tits to memory for all time. Then she had to touch them. When her tongue hit Lola's bare nipple, Lola almost screamed. Annie had been with women who'd enjoyed nipple play, but Lola seemed almost crazed with pleasure.

Annie took Lola's left breast in her mouth, flicking the tip with her tongue, sucking it like a lollipop, while her other hand squeezed, circling her pink nipple rhythmically. Annie was grinding against Lola's thigh, her own thigh between Lola's legs, Lola moving in time.

Annie's breaths came in pants. It was all so hot: Lola's blond hair splashed over the carpet. Her desperate whimpers and moans. Her tan lines. Her fucking *tan lines.*

"You feel so good," Annie whispered, Lola's nipple in her mouth.

Lola started bucking, her hands fisting Annie's hair, holding her in place.

"Oh god. Oh god," Lola panted, her voice reedy and desperate. "I think I'm going to come."

From just nipple play? Annie felt like a superhero. She increased her pressure, rubbing Lola's swollen nipple as Lola kept squirming and panting and crying out. She started to climax, her cries increasing in volume. "Yes. Fuck. *Yes. Fuck.*" Her body jerked, everything getting frantic. "Yes. Yes. Yes. Oh *fuck.*"

She was screaming. With single-minded focus, Annie kept sucking and licking and biting Lola's tits as her orgasm peaked, noisily, gloriously, then, slowly, began to recede.

They lay on the carpet, both breathing hard. Annie's mind spun in amazement. She'd never come from something like that herself or been with anyone where that'd happened. Pride ballooned into her chest and limbs.

Lola came back into herself, her golden eyes wide and fixed on Annie in disbelief. "What was that?"

Annie was just as surprised. Lying on one side, she propped her head up with one hand. "Proof I am the world's best lover?" She skimmed her hand down Lola's arm. "I didn't know you could do that. Nip-gasms. A breast-max."

"I didn't know I could do that, either," Lola said, a hand pressed to her forehead, a look of total shock etched on her face. "That was the first time."

"Really?" Annie sat up a little. "Maybe I *am* the world's best lover. Does that sort of thing have a cash prize?"

"There's definitely a medal," Lola said, "and a pin."

"Oooh, I want that pin," Annie said with a giggle, leaning over to kiss Lola on the mouth, then curling close. "God, that was so sexy. Seeing you come screaming and writhing on my carpet."

Lola stroked Annie's thigh, her gaze wondrous. "Well, it was just *so* hot. The feel of you. Seeing you so into it. Doing things we haven't done before . . ." Revived, Lola rolled herself on top of

Annie, before looking in playful confusion at Annie's outfit. "Um, why are you still dressed?"

"Hey, you still have shorts on."

"Outrageous . . ." Lola rose to her feet, extending a hand to pull Annie up. Lola backed them up to the wall, pressing Annie to it to kiss her, in between pulling her T-shirt up and off. These kisses felt different now: deeper. Hungrier. Lola pulled back, speaking low in Annie's ear. "I want to make you come."

Annie closed her eyes, her blood already singing. "I want that, too. Very muchly." *Muchly* might not be a word, but Annie's brain wasn't focused on grammar. It was focused on the half-naked woman tracing kisses down the side of her neck.

Annie shifted her weight, spreading her legs. As if reading her mind, Lola ran her hand down Annie's thigh, gathering up the material of her skirt to get it out of the way, freeing her to trace the top of Annie's satin underwear. Even just the promise of Lola's fingers touching her clit had Annie wound up, her muscles tense with need.

"Silky," Lola murmured, her fingertips easing, achingly slowly, over the front of Annie's underwear until she reached Annie's clit. Even through the material, the touch was exquisite torture. Her heart jackknifed, messy and hot.

Lola ran her fingers up and down Annie's center, featherlight, teasing. Even though each stroke was barely there, a fraction of what Lola was capable of, the anticipation was almost too much to bear.

Annie let out a strangled whimper, wanting more. Needing Lola to touch her. "More. Please."

Finally, Lola slid her fingers inside Annie's underwear, confidently stroking Annie's swollen clit. The relief was so pronounced, the pleasure so great, Annie moaned.

"You're so wet," Lola marveled. "You're so wet for me."

Annie couldn't speak, her words kidnapped by Lola's fingers, her voice, the feel of her skin.

"What do you want?" Lola murmured. "I can fuck you with my hand. With a toy. With my mouth. I want to be inside you, Annie." Moving down, she traced Annie's entrance. "I might never leave . . ."

Annie inhaled, involuntarily clenching. Now for the possibly awkward part. Maybe she should've found a time to mention this earlier, but she'd been nervous. Sex wasn't just about stripping off clothes. It was about stripping off presumptions to expose the truth.

Annie found Lola's gaze. "Not that," she said, shifting back an inch. "Not inside me. Clitoral orgasms are one hundred percent my jam. Put it on a T-shirt."

"Okay," Lola said without skipping a beat. "So, no fingers inside."

Annie exhaled. Past partners had been disappointed. But that'd been so easy. "Exactly."

Lola's fingers moved back up to Annie's clit, the touch sending fresh shock waves of pleasure up Annie's spine. "Thanks for telling me," she murmured, raising her other hand to squeeze Annie's breast.

Annie let her head fall back against the wall. Lola's acceptance had her feeling bold. "Get on your knees," she said. "And make me come with your mouth."

Lola pulled back, a pleased smile on her lips. "With pleasure, my queen. Clothes on or off?"

Somehow, Annie was still in her colorful skirt. "I think . . . skirt on." Something about keeping it on, Lola sort of underneath it, sounded unbelievably hot. "But shorts off for you."

Obediently, Lola undid the top button of her cream cutoffs, bending to slide them off over her ass, down her thighs, stepping out of them to reveal a matching sheer cream thong. Annie's head spun at the almost comically sexy sight in front of her: this blond, beautiful woman with a body sculpted as if from marble, her skin smooth and supple, her legs as long as a summer afternoon.

Life was so fucking good.

Annie gathered up her skirt and Lola dropped to her knees. Annie swallowed hard as she felt Lola ease off her pink satin panties, the material falling to her ankles.

Wedging one foot on a low stool, Annie readied herself for the coming pleasure. But nothing prepared her for the first hot stroke of Lola's tongue, licking her entire clit. Annie cried out. The sensation crashed through her like a wrecking ball, and Annie was no longer in her apartment in Rhodes; she was in the liminal place between past and present, between reality and make-believe, between the earth and the stars.

Lola moaned against Annie, her breath warm, her hands gripping Annie's inner thighs.

It was all too much. Annie's legs buckled. "I'm close." The words fell desperate from Annie's open lips. "I'm so close." It was too much to keep standing.

All at once, Lola was on her feet, one arm holding Annie up against the wall, the other moving fast to replace her mouth, the flat of Lola's hand finding a stronger, more powerful rhythm, circling even faster against Annie's slick, sticky clit. Annie started to come, the world's tallest tower collapsing. Screams of pleasure ripped from her throat. Color and light hurricaned around her, centered by breathless wonder that her body was capable of *this,* and that *Lola* was the one making it happen.

Annie's legs gave out, and they tumbled down, still wrapped together. Lola's fingers still moving, slowing as Annie's orgasm calmed. Every cell sang. Her mind was as blank as a mirror. Everything was perfect.

Reality came back into focus. The carpet under her head. The soft light of the apartment. The woman next to her, fingers moving lazily up and down Annie's arm. "So." Annie puffed. "We're back on the carpet."

Lola laughed. A bright-eyed, relaxed laugh, perhaps more generous than the comment deserved, but she was happy. "We are." She leaned closer to kiss Annie on the mouth, and Annie tasted the salty tang of sex. Lola pulled back to stare at Annie, touching her flushed cheeks. "That was everything I dreamed it'd be."

Annie couldn't help grinning. "I *am* getting that pin. But before you say another word . . ." She wriggled out of her skirt, out of her bra. Taking the cue, Lola slipped off her own underwear, which was drenched through. Kind of funny they'd both come—hard—without being naked. But they were making their own rules. Writing their own story. And the night was young. It was still only dusk.

Lola's gaze roved Annie's naked body, her fingers skimming Annie's still-erect nipples, the soft mound of her stomach, the fine hairs on her thighs. "You have no idea how often I've thought about this."

"I have some idea," Annie said, shifting onto her elbows. "What now?"

Lola's eyes were hungry. "As soon as you're ready, I'm dragging you to your bedroom." Her voice was low, with the scratchy edge of an old record. "I want to slide our wet pussies together. I want all of your fingers inside me. And I want to make you come. Again and again and again, until we can't think. Can't talk. Can't move."

Annie nodded, lightheaded, feeling like she was swimming in a vat of warm honey.

She'd done the unthinkable. The previously unimaginable. She'd fallen back in love with Lola Wilson. Uncontrollably, irrevocably, and with her entire heart. And there was absolutely no going back.

Annie could manage only one word. "*Yes.*"

27.

. . . .

Six days till the show

LOLA WOKE IN ANNIE'S BED WITH A SMILE ALREADY LIFTING HER lips. The morning sun was a cracked yolk, spilling rich and golden through Annie's funky floral curtains—Lola wanted to scoop it up with toast. Her body felt buoyant, but there was no fear of floating away, not when she was curled around a very naked Annie Lightfoot, the girl of her teenage and adult dreams. Snuggling closer, she kissed Annie's bare shoulder, letting her lips linger. Annie let out a happy *mmm* in response, rolling over to meet Lola's gaze, her blue eyes soft and sleepy.

"Morning, pretty," Lola murmured, brushing a lock of pink out of Annie's face.

"Morning." Annie yawned, cuddling into Lola, their bare flesh pressing close. "God, I slept *so* well. Like, corpse level. Usually, when someone else is in bed with me, I . . . ask them to leave immediately, of course."

Lola made her voice mock outraged. "There have been *others*?!"

"No." Annie played along, wide-eyed. "I'm a virgin, but my father will sell me to you for a few sheep."

Lola giggled. "What a baa-rgain. Well, I hope you sleep as well in New York. It's a lot noisier."

A spark of excitement lit up Annie's eyes. "When am I going to New York?"

"Soon, I hope." They hadn't talked explicitly about the future. But Lola hadn't missed Sal's not-so-subtle comment about returning to the city. It was time to start the conversation. "I know you have work," Lola went on, "and things will hopefully pick up for me, too, but I'd like for us not to go more than a few days without seeing each other."

"Really? I'd like that, too," Annie said, her face alive with hopeful excitement. "Sal's been handling the extra work great, so maybe I can drop back to five days. Spend the weekend, or something."

"That'd be wonderful!" Lola scooted up a little. "We can get bagels for breakfast, go to the MoMA, stroll in Central Park. Go out for dinner. See a Generation Women show at Joe's Pub. And, I can stay here some nights," Lola added, wanting to ensure they both traveled equally. "I've loved being back. The balance would be . . ."

"Perfect," Annie finished, gazing at Lola with so much adoration, Lola might explode. "I just don't want you to disappear again."

"That's *not* going to happen," Lola told her. "I promise."

Lola was done with second-guessing or flat-out denying her own feelings and desires. Her whole life was about playing by rules she didn't write for a game she didn't even enjoy playing. Society told her she was winning but her life didn't feel like a victory. *This* felt right. *This* felt important, the *most* important. The truth was all that mattered.

Lola sat up, facing Annie. "We promised to be honest, so here goes: I don't want a fling or just 'summer fun.' I've been so lonely, for so many years. I don't want that anymore. I want a girlfriend. A partner. I want *you,* Annie. Because you make me feel like I'm enough. You make me feel like someone I like. Someone who's whole. Who's happy just being herself. I haven't felt that in years.

Maybe twenty years. So, I don't want next weekend to be our ending. I want it to be the start of something that lasts."

Tears filled Annie's eyes. "Jeez Louise, that's the most beautiful thing anyone's ever said to me," she whispered. "I want to write it down so I never forget it."

Lola laughed softly, tugging her closer until Annie was straddling her and they were staring at each other with fresh wonder. "You won't need to write it down. I'll say it on command."

Annie smiled, looking lovestruck. "You get me, Lollie," she whispered. "I don't have to pretend I'm more interesting, or more successful, or more anything. You make me feel special just the way I am."

They sank into a kiss, the kind of kiss that buzzed through Lola's bloodstream like champagne. There was no denying it. She was falling in love. And she was certain Annie was feeling the exact same thing. Joy flooded Lola with the same intensity as the hot morning sun streaming through the window. She wanted to bottle this moment and savor it forever.

"Come to my premiere," she blurted.

Annie pulled back, eyes blinking open. "What?"

"*Saturn Rising,*" Lola said. Why hadn't she thought of it sooner? "Truly, I am not looking forward to it. The film is . . . not good. But it'll be better if you're there. We'll dress up. You'll sit with me for the screening, then there's an after-party. It'll be fun. If we're gonna do this—you and me—then let's do it. Come to my premiere."

It was next Thursday, two days before the show. Lola was leaving midafternoon, staying the night in the city before coming back for their final dress rehearsal on Friday.

"A movie premiere . . ." Annie looked adorably stunned. "I've never been."

"We wouldn't go as an official couple," Lola qualified. "Not because I don't want to—it's just too soon to be public. But I want you there, if you're okay with that. I've seen where you work," she added, gesturing in the direction of the downstairs salon, "now you can see where I work."

Annie was quiet for a full minute, thoughts racing behind her eyes. And then: "Okay." A small, cautious smile. "As long as I won't stick out like a sore thumb, I'm in."

"Perfect." Lola sighed with relief, drawing her girl close, already imagining it: Annie, all dressed up, whispering hilarious things throughout the screening, their fingers brushing in the dark.

This summer wasn't their final act. It wasn't even intermission. The curtain was rising on something new.

And Lola wanted Annie in every single scene.

28.

Five days till the show

ALL AT ONCE, IT WAS TECH WEEK. THE FINAL WEEK BEFORE opening night.

On Monday morning, Vicky stood on the theater's freshly mowed front lawn, watching a workman affix a new red and cream sign. *Rhodes Playhouse* in a classic curling font. Not a single letter missing.

Everything was changing.

"Morning, Vicky." Orchid stopped next to her, dressed in an aquamarine puffy-sleeved top, a matching skirt with a deep V-slit up the thigh, and a pair of Chuck Taylor high-tops.

"Hi." Vicky gave her a hug. "How was your Sunday?"

Jazz had given everyone the afternoon off. "So cool," Orchid said, eyes shining. "Kat, Zo, Em, and I hung out by the river, planning the talkback and swimming and stuff."

Vicky smiled, remembering those halcyon days of "stuff"—making plans and eating junk food and drinking swiped liquor.

"What about you?" Orchid asked.

Vicky had toured retail spaces for Marlowe with Dylan. At first looking around was fun, like they were a couple inspecting their first potential home. But as the day went on, the fun started to curdle.

Dylan was flying home to L.A. in a week. Vicky was going back to work. Her assistant already had a full day scheduled. This summer's expiration date was shockingly soon, something Vicky couldn't think about without getting the urge to sob.

"Odds and ends," Vicky shrugged, determined not to get emotional. "So, ready for tech week?"

"Yeah . . ." Orchid said. "But I'll miss all this." Her gaze traced the theater. "Miss doing the play. Miss Jazz's energy. Miss those idiots," she added fondly, nodding at Emery and Zoë, who were harmonizing to "For Good" from *Wicked,* and Kat, who gave Orchid an infatuated smile. A far cry from the four siloed teens at the table reading, all those weeks ago.

The trio called Orchid's name, waving her over.

"Just a sec," she called, looking back to Vicky. "Hey, I wanted to thank you. I talked to my mom about what you were saying the other day—about choosing joy. We ended up having this long chat, and, I dunno, it felt different. Like I was able to express myself a bit better and that she was listening to me in a different way. It wasn't a fight. It was actually a conversation."

"I'm really happy to hear that," Vicky said. "Parents can be tough, but we're all just human beings. Big bundles of sensitivities and trauma and hopes and dreams."

"I'll remember that," Orchid said. "Thanks."

Dylan loped across the front lawn toward them, carrying two iced coffees and a UPS envelope, hair falling over one eye, jeans slung low around their narrow waist, a crooked grin on their too-plush lips.

Vicky's heart tripped over its next beat. She'd miss those stupid low-slung jeans most of all.

"So are you and Dylan gonna do long distance?" Orchid asked.

Vicky flinched. Maybe it'd been a mistake to be so public. Move so fast. For a moment, she imagined blushing girlishly, declaring that Dylan had asked Vicky to be their girlfriend, and she was moving to sunny L.A. to be with them forever! But Dylan had not asked and Vicky hated L.A. and all that was as fictional as the play they were putting on.

"Nope," Vicky said coolly, slipping on sunglasses to hide her pain. "We're just friends."

Orchid frowned, looking confused, before heading off to join the others.

"Hey," Dylan said warmly, handing Vicky her iced coffee. "I have something to show you."

"If it's your rainbow dick, I've already seen it."

"Not that, but thanks for the visual." Dylan winked, reaching into the envelope. "I wanted you to be the first to try it."

It was a chocolate bar, the packaging designed with playful pops of glossy red. "*Hot & Sweaty,*" Vicky read aloud, recognizing the Marlowe logo. "One of yours?"

"Brand-new drop," Dylan said proudly. "Read the back."

Vicky skimmed the copy.

> Hot & Sweaty is a throwback bar for grown-ups, inspired by the taste of a crazy, hazy summer. Silky oat milk chocolate drenches a sticky raspberry compote, its sweetness deepened by agave and the warm spice of cinnamon bark. Buttery theater-style popcorn brings a playful, salty crunch, and for the pop of first flirtation, we've added a sprinkle of crispy quinoa.
>
> Layered. Nostalgic. Surprising. Just like your summer crush.

Vicky's stomach dropped. There it was, in black and white. *Crush.* As in, fling. As in, meaningless. What other interpretation could there be?

But this hadn't been meaningless to her. And there was only so long she could keep pretending that it was.

"Sounds amazing," Vicky said diplomatically, working to keep her voice even. "Can't wait to try it."

"Try it now," Dylan urged, their voice softening. "You inspired it, Vee. It's sort of for you."

Her heart, the drama queen, threw itself against her ribs. It was all too much. Vicky forced a smile. "I'll save it for later." She about-faced for the theater, gripping the bar so tight she felt it snap in two.

TECH WEEK WAS a welcome distraction. The cast wasn't just running the play now—they were syncing it to lighting and music, trying on costumes, and adjusting to the buzz of new crew members. A shy sound designer hovered in the wings, a geeky lighting tech fiddled with wires, and a chatty costume designer finalized Jazz and Lola's vision of Elizabethan with a modern twist.

Annie's easygoing Rosencrantz sported cropped striped trousers and untucked shirt with a ruffled collar, both slightly frayed. Mismatched socks added a quirky touch, reflecting Annie's and the character's playful spirit. Lola's Guildenstern was more grounded in earth-toned trousers, a fitted doublet, and worn leather boots. Her high ruffled collar had signs of wear—Lola had suggested the leads' slightly weathered looks, as those trying to climb the court's hierarchy without ever making it to the center of attention.

Maria's King Claudius exuded authority in a crimson robe with gold accents, a structured doublet, and sleek patent shoes. Deborah as Polonius was regal in a burgundy velvet doublet with gold embroidery, a cape draped over one shoulder. Mikki's Horatio kept it simple, her gray doublet and neutral hose reflecting her grounded loyalty.

Dylan, as Hamlet, became far too sexy—dark and brooding in a long trench coat with a blood-red lining.

Lola and Jazz had debated whether putting Clyde and Jamie in dresses would be distracting—too campy or tongue-in-cheek—but ultimately decided it was the right call. Clyde's Gertrude looked powerful in an emerald-green gown with gold trim, revealing matching hose and platform boots. Jamie's Ophelia wore a pastel dress with lace accents, capturing innocence, with Converse sneakers adding a subtle rebellious touch to Ophie's vulnerability. Both men came out from their first fitting with shy smiles to the rest of the cast's whoops and whistles. "I feel pretty," Clyde said. "I've never felt pretty."

Mikki inhaled on seeing Jamie, her cheeks blushing red. "It works," was her verdict.

The Tragedians wore mismatched doublets, jerkins, and hose in velvet, brocade, and leather, showcasing their plucky, resourceful nature. Vicky's look was a standout: a patched cape in jewel tones, modern combat boots, and a wide-brimmed hat with feathers, embodying the Player's theatrical elegance and scrappy charm.

The cast wasn't the only thing getting show-ready. Everyone pitched in to get the theater clean and fresh. After a few hours of scrubbing and mopping, the windows now sparkled, the parquet floors gleamed. Maria brought in her steam cleaner to get the old carpets looking brand-new. The concession food wouldn't get set up until the day before the show, but the old popcorn machine was lit up and operational. Still free for performers. One bite of the buttery, salty popcorn and Vicky was rocketed back twenty years. Seventeen going on thirty-seven.

"Careful, Vee." Dylan appeared by her side, frowning lightly at the empty bag Vicky had just inhaled. "That stuff isn't heart-healthy."

Vicky bristled. The comment shouldn't have stung—it was sweet—but who was going to look out for her next week? Who was going to look out for her for the rest of her life? "And the bar of chocolate you gave me *is* heart-healthy?" she fired back.

Dylan paused, looking caught out. "Well, I used oat milk and agave, so technically, less bad for you. But you're right—neither's getting a gold star from your cardiologist." They peered at her. "When's your next appointment, by the way?"

That Dylan kept doing and saying these protective, caring things made Vicky want to explode. "Why the fuck do you care?"

Dylan looked surprised. Hurt seeped into their green eyes. "I care. I've always cared."

Vicky bit the inside of her cheek to keep from bursting into tears.

She just had to make it through the week, then she'd be back at work, back in New York, and Dylan Rogers would be gone for good.

ON TUESDAY NIGHT, Vicky stayed late at the theater, helping finish painting the sets along with half the cast and a local artist. When she got back to Jazz's, Vicky passed Dylan's open door to sleep in her own room.

On Wednesday, the cast had their first full dress rehearsal. Things were so busy, Vicky was able to avoid Dylan all day.

They finally cornered Vicky in the green room late that afternoon. "Hey. Have I done something wrong?"

Vicky busied herself with adjusting her cape. "Kind of in the middle of something."

"Me too." Dylan stepped closer, catching her gaze. "The girl I like is freezing me out and it's making me sad and confused."

Vicky's heart folded in on itself, like paper crumpling under a heavy hand. She knew she was being a jerk, but she had to protect herself. She could not fall apart. "This isn't the right time."

"For what?" Dylan pushed. "And when is?"

Vicky let out a tense breath, willing herself to open up. "Look, Dyls, we both know—"

"Vicky." Garrett appeared in the doorway. "Need you onstage."

Vicky nodded. "Just a sec."

"*One* sec." Garrett disappeared.

"I have to go." Vicky tried to brush past Dylan.

"Tonight," Dylan said, touching her arm. "Have dinner with me, at home? Lola's staying at Annie's and Jazz said she's staying late here. We'll have time to talk."

The words sent icy chills down Vicky's spine. Vicky couldn't handle what was sure to be a painful conversation, not right before the show. But she couldn't keep avoiding Dylan.

"Tonight," she said, edging close to Dylan, looking up at them. "But I don't want to talk." She hooked one hand around the back of their neck, trying not to die at the feeling of their body so close. Their rich, dark, intoxicating smell. "This has been amazing, really. So let's go out with a bang." She pressed her mouth hard to Dylan's for a kiss so quick, Dylan barely had time to respond. Then she backed up, wordlessly hurrying in the direction of the stage.

AFTER REHEARSAL WRAPPED, Vicky went for a drive by herself, wending aimlessly through the tree-lined back roads, giving herself the gift of exploration. Her nickname at law school had been the Arrow, because she always got quickly, often brutally, to the point. While that skill was effective in her profession, one of the things she'd gained a newfound appreciation of this summer was journey as destination. A lingering, laugh-filled dinner with old friends. A movie marathon of throwback comfort watches. Doing a community theater play, not for money or career advancement or ego, but for connection and community and fun. *Take the long way home* was the idea that kept coming back to her.

So she did, arriving back at Jazz's well after dark. Light glowed from the dining room. The only sound was the soft, almost bittersweet sound of classical music. "Rogers?" she called, heading down the hall. "I'm home. Sorry I'm . . ."

The dining room was lit up with what seemed like a thousand little white lights, strung from the ceiling. The dazzling, magical sight stopped her in her tracks.

"Late," she finished.

The table was set for two, with elaborate place settings, champagne chilling in an ice bucket.

And everywhere, in a dozen different vases: red paper daisies.

It was all so achingly beautiful, Vicky felt tears prick her eyes. Her heart throbbed in her chest, spelling out Dylan's name with every beat.

She was going to miss them more than she could bear.

Dylan appeared from the kitchen. "Honey, you're home." Far from sounding irritated at her lateness, they sounded relieved. Happy to see her. "Hope you're hungry. I sort of went overboard on the food."

Vicky swallowed. This was going to be harder than she thought. Crossing the room, she wrapped her hands around the back of Dylan's neck, surprising them with a deep, lingering kiss. "Thank you," she whispered, pulling back to look up at them. "For doing all this."

"Of course," Dylan said, gazing at her with so much devotion, Vicky almost couldn't stand it. "Anything for you, Vee."

"This has been the best summer ever," Vicky said. "You've changed my life. Again. I'm going to miss you so much." She let herself feel a crush of pain before continuing. "Let's end things cleanly. For both our sakes."

All the color drained from Dylan's face. They looked flabbergasted. "What—*now?* It's Wednesday—I'm not leaving till after the talkback on Sunday!"

Vicky summoned the courage to look Dylan right in the eye.

"Why did you do that whole mock trial thing with me in the kitchen? All that play-acting," she prompted, "about me having feelings for you? Why did you tell Annie and Lola that I was in love with you?"

Dylan looked briefly shocked. Thoughts zoomed behind their eyes. Each word was a struggle. "I—was—flirting."

"Flirting," Vicky repeated softly, hiding her disappointment.

This really was a summer fling.

"Then I can't keep drawing this out," Vicky said, trying to be firm even as she felt herself unravel. She didn't want dinner. She didn't want to keep breaking up. "I want you to take me to bed."

Dylan looked uncertain. "You sure? Look, this doesn't have to be goodbye. We'll always be friends, Vee."

But that wasn't what she wanted. And yet, it was all that was possible.

Over the past few weeks, Dylan had given Vicky so much pleasure. But this night together was different. From the moment they began undressing in Vicky's bedroom, things weren't frantic or frenzied. They were reverent. They were sacred.

Harness on, Dylan positioned themself above a bare-naked Vicky, arms braced by her head. They met her gaze with unflinching eyes. "Sure you want to do this?" they asked softly.

Vicky nodded, flooded with so much emotion she could barely speak. She tugged Dylan close for a kiss, every point of contact buzzing under her skin. "Yes," she whispered. "I want to."

When Dylan rolled their hips to push their strap-on into Vicky—slowly, carefully—it didn't feel like they were just fucking. It felt like they were making love. As Dylan filled her completely, Vicky's skin shivered. Not just from the feeling of being stretched. From the feeling of locking eyes with Dylan as it happened and seeing this new, private part of them. They didn't break eye contact as they both found a rhythm, each thrust getting deeper, then deeper still.

When Vicky approached the peak, she didn't look away until her vision began to starburst and she lost all control.

There, in the moment between words and worlds, in the place of pure sensation and endless summer heat, was the place she would always love Dylan Rogers. Even if she couldn't say it, even if she'd never say it, she felt it as certain as her own heartbeat.

Afterward, Dylan drifted off to sleep while spooned around her, their breath slow and steady. Vicky closed her eyes and quietly started to cry. Salty tears leaked from under her lids, sliding down her temples to the pillow, her heart a million shining pieces on the floor.

29.

Two days till the show

"ANNIE!" SAL CALLED AGAIN FROM OUTSIDE THE BATHROOM door. "Come out of there before one of us goes gray!"

Annie dabbed on some cherry lip balm, wiped it off, then reapplied the exact same amount. "Just a minute."

"You said that many minutes ago. I have a Snatch Game special at four!"

Annie met her own gaze in the bathroom mirror, wincing at her wobbly eyeliner. Lola had booked a professional makeup artist, offering their services as a gift to Annie, which seemed like an unnecessary expense and possible inconvenience. Now Annie was wondering if she should've said yes. "Okay. Lower your expectations." She sucked in a breath, said a quick prayer to the fashion gods, and opened the bathroom door. "Ta-da?"

Out in the hallway, Sal's eyes went wide. "Ta-da indeed. You look stun*ning*! Red carpet ready, for sure!"

Annie couldn't help but squeal. Her first red carpet! In this dress, she was ready.

In preparation for *Saturn Rising*'s premiere, she'd spent every free hour scouring every thrift store in a twenty-mile radius before finding The Dress. Flapper-style, adorned with intricate art deco–style sequins and beads, and a beaded fringe that shimmied around her knees. Glitzier than anything she owned. And it was only thirty bucks! Which left just enough money to get her roots touched up, her French bob now an even, rosebud pink. Her electric blue eyeliner was on loan from Deb, a nod to the blue spandex Lola's character wore in the film. The overall look was comfortable, cute, and special. Just like Annie herself.

"It's not too . . . twee?" she asked, but truthfully, Annie was fishing for compliments.

Sal shook his head, looking like a proud dad. "No. It's perfect."

Annie glowed with excitement, imagining, once again, how her and Lola's hands might slide together in their shared popcorn. How they'd exchange a secret smile in the standing ovation. How she'd be the perfect under-the-radar date—independent and self-reliant, but on call for emotional support or shared snark.

Outside, a car honked. Sal went to the window. "Lola's here!"

Annie zipped up her overnight bag. Their driver would drop their stuff at Lola's loft, after he delivered them to the premiere. They'd then drive back to Rhodes the next morning for their final dress rehearsal.

A wave of nerves hit Annie all at once. "What if I fall on my face like Carrie in the runway episode? What if I mispronounce *Zendaya* or *Chalamet*? What if everyone identifies me as the country bumpkin I actually am and laughs me out of New York City?"

"Annie." Sal grasped her shoulders. "No one will be thinking about you—they'll be thinking about themselves. But you're not there for them; you're there for Lola. And I have to say," he added, looking a little sheepish, "maybe I was wrong about her. Her inviting you to this—it's huge."

"A huge test," Annie said. "That I might fail."

"I don't think so," Sal said. "Not if you stay true to who you are. That's who Lola likes. Now, get your shoes on. I *may* have organized a little surprise."

Intrigued, Annie slipped on her funkiest pair of dance-floor-friendly sneakers and trotted downstairs, outside to Henry Street.

Where she started to laugh and blush at the same time.

Crowding the sidewalk in front of the salon was the entire cast. Vicky, Dylan, Deb, Clyde, Jamie, Mikki, Maria, all four teens, Jazz, and Garrett lined either side of a red Persian rug, leading to a black town car. Next to it, Lola, in a caramel trench coat, stood smiling a soft, proud smile. That look lit something in Annie's chest.

Sal was right. This wasn't just an invitation to a big night. It was an invitation into Lola's world. Maybe she'd find a way to belong.

On seeing Annie, everyone broke into cheers: "Go Annie! Congrats, Lola!"

Annie elbowed Sal. "I had no idea you were such a cheeseball."

"Guess you're rubbing off on me," he joked, adding in a whisper, "I didn't tell anyone you guys are *involved.*" Stepping back, he gave her arm a squeeze. "They just wanted to wish you luck."

Embarrassed, but also low-key loving it, Annie walked "the red carpet" to Lola, who gave her a hug. "You look gorgeous," she murmured, before stepping back to open the car door.

"Have fun, darlings!" Jazz waved.

"Don't forget about us!" called Zoë.

"Tell Brett I put out on the first date!" added Sal.

Giggling, Annie slid into the back seat. Everyone waved as they headed off, their voices replaced by the quiet hum of the car.

Annie looked to Lola. Her hair was a flawless waterfall of blond. Her skin was contoured so expertly, her entire face shape seemed different. "I'd kiss you," Lola said, "but I don't want to ruin your makeup."

Annie reached across the back seat to take Lola's hand. "Nothing will ruin tonight," she said. Or really, she hoped. Because she couldn't help it; this did feel like a test.

One that Annie intended to pass.

• • •

THERE WAS A mob outside the theater in Midtown Manhattan. That's the only way Annie could describe it—a *mob,* like in a zombie movie. Wild-eyed fans waved headshots and Sharpies, cellphones hoisted like burning torches.

Gold lights pulsed along the theater's awning in time with the looping *Saturn Rising* trailer playing on a giant LED screen. A velvet rope carved a path toward the entrance, flanked by the crush of fans behind barricades and a wall of photographers shooting the arrivals.

Lola and Annie had been snuggled close for the entire ride, but now, Lola pulled back with an apologetic smile. "Showtime."

Annie wasn't upset—it was what she signed up for, and privacy made sense.

The car pulled into a cordoned-off space. A woman wearing stylish all black with a clipboard in one hand opened the door. This was Kimberly, Annie assumed, the publicist. "Here she isssss!" Kimberly crowed. "Our *star*!"

"Bet you say that to all the girls," Lola quipped. She slid out of the car with effortless grace, handing Kimberly her trench coat as they air-kissed.

Annie scrambled out less gracefully, only now seeing Lola's dress in full. Tight, black, with large asymmetric cutouts showing off her toned stomach, thighs, and back. Sexy. Chic. Annie felt a worrying ping over the dress code—Lola had said to wear whatever she wanted—before shaking it off.

This was Lola's night, after all.

"This is Annie." Lola raised her voice to be heard over the crowd.

"Of course!" Kimberly handed Annie a lanyard without breaking eye contact with Lola. "You look stunning, doll. Ready?"

They began moving toward the entrance. Everything was brighter and louder than Annie expected—flashbulbs popped like fireworks, people yelled Lola's name, a woman in a blazer shouted,

"Where the fuck is hair and makeup?!" Annie trailed Kimberly and Lola past the fans, watching Lola sign a few posters, pose for some selfies. Annie made awkward eye contact with fans whose gazes took her, then discarded her as someone non-famous—unimportant. Surprisingly painful to be deemed irrelevant.

Annie remembered Sal's words—she wasn't there for them. She was there for Lola.

The foyer was big and brightly lit. The walls were plastered with more *Saturn Rising* promo: glossy stills of muscled space captains, explosive asteroid battles, and Lola—blue-skinned, backlit, barely dressed—gazing solemnly into the cosmic void. Kimberly led Lola to the step-and-repeat—the red carpet—which faced shouting paparazzi with giant cameras. Annie watched as Lola moved into place, shifting seamlessly into finding her angles. Smiling big, then simpering with a sexy smirk. One hand on hip, then hand dropped to the side, then hip turned forty-five degrees. Annie would not be trying any of those poses.

It was almost unnerving to see Lola transform in this way, displaying yet another side of her. What sort of hidden skill might Annie impress Lola with? Her high school French? Her moderate ability to juggle?

Lola moved down the line.

Annie readied herself. "When should I go?" she asked Kimberly.

Kimberly looked briefly startled to see Annie still next to her. "Oh, you don't have to worry about that, Anna," she said with a laugh. "This is just for talent. Why don't you head inside and find your seat?"

Annie felt a swift kick of rookie shame. Of course she wasn't going to be photographed! She wasn't talent. She was just a civilian.

Following orders, she went inside.

The auditorium was massive, three times the size of the Rhodes Playhouse. Hundreds of plush velvet seats curved around in a steep stadium-style layout. An attendant directed Annie toward the back. Far from the front. "Oh, I'm with Lola Wilson?" It came out as a question. "Her plus-one?"

The attendant smiled, unfazed. "Your lanyard is general admission. You can sit anywhere up there." The nosebleed section.

Annie's instinct was to back down. But WWVD—what would Vicky do? "Lola said we'd sit together," Annie said, a little more firmly.

The attendant's smile slipped, assessing Annie as a potential crazed fan. "Your lanyard is general admission," he repeated, even *more* firmly. "But I can always check with security."

Annie found a seat up the back, pulling out her phone to text Lola. Help! I'm stuck in general admission!

Minutes passed. The theater continued to fill. Two chatty twenty-somethings dressed casually in jeans sat next to Annie, making her feel wildly overdressed.

No reply from Lola.

Eventually the lights dimmed. The energy shifted. A dozen stylishly dressed people came up the center aisle to scattered applause. The cast. Lola. The sight of her, an arrow right in Annie's heart. The group filed into the empty front row as a host appeared onstage, welcoming the crowd. Next to Lola, Brett sat with an arm around his date, a willowy blonde.

Finally Annie's phone lit up. A reply from Lola. Oh no!! One sec . . .

Squinting, Annie watched Lola twist around in her chair—every seat around her was full—then flag down an attendant, who knelt before her as they conferred. The attendant melted off.

Another text slid in. My hands are tied. I'm SO sorry. See you after? 😘

Annie read then reread the message, her surprise sharpening into dismay, then shame. She'd assumed Lola would fix this. Hands brushing in the popcorn. A shared secret look. But she was a normie stuck in coach while beautiful Lola flew business class.

Embarrassed tears pricked Annie's eyes. She blinked, embarrassed to be caught crying at a premiere.

But no one was looking at her. She didn't matter at all.

Annie thumbed a reply. No worries! Already made friends up here😊

A lie, but that was what Lola wanted to hear. She sent back a heart, then the lights went black.

Sal's words came back, uninvited: *Make sure you don't get left behind.*

THREE EXCRUCIATING HOURS later, the credits finally rolled. Lola was right—the film was a disaster: an overblown mess of CGI and space battles with a wooden script probably written by AI. Annie followed the crowd, ready to get the hell out of this theater. Maybe Lola wouldn't even stay to say goodbye.

"Annie!"

To her surprise, Lola stood at the top of the stairs, waving.

Annie waded through the crowd, half of which were shamelessly taking pictures of Lola like she was a zoo exhibit.

"I'm so sorry!" she began before Annie was even in front of her. "I didn't tell Kimberly we wanted to sit together—I just assumed . . ." She shook her head in subtle annoyance while managing to smile graciously at some well-wishers. She held up a gold lanyard hopefully. "Let me buy you some free champagne at the after-party? Start the night over?"

Annie knew she should tell Lola that of course, that plan sounded great! But honestly, it didn't sound great. So WWDD—what would Dylan do?

"Or," Annie said, raising a suggestive brow, "we could go back to yours and chill? Order takeout. Go crazy."

Lola blinked, her smile frozen in place. "I'd love to, but this is sort of a work event for me. I have to go. You can go back to the loft," she added, her tone edging into disappointment, "if you want."

Instantly, Annie regretted showing her hand. Lola wanted an up-for-anything date, not a disillusioned Debbie Downer. She strong-armed an excited grin. "No way. Let's rage! I am going to rip up that dance floor. That's why I wore sneakers."

Lola exhaled in relief, hooking her arm into Annie's. "Not sure there'll be a dance floor, but yes, amazing. Let's get out of here."

Annie let herself be led, relishing the feel of Lola's arm in hers.

Maybe the champagne would help. Maybe the night would turn around.

Or, a small, worried voice whispered, maybe this was exactly what life with Lola Wilson was going to be like.

THE AFTER-PARTY WAS at a rooftop bar in SoHo. Polished concrete floors, minimalist furniture, and tempered glass walls with staggering skyline views that everyone ignored. Violet up-lighting and flickering tea lights turned everything into a soft-focus dreamland, perfect for Instagram but impossible for Annie to read the bar menu.

"I'll have a . . . Moon Juice?" she told the disconcertingly attractive mixologist. Hopefully the drink was less ridiculous than it sounded. She turned to Lola for backup.

But Lola had spotted someone across the room. "Babe!" she squealed, arms outstretched.

"Babe!" echoed a six-foot supermodel type in a snakeskin jumpsuit. The two collided in a flurry of air kisses. "How *are* you?" Snakeskin demanded. "This dress! So fuckable."

Annie flinched, but Lola just laughed. A more animated version of her real laugh. "How was Berlin? Tell me everything!"

"Wrapped a week ago and I still have fake blood under my nails," Snakeskin said with a moan. "Director was *such* a hack. Quick pic?"

Annie stepped back as Lola leaned in. One, two, ten selfies. Then, finally: "This is Annie," Lola said, smiling at her. "My rock."

Annie lit up, as bright as the bar wasn't. *My rock.* How badly she wanted to be that for Lola—the one who grounded her.

She'd never been called that by anyone before.

The supermodel looked Annie up and down, eyes snagging on her thrifted dress. "Don't tell me you finally got an assistant!"

Annie nearly choked on her Moon Juice.

"Annie's my very good friend," Lola said quickly, giving her arm a supportive squeeze. "We grew up together."

"Cuuute!" Snakeskin declared, looking over Lola's shoulder. "Oh Christ, there's Marty. Better go kiss the ring." She vanished into the crowd.

"She had a small part in the film," Lola said, nodding at Annie's drink. "What'd you get?"

"Moon Juice."

"Is it good?"

"It is not."

Lola laughed. Her real laugh. "I kind of just feel like a beer," she admitted.

A warm pulse of relief eased the tension in Annie's shoulders. Lola might be friends with supermodels wearing dresses straight from the Kardashian playbook, but she was still a girl who opted for a beer at a fancy after-party. She was still Lola. "Me too," Annie said.

Maybe they really would have fun.

They turned in the direction of the bar.

Kimberly appeared in front of them. "Hi, doll. Can I steal you for a sec?"

Annie half expected Lola to say she was getting a drink, she'd just be a minute.

But Lola nodded, straightening like an activated sleeper agent.

"Sure." Then to Annie, while already getting shepherded off, "I'll be back as soon as I can. Mingle! Have fun!"

And then she was gone.

Ordinarily Annie was good at mingling and having fun. But this was no ordinary party. The women were preternaturally thin, with teeth as white as porcelain and stomachs like tanned leather. The men wore leather oxfords or pristine sneakers and were intimidatingly hyper-confident, mostly talking to other men wearing expensive-looking watches. Annie was pretty sure she was the only person at this party who shopped secondhand.

Still, she was determined to try. Life began out of your comfort zone—she'd seen that on a bumper sticker. "So, what'd you think of the movie?" she asked some tatted-up hipsters who were both wearing shades and smelled like weed.

"What?" they replied, dissolving into giggles.

"What'd you think of the movie?" she asked a guy her age in a button-down.

"I think they buried the third act pivot to save face on the Burns cut, but you can't salvage back-end points if the streamers don't window it internationally." Pushing past her, "Marty, my guy!"

And so on.

After an hour of glimpsing Lola through the crowd, Lola finally returned to Annie's side, looking frazzled. "Jesus, this place is packed with everyone I've ever met, apparently." Someone pushed a glass of champagne into her hand; someone else hovered nearby, trying to catch her eye. She touched Annie's arm, looking worried. "How are you?"

Annie considered the truth—over it, ready for bed—but that seemed radically uncool. "Living my best life. Did you know there's a whole company that just does CGI smoke?"

"Huh?" Lola blinked, as Kimberly reappeared.

"Doll! Chloé Zhao just arrived!"

Lola whipped around. "Really?"

Annie knew it was important for Lola to meet a director even she had heard of. "Go!" she said, forcing a laugh.

Lola gave her a grateful smile, allowing herself to be once again tugged away.

Annie gave a tight-lipped smile to the cool chick in a micro dress and go-go boots who asked, "What do you do?"

"I'm a dog groomer," she replied. "I'm Annie."

"A groomer?" Go-Go Boots frowned, leaning in. "Like a stylist?"

"No, for *dogs,*" Annie almost shouted.

"I *know.*" The girl made an empathetic face. "Men are dogs."

Annie tried one last time. "No, a *dog groomer.* I have my own salon, Upstate."

"Ooh." The confusion on Go-Go Boots's face cleared up, her gaze tracing Annie's dress and sneakers.

The wrong dress. The wrong shoes. Bumpkin alert. Why hadn't Lola given her a proper heads-up?

"I'm here with Lola Wilson," Annie added.

"Cool," the woman said, waving to a sleepy-eyed rocker boy loping toward them. She gestured at Annie. "This is Lola Wilson's dog groomer."

Annie balked. Shame rose in her throat like bile, making her feel small.

She wasn't Lola's date. She was a comfort blanket. The soft old thing from home you keep by your bed, not because you love it—because it's familiar and nonthreatening and safe. A reminder of where Lola came from. Not a part of where she was going.

The truth was Annie didn't belong here and she never would.

30.

LOLA FELT LIKE SHE WAS ON AN OUT-OF-CONTROL CAROUSEL, and every time she tried to get off, someone was handing her another glass of champagne or needing her to pose for a picture or taking her to someone she just *had* to meet. Inviting Annie to the premiere was starting to feel like a bad idea, but at least every time Lola saw her, her date was chatting with someone new. Maybe she was having fun?

Lola got dragged into a long conversation with Brett's annoying girlfriend—a twenty-five-year-old influencer launching a line of "intuitive workout wear" that she wanted Lola to support. As Lola nodded along to the pitch, she was reminded, once again, of why she was falling for Annie.

Annie, who reminded her that success might dazzle, but happiness was homemade.

Annie, who never asked for more than honesty and presence, and gave both in return.

Annie, who, Lola realized as she scanned the crowd, was gone.

THE NEXT MORNING, Lola awoke to the unfamiliar sound of a siren. An unfamiliar hangover. But—thankfully—a very familiar woman in her arms. Lola relaxed with a contented sigh. She was in New York City in bed with the girl of her dreams. The dreaded premiere was in the past. And their play was tomorrow! Life was very, very good.

Annie shifted, rolling over. She was already wide awake.

"Morning, pretty." Lola kissed her, letting it linger.

Annie cut it short, wiggling back. "I need coffee."

"No," Lola groaned playfully. "Don't leave me."

"*I* won't." Annie gave Lola an oddly complicated look that Lola was a bit too hungover to parse. She swiped at her eyes, her hand coming away black. She'd forgotten to wash off her makeup last night.

"Yeah, you wrecked your pillowcase." Annie pointed to Lola's silk case, now streaked with mascara.

"I'll get a new one," Lola sighed, unconcerned.

"Right. You can just . . . do that," Annie said lightly. Almost too lightly.

Annie was annoyed.

"We didn't leave together." Only now did Lola remember. Annie had texted—Grabbing some beauty sleep! I have the door code—have fun! 🩶 She'd been asleep when Lola got home, curled into the far side of the bed. "And we didn't sit together," Lola recalled, the pieces of the night clicking into place. "Oh god. I'm so sorry."

"That's okay."

"I barely got two seconds with you."

"It's fine."

Lola sat up, wanting to face whatever was happening head-on. "It's just, you sound a bit . . ."

"What?" Annie's voice had an almost undetectable edge, which seemed to prove the point.

"You're disappointed," Lola concluded. "With how it all went. Honestly? Me too. I thought we'd be able to sit together. I thought we'd have more time at the party. I guess I didn't realize how much they'd need me to work the room. But I still really liked having you there." Lola reached for Annie's hand, wanting to convey the sincerity she felt. "I hope I haven't scared you off."

"Never." But there was something tight in Annie's smile. "Did you have fun?" she asked. "Was it a good night for you?"

Lola considered it, wanting to be completely honest. "I like being back in the city. New York's still New York. Gorgeous and impossible, like always." She smiled, still thinking. "The turnout was good. People liked my dress."

"But did *you* like your dress?" Annie asked, her expression intent.

"I mean, it's not what I'd wear on the weekend but it did the trick," Lola said.

Annie picked at her nails. "It looked uncomfortable."

Lola laughed in confusion. "Dresses like that aren't supposed to be comfortable—they're supposed to look good and photograph well, which it did." Lola sensed Annie didn't like her dress but maybe she was misreading things—she was a bit more hungover than she'd planned. "More importantly, did *you* have fun? Apart from not spending enough time together. Was it okay?"

Annie gazed back, her big blue eyes flickering fast between Lola's own. Lola held her breath. Then Annie started nodding. Started smiling. "You know what? I did. I really did." She relaxed back into Lola's arms. "It was *so cool* being at something like that. Like, a party at the center of the universe. I loved my dress, felt great in it all night. And I had some surprisingly fun convos."

"Really? Who with?"

Annie laughed self-consciously. "You know, not sure I even got names. But seeing you on the big screen?" Annie fanned herself. "I think I have a blue skin kink now."

Lola laughed, pleased and grateful. "You promise? You promise you had an okay time?"

Annie met her gaze, speaking with soft sincerity. "I promise."

"Thank god," Lola said in relief, pressing a kiss to Annie's mouth.

"It's already eight." Annie pulled back. "We need coffee, and very greasy breakfast sandwiches, if we have any chance of making it back on time."

THEY ARRIVED BACK in Rhodes just before twelve. It seemed every streetlight, every shop window, had posters advertising the play: STARRING LOLA WILSON FOR ONE NIGHT ONLY!

Pushing open the playhouse's large front door, Lola was greeted by the smell of popcorn. The concession stand was fully stocked with old-school treats: Jujyfruits, Junior Mints, Milk Duds.

A stack of folded black-and-white programs with a grainy photo of Lola and Annie in costume sat on the counter. It was far from being a colorful, professional playbill, but to Lola it meant so much more. She scanned the list of cast and crew members, knowing every single name. She turned to Annie. "Let's get this framed."

But Annie had already gone inside.

Garrett's voice sounded. "Final dress rehearsal starts in ten, people!"

Lola refocused shifting into director mode. She pushed open the doors to the theater.

Inside, the cast and crew were buzzing about. Reminders flew from Lola's lips as she strode up the center aisle feeling energized and purposeful. "Morning, Clyde! Don't forget to let the line *as fits a king's remembrance* linger. Deb, you're stage *left* for that second entrance, not stage right. Jamie, hi, your wig is on backwards but loving the dress. Can we bring the lights to preset one? Thank you!"

• • •

THE FIRST HALF of dress rehearsal went well enough, but Vicky and Dylan were off their game, dropping lines and missing cues. Vicky was clearly underslept and Dylan was distracted. Lola tried to connect with both of them, but Vicky was tight-lipped. "I'm fine," she'd snapped, brushing Lola off, and Dylan simply disappeared during their lunch break.

Had they had a fight? Broken up? The idea had her reeling. She'd assumed they were together for good.

Lunch hour passed in a snap. "Five minutes till we start act two!" Garrett called from center stage.

"Shoot, I still need to post on social," Lola told Jazz. They still had a few tickets to move. "I'll be quick."

Lola hurried up to the balcony seats, intending to post about the show, wolf down a chicken salad sandwich, and check out the obstructed view seats. She sank into the last seat in the very back row. From here, the stage was distant. A diorama of itself.

Lola pulled out her phone for the first time all day.

Her screen was a mess of notifications.

Ten missed calls. All in the last hour. All from Kevin. Multiple texts, too. Another arrived before she'd even swiped her phone open.

JOIN THE ZOOM WILSON!!!! NOW!!!!!! Followed by a link.

Zoom? Her stomach plummeted before her brain assured her she definitely did *not* have a meeting, today of all days.

Jamming the rest of her sandwich into her mouth, she thumbed a reply. Busy. Talk next week.

Her agent's response was immediate.

NOW!!!!!! FUCKING NOW!!!!!

Irritation boiled. Still chewing, Lola tapped on the link, ready to channel Vicky Fang and give Kevin a curt piece of her mind.

The Zoom connected. Kevin's face popped onto the screen. His hair was rumpled and he looked oddly flustered. "So sorry about the hold-up, folks, I know she's beyond *thrilled* about—ah, here she is!" His relief was pronounced. Her agent's tone became kingly. "The woman of the hour: *Lola Wilson.*"

Lola froze, mid-chew. On the screen, her own image was shadowed, barely visible. She was still in her costume—the Elizabethan-style fitted doublet.

"Lola, *hi.*" A woman in her fifties Lola didn't recognize spoke with a mid-Atlantic accent. "Fran Woods, one of the EPs. *Wonderful* to meet you! And thank you for being *so* understanding."

A Greek chorus of agreement followed, faces popping chaotically on the screen as they spoke over one another: *Really appreciate it—So last minute—You're in New York, right?*

Lola straightened, alarm making everything tight. It was like walking into her own surprise party, but finding it full of strangers and not on her birthday. She choked down her mouthful. "Sorry, I've, um, been in rehearsals," she managed, "I'm not totally sure . . ." *What the fuck is going on.*

"Roll call!" Kevin called cheerily, although she knew him well enough to hear the stress in his voice. Faces popped up as he introduced them—execs, a lawyer, another EP—most unfamiliar, some vaguely recognizable, but a disorientated Lola couldn't pick from where.

"And last but certainly not least, our director—or should I say, *your* director—the one and only . . . Kris Mack!"

"My director?" Lola repeated dumbly as Kris Mack himself appeared on Lola's phone screen.

"Hello again, Lola," Kris spoke with warm authority. He appeared to be on a soundstage, burly men pushing giant lights behind him. "Awesome to see you again, albeit under pretty unusual circumstances."

"Good to see you, too, Kris." Lola was not quite inside her own body as she spoke.

Kris went on, emphasizing how special she was, how she was the only one with the experience, the chutzpah, the *grit* to make this work. "I know this must be incredibly disorientating," he added, "but everyone believes in you, especially me."

"That's—" Lola scrambled for purchase, the ground underneath her shifting. "Thank you?"

"So, whaddya say?" Kris gave her an easy smile. "Ready to come onboard *Hood* and be our new Maid Marian?"

Lola blinked fast, utterly speechless.

A text from Kevin slid onto her screen. SABINA IS OUT. YOU'RE IN.

Everyone began talking at once, layering compliments over assurances over next steps: *Fast-track the contract—Need your measurements—Throwing you in the deep end, but we know you can handle it.*

"Lollie!"

Lola jumped at the whisper-yell.

Annie stared at her quizzically from the other end of the row. She pointed to the stage below where the cast was waiting, mouthing, "*We need you.*"

Lola nodded back, trying to force a smile, mouthing, "*One sec.*"

Annie frowned, unsure, but she backed off, heading for the stairs.

Lola refocused on her phone, trying not to pant with the adrenaline.

"So," Fran was saying, "your handler, Jess, will be arriving to take you to the airport in—let's see—about an hour. We'll send your belongings on if you don't have time to pack."

"An hour?" Lola shook her head, everything sharpening into focus. "No, I have a show tomorrow."

There was an awkward pause. No one spoke.

"And I haven't actually said yes yet," Lola pointed out.

Fran's face screwed into disbelief, as if Lola had just passed on the secret to eternal youth.

"I don't think we can move Haejun . . ." someone murmured, to which someone else said, much more firmly, "We cannot."

Haejun? Who or what was Haejun?

Garrett's voice called from below. "Lola Wilson to the stage!"

Then, Jazz. "C'mon, kid, break's over!"

"Lola," Kevin said. "You and I will chat. Team, I'm *very* confident we can make this work. Wheels up in a few hours. London calling, pip pip!"

A flurry of farewells, then the Zoom ended.

Lola's hand cramped from holding her phone so tightly. She rose unsteadily to her feet, still trying to process. She hadn't made it two steps before her phone lit up again. *Kevin (agent) calling.* She tapped to accept, pressing the phone to her ear. "I can't talk right now—"

"Production's a mess," Kevin began, breathless. "Sabina broke her ankle doing a sword spin and now they're panicking. They need someone to pull the whole thing together and Russo told them you have vision."

"Vision?" Lola's interest poked its head up like a gopher. "What—like, I could help with directing?"

Kevin blew out his cheeks. "They didn't say that *explicitly.* But, yeah, sure. Maybe!"

That just made things more confusing. "But right now, the film's a disaster?"

"A *high-profile* disaster that'll open on three thousand screens. And that's *still* better than obscurity."

"Is it?"

"Of course it is!" Kevin's voice jumped an octave. "*Of course it fucking is!*"

"Kevin, my god." Lola stumbled down the carpeted stairs to the second-floor landing. "Calm down."

"I *won't* calm down. My client has just been offered the biggest deal of not just *her* career but also mine. Wilson, they are quadrupling their initial offer. *Quadrupling.*"

Lola pulled up short. She hadn't thought about money. The initial offer flashed in her mind. Times that by four and . . . Reality teetered. "That's a lot of money," she mumbled.

"That's a *fuckton* of money, Wilson," Kevin cried. "It's, like, double the GDP of most countries!"

Lola did not want anyone else hearing this insane conversation. She hurried toward a supply closet, switching on the single fluorescent bulb inside and pulling the door closed.

"So, Sabina's out and they want me," she clarified.

"They don't just want you, they *need* you." Kevin sounded equally gleeful and crazed. "They agreed to *everything.* Your points on the backend are *unprecedented.* They're giving you top billing. Above Russo, above *anyone.* Congratu-fucking-lations, *A-lister.*"

The supply closet had no AC. Sweat slid down Lola's back. "I don't have much time, but send me the script. But, Kev, I cannot miss my show tomorrow."

"Yes, you can."

"No, I can't." Lola switched her phone to the other ear, the glass slick with sweat. "It's the first thing I've done in forever that feels like mine. If they want me that badly, they can wait thirty-six hours."

"No, they can't. They've landed a cameo with that massive K-pop star, Haejun, that a bunch of the funding is tied up with. He's on tour and the *only* time he can do it is tomorrow. Ergo, you fly to London *right now.*"

Anxiety crushed Lola's ribs. She couldn't get a good breath. "But I really care about this play. The cast, my friends, the town. Jazz." *Annie,* she added in silent anguish. "We've spent the whole month rehearsing—"

"For community fucking theater!" Kevin shrieked. "Wilson! This isn't just an offer. This is a *seat at the table.* Yes, you'll miss the show, but you can't make an omelet without breaking a few eggs and this is the chance to make an omelet fit for a queen!" His voice took on more urgent insistence, rising in volume. "You *cannot* say no to this. This isn't just a paycheck and it isn't just a role. This is what every sacrifice has been for. Lola! This is the start of *everything.*"

The supply closet door opened. "Lollie?"

Lola whirled around so fast she lost her balance.

Annie stood in the doorway, looking baffled. She took in Lola's appearance with alarm—no doubt her stage makeup was smeared, her eyes wild and frantic. "What are you doing?"

"I'm—coming," Lola choked.

"One hour!" Kevin shouted, his voice tinny through Lola's phone. "Be ready in—"

Lola stabbed the screen to hang up. Sweat stains circled under both armpits. Her muscles shook with adrenaline.

"Who was that?" Annie stared at her in concern. "Are you okay?"

Lola stared back, her mind galloping in five different directions like spooked wild horses running for their lives.

She should tell Annie about the offer. Annie would then ask what she was going to do. Lola had to pass, obviously. Right? Was there any other option? Would Annie agree with that? What would Jazz say?

What the fuck should she do?

"I'm fine." Lola blew out a shaky breath, stepping out of the closet. "Just—work stuff."

She absolutely could *not* cancel the show. But she also couldn't pass on this once-in-a-lifetime offer.

Lola gestured limply in the direction of the stage. "The show must, y'know . . . go on?"

But it was no longer a statement. Now it was a question.

31.

One day till the show

THE SECOND HALF OF THE FINAL DRESS REHEARSAL OF THE Rhodes Players' production of *Rosencrantz and Guildenstern Are Dead* began with Lola Wilson missing her cue. She'd always been good at retaining dialogue, able to spout off monologues from things she'd been in years prior. But now, sweating under too-bright lights, the words were gnats she couldn't grasp, only swat at in confusion. Where were they up to? "L-line?"

Offstage, Jazz let out a tense puff. "*Has it ever happened to you that all of a sudden . . .*"

"Right. Sorry." Lola willed the line into existence. "*Has it ever happened to you that all of a sudden and for no reason at all you haven't the faintest idea how to spell the word 'wife'—*"

If she did *Hood,* she could offer Annie the kind of financial security one would expect of a wife.

"*—or 'house'—*"

If she did *Hood,* she could buy Annie a house with a big backyard and a rambling garden and guest bedrooms galore, just like she'd said she wanted. A house, *and* a holiday house *and* the salon. Whatever Annie wanted. And it didn't matter if this show was a success or not, she could keep Jazz's theater running indefinitely.

"*—because when you write it down you just can't remember . . .* um . . ."

The rest of the line vanished like a trick of the light, replaced with a twisted kaleidoscope of faces: Kevin and Kris Mack and Clay Russo.

Vicky and Dylan. Clyde and Deb and Maria and the teens. Jamie and Mikki. Garrett and Jazz.

Annie.

Annie.

"Lola?" Now Jazz sounded less annoyed, more worried. "For chrissakes, get her some water. Cut the lights!"

Lola swayed, planting her hands on her knees. So much emotion boiled inside her, she couldn't pick out each individual feeling. She might start to cry.

The stage swam. Her knees trembled. And then—

And then she was fifteen years old again, auditioning for *Our Town,* equally in love with and intimidated by acting. After performing her sides, Lola was in the small group asked to stay and read again after lunch. The rest of the hopefuls had been kindly dismissed.

On her own on the theater lawn, Lola scrabbled in her bag. She'd forgotten her lunch. She'd had only an apple for breakfast—her always-exhausted mom worked nights and hadn't gotten groceries in a week. Lola was ravenous, but she had no money. All the kids around her were tucking into store-bought salads and savory-smelling rolls. Her stomach rumbled.

"Everything okay?" A girl with a ski-jump nose and Disney-blue eyes smiled at her. Lola recognized her as one from the dismissed group. She wore brightly patterned flares and a yellow tee, her hair in two messy bunches atop her head.

Nervous, Lola nodded, affecting assurance.

The girl looked to Lola's empty hands, eyes narrowing slightly.

She dug in her backpack and pulled out a foil-wrapped sandwich. "Do you want this?"

Lola was so shocked at being casually offered the thing she needed most, it took a long moment to reply. "Oh, I'm fine."

"Honestly, you'll be doing me a favor," the girl said. "My gran makes them—roast chicken salad, really good, but I think I'm destined to be a vegetarian?" She cocked her head thoughtfully. "I care way too much about chickens."

Lola giggled. This girl was funny and it felt like a balm. Lola readied to politely decline again, but her stomach growled, loud enough for them both to hear.

The girl laughed. "Here," Annie had insisted, her smile as warm as the summer ahead. "Please."

Even back then, Annie Lightfoot had seen past her mask and offered what Lola needed most. More than two decades later, nothing had changed.

"Lola!"

She snapped back to the present. She was thirty-six and onstage, in costume, in the middle of a run.

Annie was hurrying over. "Hey, what's wrong? Who was that on the phone?"

"No one," Lola said, trying to breathe.

"Why won't you tell me?" Annie begged. Fear shone in her eyes. "Is someone hurt? Did you get bad news?"

Vicky strode onstage, handing Lola a bottle of water. "What's going on?"

"She was on the phone," Annie told her helplessly. "Something's happened."

"I'm fine," Lola croaked.

Dylan crouched beside her, peering up into her face. "Dude, you're white as a ghost."

"Put your head between your legs," Vicky said, feeling for Lola's pulse. "Give her some space!"

"I'm okay!" Lola insisted, a tear slipping down her cheek.

The creak of the theater doors split the tension like a snapped string. A young woman came up the center aisle. Car keys dangled from one hand, a phone in the other.

"Excuse me?" Garrett called. "We're not open to the public yet."

"I'm Jess," the woman said, voice cool, practiced, edged with vocal fry. "I'm here to pick up Lola."

Lola froze mid-breath, as if the lack of motion would stop her two worlds smashing into each other.

This couldn't be happening.

"Pick her up?" Garrett repeated, sounding certain this was a mistake. "We're in the middle of our last rehearsal."

Jess looked to Lola. Deferring to the talent.

Lola felt like a criminal sprung mid-heist. "I just need . . . another hour."

Jess's eyebrows pinched. She looked at her phone, then back to Lola. Pointedly.

"We're not open to the public," Garrett repeated testily, looking between Lola and Jess. "You'll have to wait outside till we're done, Jess."

"Can't leave without Lola or I'll lose my job." Jess spoke in a kidding-not-kidding voice.

"What?" Vicky stepped forward, her cape trailing behind her. "What do you mean?"

"Where are you taking Lola?" Dylan asked Jess slowly.

Lola met Annie's gaze.

Annie stared back beseechingly, moving close enough to give Lola's hands a squeeze. "It's okay," she whispered. "You can tell me."

The words cut Lola's heart out of her chest and flung the still-beating organ onto the stage floorboards.

Lola forced herself to straighten. Look the cast in the eye. Start talking. "I just got a call." She stumbled over explaining the film. The accident. The offer. "They want me to step in. As Maid Marian, one of the leads."

"Opposite *Clay Russo.*" Zoë breathed, crossing herself. "And Kris Mack! No one blows up a gas station like Kris Mack!"

Lola licked her dry lips. "The first thing I have to do is a scene with . . . Haejun."

This electrified half of the cast.

"*What?*" Mikki squeaked.

Zoë stepped forward, eyes like basketballs. "Are you serious?"

"Now, who's that again?" Clyde asked.

"He's the biggest K-pop star in the world," Emery said. "Harry Styles is basically a white Haejun."

Orchid squealed, clapping. "Can we meet him?"

"If anyone is meeting Haejun, it's me," declared Maria. "He's a cutie patootie."

"Yes—well done, Lola," Jazz announced, leading the cast in a round of applause, her armfuls of bracelets clanking.

Annie still hadn't said a word. As if she sensed there was more to come.

Lola willed herself to keep going. "The Haejun thing . . . it has to happen tomorrow. In London."

"Tomorrow?" Jazz repeated. "But the show's tomorrow."

"And we're not in London," Clyde added shrewdly.

"I know," Lola whispered, glancing guiltily at Jess.

Like a group of meerkats, the cast followed her gaze to the handler, who smiled back awkwardly.

"So, *Jess,*" Vicky said, "is here to take you . . ."

Lola gulped. "To the airport."

The mood in the theater transformed, a freezing gust of wind announcing a pending storm.

"Oh," Dylan said quietly.

"But, surely they can shuffle things around for you," Deb said. "I mean, you're *Lola Wilson.* Aren't you?"

In that moment, Lola truly didn't know who she was.

"How can we do the show without you?" Clyde asked.

"We can't," Kat answered bluntly. "She's ditching us."

Half the cast gasped. The other half froze.

"I'm *not* ditching you," Lola assured everyone. "The show *isn't* off. Look, I only just heard about this. I don't know what to do."

"Well, you *have* to do it," Zoë said incredulously. "It's Clay Russo and Kris Mack and hello, *Haejun*."

"Doing it means *you* don't get to perform," Emery told her. "Don't you have family flying in?"

"Understudies!" Jazz shouted, one finger raised jubilantly. "Lola, who's your understudy?"

Everyone looked hopefully to Zoë, the teen who'd made the most effort all month.

But it was a white-faced Kat who shakily raised her hand. "Um—me."

"Ah," Jazz said, a bit less confidently. "Rightio . . ."

Lola gathered every ounce of strength she had and looked at Annie.

Annie stared back, wounded, her lips pressed into a hard line.

That was it. Lola couldn't do it. Annie was more important than anything else.

Lola stepped toward her, touching her arm in a way that pushed the *just friends* believability. The least of her concerns. "Can we talk?"

Annie followed Lola through the wings to the green room. Lola shut the door, expecting Annie to be a teary, panicked mess.

But Annie's face was oddly blank. Cold. "So," she asked, folding her arms. "What are you going to do?"

"I don't know," Lola said carefully. "We'll decide together."

Annie let out a short, humorless laugh, glancing up to the ceiling with a tense jaw. "Lola. What do you *want* to do?"

The question sounded like a riddle Annie already had the answer to. Lola took a beat to untangle her ambition, her desire, her responsibility, her—

"It's not a complicated question!" Annie exclaimed. "What do you want?"

"It's not that simple," Lola shot back.

"Yes, it is," Annie said, eerily calm. "Do you want to do this movie? Or is this just like the dress?"

"What dress?"

"The dress," Annie spoke slowly, "that you wore last night. You didn't like it. You only wore it because it was what other people wanted you to wear."

A scalding flush of emotion burned Lola's cheeks. Deep down, a part of her knew Annie was right. But another part decided Annie was being simplistic. Didn't understand how the industry worked. Couldn't see the whole picture.

Lola knew how this looked—jetting out of her small town for a big-budget overseas shoot. She'd promised Annie that she wouldn't disappear.

The solution arrived fully formed. "Come with me."

Annie blanched, incredulous. "What?"

Lola moved closer, taking Annie's hands, speaking fast. "Come with me. To London. Come for the whole thing. Stay with me. Come to set. I can even pay you! As my, I don't know, assistant producer or something."

Annie's jaw had loosened, her eyes as huge as the London Eye. Her voice was soft. "Are you serious?"

"Yes!" Lola exclaimed, getting excited. She could *see* it. "Late summer in London is gorgeous. I'll make them put me up in a suite at Claridge's. We'll eat crispy duck salad at the Ivy, go shopping at Harrods. High tea at the Ritz? Heaven. Oh, it'll be so much better if you're there!"

Annie cocked her head. "Like the premiere was better by me being there? Even though we were apart all night?"

Lola waved this off—a minor misstep. "I learned my lesson. I'll tell Kimberly we're a couple as soon as we get on the jet."

"And what about the play?" Annie asked in a low voice. "What about Rhodes?"

"I know it's far from ideal," Lola said, "but I'll cover the cost of every ticket and then some. Maybe we can try again next summer!" Unlikely, given everyone's schedules, but anything was possible, right? "Look, you can't make an omelet without breaking a few eggs and this is the chance to make an omelet fit for a queen!"

There was a long, long pause. "And, in this instance"—Annie's voice was cutting—"the queen . . . is you."

Lola blinked, unsure.

Annie let go of Lola's hands roughly, taking one, two steps away before spinning around. Her eyes glittered with rage. "Are. You. Kidding. Me?"

"Annie, I—"

"Are you *fucking* kidding me?" Annie screamed.

Lola swayed back in alarm. She'd never seen Annie look this mad.

"I would never, in a million years, for a billion dollars, abandon this town!" Annie shouted. "No, I don't want to go to London with you as your *assistant.* Do you have any idea how patronizing that is?"

"I said assistant *producer—*"

"High tea at the Ritz? Crispy duck salad?" Annie laughed manically, even as her eyes filled with tears. "Have we met? I bring my own *vegetarian* lunch every day because I'm *dead broke.* Christ, I spent thirty bucks on that stupid dress last night and *that was a splurge.*"

Lola floundered, grasping for the right thing to say. "But you—looked great last night."

"I felt great, until I arrived and realized I looked like Little Orphan Annie next to a family of Warbucks!" Annie exclaimed. "Last night was *awful.* I've never been made to feel less consequential *in my life.* Why would I want to go to London as your underling to feel that way *for months*? I had a perfectly good life here until you came back into it!"

Lola's mouth was open, her shock making it hard to reason. "But . . . you said you had fun last night. Great conversations. Being in the center of the world."

Annie gave an exaggerated shrug, lips pressed, eyebrows all the way up.

Something inside Lola broke. "You lied to me. Right to my face."

"I was trying to protect you!" Annie cried, but her voice had taken on an edge of contrition. "I didn't want you to feel bad on opening night!"

"By *lying* to me," Lola said, now feeling some fury of her own. "Just like when we were kids. When you broke my heart and made me wonder what I'd done wrong for twenty years."

"It's not the same thing," Annie exclaimed.

"Yes, it is! My trust issues are your fault and then you lied *again* after we *promised* to be honest. You haven't learned a thing."

"Have *you*?" Annie cried. "In case you've forgotten, you love doing this play. You hate your life. You swore to me you'd choose being here over *Hood*! The only reason you'd do this stupid film—another bad choice by the way—is for money and power and those are two of the shittiest reasons to do anything—"

"Enough!" Lola shouted, shaking with anger.

She stared at Annie, speechless over her lack of honesty, her lack of respect.

Maybe Kevin was right—maybe this *was* all a delusion. Vacation goggles. Summer fun. Maybe she was insane to think there was a future for her here. Annie *lied to her.*

The crossroads ahead of Lola blurred, each path equally right and wrong. Her pulse banged out of rhythm, her chest clenching like a fist. A panic attack, barreling at her with full force.

"I don't trust you." Lola stumbled, speaking on a gasp. "I have to get out of here."

Without waiting for Annie's response, Lola lurched out of the green room.

Back on the stage, the cast was mid-conversation.

"We've been talking," Vicky began ostentatiously, "and we agree that you should—"

Lola's panic whipped into fury, rising fast. "I don't care what you think," she snapped, voice edged with too many years of being managed and molded and misunderstood. "I'm in charge of my life, not anyone else."

"Lols, dude, chill . . ." Dylan said, but Lola was already heading for the stairs.

"Let's go," she hissed to Jess, who obediently fell in step behind her. Vision blurring, Lola hurried up the theater aisle before she did something stupid like pass on the opportunity of a lifetime.

"So—that's it?" Jazz called, her tone full of disbelief.

Lola paused at the doors, turning back one last time. "I'm sorry, everyone. I wish this wasn't our end. I really do."

The Rhodes Players stared back at her, aghast. Their expressions were enough to wobble her resolve.

But then Lola saw Annie on the edge of the wings, mouth tight, arms folded, face cold.

The face of someone she could no longer trust.

Lola's heart shattered. It felt like forgetting how to breathe. To live.

Her agent was right. This was the start of everything. The end of everything else.

Lola's voice broke as she addressed the cast. "Break a leg."

Then she turned and walked out of the Rhodes Playhouse, not sure if she'd ever have the courage or will to return.

PART THREE

We Regret to Inform You that This Is the Show

32.

ANNIE'S GRANDMOTHER HAD DIED ON AN UNFAIRLY BEAUTIFUL summer afternoon, and though the end had been long and expected, the grief still gutted her. That same suffocating despair returned now, seated silently in Jazz's office while the others talked, their voices like storm runoff she couldn't absorb.

Lola was gone. Because Annie had done the wrong thing.

Why didn't she just tell the truth this morning? Why was she so insecure, so reactive, so *mean* in the green room?

I had a perfectly good life here until you came back into it.

Was that even true?

Annie tried not to think about Spaghetti à la Spontaneity, and the McCormacks' water hole, and movie night banana splits. She tried not to think about bringing Lola a flower in the green room or an afternoon in Jazz's overgrown backyard or group dinners at Rock Around the Clock. She tried not to think about Lola's lips and fingers and the way they could make her feel. She tried not to think about the show, their show, and everything it meant. And she tried not to think about all their pillow talk about splitting their time between New York and Rhodes, and how this summer would be the start of their forever.

But, of course, Annie would never forget any of those things. They would torture her for all time.

Lola had left and Annie felt like she might die.

All she wanted to do was go home, get into bed, and weep until her throat bled. But her sheets would still smell like Lola's lemongrass, and blood was notoriously hard to get out, and Annie felt she had a responsibility to be here, making a plan.

But what plan was there to make?

"How much of the play *do* you know?" Garrett was asking Kat.

Kat's nose was stuffy, her eyes red rimmed. "I've been so busy planning the talkback," she whimpered. "I never thought Lola would bail."

"How much?" Garrett repeated.

Kat shrugged miserably. "I know *my* part."

Everyone puffed out tense sighs.

"Kat, I'm disappointed," Jazz said curtly. "You can go."

"I'm so sorry," Kat whispered, beating a hasty exit.

"Why didn't I have *Zoë* understudy Lola?" Jazz muttered. "Zoë's completely off book, just as the wrong character!"

"What about you?" Vicky asked Jazz. "You've run the play a million times."

"No," Jazz said with a tired laugh. "I don't know it that well. Maybe I could manage half of act one. But not the whole thing."

Dylan leaned forward in their chair. "What if—I dunno—we find another actor and they, um, video call in? Like a projection, sort of high tech, and . . ." They sagged in defeat. "No, that's stupid."

"What if I read Lola's part?" Garrett suggested. "I know pretty much all the blocking."

"What, you onstage with a script?" Dylan asked doubtfully.

"In our *gender-swapped* production?" Vicky added.

"Yeah, might be a *Cats* level of bad idea," Garrett conceded, kneading his temples. "What if we push the show to after Lola's film wraps?"

Everyone looked highly doubtful.

"I'm not sure Lola will be doing the show." Dylan glanced cautiously at Annie. "Ever."

It stunned Annie that her body still had tears to cry but yep, here they came. She swiped them away, speaking through her stuffy nose. "I don't think we can count on Lola."

Vicky gave her another sympathetic smile, another side hug. "It'll be okay," she whispered.

Annie couldn't even fake a resilient smile back. Vicky was wrong. Things wouldn't be okay.

"I just can't believe it!" Jazz popped a fist onto her desk, rattling her bangles. "I *don't* believe it. Lola Wilson is a professional. I've never known anyone more trustworthy, more committed. She gave me her word!"

Annie reached for a tissue from a box on Jazz's desk. "People change."

"Not at their core," Jazz insisted. "You lot haven't!" She waved at the trio. "You've grown up, have new careers, have new haircuts. But in your hearts, you're the same."

Was that true? Vicky was the same, maybe Annie was, too, but Dylan had changed, not just looks-wise but in their confidence and sense of self.

Or maybe Dylan had just become the person they were always destined to be—and so had Lola. And that person belonged in blockbuster movies, not community theater.

"So, what are you saying?" Dylan asked. "Lola hasn't changed and . . . she'll be back?"

"That's exactly what I'm saying!" Enlivened, Jazz got to her feet. "Lola Wilson did not get on that plane. She'll be walking through my door, full of apologies and ready to get back to work in five seconds!"

They waited five seconds.

Nothing happened.

"Sorry to burst your bubble," Vicky said, "but it looks like she *did* get on that plane."

Vicky held up her phone, showing the tagged section of Lola's Instagram. A grainy, zoomed-in video showed Lola and her handler boarding a small, sleek plane at the nearby Albany airport. Annie's heart quivered like a wounded animal at the sight of Lola still, bizarrely, in her theater costume, disappearing into the private jet. The video sped up a little, returning to a regular speed when the plane lifted from the ground, into the clear afternoon.

The candle of hope Jazz's premonition had lit flickered out. Lola was en route to London. There was no workable plan. It was over.

Hope Irish-exited the room.

"Should I tell the rest of the cast?" Garrett asked Jazz quietly. "Start refunding tickets?"

Jazz didn't reply. Seated behind her enormous desk, Annie's mentor looked half her size. Tears filled her eyes, her lips twisted in pain.

Next to her, Annie heard Dylan sniffle.

"Jazz?" Garrett prompted.

"I'll do it," Jazz said, her voice cracking, "I'll tell the cast." She took off her glasses with a shaking hand, wiping at her eyes. "It was going to be so wonderful. It wasn't supposed to end like this."

Annie sank to a new level of despair. Not only was Lola gone, off to the big, bold life she was always going to return to, but Annie's heartbreak was the end of Jazz's dream, too.

Jazz went on. "I've always had so much faith in people. Maybe that's naïve, maybe that's stupidly optimistic, but I've always believed people will do the right thing. Show up when the going gets tough. I have always believed that *we* are the answers to each other's prayers. But today"—and now Jazz began to cry, her words coming through choked sobs—"today I've lost that faith. Today I'll stop believing that. I'm just a stupid old woman who doesn't know when to quit. Well, today I quit. I tried and I failed and it's over. I give up."

Now everyone was crying.

"Jazz," Vicky pleaded, her throat thick with tears, but Jazz just turned away from them, saying, "Go."

"But Jazz—" Dylan tried.

"*Go,*" Jazz said, and so silently, they all did.

THEY ENDED UP at Rock Around the Clock, squeezed into a smaller window booth. Annie stared blankly outside while Vicky and Dylan ordered too much food and booze.

Soon, Annie would return to her life of domestic tedium—washing dogs, doing laundry, making dinner for one—while Lola was gallivanting around London with Clay Russo and a K-pop star, beginning a thrilling new chapter. The town would find out that the play was canceled, in part, due to some drama between them, but eventually, even that would fade, and everyone would forget about Annie and Lola and what might have been. Everyone except Annie. Annie would never forget. The barbwired scar tissue around her heart was permanent.

"Annie?" Vicky's voice broke through the grim monologue in her head. "Food's here."

A surprise to see a table full of burgers and glasses of wine.

White wine. That's what Lola used to drink. "I'm not hungry," Annie said, pushing her food away.

"Can I ask," Vicky said delicately, "what happened?"

It wasn't as if Annie was dying to spill, but what difference did it make now? As briefly as she could, she summarized their fight: her stupid lie about enjoying the premiere, which had somehow blown up into proof Annie was untrustworthy, triggering all of Lola's anger about the past.

Understanding and sympathy unfolded over her friends' faces.

Annie grabbed some napkins to wipe her face, blow her nose. "Have you guys broken up, too?"

Vicky and Dylan traded a pained look, shifting awkwardly. Dylan hazarded, "We're still . . . talking," but Vicky just said, "Yes, we have," and that was it.

So, neither couple lasted. Annie slunk lower in the booth. This time-traveling theater reunion had brought nothing but suffering and sadness and regret. She never should've agreed to it.

The jukebox kicked in with "Do You Realize??" by the Flaming Lips and Annie wanted to scream. Lola's face filled her mind. She'd give anything for headphones.

"Jazz was right," Annie muttered. "The world is doomed."

Vicky snorted in agreement.

"Hey, come on," Dylan said. "You don't mean that."

"I do mean that," Annie said darkly.

"Not to put words in your mouth," Dylan pushed back, "but this is just a very, very bad day. You don't really think everything is 'doomed.'"

"Not to put words in *your* mouth," Vicky said to Dylan, "but Annie can believe whatever she likes. We're not impressionable kids anymore—we have a right to our opinions, even if they're completely dystopic."

Annie wished again for headphones. "Not to put words in *anyone's* mouth," she snapped, "but I can speak for myself and . . ."

Out of nowhere, Annie had an idea. A solution. It hit like a power surge, jolting her upright.

Was it crazy? Yep. But could it work?

Vicky and Dylan kept bickering as Annie's mind started to race.

Lola had made her choice and yes, it'd cut Annie's heart out of her chest like an eighteenth-century unanesthetized surgery. But it hadn't robbed her of *all* her organs. She had her brain and she had her guts. She could still be strong. Little Orphan Annie still had some fight left.

"Guys?" Annie interrupted the others. "I think—I think I need to call Garrett." Her heartbeat careened, breath catching like a car slamming into reverse. "I think I have an idea."

"An idea for what?" Vicky asked.

Annie was already getting out her phone. "An idea for how we can save the show."

Annie called Garrett. She needed him and all four Tragedians back at the theater, right now. She'd explain everything then.

She could do this.

She could absolutely do this.

"And while we wait for them to come back," she told a bewildered Dylan and Vicky, "we eat." She surveyed the table of food, her appetite galloping back with gusto. "I'm absolutely *starving*."

LESS THAN AN hour later, all four teenagers, Jazz, Garrett, Vicky, and Dylan stared at Annie on the Rhodes Playhouse stage. It was past nine P.M. but everyone was wide awake.

Annie's heart thumped. Next week, she could fall apart. Tonight, she would stand tall.

"I have an idea." Annie made her voice strong and confident. "Zoë, I know you're off book for my part, not Lola's. But what if we switch? You take Rosencrantz, and I take Guildenstern."

Zoë's face screwed into confusion. "But you don't know all of Lola's lines, do you?"

The collective hope dwindled. *That* was Annie's big idea?

"I don't," Annie said, "but what if I wear an earbud onstage and have Garrett feed me the lines?"

A pause as Annie's suggestion sunk in. A single earbud, relaying a phone call. Garrett reciting the lines, Annie performing them.

"What, like, a Cyrano situation?" Garrett asked.

Jazz cocked her head. "From backstage?"

"Exactly," Annie said. "You know all the blocking, don't you, Zoë?"

"Yeah, I mean, maybe?" Zoë hedged. "I'd have to practice, but it *might* be possible?"

"What about us?" Kat indicated Emery and Orchid. "We're *four* Tragedians."

"Now you're three," Annie said. "It's too late to bring someone else up to speed so you'll have to re-block and relearn everything."

"The whole play?" Orchid asked in disbelief.

"All the swordplay," Emery said, "the clowning, the tumbling . . ."

"Yep." Annie nodded. "It's not a perfect plan but it's our only shot." She met everyone's gaze, one by one. "Jazz and Vicky, you work with the Tragedians. Dylan, you work with me and Zoë. Garrett, you're reading me Lola's lines." Annie addressed the group, her heart still beating fast. "What d'you say?"

Everyone looked to Zoë. The teenager took a deep breath, her expression serious and committed. "Not gonna lie, I'm totally freaked. But I'm in."

"I'm in," said Kat.

"In," said Orchid.

"In." Emery nodded.

Annie looked to Vicky.

"Well, the earbud might fall out," Vicky spoke practically, "the call might drop—reception's never been great in here. Garrett might go too fast or too slow and this isn't the kind of play where you can improvise. But obviously," she added, "I'm in."

Annie's mouth was dry. She didn't know the lines. Didn't know if the earbud would work. But she had a pulse and a stage and a story to tell. Annie met Garrett's eye.

He looked doubtful. "It's risky. But theater isn't about playing it safe. It's about . . ." He paused, allowing a brief, anticipatory silence. "Taking the leap. It's about defying gravity."

Like soldiers receiving a call to arms, Zoë and Emery broke into song—"*It's time to try defying gra-vi-ty*"—but Annie cut them off. "Guys, no. We have work to do. Call your parents—we need you here as late as they'll let you." Annie inhaled the deepest breath of her life. "We may not have Lola. But we have this play. And this cast. And this chance. I'm not giving up."

"I knew we'd figure it out!" Jazz declared. "The show must go on! It simply *must*!"

"Yeah!" Dylan pumped a fist. "Let's do this!"

Energized, Annie stuck her hand into the center of the group. "*Theater kids* on three! One, two, three—"

"Theater kids!" everyone cried, throwing a hand up.

And just like that, hope reentered the chat.

33.

. . . .

Show day

THE NEXT MORNING, ANNIE WAS TUGGED INTO CONSCIOUSness by a waft of lemongrass. "Lollie . . ." Annie smiled, reaching for Lola's side of the bed.

Which was empty.

Annie blinked awake, scanning her room. No coffee brewing. No shower running. No Lola, just the memory of her written in ghostly essential oil. Annie whimpered, curling back into herself like an injured dog. She wanted to stay like this for the next hundred years, cocooned in bed. But she couldn't. Today wasn't just the first day of being single and heartbroken—again. It was also the day of the show. The last Saturday in August. Their one-night-only engagement was finally here.

She could break down tomorrow. Tomorrow she would eat an entire pint of Chubby Hubby and rewatch all the magic-gone-wrong episodes of *Buffy*—only Randy and Joan could save her now. Tomorrow, she would pine for the love that'd slipped through her fingers. Today, Annie Elizabeth Lightfoot had to get shit done.

• • •

ANNIE ARRIVED AT the playhouse just after ten A.M. with a box of takeout coffee, her lucky truck-stop doughnuts, and a fiercely resilient smile. Originally, the cast had been given the day off, but Garrett had promised to wrangle whomever he could. Annie pushed open the double doors, expecting to see half the cast.

Instead, almost everyone turned to face her: Jamie and Mikki. Deborah and Clyde. Vicky and Dylan and Jazz. Garrett and all four Tragedians—who, despite having rehearsed until one A.M. last night, looked enviously well rested. (Oh, to have the constitution of a teenager.)

The group was gathered by the front row, urgently mid-conversation. As Annie stepped inside, they abruptly paused. Annie had the brief, uncomfortable feeling of walking into a meeting she a.) wasn't invited to and b.) was all about her.

Steeling herself, she walked up the center aisle, head held high. "Morning, everyone!" she called, making her voice as cheery as she could. "Great news!"

"Lola's coming back?" Zoë looked hugely relieved. "Oh, thank god. We're not sure this earpiece idea will—"

"Nope," Annie said quickly. "The great news is I have doughnuts and coffee—and *belief* in all of us."

She sucked in a shaky breath and faced the listening cast. "I know what we're planning for tonight is unconventional and risky and might go totally off the rails. But that's the beauty of art. That's the beauty of *life*."

She hadn't planned on a speech, but it felt right—the cast needed hope. Assurance. Inspiration. Being a leader wasn't about self-importance or delusions of grandeur. It was understanding what a group needed most and helping guide the way there.

Annie's voice stayed clear and confident. "Life doesn't always go as planned, but it's not about what happens. It's about how we handle the setbacks. And we're going to handle our setback by staying positive." She met Jazz's eye, who beamed back. "Staying sharp." Annie looked to Vicky, whose cat eyeliner had never been crisper. Vicky nodded back, her gaze unwavering. "And having *fun*," Annie went on, smiling at Dylan, who grinned, running an easy hand through their flop of dark hair. "Because together, as a team, we're creative and inventive and we've got each other's backs. Any questions?"

Annie readied herself for a snarky comment from Kat or a crazy curveball from Clyde.

But no one said anything. Everyone just smiled, eager and hopeful.

"Okay." Annie clapped her hands, the sound echoing around the empty theater. "Then let's get to work."

The final day's rehearsals kicked off with a renewed sense of determination. But as soon as they began, cracks started to show. Zoë knew most of her lines but not every one, calling for prompt after prompt, which visibly undercut her confidence. The remaining trio of Tragedians kept slipping back into their original choreography, muscle memory overriding the new blocking. But worst of all was Annie's attempt to perform with the earbud.

By the time Garrett fed her a line and her brain translated it into action and delivery, the moment had passed. Her performance was stiff and halting, her body tense, her movements unsure. And the call dropped out. Twice.

The strain rippled outward. Other cast members began missing cues, stumbling over lines.

Their makeshift miracle was unraveling, stitch by stitch.

BY THE END of the day, doubt hung over the group, as dark and heavy as the clouds rolling in. A storm was coming. The news that they'd sold two hundred and seventy-five tickets inspired worry, not triumph. "Two hundred and seventy-five people are gonna watch us fall on our ass," Emery muttered.

Annie didn't have the energy to correct them—they may well be right. "We'll just do our best," was all she could manage, before everyone slunk off to grab dinner and get show-ready. Far from the excited, celebratory mood Annie recalled from other opening nights, the vibe was funereal.

Annie was the last to leave the stage. She surveyed the sweep of empty seats, her hard-won hope fizzling out like a wet firecracker. The Rhodes Players weren't ready for their revival. Not in this form. Not—she had to admit—without Lola.

Lola, who at this very moment was charming a handsome K-pop star on a professional film shoot, an ocean away.

The idea could make her weep, but Annie didn't let herself. She'd go down with this ship. She'd be the last one on deck as the freezing water rushed to claim them.

Annie didn't leave the theater, opting to stay close and put on her makeup in the green room, trying not to replay yesterday's awful fight. She was too nervous to eat or drink, refusing both the takeout burger Vicky brought back for her and the flask that Dylan, in costume as Hamlet, took a nip from.

"I don't think being drunk will help things," Vicky told them witheringly.

"And being a Goody Two-shoes will?" Dylan flipped back.

"Fuck off!" Vicky whirled on them, her half face of stage makeup making her look weirdly broken. "*I'm trying!*"

"You think I'm not trying?" Dylan sounded outraged. "Jesus Christ, Vicky, *I'm* the one who—"

"*Guys!*" Annie cut them off, her voice sharp with tears. "Please. Let's just get through tonight, then you never have to see each other again."

She meant it as a light at the end of the tunnel but instead Vicky and Dylan both flinched, their anger collapsing into devastation.

Vicky was the first to recover. "Perfect," she said, swiveling back to the mirrors to furiously sponge on foundation.

Dylan's gaze was pinned to the carpet for a few painful beats. "I'll check on the box office," they murmured, melting off as Jamie and Mikki came in with the news that the theater was officially open; the audience had begun to arrive.

"My whole moms group is here," Mikki said. "I thought I'd be excited but . . ." She exchanged an uncertain look with Jamie, who gave her shoulder a reassuring squeeze.

"It's going to be great," he said, sounding thoroughly unconvinced.

Annie focused on her makeup, trying not to meet her own eye in the mirror.

Maybe they should've canceled. Maybe her big idea was just another big mistake.

Garrett rapped on the doorframe. "Thirty minutes to places."

"Thank you, thirty," everyone chorused, but not even the backstage lingo could assuage Annie's ballooning doubt.

Garrett caught Annie's eye, gesturing for her to join him in the corridor. There, he made sure none of the cast was in earshot. "Annie," Garrett began, "I hate to say this, but I think we should mentally prepare to call it at intermission."

"Call it? Call what?"

"Call it off," Garrett said. "Cut the play."

Annie's jaw just about hit the floor. "What? Why?"

Garrett let out an agitated breath. "Zoë and I have been running lines nonstop in Jazz's office but she's getting in her head. Her performance is getting worse, not better. And I just don't think this earbud thing will work."

Annie stared back at him, aghast. Calling it off, halfway through, was worse than no show at all. It was like a bride running out on a wedding halfway through the vows. "We can't *call it,*" she whispered in horror. "We absolutely *cannot.*"

"We might not have a choice," Garrett said bluntly.

Panic seized Annie's muscles, blanked her mind. What was her first line? What were any of her lines? What was she doing here? There was no way she could do this. There was just *no way.*

"It's filling up out there!" Deborah bustled past, sounding upbeat.

"The whole town showed up!" Clyde added, following Deb into the green room. "Despite the rain!"

The whole town. Would see. Her failure.

Time sped up. Minutes blurred. Backstage became a frantic mash of voices.

Fifteen minutes to places—Where's my sword?—The box office says we're about to sell out—Five minutes to places—Help me with my cape?—Okay, we're officially sold out!—Places, please!

And suddenly Annie was on the side of the stage, the chatter of the waiting audience as loud as the rain pounding the roof. Her heart was beating so fast she felt like it might explode. With a shaking hand, Annie edged back the tall red curtains, peeking out. *Every seat was full.* Even the nosebleed seats in the balcony. She recognized so many faces—locals and acquaintances and friends. All her favorite clients. The waitress with the micro bangs. Sal sat in the front row, proudly pointing out her name on the program to the cute boy he was with. Next to him, Annie recognized Dylan's mom. An expectant smile lifted Celine's makeup-free face.

But there were plenty of people she *didn't* know. Nonlocals who were there to see the famous Lola Wilson. Nonlocals who were supposed to see the show, fall in love with Rhodes, and keep coming back, per Jazz's vision. A vision that was fading by the second.

A crack of thunder boomed directly overhead, so loud it rattled the chandelier. A few audience members squealed.

The storm wasn't just on top of them—it was inside Annie, electrifying every nerve.

Garrett's voice cut through the chaos. "We're having an issue with reception." He held up his phone. Zero bars. "There is none."

Next to her, Zoë was all but hyperventilating.

"Calm down, dear," Jazz soothed. She was dressed head to toe in shimmering gold, from her muumuu to a pair of glittery sneakers.

"We can do this, Zoë," Annie promised, deeply unsure that they could.

Zoë grabbed the front of Annie's costume. "Don't make me do this. My whole family is out there and *three* casting agents. If they see me bomb, I'll never get another shot."

"But the show must go on," Jazz said, as if it was obvious. "It simply must."

But Lola was gone. Zoë was panicking. The earbud plan was a bust.

Annie found Vicky's eye, then Dylan's. Slowly, Vicky shook her head. Dylan folded their arms and let out a long sigh of defeat.

"Jazz," Annie said quietly. "It's over."

Jazz stared back uncomprehendingly.

Beyond the curtains, a playful chant had started. "*We want the show! We want the show!*"

"We can't make Zoë do it if she doesn't want to," Annie said. "We have to cancel."

"*What?*" Jazz choked out a disbelieving laugh. "But we're so close. Everyone came." She waved a hand in the direction of the sold-out audience, then at the gathered cast. "We're all ready."

The chant gathered momentum. "*We want the show! We want the show!*"

"But we can't do it without Lola," Annie said. She looked around the cast, wondering if they'd push back or if someone had a last-minute solution. But no one did. They just looked resigned, faces slackening into despair.

Annie fortified herself. The idea of stepping onstage to disappoint three hundred people, many of whom she cared about, was her own personal nightmare. But this was her responsibility. "I'll do it."

"Do what?" Jazz asked, the color draining from her face.

"I'll tell the audience we're unable to do the show," Annie said.

Jazz's eyes filled with tears.

Mikki let out a sob, turning into Jamie, who was stone-faced. Clyde swallowed hard.

All their work. Their once-in-a-lifetime opportunity. Gone.

Annie took a breath, pushed back the curtain, and stepped out onto the stage.

The crowd erupted into joyful applause, a sound so sudden and loud, Annie stumbled back. The stage lights were blinding. She winced, raising a hand to shield her eyes. "Uh, hi . . ." Her tiny words were swallowed up by the cheers of the frothing crowd.

A supercut of the past month flickered in Annie's mind: the shaky table read. Maria singing "A Natural Woman." Awkward rehearsals turning into magic. The way the whole production came alive.

Lola storming off.

Everything falling apart.

The crowd began shushing itself until the applause died out, giving way to a suffocating attentiveness. Annie cleared her throat, forcing herself to speak. "I'm, um, Annie Lightfoot," she began.

"Go Annie!" someone yelled, prompting a wave of supportive laughter.

Stoically, Annie continued, "And I'm here to tell you that . . ."

The play was off due to a . . . casting issue? Personal emergency? Another pandemic?

"That . . ." Annie went on. The room was pin-drop quiet, hanging on her every word. "Well . . . that the play is—"

The doors to the theater burst open, banging loudly. The audience jerked in the direction of the sound.

A strong female voice rocketed into the room. "*Wait!*"

Annie's heart stopped. Rain-soaked and breathless, *Lola*, in full costume, sprinted up the aisle.

The audience erupted in delighted applause, mistaking it for part of the show.

Lola ran up the stage steps, joining Annie. She was shaking with adrenaline. For one breathless moment, it was just the two of them, standing together in the storm's eye. Then Lola addressed the crowd. "Sit tight, folks! The play is about to begin!"

She grabbed Annie's hand, tugging her behind the curtain, backstage.

There, Annie could only blink at her, overwhelmed. She wondered if she was dreaming. "You came back."

"I had to." Lola's eyes were wide, frantic, burning gold. "I had to be with you."

"Thank god!" Zoë had transformed from panicked to overjoyed, hugging Lola with a squeal. "I need to change costumes!" She bolted off, flanked by the teens.

"I knew it!" Jazz declared, one finger jabbing the air, bangles jangling. "I knew you'd come back!"

"You're doing the show?" Garrett confirmed.

"No, I flew from London for the free popcorn," Lola deadpanned. "Of course I'm doing the show! I've been trying to call. I couldn't get a signal with the storm!"

"Thank Britney!" Garrett moaned, tossing an earbud into the wings. "Then, places! Let's start before this audience eats us alive!"

Annie was speechless. Her heart was staging a full-blown production, complete with fog machines and overture.

Vicky swooped in with a towel to dry Lola off, straighten her costume. "Your timing is impeccable."

"*Actors,*" Dylan added, rolling their eyes and socking Lola's arm. "Always making an entrance."

Lola gave them both a grateful, apologetic smile, before turning her full attention to Annie, taking her hands. Despite the swirling chaos, despite the noisy audience, despite the prospect of the two-hour play ahead, all of her attention was poured solely onto Annie.

"Annie, I am so, so sorry," Lola said. "I never should've left. I never should've invited you to London as my *assistant.* God, what was I *thinking*?"

"Hey, I'm the one who lied. Who also said some pretty terrible things." Annie squeezed Lola's hands tight, her heart still pounding. The apology speech she'd dared to imagine fled her brain. All she could manage was, "I totally shit the bed and I'm sorry, too."

"You were right, Annie," Lola said. "I don't want that life. I want this one. With you." Her hazel eyes shone with courage and truth. "I was scared. Of what that meant. Of admitting how wrong I'd been. But I'm not scared anymore."

Annie let out a shaky breath, blinking fast. "I—I don't know what I'm doing half the time," she admitted. "I try so hard to make everything okay, keep everyone happy, because it's like—if I mess up, they'll leave. Or think less of me. Or . . ." She wiped at her eyes. "Sometimes I shrink myself down so small trying not to be a problem that I forget how to be a person. I don't want to do that anymore. I don't want to disappear."

Lola's voice stayed steady. "And I'm going to work on trusting my gut. And trusting what we have—what we are. You and me—we're the story I want to tell for the rest of my life. When I'm with you, I know what home is."

Annie let out a hiccupping laugh, her heart overflowing. "You're my home, too," she whispered. "You always were."

Lola let go of Annie's hands to frame her face with both palms, gazing intently into her eyes. The rest of the world faded into static as Lola spoke, her words firm and clear. "Annie, I love you. I should've said it much earlier but I'm saying it now. I'm sorry and I love you."

Warm, golden light gushed into every cell of Annie's body. "I love you, too, Lollie," she whispered. "I love you, too."

Lola leaned forward, pressing her lips to Annie's. For a few beautiful seconds, Annie sank into the sweetest kiss of her life, the world spinning away until it was just the two of them, tethered together.

Everything became clear.

It had never been a big, bold *life* she'd wanted. It had never been a big, bold *life* that felt like it passed her by.

What she'd wanted—what she'd dared to hope for—was a big, bold *love*.

A love that was right here, in her arms. A love she would spend the rest of her life protecting and growing and cherishing as best she could.

They broke apart, smiling big, giddy grins, then swiveled to face the curtain. Find their marks. Focus.

"Ready?" Lola asked.

When Annie answered, she wasn't just talking about the play. She was talking about everything that lay ahead. "I am."

The opening music played.

A hush fell over the playhouse.

The tall, red curtain swept aside.

Lola and Annie stepped forward, into the light. Together, they began.

34.

WHEN DYLAN WAS FIFTEEN YEARS OLD—SEARCHING AND SHY and misunderstood—being in the cast of *Rosencrantz and Guildenstern Are Dead* cracked open their entire world. Performing in a play unlocked the concept of performing in one's own life, something Dylan eventually realized they'd been doing—playing a girl, not existing as one. It introduced Dylan to the importance of friends you could be yourself around, and role models who inspired. It introduced Dylan to summers being fun and adventurous, not just extended time to avoid their mother. And, most important of all, it'd introduced them to Victoria Mei Fang. They'd never met anyone like Vicky, not then, and not since. It'd been a risk to return to Rhodes. But as Dylan performed the role of Hamlet in this sensational play, on this rainy night, in this quirky small town in front of a crowd who included their mother, they'd never been more certain that this was a risk worth taking. That risks, of all kinds, were worth it.

Dylan had never felt so alive. The audience's laughter and gasps fed the cast's energy, blurring the lines between performance and reality. Lola was clearly the best actor in the production but she never stole the show—she shared it with everyone else. Annie didn't miss a mark and the rest of the supporting cast committed just as hard, especially the teens. But performing with Vicky was what made the night unforgettable.

In between scenes, however, the distance between them was palpable. Vicky pulled away, keeping conversations brief, smiles tight. But onstage, when their eyes met, their chemistry sparkled, undeniable.

"*Think, in your head,*" Vicky spoke as the Player to Annie and Lola, "*now, think of the most private, secret, intimate thing you have ever done, secure in the knowledge of its privacy.*" A pause, for Rosencrantz and Guildenstern—and the audience—to imagine such a thing. "*Are you thinking of it?*" Vicky whirled on them, the mirrored moons and stars sewn into her cape catching the light, her next line a roar, "*Well, I saw you do it!*"

This beat muddied the line between reality and illusion, but as Dylan pondered it anew, they realized how interwoven Vicky was in their private, intimate moments. Making love. Accepting comfort. Giving care. Letting someone in. Trusting them completely.

It was over far too quickly.

One minute they were onstage, performing under lights, the next they were standing in a line with the rest of the cast, bowing deeply to an exuberant audience who was on their feet and shouting for more. Jazz emerged for the final curtain call, and Dylan had never seen someone look so ecstatic. So proud. She'd had a vision, and—after a lot of work and a few leaps of faith—that vision was reality. The world needed more people like Jazz Whitaker.

Dylan wanted to talk to Vicky but she disappeared as soon as the curtains closed. The first person to approach after they emerged from backstage was their mother, hugging them with uncharacteristic warmth. "Darling, you were magnificent! Astounding! Sublime!"

"Calm down," Dylan said with a chuckle, hugging her back. "Put your thesaurus away."

"I'm just endlessly amazed by you." Celine beamed, smile lines creasing her face. No makeup, no designer outfit or heels. She'd never looked better. "My brilliant"—tiny pause—"child."

That she didn't say *daughter* felt like a win. Dylan knew their mother was trying. "Thanks, Mom."

"Every town needs a good playhouse," Celine said. "Who knows, maybe I'll audition."

Dylan laughed in surprise and Celine joined in, and Dylan wasn't sure if they'd ever done that before—laughed, simply and easily, at something wonderful the future might hold.

The after-party was meant to take place in Jazz's backyard, but it was still pouring.

"Why leave?" Jazz swept a generous arm around the buzzing space. "We're already home!"

Volunteers ferried all the food back to the theater, setting it out picnic-style on the edge of the stage. Tomato and basil crostini on crispy baguette drizzled with olive oil; cucumber and cream cheese pinwheel sandwiches; herbed white bean dip. Warm cheddar and chive biscuits were piled on a plate next to bowls of rosemary and sea salt spiced nuts. For dessert, berry and cream tartlets and decadent iced chocolate brownies.

The teens put on their playlist, Jamie popped champagne, and just like that, it was a party. The theater remained crowded as everyone's loved ones mixed and mingled, basking in the glow of the play's success.

Lola and Annie were inseparable, chatting with all of Annie's friends in between egregious displays of PDA that confirmed the current state of their relationship.

"Congrats, lovebirds," Dylan offered, in one of the rare moments they weren't fused at the mouth. "Invite me to the wedding."

Annie blushed, her smile as big as the world, but Lola just looked a thousand percent certain, as she said, "Of course. You'll be my best man."

Every time Dylan tried to corner Vicky, she slipped away, so

Dylan connected with their inner child by playing hide-and-seek with Flora, Mikki's three-year-old. "We can't stay too late," Dylan overheard Mikki saying. "My boyfriend will drive us home."

"Boyfriend!" Dylan whirled around, all but shouting the word.

Mikki twinkled, dimples popping, as Jamie draped an arm around her, looking equally besotted. "What can I say?" She patted his chest. "I can't resist a man in a dress."

Dylan chuckled, giving them both a high five. Then they scanned the theater again for Vicky, finally spotting her heading into the wings. With single-minded focus, Dylan vaulted through the crowd, not stopping for anyone. There was only one person Dylan wanted to see.

They caught up with her as she came out of the green room, back in pleated slacks and a crisp button-down, bag over one shoulder.

"Hey," Dylan panted. "You're a hard woman to pin down."

It was ripe for double entendre, but Vicky didn't take the bait, instead checking her phone. "It's late. I gotta motor."

"Back to Jazz's?"

Vicky met Dylan's gaze with an expression as hard as steel. "Back to Manhattan."

Dylan flinched, feeling like they'd just been punched in the face. "Now? But . . . what about . . . the talkback?" Not the most pressing reason, but better than nothing. "Tomorrow's talkback!"

"You don't need me for that."

"I need you," Dylan blurted, panicked by the idea of Vicky about to disappear. "I very much need you."

Vicky's expression stayed cool. "My car's packed and I've already said my goodbyes. So"—she shrugged bloodlessly—"see ya."

"*See ya?*" Dylan was so taken aback they almost laughed. "*See ya?* That's how we're ending things?"

Vicky's mask cracked, just for a microsecond. Pain and longing rushed over her face, her eyes becoming glassy. She blinked, and it was gone. "Have you got a better idea?"

Shrieks of laughter sounded up the corridor. The four Tragedians, running for the green room. "We almost forgot," Zoë cried as they all tumbled past, "to write our names!"

Dylan and Vicky watched as the quartet squished together under the bench. Giggling, Zoë passed Emery a pen, performing the same tradition Dylan, Vicky, Annie, and Lola had, twenty years ago. Emery glanced back at Dylan, giving them a brief, heartfelt smile before turning their attention back to their friends. Orchid's hand was on Kat's thigh. Kat smiled at Orchid, holding her gaze. Young love. Society dismissed it as naïve, but Dylan knew better.

Dylan refocused on Vicky. Did they have a better idea of how to end things? "Yeah," they said. "I do."

OUTSIDE, THE NIGHT air was damp and floral. The clouds were thinning, scudding west.

"Oh." Vicky looked up at the patches of sky, freckled with stars. "It's stopped raining."

It took every ounce of Dylan's strength not to cup Vicky's cheek, duck close enough to find her mouth. "Wanna go for a walk?" they asked.

Vicky crossed her arms. "With you?"

Dylan bit back a smile. Why did they find this side of Vicky so damn adorable? Maybe because they knew that while Vicky was a legit bad bitch, underneath that armor was a total softie. A caramel chew with a hard shell, undeniably sweet.

Without breaking eye contact, Dylan wandered back a few steps, giving Vicky the crooked grin they knew she couldn't resist. "Come on a walk with me."

Their shoes squelched in the sodden grass as they crossed the quiet lawn together toward Myrtle Street. They passed the overgrown lot, now full of puddles that shone like spilled mercury. They passed the silent, freestanding houses, their upstairs windows gently glowing gold. The night air smelled of rain, of the tang of asphalt and the sweetness of crushed honeysuckle.

"You were incredible, by the way," Dylan said. "In the show? You nailed it."

"I know," Vicky said, "I was there."

Dylan laughed and it felt a bit like flying, like their bones were filled with air.

The celebration in the theater faded, until the only sounds were their shoes on the sidewalk, and their breath, pulling in and out. Above them, revealed by a shifting cloud, the moon. As full and shining as Dylan's own heart drumming in their chest.

"I never thought I'd come back to Rhodes," Dylan said. "Never thought I'd be in a play again—certainly not here, and certainly not with you." They came to a stop, facing Vicky on the sidewalk. "And I didn't think that, when I did those things, I'd discover everything I felt for you, as a kid, never went away. If anything, those feelings just got more powerful."

"Dylan." The word was half a sob. Vicky's eyes filled with desperate tears. "We've already broken up. I'm already broken. Please don't draw it out."

Dylan sucked in a long breath. This was a risk and they knew two things about it.

One. They couldn't take it back. Not tomorrow. Not ever.

Two. They could not wait another second longer to say it.

Dylan wiped away one of Vicky's tears with their thumb. Their voice was low but resolute. "What if I didn't go back to L.A. tomorrow?" A beat. Then, "What if I stayed?"

"Stayed where?" Vicky asked.

"What if I stayed," Dylan repeated, "in New York?"

Vicky froze, her eyes flickering fast between Dylan's. "For how long?"

Dylan smiled at the girl they were pretty sure was their best friend. "For as long as you're there."

Vicky's breath caught. Something like hope tiptoed into her eyes. "You'd stay and we'd—what—date?"

"Yeah," Dylan said. "For like a week, then I'll ask you to be my girlfriend and I'll move in. You got a dope place, right?"

Vicky shoved them, but only lightly and she was starting to smile. "Are you serious?"

"As the heart attack you'll never have again," Dylan said, cupping Vicky's face with both hands. "Not on my watch."

Dylan planted a soft, slow kiss on Vicky's parted lips, feeling a well of emotion at the tiny whimper in the back of Vicky's throat.

Vicky opened her eyes. The streetlight behind her made a shining crown of her hair. "So I'm not just your *summer crush*?"

It took several seconds for the meaning of Vicky's question to land. *That's* why she'd seemed so disappointed over Hot & Sweaty. Vicky still thought this wasn't the real deal. "You're not just my crush, babe," Dylan said. "I mean, you are, but you're so much more than that."

Vicky hesitated. "But what about the beach, and tacos, and sexually curious smokeshows?"

"Ho*ney.*" Dylan brushed strands of hair out of Vicky's face. "The only sexually curious smokeshow I'm interested in, now and forever, is you." They moved even closer, one hand on Vicky's waist, the other touching her cheek. "I'm in love with you, Vicky. I've always been in love with you and I will always be in love with you."

Vicky's entire being lit up. Her question was disarmingly sweet. "Really?"

"I think it's pretty obvious," Dylan said. "Never had much of a poker face."

And with that, Vicky melted against Dylan, the last vestiges of armor dissolving like sugar in water. Her voice was muffled, even a little huffy, as she pressed her face into Dylan's neck. "Well, obviously, I've always been in love with you, too."

Joy fountained inside Dylan. They grinned, floating, and squeezed Vicky teasingly. "I think I might need to hear it. Those three little words?"

Vicky lifted her head, both arms still wrapped around Dylan, and smiled. "Okay. Here goes: I. Love. You. I *love* you, Dylan Rogers."

And Dylan just about died, right there, on the rainswept street. It felt like the whole world had been waiting for them to find their way back to each other, and now they had. "I love you, too." Dylan tightened their arms around Vicky, vowing to never, ever let her go. "Hope it was worth the wait."

"It was," Vicky said, lifting her mouth, eyes drifting shut.

Just two people, on a quiet street corner, kissing. Two people, with hearts the size of planets and hope as unspoiled as the dawn.

They broke apart, smiling giddily.

"I can't believe it took us twenty years to get here," Vicky said. "I guess I really did take the long way home."

"At least we got here in the end," Dylan said.

Vicky glanced around. "I can't believe I'm saying this, but I want to spend more time here."

"Because we crushed it in the play and we'll be local heroes forever?" Dylan kidded.

"Sure." Vicky smiled. "Also, country life is good for my health."

"I wanna spend more time here, too. Shame I never found the right space." Dylan buried their nose in Vicky's thick hair inhaling her sweeter-than-usual smell. "Did you change your shampoo?"

"No way, I'm loyal. I think it's the honeysuckle." Vicky nodded at the wild, flowering vine climbing the iron railing of the abandoned storefront beside them.

They both turned to look at the building. Once Upon a Time. The long-abandoned bookstore.

The *bookstore.*

Their eyes met again, wider. The flare of possibility Dylan felt was mirrored in Vicky's expression.

Dylan took her hand, their fingers intertwining with ease. Together, they stepped closer to the window, peering in.

"Good bones," Dylan murmured, scanning the wide plank floorboards and generous square footage.

"The theater reopening will mean more foot traffic." Vicky touched the decorative window frames, chipped but sturdy. "These old fixtures might qualify for a historic restoration tax credit." She indicated the neglected patio. "Clean this up and you could argue for an extended-use permit. Tables and chairs for people to gather." She looked up at Dylan, eyes bright. "Like a real community space."

That Vicky remembered their dream made Dylan swoon. They nipped at Vicky's neck. "Your Honor, is it possible that what I've been looking for has been in front of me all along?"

Vicky smiled back, her eyes warm and steady. "I think that's entirely possible." She nestled against Dylan, letting out a contented sigh. "The defense rests."

BACK INSIDE THE theater, the after-party was winding down. Deborah was promising Maria free manicures for life. Clyde posed for a selfie with all four teens. Jamie held a sleepy Flora as Mikki hugged Garrett, promising they'd all get lunch.

Dylan and Vicky found Jazz by the edge of the stage, bidding some friends goodbye. "You're both still here," Jazz said in happy surprise. Her gaze dropped to Dylan's and Vicky's intertwined hands. Satisfaction bloomed over her face. "I've always had a sixth sense about casting," Jazz said slyly. "I know what'll work."

"Hold up," Dylan said. "Was all this—a setup?"

Jazz was tight-lipped. "Let's just say I knew that everything would work out. It always does."

"But, how did you *know* that?" Vicky asked. "You were absolutely certain that this play would happen, even when we all thought it wouldn't. How did you *know*?"

"I didn't." Jazz trilled a laugh. "I'm white-knuckling it, just like everyone else. But here's a secret: I always bet on something powerful that never lets me down."

"What do you bet on?" Dylan asked.

"People," Jazz said with a fond smile. "I bet on you."

Dylan's chest went shuddery-warm as they bashed away a tear.

The crowd continued to thin. Everyone's loved ones picked up their wet umbrellas and folded programs, saying their goodbyes. Dylan convinced Jazz they could all clean up in the morning before the talkback, sending their director home for some well-earned rest.

"You didn't just save my theater," Jazz said, hugging them both. "You saved *me*. And trust me, I'm not done yet."

And then it was just Dylan and Vicky, sitting on the edge of the stage, dangling their feet, shoulders pressed together.

"I promise I won't be a bitch," Vicky said. "Much."

"I promise I won't be a flirt," Dylan replied. "Much."

Vicky giggled. The cutest sound in the whole world. Dylan leaned over to kiss a fresh coat of gloss off Vicky's lips.

"Get a room!" Annie plopped down next to them, followed by Lola.

"You guys made up," Lola observed, her fingers folding into Annie's.

"We did." Dylan nodded, unable to keep a lovestruck grin off their face as they slung an arm around Vicky's shoulder. "You too."

Annie and Lola exchanged an infatuated smile. They'd changed out of their costumes and into a funky saffron-yellow dress for Annie, boyfriend jeans and a tee for Lola. "Sure did," Annie said.

"I'm so sorry again," Lola said to them all. "I can only imagine how hard and stressful the last twenty-four hours were."

"The important thing is you came back," Vicky said generously, and Dylan loved her for it.

"Dying to know," Dylan said, "what'd Haejun say when you dined and ditched?"

Lola shook her head. "We never even met. I knew I'd made the wrong decision as soon as we took off. When we landed at Heathrow, I ran like a maniac through the airport to get the first commercial flight back, while my agent screamed at me that I'd never work again." She shrugged. "Maybe I won't."

"Ouch." Dylan winced in solidarity.

But Lola looked unconcerned, her gaze on Annie. "I know I made the right choice."

Annie smiled back, the living embodiment of the heart-eye emoji, and Dylan wasn't sure if they'd ever felt this happy.

The Rhodes Playhouse was completely quiet now, every red velvet seat empty. No more rehearsals, no more notes, at least, not for this show.

"Where to?" Dylan asked.

Annie and Lola shrugged, looking as awake as Dylan felt. "Diner?"

"I didn't have dinner," Lola added. "Dying for a bite."

"Lemme guess." Vicky hopped off the stage, tugging Dylan with her. "Something that's roast chicken—"

"And salad—" Dylan added.

"And a sandwich," Annie finished with a cackle.

"Yup." Lola laughed, sliding off the lip of the stage. "You guys know me so well."

And what a wonderful feeling that was—to know and be known. To be seen and understood and loved.

The quartet wandered up the aisle, taking in the reawakened grandeur. The gold and rose gilded plasterwork of the ceiling. The grand old chandelier. The reverent hush that only theaters have. Dylan lingered in the doorway, fingers poised over the light switch.

What magic they'd made in here, what wonder. What damn good fun. It wasn't the end of their time at the Rhodes Playhouse, but it was the end of something. Their one-night-only show was over, never to be repeated. But so many other, even better things were just getting started.

"C'mon, Rogers!" Vicky called from the front entrance. "The night is young! Just like us!"

"Curly fries!" declared Annie, galloping onto the front lawn, chased by a giggly Lola. "We must have curly fries!"

Dylan cast one more look around the beloved old theater and switched off the lights. Crossing the foyer to join the others, they stepped out of the darkness and into the starbright summer night.

EPILOGUE

Nine months later

ANNIE KNELT ON HER LIVING ROOM FLOOR, SURROUNDED BY the joyful chaos of half-packed boxes, trying to decide if her ugly-charming knitted tea kettle cozy belonged in *Kitchen Essentials* or *Just a Bit of Fun.* Around her, delicately cracked teacups, notebooks of pressed flowers, and magazines from the mid-aughts—that is, very precious objects she could never, ever part with—cluttered her apartment.

"Baby?" she called to Lola, who was bubble wrapping Annie's animal-shaped glassware collection in the kitchen. "Need your opinion."

Her girlfriend popped her head around the doorway, holding a juice glass shaped like a fish. "Yeah, baby?"

Annie held up the tea cozy in question.

"Chuck it." Lola wrinkled her nose. "Glad you asked."

In the past, Lola's disapproval would've been a cue for Annie to donate the cozy. These days, she was getting a lot better at standing up for what she wanted, even if it wasn't what other people preferred.

"*Essentials,*" Annie decided, tossing it into the box. "Whimsy *is* essential, don't you agree?"

Lola laughed softly. "I do." She stepped around the boxes to press her lips to *that* spot on Annie's neck.

They didn't really have time for another round of afternoon delight. But as they collapsed onto the sofa, it became apparent they'd have to make time.

And soon, they'd have even more room to roll around in.

Annie and Lola had just closed on a century-old stone cottage, just outside of town. It wasn't the sprawling country estate a *Hood* paycheck would've afforded, but it was better—charming and human-sized, with hand-carved beams and a porch tangled in purple wisteria. It reminded Annie of her grandmother's old place: a life built on small comforts instead of overblown grandeur. A perfect balance to Lola's newly decorated New York loft, where they'd spend the rest of their time.

Lola had offered to cover the down payment. But Annie insisted they split it, funded by selling half of the Groom Room to Sal. He was eager to run it full-time, while Annie worked select shifts as it suited her. In her free time, she was laying the groundwork to franchise the brand, starting with Groom Room pop-ups at farmers markets and Pride events—anywhere a dog and a dream were welcome. Still, she'd miss being in the weeds with Sal, who she assumed was the one currently knocking on her apartment door.

"Hang on!" Annie looked around the messy room for her underwear. "Just a sec." Giving up, she buckled herself into her blue overalls, opening the door with a hearty "Hello!" just as Lola tossed her the missing undies, which landed squarely on her head.

Jamie, Mikki, and little Flora all stood on the doormat.

Calmly, Annie removed the underwear from her head. "Welcome," she said. "Obviously things are going well."

Mikki and Jamie exchanged an amused grin. The couple had jumped at the chance to take over Annie's lease. Annie would miss living above the shop. But she was more than ready for her new chapter to begin.

Jamie and Mikki left with a set of keys, promising to have Annie and Lola over for dinner soon. "It's so nice out," Mikki added, as the young family headed down the stairs.

Annie exchanged a look with Lola. "Finish up later?"

"You read my mind," Lola replied. "Let's get our skates on."

Outside, tender May sunshine softened into dusk. The buds on the trees swelled with promise.

Annie and Lola paused by the salon's open door to wave inside. At the wash stations, a pink-suited Sal was up to his elbows in suds, alongside their new hire. One who always pinned a cheery *Spay and Neuter the Patriarchy!* badge to her jumpsuit.

Kat gave an enthusiastic wave. "Salon's hoppin'! I'm thinking of unionizing the poodles."

Annie chuckled, plopping down on the curb to begin lacing up her favorite pair of shoes.

Roller skates. Lola had bought herself a matching pair. After many a wobbly fall, they'd both found their balance.

Lola stood up, gliding in an experimental circle. "Ready?"

Annie nodded with a grin. "Last one there buys!"

She set off quickly down Henry Street, Lola hot on her heels.

They passed Clyde's Grocery, now stocking queer-owned brands and plant-based everything. They passed You Nailed It, now offering poly-friendly packages and gender-affirming glitter gels, and French Kiss, serving Pansexual Panna Cotta and Safeword Shortbread.

In every other window, colorful posters advertised the upcoming Big Gay Summer Stage at the Rhodes Playhouse. The programming featured a dozen new plays by queer writers, curated by Lola, as creative director. She'd also picked up a new gig in the city, assistant-directing a staged reading at the Public. She'd been busy. They all had.

Annie spread her arms wide, warm air on her face, and it felt like she was flying. Like she had the power to go anywhere. Do anything. And even with that power, she wouldn't trade this moment—this street, this town—for anywhere else.

They could smell Marlowe before it crested into view. Dylan's new chocolate shop had opened in late fall. After a quiet few months, word got around. As Lola and Annie glided to a stop, the former bookshop bustled with life. Couples sat on the neat little patio surrounded with flowering honeysuckle, nursing tasting flights of Marlowe's famous hot chocolates—white, dark, and milk. Or customers could make their own blend. Dylan did not believe in chocolate binaries.

Changing into sneakers, Annie and Lola went inside.

Dylan was behind the counter, ringing up a starry-eyed young woman who seemed more interested in the founder than their wares. But Dylan's smile was purely professional. The less professional ones were saved for someone else.

Spotting Annie and Lola, Dylan waved. "Hey, guys! Check out the new drop."

Annie hurried to the far end of the counter, where Dylan was slicing open a box. Inside sat one hundred stacked bars of the newest Marlowe flavor.

"*End Game*," Lola read the opening lines, "*is a slow-burn bar, crafted for commitment-curious smitten kittens.*"

"Cute!" Annie swooned, reading from her own bar. "*Dark chocolate spoons brown sugar cookie crumbles—deep, sweet, and just a little salty. Toasted sesame, a symbol of longevity and luck, brings a nutty warmth. Vanilla bean lingers at the end, soft and sure.*" Then, the final lines. "*End Game is for those who know: True love is worth the wait.*"

"Aw," Lola and Annie chorused, while Dylan blushed, looking proud.

"Has Vicky seen it yet?" Lola asked.

"Of course," Dylan exclaimed. "We've . . . done a lot of tastings."

"TMI," Annie deadpanned, and Lola elbowed her with a chuckle.

"Still the funniest girl I know," she murmured, eyes shining with affection.

Lola and Annie waited outside for Dylan to close up, then the trio walked the short distance to the diner, crossing the rainbow crosswalk—their own yellow brick road.

The diner was packed. Rock Around the Clock had leaned into the town's queer rebranding, adding framed posters of Rock Hudson and Judy Garland, and a colorful *Rhodes: Small Town, Big Pride* poster board out front. The flipside of progress—the days of walking in to their empty back booth were over. Fortunately, the diner now took reservations.

The trio weaved through the crowd to their table. Now it wasn't just Lola the patrons looked twice at—it was also Annie and Dylan, hometown heroes. A framed cast photo of the revival had also been added to the cheerful clutter.

They all slid into the vinyl booth, chatting about the upcoming theater festival. "We haven't even finalized the line-up," Lola said, "but Jazz is already planning a queer arts walk. I can't keep up with her!"

"She was talking to me about turning her house into a gay inn," Dylan said. "The woman is unstoppable."

"Speaking of unstoppable, where's your better half?" Annie asked Dylan.

Dylan checked the time. "Well, it's seven so I'm expecting her—"

The front door swung open.

"—now," Dylan said, their face softening into an infatuated smile.

Vicky, in a white button-down and pleated slacks, plopped down next to Dylan. "I had to park *one block down*!" she exclaimed. "Never thought I'd say this, but we out in Rhodes."

"We sure are." Dylan smiled lazily, tugging Vicky in for a kiss.

This was their new routine—Vicky spent weekends in Rhodes with Dylan, and Dylan headed down to New York midweek to do a few nights at Vicky's. Vicky had even relaxed her stance on L.A., enjoying some long weekends of tacos by the beach.

Soon, the quartet had their meals—a classic Rockin' Roast Chicken Salad Sandwich for Lola and a Big Bopper Bacon Burger with plant-based meat for Annie, plus some new menu additions of the Lipstick Les-bean Burger for Vicky (hold the mayo) and the Soft Boi Club for Dylan.

And wine. Sauvignon blanc. It wasn't yet summer. But the promise of it hung in the air.

"What are we drinking to?" Dylan asked, as they all raised a glass.

"Old friends," Lola said.

"New adventures," Annie added.

"To the playhouse," Dylan said, "for bringing us all back together." They looked to Vicky, prompting her with a raised brow.

Vicky wrenched her gaze from Dylan's mouth, blushing. "To . . . Jazz. And all that lies ahead."

"To all that lies ahead," the others echoed, clinking their glasses.

The love Annie felt was almost too much for one person. It rushed up her throat, hot and sparkly, and for a moment she thought she might cry, or cackle, or let out a ridiculous sort of screech. She settled for a sigh, big and shuddery.

She was happy. She was home. She was in love. It would never get any better than this.

ACKNOWLEDGMENTS

WRITING THIS BOOK WAS A JOY AND A PRIVILEGE. HOW LUCKY am I?

THANK YOU TIMES A MILLION BILLION to:

My genius agent, Allison Hunter, and her incredible assistant, Nat Edwards, for steering the pitch from "a group of women redoing a thwarted mid-aughts beach volleyball championship" (lol) into the book I was actually meant to write.

My phenomenal editors, Katy Nishimoto and Emma Caruso, for your expert, loving guidance in making the heart, humor, and heat of this book shine brighter than a sequined jumpsuit. And to Talia Cieslinski, who stepped in while Emma was on mat leave (welcome, Maren!).

The whole Dial Press dream team—Whitney Frick, Andy Ward, Avideh Bashirrad, Debbie Aroff, Maria Braeckel, Raaga Rajagopala, Rachel Parker, Madison Dettlinger, JP Woodham—publishing's own heist crew.

My tireless book-to-film agents, Addison Duffy, Jason Richman, and Maialie Fitzpatrick, for championing my stories from page to (hopefully) screen.

My generous early readers: Angelica Guarino, Emily Herrell, Jenna Becker, Jenna Britton, Jess Pascale, Katy Stankevitz, Kyla

Gizzi-Najjar, Michelle Hickey, Rachel Grate, Shannon Whitney, and Stephanie Spear—this book was cute; you made it hot.

My devoted Generation Women community and team—I love that we get to do this together.

My brilliant writer friends—thanks for being cool, kind, smart humans who get it.

My readers, and everyone who waves the book-nerd flag online and IRL—#bookstagram, BookTok, booksellers, librarians, podcasters, reviewers, book clubs—you're the real main characters.

My hilarious friends—I love you guys so much. All I wanna do is make dumb jokes with you.

Thank you to my family—my wholesome in-laws and the cheeky Clarks. I love you all.

I am eternally grateful to be Mum to my sweet, sassy, in-all-ways wonderful daughters, Rozella and Lulette—you two changed my life in the most profound and tender way, and I'm so glad you did.

And finally my sunshine wife, Lindsay—thank you for letting me a.) give our kids wackadoo names, and b.) live a real-life love story that just keeps getting better. I love and admire you, boo.

Play It Again

GEORGIA CLARK

Dial Delights

Love Stories
for the
Open-Hearted

Dear Reader

THANK YOU SO MUCH FOR YOUR INTEREST IN MY LATEST FLIGHT of fancy! I'm always curious about why writers wrote the books they did—if you are, too, here's a snapshot of the origin story of *Play It Again*.

It began with my own teenage stint in community theater. My high school on the Central Coast of New South Wales, Australia, didn't actually have a theater program, so if you loved performing, you had to go hunting for it. I found my way into Marian Street Theatre, a Sydney company still in operation today, with an adult troupe upstairs and a youth program downstairs. Every school holiday, the teenagers would put on family-friendly shows for little kids. It was super competitive to get cast, but somehow, I managed to snag a spot. Twice.

Over two productions, I played a naughty Scottish fairy in *The Woman Who Flummoxed the Fairies* and—my true claim to fame—the Goose That Lays the Golden Egg in *Jack and the Beanstalk.* My first interpretation of the goose was . . . a lot. I burst on stage like a manic poultry tornado, flapping and honking with gusto. After a few performances, my director pulled me aside and gently said, "Georgia, you're scaring the children."

So I reinvented myself. Out went wild-eyed barnyard chaos; in came a timid goose, nervously honking and laying that golden egg like it was the scariest task in the world. And the kids adored it. Lesson learned: Sometimes pulling back is more powerful than going full goose.

But what really stuck with me wasn't the roles, as highbrow as they were—it was the life around them. Over the holidays, our misfit cast of thespians would perform once a day on weekdays and two shows on the weekends, subsisting on candy-bar junk food and endless rounds of Spit in the sacred green room. After shows, still on performance highs, we'd take the train one stop to a café, crowd around the biggest table, order the cheapest things on the menu, and stay for hours talking about everything and nothing. Halcyon days of crushes, drama, gossip, inside jokes—the kind of all-consuming friendships you get only when you're a Young Actor.

It was the first time I experienced the magic of community: a group of people coming together to create something fleeting, taking it all *so seriously* even though the stakes were hilariously low. To me, it felt like everything.

My love for the dramatic didn't end there. At university, I was cast as Bérenger in a gender-swapped production of Eugène Ionesco's Absurdist classic *Rhinoceros.* The play is a satirical fable in which a small French town's residents turn into rhinoceroses (yep, you read that right!)—a comment on conformity. I was eighteen, and our director wasn't much older. For some reason, he decided to advertise the play with posters that said only *Feeling Horny? Need Relief?* alongside the time and place of the show. A marketing genius he was not, but doing the play was a riot. Around the same time, I stumbled across Stoppard and *Rosencrantz and Guildenstern Are Dead* and fell in love with its similar mix of humor and hubris. When it came time to decide on the play in this book, it was my first pick.

After moving to New York City in my late twenties, I discovered improv and oh boy, did I chug that Kool-Aid straight from the bottle. Ob. Sessed. If I wasn't at shows I was taking classes at UCB (Upright Citizens Brigade). My 201 teacher put me and seven other promising students on an indie team. We called ourselves Dreamboat and performed monthly shows at various basement and black box theaters around Manhattan for about seven years. "All we need to get started is a suggestion" will still winter-soldier me back to the stage.

During that time, I also co-wrote a totally nutso Off-Off-Broadway play, *Pickles & Hargraves and the Curse of the Tanzanian Glimmerfish,* with fellow improv team member (and then-roommate) Ryan Williams. It was a delightfully off-kilter locked-room comic murder mystery centered on an invisible talking mouse detective solving a whodunnit at an international fish fanciers convention. Once again, I was back in rehearsal rooms with lovable weirdos, handmade props, and the joy of doing something purely for fun.

Eagle-eyed readers will catch a reference to my current theatrical offering, Generation Women, a multigenerational storytelling show that performs monthly at the iconic Joe's Pub in New York. Our show invites women and nonbinary performers in their twenties, thirties, forties, fifties, sixties, and seventies-plus to share a story on a different theme. I founded and host the show, and we now have sister productions in New Jersey, D.C., Montreal, Sydney, and Melbourne. Recently, one of my favorite performers told a beautiful story about falling in love *in her nineties.* Taking the stage each month with a different group of storytellers opening up their hearts gives me a real sense of purpose and joy.

I wanted to capture all of that in *Play It Again.* The intoxicating thrill of performing, the sweet power of human connection, the glorious silliness of Zip Zap Zop. The way community theater or an indie show can feel like the beating heart of the entire universe.

I'll always love sharing stories onstage, and those nineties-era summers as a scared little goose are still some of my happiest memories. I hope this book leaves you with a golden egg or two of joy, too. If it did, let me know—I'd love to hear from you.

—Georgia Clark

© PHOEBE WEEKES

GEORGIA CLARK is the award-winning author of *Most Wonderful, Island Time, It Had to Be You,* and more. She's the founder and host of Generation Women, a beloved multigenerational storytelling series that performs monthly at Joe's Pub in New York and in cities across the U.S., Canada, and Australia. Georgia creates transformational experiences for writers and creative communities through retreats, workshops, storytelling events, and My Novel Year, her signature twelve-month mentorship program. A native Aussie, Georgia lives in Brooklyn with her wife and daughters.

georgiaclark.com
Instagram: @georgialouclark

ABOUT THE TYPE

This book was set in Minion, a 1990 Adobe Originals typeface by Robert Slimbach. Minion is inspired by classical, old-style typefaces of the late Renaissance, a period of elegant and beautiful type designs. Created primarily for text setting, Minion combines the aesthetic and functional qualities that make text type highly readable with the versatility of digital technology.

Discover more books by

GEORGIA CLARK

Available wherever books are sold